BOOK FOUR OF THE PALATINI SERIES

BLUE EDGE

BOOK FOUR OF THE PALATINI SERIES

BLUE EDGE

Vigilante—He cannot be bought and cannot be bargained with

Lyle O'Connor

The New Master of Crime Thrillers

ISBN: 978-1-59433-783-3
eISBN: 978-1-59433-784-0
Library of Congress Catalog Card Number: 2018945763

Manufactured in the United States of America.

Dedication

Legacy is about far more than material things—

Kasydi

Ava

Kaydence

Cheyenne

Shiloh

Raegan

Barrett

William

Acknowledgements

"There are three rules to writing a novel.
Unfortunately, no one knows what they are."
—W. Somerset Maugham

I'm thankful for all those that have contributed to my journey as a novelist.

First and foremost, I'm thankful to my wife Gena, for her love, support, and belief in me.

To Author Walter Allen Grant, a heartfelt thanks for mentoring and encouraging me.

My deepest gratitude to B.J. Wood for her collaboration on the manuscript.

Evan Swensen, my sincere appreciation for the golden opportunity to fulfill my dreams as a published author.

Other books by Lyle O'Connor

Due Process
Lawless Measures
Blood Appeal

CHAPTER 1

*"The edge...there is no honest way to explain it because the only people
who really know where it is are the ones who have gone over."*

—Hunter S. Thompson

October 31, 2003
Squaw Lakes, Oregon

Halloween. What better way to celebrate the Festival of the Dead than
to add to their ranks another wicked spirit? I didn't give a flip about the
traditional significance mythology had assigned to the date. Olin Boe
was out on bail, and that was significant in my book. I thought back on
the events that had led to this night.

Boe had worked hard to convince the court system of his
trustworthiness and that it was in his best interest to continue
employment and his community standard until he was acquitted. The
judge bought his spiel and released him back into society while he
awaited trial. I disagreed with the magistrate's decision and appealed the
matter to more capable judgement—mine.

At the ripe old age of sixty-six, Boe's alleged crime of child pornography wouldn't get him enough time behind bars to suit me. Electronic digital images were the up and coming rage among perverts, and unique to the modern day and age in which we lived. But Boe was old school and liked to trade and own physical photographs. According to the arresting documents, he had dozens of photos of young children in sexually explicit positions, and some were allegedly infants. The details of his crime had stuck in my craw, but that wasn't the whole story.

Boe was a felon. Twenty-three years earlier he'd been convicted of child molestation and had served a measly two-year sentence. An unfortunate standard assigned to such a crime during that stage in America's history.

Versed in the criminal justice system beyond what the average citizen knew, I was aware of the policy of public pacification. Getting the story off the front page was the objective—not justice. Understanding the system as I did, prompted serious doubts that with the passing of time, his criminal history would be taken into thoughtful consideration—if mentioned at all. Most likely it would be overlooked or brushed under the carpet to appease the citizens—giving the community a false sense of security. Boe's current offense would not likely extend his incarceration—it should.

Playing the devil's advocate, I had to admit there was no proof that he'd continued his life of crime as a child molester. Likewise, there wasn't any evidence that his ways had changed. Being a drifter and an unknown entity Olin was free to prey upon the unsuspecting innocents wherever he went. The fact he hadn't been caught wasn't proof that he'd had a life-changing epiphany from his first go around in the rebar hotel. If he had changed, why was he packing a pocket full of kiddie porn?

Experience had been a cruel teacher in the past when it came to the judicial system. In each case, I considered the lessons taught to have been building blocks to a stronger foundation upon which to pursue righteousness. Having exercised my trust in the courts to do the right thing, more times than not, resulted in a disappointing outcome. I was in a position to take advantage of Boe's new-found freedom and mete out the justice deserved and overdue by twenty-three years.

By happenstance or fate, Olin's path and mine had crossed at a West Linn diner a few months earlier. Anna Sasins had invited Tom Kuhl and me to meet in preparation for our Alaska trip at the joint where Boe worked as the chief fry-cook and head bottle washer. I'd never met the guy before that day, didn't know his name or who he was, but I took exception to his presence.

My first impressions of Boe I attributed to a manifestation by Destiny—my familiar Spirit. She wasn't happy, and her reaction to Boe was notable. I suspected she had, as was her nature, instilled within him a reminder of the pain and suffering he had perpetrated on the innocent while in my presence and that I could look into his soul and see his evil. He didn't appear to understand why he reacted toward me in such a rude manner, only that he'd experienced a supernatural clash within that didn't make sense. I didn't have the time at our first meeting to follow up on who this creeper was, or what made him tick, but when the Alaska project had finished, I'd cycle back and pay him a visit. I was sure we'd get to the bottom of why he'd given me the heebie-jeebies.

It was on my return from Alaska that Anna suggested we reconvene at the diner to tie off the operation and subsequently learned Olin's name. We filed into Peg's Diner where I looked to see if the old geezer was at the grill. Almost instantly I noticed the stillness in the spirit and knew something had changed. I inquired of our teenage waitress if she knew the whereabouts of the old cook. With the slightest prodding, she divulged his name and the turn of events that had befallen him. Boe had been arrested, in jail, and no longer worked at the diner.

Since those early visits to Peg's, I'd made the inconsequential little place my favorite stop to grab a cup of coffee, relax, and hang out. The young waitress, Sondra, and I were soon on a first name basis. As it turned out, she was a chatterbox who held nothing in reserve. Most of the jabber was nothing more than what teenagers usually focus on when they start out in life and living on their own. As she would ramble, the occasional vague memory from my childhood would cross my thoughts and shine a light on the meaning of the good old days.

I took my seat at the table at the rear of the diner, Sondra, brimming with excitement, met me there. "Do you remember Olin Boe?" Before I could answer, she continued. "The old guy you talked about?"

"The ol' pervert?"

"Yes."

"How could I forget him?"

"Well, like he came in here yesterday. He scared me so much. Seeing him made my heart race. He asked for the owner's phone number, and for the rest of the day, every time the door opened, I would jump thinking it would be him, even dropped a couple of orders. It was horrible."

"He must have made bail."

"He said Peg promised him a job and he'd be coming back to work soon. I hope not. I don't want to be around someone like him."

"You could tell Peg how you feel about the guy?"

"Oh, I don't think so. She'd fire me."

I hadn't spoken with Peg, but if she shared the foolhardy theory many of my former co-workers at the aluminum plant believed she was a victim waiting to happen. "Not discussing Boe won't make him go away. That's an ostrich approach."

"Ostrich?"

"You know, they have their heads buried in the sand." I spoke from experience. Urbanites considered crime to be part of big city life and best accepted or ignored. I'd heard all the comments, "Nothing I can do about it. It doesn't affect me," and so on. I didn't see it that way. I had the power to fix it for Sondra and for the world at large, and had every intention of doing so.

"Don't give him a second thought. He's an old creeper that's after little kids."

"That's easy for you to say you don't have to work around him." She shrugged as her lips pressed tightly into a bitter smile.

"He'll be gone before you know it."

Her head dipped slightly. The grimace more pronounced as she said, "Sure."

She didn't believe me. As much as I wanted to tell her my intentions, it wasn't possible. To her, I was another talking head. I let her have the last say.

"I thought you'd be more interested."

A long few seconds dragged out until the diner's wall phone rang and saved us both from the moment's awkwardness that had set in.

Olin Boe hadn't been on an active target list since I learned of his incarceration. A guy like him didn't have many friends with money and to my way of thinking it was highly questionable whether he'd make bail. But somehow he'd managed and I suspected Peg was behind his new lease on life.

Unbeknownst to Boe, he'd become fair game and made a significant move to the top of my project list. I doubted he would celebrate the honor that I'd bestowed on him. As for my part, speed was of the essence. Not so much for Sondra, but because Boe was foolhardy enough to commit another criminal offense and end up with his bail revoked.

The conversation with Sondra had brought to mind that I was a member of a secret society known as Palatini. They represented the resurrected knighthood of freelancer's—champions of the people, paragons of virtue, chivalrous, and all that heroic sounding stuff. Simply put, the Palatini Knights never called 9-1-1. They took care of business their way—the vigilante way.

Palatini contributions to justice were large-scale operations. Our mission was to take out human traffickers, destroy child pornography rings, and rescue as many children as possible who were in harm's way. It was a numbers game, and satisfaction came as we wrapped up each leg of a project.

On a personal level, there was nothing more satisfying than assassinating an evil individual. It wasn't a yearning to step back in time and relive the earliest stages of my Calling or any need I felt to get in touch with my roots. That was pure psychobabble. I enjoyed a personal, one on one encounter. It fulfilled the deeper need in my life—that of love. Yes, love. There, I said it. The killings were demonstrations of my love. My mission, long before my affiliation with Society Palatini, was to protect and defend the innocent like Sondra. Children, elderly, feeble, and weaker of our society; status made no difference to me. If and at what time they might have a need for my brand of love was all that mattered.

A warrior stands in the gap and fights the battles to save the innocent from their enemies. I'm not one to hope for a better and more compassionate world. Hope applied with faith may be a viable attribute, but concerning the evil in human nature, it falls short of eradicating the problem.

Society's misguided concept of evolving humankind doesn't lend itself to the understanding of the base nature of humanity. We are wealthier and better educated, but more capable of violence and wickedness. Sympathy and kindheartedness shown by our judicial system toward the vilest of criminals are the breeding ground for the growth of evil. Whatever peaceful coexistence we've obtained with evil was delivered at the hands of good people who were willing to do great violence upon the wicked.

Olin presented such an opportunity to right a wrong. However, Sondra needed protection from the knowledge a creature like me existed. She could not be made aware of my objectives.

Meanwhile, Anna was deeply immersed in the piece she was writing on a local Sunni cleric that held extreme views of Islam and spouted them freely in and around a Corvallis, Oregon mosque. A Pacific Northwest publication had approached Anna suggesting her style would give the proper attention and slant to the story. The editor believed their brand of religion placed them in the crosshairs for a human rights investigation and wanted Anna to raise a red flag. The ploy was nothing new in the world of media. After Anna briefed me about the Iman's activities and his anti-western ideologies that were opposed to our American culture I had to agree with their agenda on this one.

To complicate matters, as Anna delved into the investigation she saw a possible Palatini intervention in the offing. She'd been placed in phone contact with an anonymous informant who'd given her raw video material on the Iman. Not realizing the stress level she was under, I asked her to add Boe to her fieldwork.

She made quick work of my request, so she could move forward with other items on her plate. Her fact-finding revealed one significant detail of interest—his previous conviction for sexual assault on a minor. Anna noted from his work history he'd been a drifter. His residence and employment changed frequently, but rarely outside of Oregon. His forte was unskilled labor. He'd pulled green chain at different lumber mills up and down the Oregon coast, worked as a roustabout on the Portland docks, and most recently, a cook at Peg's Café. Armed with the information she'd obtained, I decided to ask more of Anna by involving her in my plan.

Over dinner I said, "Olin has to go."

"I'll be there for you as best I can, but I'm knee deep in Islamic honor killings and pedophilia right here in America. I must get something in by the deadline, and I will likely end up with a series of articles featuring the Iman."

I didn't have to tell her to be careful what she wrote on the Iman. If we initiated a Palatini operation against him, we'd be better off with less said in the public arena. There was no reason to tip off the FBI with something in print that would pique their curiosity. They would want to get in on the action and take the Iman down.

"We can avoid things getting messy if we launch the project. Every one of us will relentlessly pursue him to his grave."

Anna blew strands of hair from in front of her face. Her frustration showing as she briefed me on another matter that she'd held in reserve for the right moment. "On top of my deadline, Maximilian called asking for my assistance with additional Palatini issues."

At three in the afternoon on the twenty-eighth, I slipped into Peg's for a cup of java and immediately saw Boe behind the grill. I'd never laid eyes on the older waitress that made her way to the back table where I'd settled in with my back to the wall. She sat a menu on the table and opened the cover page. "Coffee," she asked?

Emblazoned on her blouse was, "Peg." It wasn't a stretch to ask, "You the owner of this place?"

"Nineteen years, Hon, nineteen long years."

"Coffee—black." Surprised that Sondra wasn't working the floor, I suspected her absence was based on Boe's attendance. "Where's Sondra today?" I asked.

Without making eye contact, she replied, "Sondra moved. I'll be right back with the coffee and give you time to look the menu over."

"Thanks, I'm going to miss her. She was a good kid."

When Peg turned away, I fixed my sights on Boe. Sondra couldn't stomach the idea of working alongside the likes of this pervert and had no idea help was on the way.

That evening, Boe along with a middle-aged, heavyset waitress, with her hair pulled up in a topknot, closed the café. The waitress hurried across the parking lot toward a city transit bus while Olin climbed into a GMC Sonoma pickup that had seen its better days. He let the clunker idle while he fired up a smoke and dangled it out the driver's window. I counted the minutes. When he finished his smoke, he crept the pickup forward to the lot's exit.

I watched the following night as Boe closed the diner, repeating his previous routine to include smoking a cigarette in his heap before he left the lot.

Early Thursday evening, I told Anna, "I have to take out the trash."

"The trash went out last night, Walter."

"No, I really need to take out the "trash," that's why I'll need a ride to Peg's café tonight."

Anna watched as I prepared my Glock and Walther for action. "Expecting more trouble than usual from that old man?"

I shook my head and smiled. "The best-laid plans of mice and men often go awry."

We pulled into the parking lot and looked for Olin's red Jimmy pickup. It was nowhere in sight. Anna slipped into the diner and confirmed that two women were working the shift. We'd have to wait for another day.

On Friday afternoon, I swung the Avenger through the strip mall's parking lot and spotted Boe's Sonoma in the general parking area. That was the good news; however, there was bad news too. At five o'clock, activity levels were higher than on other days that I'd set up surveillance and for good reason; Halloween was in full swing. Children were dressed in costume attire, some in groups while others were with their escorts, mobbing mall shops trick-or-treating. I called Anna, "We're on for tonight if you're free."

"I don't have time for a date, you know—"

I quickly interrupted, "You can call it what you like, but if you're too busy, say so. I can take care of business by myself."

For a moment, silence filled the airways. Finally, it dawned on Anna what I was saying. "I would love to join you this evening. Why don't you leave your car at home and we will take mine?"

It wasn't easy to communicate our plans over an unsecured network. We had developed a form of informal code talk that sounded like bantering and was taken in good fun but carried a hidden message that accomplished what needed to be said. A cloak-and-dagger sounding conversation had a way of attracting federal agencies that monitored the airwaves in this post 9/11 atmosphere.

"My plans exactly," I responded.

As the strip mall closed for business, the trickle of kids dwindled to an occasional goblin or princess. Boe and the bun-headed waitress closed the diner a few minutes early and cleared the building before nine. Boe climbed into his pickup and lit up while the waitress scurried across the parking lot to the bus stop. A quick scan of the area and confidence set in. The coast was clear to advance the project. Anna's Lexus purred as I climbed out and began my clandestine approach. I had eight minutes to engage my prey. It took only five.

Boe, with his driver's window down and arm outstretched, had no defense as he held his smoldering cigarette. Casually I walked toward the mall with my hands hidden and then angled toward Boe's junker. A driver's side blind spot was as good as a tree blind during deer hunting season. All I needed to do was stay in the sweet spot until I was within arm's reach.

Only a few feet from the pickup I pulled my knit ski cap down, positioned the eyeholes, thus turning it into a face mask.

One step then another, one last quick step and the door flew open as I jerked the handle. Boe, caught off guard, tumbled partially from his vehicle and into my waiting arms. As he hung onto the open door and the vehicle seat, I pushed the muzzle of my Walther against his face and said, "Sssh."

He stammered and stuttered while I pulled him to his feet, spun him around and gave him a love tap with the muzzle of my weapon to gain his cooperation. At my command, he moved his hands behind his back. He'd been there before only this time there wasn't a police officer present to protect his rights as in times past. The zip ties I'd brought especially for this occasion secured firmly onto his wrists.

"You're no cop."

I pulled a piece of Duct tape from the back of my leather glove and slapped it over his mouth then shoved him back into his ride and across the bench seat to the passenger side. Once I'd secured Boe with the seatbelt, I locked his door. I didn't want anything tragic to befall him. I situated behind the steering wheel, but before putting the pickup in gear, I pulled the knit cap from my head and looked him square in the eye, and prepared for a formal introduction. Expecting a nasty reaction when he saw my face I was surprised when there wasn't an indication that he recognized me from our previous contact. However, I gathered from his blank stare he knew why I was there and how the night would turn out.

Some people have lived lives they figure sooner or later will catch up to them. Boe was one of those individuals who knew what he was and that perdition nipped at his heals.

We drove the route through Estacada to North Fork Reservoir and hooked a left that soon turned into Abbott Road and on into Squaw Lakes. Anna followed closely until I slowed the Jimmy to a stop at a forest road junction. Anna's car crept alongside the pickup. When she dropped the passenger window, I said, "Hang tight right here until I get back."

"Be careful; it's terribly dark."

What about the darkness was disconcerting? Could it be Anna's orientation to her living conditions? A city girl who found comfort surrounded by neon signs, street lights, and headlights from passing vehicles? My orientation was altogether different raised on a ranch and tucked away at the head of a valley. I learned to trust darkness more than light.

The Squaw Lake area was hidden amongst a mixed conifer forest and perfect for what I had planned. Boe and I continued in his pickup to a turnaround at the end of the dirt road. The vehicle swung a wide circle, the headlights illuminating a small camping area. We were alone. I turned the ignition off but left the lights on. Opening the driver's side door, I stepped out and turned to face Boe.

For a long minute, I enjoyed the peace and tranquility the forest brought to what would become a chaotic scene if I pulled the tape from his mouth. With my Walther in hand, I found no reason to upset the ambiance. As he squinted and grimaced, I made my first shot count. The second round blew a portion of his skullcap off and took the passenger side window out.

From the pickup's floorboard, I heaped together a pile of trash positioned to ignite the seat and eventually the gas tank. Newspapers scrunched together, and a brown paper bag filled with used tissue made perfect fuel for the fire. A stroke of convenience saved one step in the process as I used his lighter from the ashtray to ignite the pile. I rolled the driver's side window partially down to allow oxygen to work its magic with the flames.

When the blaze roared, I tossed my empty Glock under the driver's seat. No sense wasting valuable ammo on the setup. Unexpectedly, I caught myself saying, "Goodbye pal." I never considered myself sentimental, but after I had dropped the gun on the floorboard, a tear welled up in my eye. I would miss my close friend.

The cold, fresh mountain air sent a burning sensation into my lungs as I ran the distance to Abbott Road and my connecting ride. In the light of a waxing crescent moon, I experienced freedom like never before. As I picked up the pace and ran as fast as I could, a howl caught in my throat. I felt like a wild animal running free. The impulse rose inside again to let out another, but if Anna overheard the sound, she might not understand what I was feeling.

Anna's Lexus sat idling on the gravel topped turnout. She smartly avoided leaving tire prints on the soft forestry road that Boe and I had taken to its end, and his. She saw me approach and sprung the electric locks allowing me access to the passenger seat. Rather than boast of my exploits with Boe a tune came to mind and I belted it out with gusto, "Another one bites the dust, another one bites the dust, dah, dah, dah…"

"You don't know the words, do you?" Anna asked.

"Not a chance, honey," I responded proudly. I didn't know the lyrics or what the original meaning of the song was, but it came to mind, and I thought it was apropos for my mood.

Anna swung a three-point turnaround and gave her car the juice. Traveling back through the mountain passes, I was surprised she hadn't asked questions about how the kill went. She had interpreted my return to the car alone and happy as a lark, to be enough evidence the operation had gone off without a hitch. Perhaps she was preoccupied with more pressing feelings.

"When are you going to finalize your move from the trailer house to our condo?" She asked.

"I've been working on it. I want to unload the place, but I'm concerned about Detective Sergeant Ware snooping around."

"He's no longer an officer."

"Tell him that. Sale of the property might make him more suspicious and provide a traceable transaction to my identity."

"I'll give Maximillian a call. He has financial resources that might be helpful. I'm sure we can run it through our offshore Palatini accounts."

"Ware will still be a problem, and he's not likely to go away, right?"

Anna nodded, "He was a tenacious detective. It would be uncharacteristic of him to fade away."

"Right, so I propose to muddy the waters. I left my Glock in Boe's pickup."

Anna slowly applied the brakes. "I hope you can retrieve it quickly."

"Listen to me for a second, and I'll let you in on the game plan. I left the gun for law enforcement to find. Boe was a criminal, a felon no less, and out on bail. When his murder is investigated, the weapon will be found under the seat on driver's side of the pickup. Ballistics won't match the Glock as the murder weapon used to kill Boe. If the shooter didn't drop the weapon after it was used, it might be assumed Boe was the one illegally in possession of the Glock."

I let it sink in for a minute then continued. "When you ran Boe's name and information you said he hadn't racked any other jail time besides the chomo charge twenty-some years ago,"

"Chomo?"

"Child molester, baby."

Anna sighed.

When I talked code, she picked up on the meanings. When I spoke slang, it would pass over her head. I'd managed to convey to her the meaning of "perps" to broadly cover all classifications of criminal behavior. However, jargon and contractions frustrated her and ultimately lost its effectiveness to communicate what I wanted to say.

Anna responded, "No additional incarcerations. He stayed close to the Portland community occasionally traveling around the state for employment."

"My Glock has been used over the past few years to kill several of these criminal predators. I don't know what the cops have for forensic evidence to tie the gun to murders, but it's time to move it out of my inventory."

"Why now? Why not before?"

"I figured getting caught was in my future. When that day came, I wanted to stand up in court, and admit I'd killed every one of them. I did the job the courts refused to do the first time around. Maybe it's selfish on my part, but I didn't want someone else taking credit for my kills."

"What's changed?"

I felt Anna was fishing for confirmation of my feelings for her or our relationship. "The scenario has changed—I've changed. If Boe is linked as a suspect in the executions I've committed, it'll take the heat off the search for the killer. In any case, the weapon is no longer in my possession, and can't be connected to me."

"I think you're right. The police will recover the weapon and launch an extensive investigation to link Boe to the weapon, if for no other reason but to close the books on a few cold cases."

"I'm counting on it."

"What about Boe's motives? Why would he kill people who were child molesters and criminals like himself?"

"Like I said, I'm not after a clear picture of why Boe killed them because he didn't. All I want to do is muddy the waters."

There are no perfect crimes, and it's always a mistake to try and rig a perfect frame. The beauty of my old Glock was it had never been traceable to me. If I wasn't caught with it in my possession like Olin Boe, I couldn't be connected to it. "I'm also going to unload the Avenger. It's been a good ride, but it's been at too many kill sites."

"The Avenger?" Anna questioned.

"Don't you remember? It was your idea."

When the light came on, she was quick to agree. "That's a good idea, I can help you sell your car. I have a mechanic friend who buys and sells used vehicles. I'll give you his name and number. After that, we can find you a suitable vehicle for a replacement."

"Thanks, honey, I knew I could count on you."

The two-hour trip back to Portland seemed faster than our trip to Squaw Lakes although the distance hadn't changed. As we neared the condo, I had one more favor to ask, "Do you still have your police sources?"

"Yes."

"I'd like to find out if Ware has snooped around in those cold cases of mine or if he's calling in favors on the old cases. He had one or more of my business cards that he could only have picked up from one of my projects that ended with a kill."

"You interviewed family members and gave them cards. Do you suspect he's been in contact with one of them?"

"Maybe…he's a private investigator. The fact he has one of my business cards in his possession tells me he's still working the vigilante cases the same as when he was a cop. Maybe it stuck in his craw from when he was on the force. It's got to be hard for a seasoned veteran like Ware to almost solve the case, and then have the FBI slap him down, take the case out from under him, and then lose the scent."

"I imagine it was a blow to his ego because he was a good detective and he knew it."

"Still, I want to find out what he's up to before he deals the trump card of our game."

"The fastest way is to let him interview you. Until then, I'll check with my sources. What about the move to the condo?"

"Tomorrow I'll gut the trailer while you work with Max to unload it."

The spirits of the dead that haunted Halloween night had returned to the netherworld taking Olin Boe with them.

Relaxing on the sofa, I mused on how to contact Sondra. She'd be excited to hear that Boe was gone—forever. If she wanted to return to her employment, the way had been cleared. She would be shocked to learn her co-worker had a previous felony conviction for child molestation. She would be further devastated to discover, her friend who she'd frequently shot the breeze with, was a cold-blooded killer. She was better off searching for a new job and naïve to the ways of my world.

CHAPTER 2

After breakfast, I gave Anna a quick kiss. "I have to roll. By getting an early start, I can finish clearing everything out of the trailer and be ready for market before day's end."

"How many trips do you think it will take?"

"I'll run the Avenger to the storage lot and grab my pickup. I doubt if there is more than one full load to bring back."

"All right, I'll go ahead and contact Maximillian about his financial sources. I owe him a call to find out what he needs."

I pulled Anna into my embrace and gave her a kiss worthy of our relationship. I thought I was holding a cold fish. I was going to ask if she had something on her mind, but I needed to rock-n-roll.

The '57 fired up and rolled off the storage lot without issue. The old pickup had set for weeks and yet started on the first try. I made my way south through Portland Metro, and up on the Interstate. I placed a phone call to Shelly who lived in the park across the street from my trailer. Casual chatter ensued as we shot the breeze, saying nothing substantive, and going nowhere. Finally, Shelly asked, "How is the transition going? Do you still plan to sell the trailer?"

"I'll have everything moved out today. Maybe you know someone interested in short-term employment. I need to get the trailer spotless and the lawn looking manicured."

"I'd be glad to take care of that."

"That would be really great! I'll make it worth your time. I'll be at the trailer in a half hour."

Shelley smiled and waved from across the street as I backed my pickup into the driveway. Her friendliness was a good sign. Maybe Ware had ceased to pester her about my comings and goings.

Moments later she walked across the trailer park hardtop to my doorstep. "Mister Goe, I'd like to do a walk-through of the trailer to ensure I understand what you'd like done."

"No problem," I said. I didn't want to rush her, but there was the matter of Ware showing up that I wanted to avoid and slip away into the proverbial sunset without his knowing where I'd disappeared. Two bits of information I wanted before a chance encounter occurred with him. First, I wanted feedback from Anna's resource at the police station. Secondly, Max's input on the secretive purchase of the trailer. "Let's do the walk through now, and I'll leave you with a door key. You can take care of the cleaning at your leisure. Don't worry about the mail this time, I'll have it forwarded."

Shelly liked to talk. I hadn't noticed it before, but the dilly-dallying at the trailer had given time for a blue Chevy Impala to park crosswise of my driveway, blocking my exit. Private Snoop, Brandon A. Ware was back, and this time he wasn't wearing a friendly smile. I said goodbye to Shelley, who had turned to see Ware stepping from his car. She wanted to avoid Ware too and hurried across the street to her home.

I turned my attention to the private investigator.

"Mister Goe, Brandon Ware, you might remember? We met—"

"I remember."

"I was hoping we could talk for a few minutes."

"About?"

"I represent a client that's looking for answers to his daughter's death, and I believe you might be able to shed light on the case."

"How's that?"

"Is there a place we could sit and talk?" Ware motioned toward the trailer.

"Not here," I said.

His lips pursed together as we stood face to face and sized each other up. The easiest way to shape the dialogue was to first control the location. Neutral ground that was open to the public and one where I could walk out when I wanted.

"How about you buy me a cup of coffee?" I watched for his response.

The hint of a smile crept up Ware's cheek as he nodded, "I could do that. Where?"

"The big mall where the road branches about a half-mile from here will work. We can meet there in ten minutes."

"Mister Goe, I do not want you to feel rushed. If you need more time, I don't mind waiting here in my car until you're ready."

"Ten minutes."

Ware nodded and opened the leather-bound notebook that he carried tucked securely under his left arm, annotated momentarily then closed it. The last time Ware and I had met his notebook held one of my business cards that he promptly displayed in my view.

Detective Sergeant Ware had retired from Multnomah County Sheriff's Department after thirty-two years of service. He didn't have to stay that long to retire, but I surmised he couldn't handle life not being a cop. He was true blue, and it ran to his core.

Flashing a business card in my face was nothing more than a fact-finding mission. He wanted to watch my reaction and show that he possessed something of mine that connected me to his case. He saw it as a leverage technique; I saw it as an old trick executed by an old cop.

Ware was seated in the food court of the mall when I arrived. I pointed to one of the fast food joints that served coffee and said, "Large, black." When Ware returned to the maze of tables clustered in the food court, I'd taken the liberty of moving our seating arrangements from the sheltered corner he'd chosen for our conversation to a small center table. Although the location exposed my back adding to my discomfort, it likewise created uneasiness for Ware. He'd lost the first battle for control.

"So, Detective, why are we here?"

Ware paused and chuckled before proceeding. "I'm investigating the murder of Mona Lott. I have reason to believe you may have interviewed her for one of your writings."

"Yeah, I remember talking with her. What about it?"

Ware opened his notebook and made a notation. "I'm sorry Mister Goe, I searched extensively for your published article on the victim and was unable to come up with it."

"That's right; I didn't pursue the article because of her untimely death."

"How long after the interview was she murdered or that you were made aware she had been killed?"

I took a deep breath before answering to slow the pace. After a few drawn-out moments, I responded, "I don't remember any of the details surrounding her death." Again, Ware made a notation in the leather-bound notebook. I decided to challenge his position for control. "Aren't murder investigations conducted by law enforcement?"

"Yes, generally, but private investigators are commonly employed to look into both criminal and civil matters of the law."

A vague answer and I doubted private eyes were frequently involved in criminal cases. It's a money racket. Nonetheless, Ware was a tough, experienced, tight-lipped, no-nonsense investigator who had notoriously run roughshod over journalists and reporters alike when he was with the County Mounties. I remember having great admiration for him and the way he manhandled the press. His looks hadn't changed much, maybe slightly heavier and older-looking with the same drab suit jacket and matching tie that he wore on his rare television interviews. His behavior hadn't changed either. He continued to approach his new-found career from his tainted blue perspective. The only problem I had with his bulldog tenacity was that he'd been closer to catching the vigilante than any other law enforcement agency. That made him dangerous.

I leaned forward. Running my fingers across my mustache and goatee to the bottom of my chin, I asked, "Who's financing this gig?"

"The Lott family has unanswered questions."

"As I recall the Lott's had plenty of money. A private investigator like yourself would be in line for a pretty good grub-steak if you milked it out."

"It's not about the money, Mr. Goe."

That's what I wanted to hear. The motive and driving force behind his pesky quest was ego. Ware had given me a window into his soul, but I couldn't let on that I understood. "It's always about the money."

Ware's bruised blue pride was exploitable. In his tenure with the MCSD, he had a series of unsolved murders in his jurisdiction and the weight of responsibility to solve them he continued to bear. That was a weakness.

As a private eye, maybe he'd discovered additional evidence in Mona's murder. Knowing there was a personal motivation to the investigation, I continued to control the speed and intensity of the interview.

Once again, Ware opened his notepad revealing my business card. Game on, I thought. He upped the ante. It wasn't until he slid the card out of the plastic pocket that I was made aware he had at least two cards in his possession. Troubling. Where had the other one come from? Were there more? I had to shake the concern and keep my cool. Ware pushed the card across the table, his eyes measuring my every move. "Did you leave this business card with Mona Lott?"

Picking up the card I looked it over and flipped it to see if any notes were on the back. I had taken extensive care to ensure no fingerprints were on the card when I gave it to Mona. In Ware's presence, if it was the same card, I didn't want to come off careful about getting prints on the card. I tossed it back on the table and said, "Can't say if this is the same card I left with Mona. I can tell you, as a professional journalist, I wouldn't have left without leaving a card. Where was it found?"

"Family members recovered the card at Mona's apartment when they were cleaning it out." The big man leaned forward. The imposing view intended to intimidate. "Did you meet at Mona's apartment for the interview?"

"No. As I recall, we met at a local diner."

"Do you remember the name of the place?"

"Not at all...I fail to see how any of these questions can help you answer questions for the Lott family."

I had respect for Ware, but respect and trust didn't go hand in hand. He was an adversary in the greater scheme of my life's work, and I had to treat him as such. "I haven't followed the case, but if you're still looking for the killer, maybe you should look at her loser boyfriend or the crowd she ran with?"

"Owen Moore was incarcerated at the time of her murder, and neither of them had many friends."

"Is that right? My impression was anyone with a needle was her friend." Moore had people that cowered at his every demand. It wouldn't be a stretch to believe Moore caused her death. "Maybe he used a surrogate, maybe he didn't, either way, he was ultimately responsible."

"You seem sure that Moore was behind her death."

"Nothing is certain unless you can prove it. It's the way I remember Mona and the case, that's all."

With a genuine laugh, the big guy said, "I take it you had a relatively low opinion of Mona and her lifestyle."

"Very relative. She was just another story—plain and straightforward. She didn't mean anything to me. Listen, I need to get back and finish up."

Ware responded, "I have a few more questions I'd like to ask?"

"Not today." I scooted the chair out and said, "Thanks for the coffee—I had a delightful time."

I knew Ware had a few tricks up his sleeve, but so did I. One of the best Palatini operators in the business, Thomas Orlando Kuhl, had taught me counter-reconnaissance maneuvers. In the past, when I operated as a lone wolf, I only considered dodging law enforcement's efforts to snare me. But as a pack hunter, I'd learned to move in ways to protect the Palatini from discovery by criminal organizations as well as cops. Kuhl was a stickler about following steps to change routes to and from home or safe houses. Dumping a tail or ensuring you didn't pick one up was more involved than taking different streets to a destination. The route included multiple stops at malls, diners or coffee shops, and a bookstore or public library. If you were being followed by someone skilled, like Ware, at some point they were either detected or unable to stay up with the movement.

I contacted Anna by cell phone soon after I cleared the mall parking lot. "Had a talk with a stalker. Heading home late." It went without saying since Ware had made contact that I'd be a few hours in the process once I'd finished at the trailer. I wasn't worried about Ware tailing me to the trailer, only when I left for Anna's condo.

"I have news too…an agreement was reached on the mobile home."

"Wow! That was fast." My past was about to be left in the dust. With the transaction being run through an overseas account, my future looked more secure than ever, and I'd likely be clear of Ware's ability to follow my paper trail. Any dead end was to my advantage in our cat and mouse game. Anna's long silence raised my concern. "Maximilian asked for my assistance managing projects."

It was my turn to respond in silence.

Shrouded in coolness, she continued, "I've accepted the challenge."

It sounded like a monkey wrench was being tossed into our plans of cohabitation. Max was constantly on the road facilitating the needs of Palatini operators. How was Anna going to pull that off without causing considerable disruption to our living situation? Was she going to find happiness in being a facilitator? She enjoyed the hunt and the kill as much as the next operator. Maybe she was planning to drag me along with her? I hoped not. I couldn't survive being out of the projects and living like a cabin boy. Too many questions came to mind, and the airway wasn't the venue to explore the answers. I had cut the call before we said anymore. Unfortunately, the thoughts persisted. I resolved the issue by readdressing the bottom line for all Palatini. Mission first. Anna could do what she wanted, it was her life, and likewise for me.

After muttering a bon voyage to my trailer, I locked the door and slipped one of Ware's old business cards he'd left on a previous call, under the glass panel on the screen door. A subliminal message if Ware returned. The bridge that linked us was about to be buried. Anna wanted me cloistered at the condo to avoid accidental contact with Ware until the heat died down. I couldn't argue with her logic, it was the simplest solution to the problem.

Engaging in counter-reconnaissance tricks on the way to Anna's condo, I stopped by a tavern for a shot of Jameson's then off to a Fred Meyers grocery store for a fifteen-minute jaunt. From there I caught the Interstate south until traffic thinned on the city outskirts. A lonely

Mom and Pop's gas station looked like a good place for a stale cup of coffee. After fueling my pickup, I slipped east onto a state highway and headed north, back toward Anna's home. Ware, my worthy opponent, didn't turn up at any of my stops.

When I arrived at Anna's place, I'd missed the five-thirty local news broadcast. By now, the cops were bound to be scouring over the remains of a dead man at Squaw Lakes. I wanted to hear the breaking news for myself. In some sense, the broadcaster announced to the audience that the playwright's work was ready to view. Portlanders would be tuned into the news for entertainment, and I wanted my work showcased for all to see.

I looked around the condo and noticed Anna had many nice things from brand-name furniture to designer curtains. The more I saw, the more I realized my new setting made me uncomfortable. I didn't need ritzy hotels or luxurious accommodations when an economy motel would do just as well. Anna's Lexus was an expensive, beautiful car, but I didn't need to impress or be noticed by anyone.

Often, I had holed up in my mobile home and drew upon spiritual dimensions to keep me company. Each time, Destiny guided my steps to a viable target. There was a time when I didn't report to anyone, but now I'm held to account daily by Anna and Max. I'd lost my identity once, replaced by a façade, only to find myself faced with the same issue—traceability since Anna had legitimized Walter Eloy Goe. If I fit into my new surroundings and Anna's world, I did so like a chameleon, as I would have done in anyone else's world—it will never be my world. Do I love Anna? Yes, but love may not be enough.

The late edition news broadcast mentioned the torched pickup and homicide that I'd staged. But I'd misjudged the gravity of the execution. Had I killed Boe at a local park and torched his ride, maybe then it would have garnered the media attention. Given the nature of crime in the Portland area, I surmised an old man burned to a crisp at a remote mountain lake area was meaningless to the metro area.

CHAPTER 3

"Good and evil grow up together and are bound in an equilibrium that cannot be sundered.

The most we can do is try to tilt the equilibrium toward the good"

—Eric Hoffer

Time crawled. For the past three weeks, I've lived like a fugitive on the lam. Cooped up in a posh condo wasn't the dreamy life I'd hoped for with Anna. A fancy cage was all it was. I adored Anna and enjoyed being with her, but the idea of hiding from Brandon A. Ware gnawed at me. I suppose from time to time my discontent showed, but if so, Anna never seemed to notice. She had her nose to the grindstone and rarely looked up. She had quelled my concerns for being underfoot, but there were signs. During her adult years, she'd been a single dweller; I came at a price—her freedom. Never had it been more evident than when she was busy searching the Internet or conversing with Maximillian on her newly assigned duties.

Safely hidden at Anna's condo, I was lonelier than I'd ever been in my life and I'd spent most of my life alone. Work dominated Anna's life, and at times she'd given me the cold shoulder. She had taken time from her busy schedule to include me in a brief rundown of the progress she'd made handling Palatini finances under Max's tutelage. I'm sure her goal was admirable; she wanted me to feel included. But, at the end of the day, the realization had set in that I had become a bystander in Anna's world. Struggling to adapt to that world had become too cramped of a lifestyle, and I wasn't ready to accept being sidelined. I had to find a way back to vigilantism.

The status of Anna's mission recaps provided an opportunity for discussion. Three Palatini projects were currently underway stateside and another half-dozen internationally.

"Is that all?" I asked.

"Two of the operations have had multiple legs taken out over the course of a year and one action overseas is in its third year. We are facing some very complex organizations."

"Considering the magnitude of human trafficking we are facing don't you think we need all-hands-on-deck?" In my way of thinking, hiding from Ware was counterproductive to our mission.

Anna wasn't blind to my inference. "We are in league to elicit justice, and you are a liability to the organization right now. The only project I can put you on is international. Is that what you want, to leave already?"

"Mission first," I chimed back.

Anna's orientation to Max's facilitator position had started with the three American-based projects. These were typically small-scale projects, garden-variety, easily financed, and coordinated.

Only in the past few days had Anna taken on the International element too. Funneling money to the hitters and handling communications overseas was Anna's forte. She loved the challenge of the new facilitator position and didn't let on she was stressed, but I saw through the veneer. She'd become unable to devote time or energy to a local project that she'd sat on for a month. She could have passed the project to me, but she was unwilling for fear Ware would find my whereabouts. I didn't have the same concern.

Outside of the evening recap of Palatini business, Anna and I didn't speak much or often. With the passing of each day, we ran out of hours to have any time for ourselves. Consequently, I withdrew into my own world where I was comfortable.

Thanksgiving held no special place in my heart as far as family gatherings went, but it was on the horizon, and Anna hadn't mentioned plans for a festive occasion. I made plans to celebrate the event out on the town. If Anna didn't want to go, that was all right too. The excuse was more of a ploy to get out of prison for a night than it was to celebrate. Before the evening recap of events, I hoped to trigger Anna's thoughts on the holiday. As we sat next to each other on the sofa, I tossed out the idea we could make a day of it, together, just the two of us without the Internet or a phone. Anna was silent.

Anna gave the impression she'd rather avoid the topic as she launched into the recap, an abbreviated and lackluster spiel on the operations in play. Something had changed. I considered the thought we'd jumped the gun on cohabitating and concluded that if she was of the same opinion, I'd pack up and go.

"Do we need to make a change to our living arrangement?" The question sounded softer rolling around in my head than when it crossed my lips. It came out harsh.

"I'm torn over a situation." Anna's pause brought further uneasiness to our nightly ritual. "Maximilian's health is failing."

I nodded, "He's definitely no spring chicken, and the job carries a lot of stress."

"Walter, he's asked me to join him. He has materials that must be transferred into my possession."

"It's the right move. If something happened to him, there is no one ready to assist the operations—we'd be in a world of hurt."

Anna reclined under my arm and laid her head on my chest. "I would be flying to the Isle of Mann if I go."

"Not if, honey…Go! No need to think twice about it." There were no viable options. The greater good of the Palatini came first. "Look, he trusts your abilities to carry on the organization's mission in his absence."

She nodded her agreement.

Anna smiled. An expression I hadn't seen from her for the past few weeks. My motive, as pure as it sounded, had a self-serving aspect to what I'd said. Anna had hatched the idea for me to lie low at the condo until Ware gave up the chase. But, in her absence, the leash would be off. My craving could be fed.

It was a long minute before Anna responded. "I'll book my flight for this weekend."

I could hear the sound of relief in her voice, but she wasn't ecstatic. There were no five-star resorts in her immediate future like our trip to Italy. Life on the Isle of Mann would be much different from Portland and restrictive in many ways. It sounded perfect for me but not all that cozy to her.

"When I expanded from the stateside operations to funding the international projects one of the people I spoke with was Thomas."

"What's ol' Kuhl up to?"

"He is in Mexico. Thomas couldn't go into detail, but it involved the Los Zetas Drug Cartel."

"He's working drug runners?"

"Los Zetas is a cartel comprised of ex-military and police. These people are extremely violent and have a lot of irons in the fire other than drugs."

"All Mexican cartels are deep in narcotics and murder. One's not better than another. They all need to be taken out."

Arm in arm, we reclined on the leather sofa, but instead of relaxing, I sensed a heightened level of anxiety with her. It didn't mingle well with the excitement I felt. Images swirled as I conjured up drug lords, kingpins, and pushers with the crosshairs of my scope on each of them. Kuhl was a lucky cuss. No leash held him back. I wanted to let out a howl, but Anna wouldn't have understood my happiness.

Anna had pushed hard for my commitment to her living arrangement. She knew I was a man of honor and integrity, but other elements were at play, and the tide of life changed direction. Unforeseeable, was where it had swept us. Apart. Alone.

Anna ran her fingertips across my chest. The featherlike strokes weren't the result of a mechanical calmness, but a sign of preoccupation. There were no prompts that could be given to bring out whatever lingered in Anna's thoughts. I had to wait.

Slowly, Anna let slip her last concern. "I have confidential informants and professional connections. If they come across an urgent matter, they will try to make contact. In my absence, I will need your help to respond to their situations if an issue arises." Anna rose from where she lay cradled in my arm and searched my eyes.

"Absolutely. You know you can count on me."

It was apparent from the beginning of her new responsibilities that a project was out. A hitter in the field would find themselves frustrated if they had to round up supplies, money, or Palatini operators when in dire need. That's what Max was for. She had chosen between active engagement in a project and the facilitating of projects for others.

I reinforced my position, "You can't do field work and do justice to the project. That's how mistakes are made and cost operators their lives."

"I will make calls tomorrow and let my people know you are a trusted associate."

"You're a news reporter. You can tell them I'm your investigator."

"I write human interest stories."

"More reason to have a research team."

My mood continued to brighten in the light of a purposeful existence. Receptionist and secretarial duties were what Anna had in mind for me in her absence. Judge, jury, and executioner were more to my liking. She could attach whatever label she liked to me, in the end, what it amounted to was a "get out of jail free" card.

"A man who identified himself as, Matt Thaman, has information I'd like a file started on. Briefly, he said that he was speaking for his dead brother who he claims had been murdered and his organs harvested."

"Somebody butchered his brother? That's downright gruesome—but fascinating."

"He made contact after reading an article I had written on vigilantism. He intends to expose the story."

"Why not the cops. Your article would only scratch the surface of the problem."

"Thaman is a former law enforcement officer. According to him, police worked his brother's death. It's since grown stale and was moved to cold case detectives. He thinks they dumped the investigation in file thirteen."

"Where did this go down?"

"Southeast Portland in Lents."

"Lents! His brother was either poverty stricken or a bum. I'll check it out. If it rises to our level, I'll crank up an operation. If not, Thaman and I can have a nice chat about what interventions are necessary from a journalist's perspective."

I bedded down for the night and pondered the challenge that I'd accepted. I didn't know much about organ smugglers or how they selected their victims. Further, I'd likely need Thaman's help as a confidential informant or asset to weave through where his brother had come into contact with the butchers. Taking a cold contact like Thaman and turning him into an asset would test my skills in a way never before imagined. Other Palatini had developed assets and resources; I'm sure I could too. But I had a slight roadblock to overcome. To my way of thinking, handling new talent was like going on a blind date. While you chat with your date and become acquainted, you look for signs of chemistry forming. Without the right connection, the relationship that formed lacked the essential element of trust. Without trust, an asset was useless, unless you planned to use them as cannon fodder.

Before I was willing to expose myself to Thaman, I had another change to make. Walter had unfortunately become a valid entity and would take a backseat to a new façade—Hunter. It was the only way I could protect myself.

Anna understood that this time there would be no legitimizing my character. Hunter would be known on the street, and amongst the criminal elements by one name, first or last, it made no difference—Hunter.

Anna pounded away on the keyboard and barely acknowledged my kiss on her ear as I whispered, "See you later."

"Goodbye, and stay away from Ware."

I was going to wave goodbye from the door, but her eyes hadn't left the laptop to look in my direction. In the broader scope, it only made what I was going to do that much easier. Separating from who I know myself to be in Walter's world was a step in the evolution as Hunter. There could be no surreal mix of fact with fantasy. My façade would morph into the lowest of the low and I would survive amongst them as one of their own. Once my targets were defined Walter would manifest the scythe of justice slaying their filthy souls. Mentally my transformation had begun.

Hunter needed more than a name. He required his own look and attire to reinvent his new Scythian identity. Mental ascent to my façade as Hunter wasn't enough. Driving the Avenger and wearing Walter's clothing could create confusion at an inopportune moment revealing to a target that I wasn't who I pretended to be. Total immersion always in the character of Hunter was the only way to keep me safe from accidentally slipping out of my façade.

Secondhand stores were my favorite shopping experience. No pressure or expensive price tags, I cruised until I found the right combination of clothing. Walter had been decked out in casual slacks and penny loafers. Hunter wore a faded, black-hooded sweatshirt, without logos or emblems and a well-worn dark brown leather jacket over the hoodie—the bottom of the sweatshirt would hang below the jacket and over the top of ratty blue jeans. The combination worked well to protect from the wet and miserably cold Portland weather and aid my movements through cover and concealment. A heavy duty black leather belt from a Salvation Army store, and finally, at an Army–Navy surplus store called G.I. Joe's, I located a cheap pair of black jump boots with zippers on the sides. Except for the Walther, my outfit was complete.

When I returned to Anna's condo, I washed the clothes on the hottest setting sprayed the leather jacket, belt, and boots with Lysol. Twice. With everything dried, I slipped into the new look and checked it out in the mirror. It was the look I was going for. My transformation was nearly complete.

Pulling a few hundred bucks from a small safe that I'd placed under Anna's bed I separated the money into two equal amounts. With the greenbacks folded into my two front pockets for security purposes, I was prepared for a night on the town. I didn't see any reason to take my wallet with me when all I needed in my possession was my driver's license. One last thing and Hunter was ready to prowl. Into a side pocket of my bug out bag, I slipped my Walther .40-caliber and waited.

Running surveillance in the dive districts early in the evening had proven profitable from a reconnaissance perspective. Portland's Lents District was urban decay at its finest and had its own special circumstances that could be encountered. Understanding the street action was imperative to survival.

From my earliest vigilante days as a lone stalker of prey, I was aware of the tarnished reputation of the Southeast area. As was my manner, I fired up the Avenger and descended into the environment like a chameleon. Stealthy. Blending.

I didn't know Matt Thaman, or his brother's name, where he had lived or hung out. I only knew I wanted to get a feel for the neighborhood.

It didn't take long behind the wheel to grasp the uniquely dark nature presented by the Lents district. I've been in metro areas where lawlessness loomed in the shadows of every street. In the Lents District, it was a block or street that served as the hubs for criminality. However, eyes can deceive. I crisscrossed Southeast Foster, Insley, and Ellis, connecting with the vibes understood only through intuition.

Families were drawn to Lent's in earlier times searching for life, liberty, and the pursuit of their happiness, but the downturn of economics drove the large population centers to dysfunction. Conceivably, it had been the results of winner take all politics that caused the deindustrialization of the Lents District and left it financially devastated.

Close on the heels of high unemployment came poverty and increased levels of crime. Following the devaluation of property, cheap rent and easy qualifying for welfare spurred a migration, and Southeast Portland transformed from a working-class neighborhood into graffiti filled slums. There was plenty of blame to go around, but it was unfairly placed on the people who were spawned into fractured families with little hope.

Sadly, they found a life of drugs and alcohol the easiest road to travel and the fastest way to escape their surroundings. However, there were those who defied the odds through ambition for a better life and strived to find the path that fulfilled their dreams. I respected such people where the compulsion to succeed motivated them to rise above and prevail. I often wondered how I would have made it in an environment like Lents. Would I have had the tenacity to endure until I was able to escape?

On Holgate Boulevard, an old Asian restaurant sign hung cockeyed across the front of a one-story building. The sign should have read, "Chinese Buffet," but a section was completely missing and read, "Chinese Buf." The vacant eatery sat as an Ad Hoc historic monument of the population shift into Lents that occurred during the early '70s. Many Oriental's tried to make a go of the area by opening up Asian food stores and dining facilities. But, only a remnant remained dotted across the district, although most of the Asiatic people stayed.

On Southeast 122nd Street, I watched two hookers walk short routes to nowhere. They'd staked out their territory on a crumbling sidewalk and patrolled back and forth like military troops pulling guard duty. Within minutes of my arrival to the area, a sedan pulled up alongside one of the women and rolled down the passenger window. After a brief exchange, the woman pointed to a no-tell motel located a half-block off the main drag. The vehicle pulled away and turned down the alley toward the motel. She gestured with a wave of her hand to the other woman then briskly beat feet in the same direction the vehicle had gone.

What I didn't see in Lents was perhaps as important as what I did see. Portland's Northeast side differed distinctly from Southeast. The rundown neighborhoods in Northeast were notoriously gang-infested. In Lents, it was hard to find the organized street activity. No signs of Bloods, Crips, or Mexican Mafia. Taggers were responsible for most of the graffiti, and the only gang indications were the name "EastEnders" painted on a few walls of abandoned buildings.

It was no joke that in Lent's there were more local bars than churches. Taverns were small and seedy, appearing at the edge of tree-lined vacant lots and trash lined alleyways. By midnight I had tired of the casual observation and returned to the condo.

Anna had set the alarm clock too early for my liking. On this particular morning, however, Anna resolved to get an early start on packing and other preparations for her trip while I searched the Internet to better comprehend the meaning of the term, "Red Market." Superficially, it was easy to understand the illegal organ trade and the supply and demand matrix. It's the same reason all black markets exist—money.

At two in the afternoon, Anna and I grabbed lunch together at her favorite place a city block from the condo. Anna read the Intel I'd picked up including an obituary from a Longview, Washington, newspaper from three years ago. The death and funeral arrangements for Lance Thaman was of little value other than the mention of a brother named Matthew.

"It's a good start, Walter. Call me if the project looks promising, and we will channel finances and other operators to help."

Calling a facilitator every time I open a door or stubbed my toe wasn't high on my priority list. Other Palatini operators followed the protocol religiously, but I only checked in when necessary. I wasn't big on socializing, and consequently, I never thought about calling to chat. It wasn't me. Whenever I tried to be normal, it was if I were an actor on a stage and what I presented to my audience wasn't the real me. I have a beast within that manifests as a vigilante. Our destinies are one.

Anna, in a guarded tone, asked, "When you meet with Matt, will you be Hunter?

"Absolutely. His character fits into the local scene in Southeast."

With the weight lifted off her shoulders, Anna smiled and gave a conceding nod. She was free to pursue her new responsibilities knowing I would take care of business.

Anna jotted a phone number on the back of my paperwork and folded the sheets back into the envelope. "Matt says to call anytime. He will be expecting the call to come from me. I suggest you act as my investigator for the article and not cause any concerns."

"What do you know about the guy?"

"I've completed a preliminary work up. Matt was born and raised in a remote coastal area of Washington. His father is now deceased. His mother lives in Kelso, Washington. He had three siblings, all brothers. He aspired to be a law officer and pursued a career. He hired on with Multnomah County Sheriff department fifteen years ago."

"How old is this guy?"

"Forty-six."

"Yeah, it'll be my luck he's buddies with Ware."

"His police career was cut short. He was involved in a shooting that had political overtones, raked over the coals by the defense attorney's, and the County failed to back him sufficiently."

"Hung out to dry—sounds right for doing right."

"Matt was placed on a desk without a weapon and given a reduction of pay. With a total of eight years of service, it was over for him."

"Too bad sounds like he's a regular Joe that got railroaded by the political-judicial system."

Back at the condo, Anna tied up financial loose ends and made last-minute communications with Palatini operatives before she took a flight to the Isle of Mann. I waited around with my hands in my pockets. I'd envisioned an evening with the two of us entwined as one entity through the night until dawn forced us to embark on the day. But, there wasn't any time for us in the schedule. Too many last minute details consumed my dream and, our last night that we would spend together for an undetermined amount of time, simply slipped away.

Surveying "EastEnders" street gang graffiti kept me occupied late into the evening. When I returned to Anna's condo, I quietly passed through the front room and by Anna's travel bags set poised by the main entry. Her trip to the Isle of Mann was gaining reality. In a few short hours, I would be alone. How weird would this place be without her? There was practically no reason for me to stay in her condo except to hide from Ware. Silently I slipped into the bedroom.

I was relieved to see she had fallen asleep. Fewer emotions to deal with, I surmised. Yet, sleep eluded me.

Wide-awake and out of bed before Anna's alarm sounded, I prepared to greet the solitude head on. Hidden within my thoughts was a skill I'd tapped into in my earlier days on the ranch. I referred to it as a disconnect. For me, it was as easy as changing a television channel. However, it came at an increasing cost. The more often I disconnected from my surroundings, the more difficult it was to reconnect with my emotions.

Isolation had once been my friend and had served me well. Once again, I'd adjust to being alone and concentrate my efforts on the one thing that brought me pure joy—prey.

With Anna's luggage squeezed into the trunk of her Lexus, I opened the passenger door. For a fleeting moment, I saw hesitation in her eyes, but in the distance, the mission called. Like a ringing phone, it had to be answered. Behind the wheel, I prepared to pull out of the garage that I'd named the bat cave because of its secretive nature. We moved forward and down an interior ramp of the building to the exit gate, Anna asked, "While I'm gone I would like you to drive my car."

"Why, the Avenger fits me and what I do. The Lents neighborhood won't tolerate your Lexus unless I'm going as a pimp."

"I understand, but keep in mind, Ware is looking for you."

I wised up and agreed. I'd made a pledge after Toronto to play well with others and learn to compromise. Now was that time.

We pulled into airport parking, and I helped Anna with her bags to the ticket counter. We said our goodbyes, kissed and promised each other our undying love. It seemed like the right ritual for brief separations, however, I'd already begun my conversion resulting in a surreal moment. I waved one last time as she made her way through the terminal to the designated departure gate.

Anna's Lexus was a decent ride, but I couldn't wait to shed the image that I imagined when I was driving it. At the condo, I used Anna's key card to gain entrance to the ramp and parked the Lexus back in the bat cave. With Anna out of the picture, I didn't see any further need to compromise. I took on the new façade then fired up the Avenger. What she didn't know wouldn't hurt her.

Before heading into Lents, I phoned Matt Thaman to see if we could open lines of communication.

"Hello," a gravelly male voice responded.

"Mister Thaman?"

"That's me." His voice cleared slightly, and the raspy tone disappeared.

"My name is Hunter. I'm returning your call for Anna Sasins."

"Okay."

"I'm an investigative journalist for Miss Sasins. She apologizes for not getting back to you personally, but she is out of the country. She had a tremendous interest in your story and asked me to follow up as soon as possible."

"That'll be okay...I guess."

The hesitation in his voice told me I had to sell the idea further to gain his trust. "If you would like, I can conduct a preliminary interview over the phone?"

"Do you have a clue what my story is about?"

"I was briefed by Anna. Your brother fell victim to organ traffickers, and they butchered him. That's the down and dirty version."

"That's right. They butchered him. Mister Hunter, I don't want to say anything more than I have already…not over the phone. I don't trust many people. Not after what happened to Lance. Not anymore."

"Alright, then, how about you say when and where we meet?"

"I have substantial evidence…"

"Not enough for the cops?"

"Maybe it's more of a lead, but if I don't tell someone soon, get it down on record, I may never get to tell anyone who and what happened."

"Mister Thaman…"

"Call me, Matt."

"Are you being threatened by someone?"

"I don't want to say any names. It's not over yet. They know who I am. I tried to work with the police and made a terrible mistake…you know, got too loud when the police weren't turning up any evidence. Next thing you know the cops quit working the case. It doesn't matter one iota that the case went cold. I still have to lie low. I can't let them find me. That's why I need to get others involved. The case is cold now which is why I need Miss Sasins involved real soon…before it's too late."

I had no desire to meet face to face with Thaman, but I could hear the panic in his voice, and the longer he talked, the more pronounced it became. The basis of the story intrigued me, so I made the arrangements. "What you're telling me, Matt is that you are going to put Miss Sasins in harm's way if she investigates or reports on this story."

"Probably."

"When and where?"

"Maybe I sound paranoid when I say this…I'd like to call the same day and meet if we can?"

"I can't promise you I can break free at the drop of a dime, but we can give it a try."

For the first time in my Palatini career, I gave a non-Palatini the ability to contact me via a preloaded cell phone.

CHAPTER 4

"Sometimes it's better to react with no reaction."

—Unknown

Portlander's would rather omit the fact that territorial gangs dominated the Northeast districts of their city. In the darkness of night, the streets flourished with shadowy activity, and cops were rarely seen. If nothing else, watching thugs made for good entertainment and kept me amused. Conversely, the Lents district was dull. Once the stores had closed shop for the day, traffic became scarce, and the action on the city's Southeast side was off the main drags and hidden from sight. The criminal action happened, but it was confined to the back alleys and side streets. By midnight, I decided that waiting for a phone call from Thaman in felony flats was the epitome of boredom.

Patrol cars from a nearby substation rolled past my location with lights and sirens blazing which lifted my spirit from the funk it had sunken into. The unsung heroes of the local PD deserved credit for keeping a lid on their district and not allowing Southeast from becoming like the Northeast area.

Shortly after midnight, a car pulled up behind my Avenger. A few seconds later the police cruisers lightbar flashed red and blue. After a stealthy approach, the officer asked for my identification, registration, and insurance card. Polite and with promptness, I supplied the documents for his inspection.

"Step out of the car, please."

I complied with his field interview.

"What brings you into the area at this time of night, Mister Goe?"

Any reply was likely to bring another question. I gave a distant stare as I answered, "I had an argument with my ol' lady and needed some fresh air and time alone to think."

"Next to a cemetery?"

The tone of his voice and the direction of his questions created a concern. A vague answer might be interpreted as suicidal, followed by me in cuffs, and heading to the looney bin on an ex parte order. Not the evening I had planned. I looked over at the graveyard fence and said, "Didn't notice. I drove for a while and pulled over here and have been running the arguments through my mind, you know. End the marriage or try to make it work."

After a short pep talk, the officer told me in no uncertain terms that I needed to move on.

"Mister Goe, your decision not to drown your sorrows in a vat of alcohol was the right choice. Between you and me, this neighborhood is not safe late at night to park along the street. Parking next to a cemetery concerns me too. It's not conducive to good mental stability."

"Thank you, officer, perhaps it would be best if I checked out a piece of pie and wash it down with some coffee at an all-night diner." He nodded, returned to his car, and waited for me to leave.

At one in the morning, the diner was a drag. I'd eaten cherry pie as promised to the officer and made it à la mode for good measure. The waitress, a pixie, stood all of five foot tall in her shoes and struck me as a kind-hearted soul. She'd taken pity on me after I'd given her the same spiel I'd given the cop. She kept the Java flowing, and when the mood struck her, engaged in superficial conversations that broke the monotony for both of us.

I couldn't help but wonder where Lance Thaman had been in Lent's. I wanted more to go on. He might have bummed coffee from this same waitress or drank at the bar across the street from the diner. I was right in the midst and didn't have a clue. Further, what was Matt doing? What was taking him so long to make contact? Was there somebody stalking him or had they made good their evil intentions?

Most Portland taverns stopped serving alcohol by two in the morning and closed down operations by two-thirty. A few joints stayed open longer but didn't serve alcohol after two, only water, fountain drinks, and coffee. According to my watch, it was long past four and still no call. I was spinning my wheels. I'd let the possibility of a project excite me beyond reason. It was time to slow my roll.

I'd had enough fun for the night and tossed a five-dollar bill on the counter and said, "Later, honey."

She smiled, tucked the bill into a tightly packed push-up bra, and replied, "And I was just getting to know you."

She had my attention. "I'll stop by again."

She placed the palms of her hands on the counter and leaned forward silently but still smiling with the hint of an invitation. Her clear blue eyes fixed on mine as I visually traced the outline of her exposed cleavage.

"I don't think we had a chance to formally meet…I'm Connie."

"Hunter."

"Is that your first name or last?"

"Just, Hunter."

"I can tell a lot about a man by watching. My shift ends at five if you're interested in getting some breakfast…someplace else."

I swiveled the counter seat around and said, "Heading to bed."

"Alone?"

"That's the idea."

"Pity."

I appreciated the humor as her smile broadened. I put the diner on my list of places to chill if I had another long night to endure. Besides, her not-so-subtle invitation to play had piqued my interest, that is until a twinge of conscience reminded me of Anna. I quashed the thought as I went out the door.

The following day I made my way through one-o'clock traffic to my favorite shooting range. If Thaman identified a set of targets, sharpened skills might make the difference between success and failure for the project. I burned off two hundred rounds with my primary weapon. With each squeeze of the .40-caliber's trigger, I envisioned the faceless that I hoped to meet.

Opportunities were known to knock, and I wanted to be ready with the answer. Following the pistol work, I put a box of .223 through my AR to ensure scope accuracy. Then for fun, I blasted a few rounds of Dragons Breath downrange with my Remi 870.

The range seemed to be one of the few places where I was truly comfortable. Paranoia over others watching me or standing behind me never crossed my mind. I'd never experienced an attitude from another shooter or had cross words with anyone there. It was like paradise.

For the past two nights, I'd kept my eye out for a spider hole in the area of operation (AO). I'd located an abandoned roach motel on Southeast Insley with all the windows and doors boarded shut. The place struck me as a viable alternative to a street-side parking where I could stage the Avenger. The last thing I needed was another field interview with Portland's finest.

In my way of thinking, the Avenger would be concealed from the main drag if backed into the trash-lined driveway that circled the rear of the ramshackle building. To stash my rig required manual labor. The debris had to be removed. Not a difficult task from a physical perspective, however, it wasn't my only consideration. The unpleasantness of my predicament was the need to clear a parking spot during daylight hours in the unfriendly neighborhood. I didn't want to be seen making my burrow. My actions would likely create suspicions about who I was, and most importantly, why I was intruding on their turf. I'd either receive a visit from the cops or unwanted visitors that wanted answers. The quandary led to hesitation on my part.

I drove past the roach motel and eyeballed the activity. Two young men, with black and silver jackets, sat on a concrete wall at the base of a set of stairs near the rear of the building. The two look-alike wannabe gang-bangers were near where I wanted to park and too close for comfort. With the skies darkening for another winter rain I'd wait for a better opportunity.

Until Thaman called or I hollowed out a spot to conceal my Avenger at the roach motel, I needed a place to land. There was nothing special about Lenny's Place which sat at the north end of the district.

Small and antiquated, it attracted a few working-class regulars that had bellied up to bar and only glanced in my direction when I entered the joint. A dozen tables sat empty except for a couple old coots that had set up a table nearest to the barkeep for a card game. I had them figured for Gin Rummy or Tonk; they didn't look like the poker and blackjack crowd.

I had my choice of seats and took a table against the far wall from the entrance. I moved the chair out which placed the table at my left side with my gun hand unimpeded. The barkeep took my order and returned with what he'd recommended as the best brew on tap.

With a quick flip of my sweatshirt hoodie, I covered my head, leaned back in the chair, and milked my beer for an hour and a half while I watched the locals and waited on Thaman's call.

An orientation to the physical layout of the area was crucial to the success of an operation. Secondly, knowing who's who in the area was likewise valuable. Asking questions about who ran the territory was unwise. If the area was in dispute, inquiries could draw suspicion which was counterproductive and dangerous. Ideally, Intel and surveillance would lead a Palatini to the right set of cues for understanding an area. Generally, casual conversation with the locals led to genuine insight. So far, all I had to base my perceptions on was surveillance and my ensuing observations. The criminal underbelly of the community had the advantage.

I'd moved toward the Southeast but never spent time in my own backyard. Being an outsider, I didn't have a sense of the people I referred to as locals. I had to learn who they were. Organ trafficking was big business and drew on impoverished people to sell their body parts for a fast buck, or in Lance's case, be harvested. My thoughts grew darker as I mused and waited.

The tall, long-legged blonde had barely cleared the entrance as she slipped the lightweight black leather jacket from her shoulders, revealing a sheer form-fitting blouse that was a startling aquamarine. It was a good look on her, and she knew how to wear it, with just a hint of cleavage and a promise of lacy lingerie beneath. She swept her long hair to one side and softly thrummed the fingers of her right hand along the edge of the bar's countertop as she sauntered down toward the gawkers, agile and confident, a barely discernible gleam of amusement in her eyes. Without a doubt, she'd accomplished her intentions as all heads had turned, eyes glued to follow her every move—mine too.

The barkeep smiled and said, "Morning Hope." A sarcasm perhaps judging by the lateness of the day. However, I gave her the benefit of the doubt it was the beginning of her day.

With a voice that was soft and silky, she responded, "Hi, Lenny."

I shook myself from my reverie and back to the job at hand as I opened my small memo pad and jotted, "Hope. Tall Blonde. Possibly a working girl. Arrived at Lenny's Bar—early evening." On the next line, I wrote, "Barkeep's name: Lenny." It was a start of learning the who's who of the neighborhood.

Hope stopped midway along the well-lit bar and without as much as the blink of an eye her look of bemusement vanished, immediately replaced with a wary-eyed countenance as wolf-like, she scanned the darkened table area. At that moment I recognized we had something in common and I felt spellbound once again. Mysteriously, this blonde huntress was prowling, a look of primal hunger nearly incandescent in her eyes as she stalked her prey.

Captivated, I watched her every move. The locals were to her as they were to me, a form of camouflage, but their role played a greater significance in her hunt. Bellied up to the bar, as they were nightly, they held no interest for her. They swayed back and forth like tall grasses of the Serengeti that provided cover and concealment for her predatory movement. Like all skilled predators, what she sought was uniquely different from the regulars at the watering hole. Her victims were as special to her as mine were to me.

In my estimation, she was living proof that our primitive instincts were intact. Sure, modern humans have tried to distance themselves from Cro-Magnons, but our base nature has remained the same. We fool ourselves if we believe that through generations of education and insight we evolved into a form of enlightened humanity. Different. Superior.

Buried by the murky mumbo jumbo of false beliefs, shame, and guilt, we wrestle with the self-realization of what we are. Since the dawn of time, we have shared the same innate behaviors. We have the same weaknesses and the same strengths, a capacity for love and compassion and the desire for power and control. As we were in the beginning so shall we be in the end—the same primitive creature we have always been.

Hope was a beautiful example of a perfect predator. Her eye's fastened onto mine. For a time, she showed no outward expression of her thoughts or emotions, only a steady vacant gaze. Studying and whetting her appetite. Then her eyes closed for a brief moment, and I knew when they opened I'd have my answer. Ever so slowly, a slight smile emerged. As her eyes opened, they were fixed on me. I'd been chosen.

Lovely smiles have been known to hide dark secrets, and Hope's soft and delicate jawline hid her secrets well. It was her eyes and not her lips that gave intent to her smile; her prowess, both suggestive and carnivorous appealed to my instincts. But maybe I'd read too much into her expression because I was looking over the whole package.

She approached my table, her hips rolling effortlessly under the tight leather mini-skirt. She'd left little doubt that the sleek black garment had been conceived with a woman like her in mind. Intriguing. Alluring. Bewitching.

From all appearances, she was my type of woman. Before she spoke, I awkwardly pushed a chair out from the table with my foot for her to sit. She eye-balled the offer but didn't bite. I broke the melting ice, "What are you drinking, Hope?"

She reached to my hoodie and partially lifted one side with her fingertips to peek at my face. "Do I know you?"

"Not yet." I figured I'd leave how I knew her name a mystery.

But, she surprised me with her savviness. With a glance in Lenny's direction, she quipped, "You pay attention—you must be interested." She smiled seductively as she continued her introduction. "I'll have wine. Lenny knows. You probably know Lenny, too."

"I make it my business to know everybody, that's my job. I always start with the bartender when I'm in a new place."

"A know-it-all, my-my, how exciting," Hope dryly responded, and then maneuvered the chair to her liking. Lenny who had watched, nodded when I gave him the sign for a round of drinks. Hope presented her hand for a cordial greeting. "You have an advantage on me. That can be very dangerous for a woman, not knowing the name of the man she is with."

I took her hand and returned the same cordial handshake. "Hunter's the name, and you're safe with me."

"Is Hunter a first or last name?"

"Uh, huh—"

"That sounds more dangerous than not knowing your name." Hope's smile morphed into a puzzled look. Reaching over to my hoodie she slipped it back off my head and began a detailed study of my face. I let her take her time as she checked me over like a mother making sure her toddler had cleaned behind its ears. She brushed her bangs to one side revealing a small scar high on her forehead. "You're not a bad looking man. Why are you hiding your face?"

I suppose it was a compliment and I should have said thank you. But I pulled my hoodie back in place and responded, "Not everyone that hides their face does so because they don't like their looks."

She nodded. I could see she understood I was veiled for a purpose.

Seven men and one old barfly remained at the counter while the card game flourished. Minutes before Hope arrived a couple new faces had joined the people at the table and had been dealt in. The game was in full swing and gaining strength with every hoot and holler. One guy had his eye on Hope and attempted to gain her interest, but she ignored his obnoxious behavior. I found it more difficult. He was using up perfectly good oxygen and needed to stop.

One-upmanship in an alpha driven world was a dominant trait and one I intended to display for my new façade. When Lenny arrived at the table with our refreshments, I employed my alpha-male performance. "Make it a round for everyone and include yourself."

My status around Lenny's bar had immediately elevated from the level of accepted to preferred. By spending a few bucks, I'd become a big fish in a little pond and the guy that everyone liked. The card players all yelled thanks one after the other, even the dimwit that I had bested. The locals turned from the bar's counter and waved their beer mugs in appreciation. I was king of the boozehounds—as long as the money flowed I had command of the floor.

Hope sat tall in her chair and scanned the room from side to side. A striking look of pride beamed from her widening smile. Less than a hundred bucks spent had bought a lot of respect with this crew. I'd practically become their friend with one small financial transaction. To solidify my newfound friendships all I had to do was be introduced.

The longer I looked at Hope, the more I liked what I saw. Delicate. Shrewd. Confident.

"You almost missed your chance with me, Hunter. Sitting in the dark and all, I almost didn't come over."

"It's your story you can tell it any way you want to, honey."

She laughed. The ball field was level, and we were on equal footing—we both knew how to play the game.

"Why'd you choose Lenny's tonight?" She asked between sips of her wine.

I grinned, took a long, slow drink of my beer and responded, "I saw you in a dream, and trusted in Destiny." She could not yet have known my double meaning.

"Hmmm, a smooth talker I see." She mirrored my performance with the same coolness and calmness I'd offered. With another sip of her wine, she continued, "I'll bet you're here because your business exec lifestyle bores you to tears and you're flirting with a walk on the wild side."

"Good guess."

"I'm right?"

"Not even close, honey, I'm in waste management. My job is to clean up the trash. But, while we're on the subject, what brings you out on the town?"

"I enjoy the nightlife?"

I looked around the joint then threw a glance back at her, "Yeah, it's crackin' 'round here."

Her smile returned as she continued her study of my façade. "I'll bet it's every bit as good of a reason as you have for being here."

"Save your money, honey, I'm too expensive. Besides, I ain't got the time."

She scooted her chair close until her leg rested against mine. "You should find the time. I guarantee you'll be pleased."

I was the sort of guy that found it hard to walk away from a challenge. Taking a bigger gulp of my beer, I said, "I have my reasons. I have to leave it at that."

With a note of sarcasm, she replied, "You're worried Mrs. Hunter wouldn't approve?"

A fact-finding expedition, I thought. I'd give her the lead. "Wrong again, honey. Ain't no Mrs. Hunter in the picture."

Her suggestive smile broadened as if it were scripted. "Don't worry, Hunter. I won't bite—hard." She softly laughed. "Men that I date are guys that don't want the baggage that comes with finding a regular girl."

"Not this guy, honey. You're barking up the wrong tree." I didn't want to leave her with the false impression. Hunter, my new façade, was a man of action who made things happen. An alpha male, loathed by men and adored by women. At least, that was my goal to portray. I didn't have any Grant's or Franklin's with her name on them and figured that's what it would take to secure the deal. Hunter wasn't the kind of guy that needed to pay. It wasn't that I held a moral objection to enjoying the company of a woman, but it had to be the right one. I had standards. However low they may have been. To prove to Hope my manly strength, I threw out a morsel she could chew on. "I love the women, honey. I can handle any action that comes my way, but I'm not the kind of guy that needs one in tow."

Hope looked toward the bar as she uttered her response. "I love the women too."

What was that? Her words hung in the air as I was caught off guard, had she really meant that the way it sounded?

"Did I hear you correctly?" I wasn't naïve but something resonated in her words. Maybe she wasn't a typical hooker, but she was in the market for someone, and I figured it had a price tag attached.

Hope leaned back as if she heard my thoughts. Looking somewhat coy she said, "What are you asking, Hunter?"

I shrugged, "I'm twice your age. What do you see in someone like me?"

Hope sat quietly and looked hard into my eyes. She appeared comfortable with what I'd asked. Suddenly, she broke eye contact and laughed. She wasn't making this easy. I didn't want to ask the question because I didn't want to think of her as a working girl.

"I'm a kept woman."

"You have a husband?"

"No, she's my life partner, and yes, before you ask, she is okay with what I do."

"What is it that…what you do, I mean?"

"You don't look like a man I have to spell it out for? I'm bisexual."

Wow, I didn't see that coming. In some sense, I was relieved it was a sexual orientation, but it still didn't explain her interest in me. Probing with a statement, I responded, "I'm hard-wired heterosexual, baby. I don't swing any other way."

"Oh, good, I was trifling with the idea you might be gay or something."

"No you weren't or you wouldn't have hung around as long as you did." We both laughed.

"I'm open about my sexuality. I love Samantha, but I enjoy sex with men. Is that so odd? It's the best of both worlds."

"Odd? In a word, it's different. But, hey, it's your world. You can do whatever you want." Hope's life didn't affect me one way or the other. Not as long as she wasn't asking for my approval or to embrace her alternative lifestyle.

"I'm trying to do what I want, but I'm not getting much cooperation. If you know what I mean?"

"I thought we were just having a drink together."

We talked for another half-hour getting to know each other. I was impressed with Hope's skills. What she'd learned she didn't learn from a book. Her abilities were displayed and transparent in every action and word. She wasn't hiding a thing. In my view, her lifestyle wasn't to my tastes, but she was an okay kid, and I liked her.

"You're fun, Hunter."

"I've heard a lot of things said about me, but fun ain't one of them."

Her smile broadened, "I'm saying I dig you." She slipped her hand on top of mine and whispered, "I only have one rule; No kissing on the lips."

"Lips! How many ways does a guy have to tell you, I'm not interested?"

"If you're worried about a long relationship, don't. I have Sammie to go home to."

I caught a glimpse of Lenny returning to our table with drinks in hand. I whispered in Hope's ear, "You can save the list of rules, honey, cuz I'm not in the market—not even for a freebie."

She whispered back, "I didn't offer one."

When Lenny arrived at the table with a second round, I slipped my hand away from Hope to give him a ten-spot and said, "Keep the change."

Hope sipped the fresh glass of wine, "Wow. I've never met a man that could turn down a freebie. I didn't think they made men like that—that were straight."

"Tell me about this gal you're shacking up with?"

"Shacking up? Sammie and I have loved each for a long time—"

"Whoa, whoa, whoa," I interrupted her. "You've loved her a long time? What are you, all of twenty-five or twenty-six?"

She softly laughed, "You know it's not polite to ask a girl her age. Sammie and I are far more involved than shacking up as you called it."

I offered a toast with our fresh drinks. After a quick sip, I opened the conversation up further. "I bet you've got a great story to—" A lumbering shadowy figure filled the entryway and distracted my attention. I glanced around the tavern to see what response the man at the entrance received. All eyes looked as they do in small joints like Lenny's, but no one acknowledged the strange visitor. He quietly shut the door behind him and made his way to the corner of the bar. However, there was one person that knew him well, maybe too well. Brandon A. Ware had somehow found me. I wasn't excited at the prospects of what it meant for my evening. I'd made headway getting to know Hope and preferred her company to his, but I figured that was about to be interrupted.

Hope looked the man over then turned her focus back to me. Wiry predators share many things in common, one of which is the ability to read a situation. "He's a cop," she said.

"You know him?"

"You don't have to know him to know he's a cop." Maybe she'd caught my expression when he came in, or it was how quickly I'd tossed my hoodie back over my head, either way, she knew he was trouble for me. "Your friend?" She asked.

I shrugged, "Not exactly, but I know him."

Ware picked up a drink from Lenny, turned toward the table I shared with Hope and walked in our direction. Ware's rotund waistline protruded through his suit jacket, and his tie hung loosely around his neck. What caught my attention the most was the absence of his leatherbound notepad. Why wasn't it tucked under his arm or being carried in his massive hand?

Ware stopped in front of our table and stood expressionless looking at Hope. He turned toward me and said, "Mind if I join you?"

"I'm entertaining a guest right now," I said. "Maybe later."

Ware picked up Hope's drink and set his beer on the table. Using his knee, he bumped her chair, handed her the drink, and said, "Beat it."

If I was ever going to ditch this guy, I needed to find out how he found me. Portland was a big enough city to know our meeting wasn't an act of divine providence or even a coincidence. He had Intel on me. I looked toward Hope, "Give us some space for a minute."

Sporting an indignant look, she shrugged, stood, and turned toward Ware, but addressed me. "Tell your friend he's rude." I was impressed. She had moxie. "Later, Hunter."

"It won't take but a minute."

Hope slowly sipped her drink as she glared into Ware's eyes. Calm, cool, and collected, she set her drink on the table and strolled to the bar as if nothing had transpired. Ware moved Hope's chair away from the table making room for his larger frame before he sat down. I would've done the same thing but for different reasons. Ware was a big man that needed to breathe.

Ware took a drink from his frothy mug of beer before he uttered, "Hunter," followed by a hardy laugh.

I jockeyed my chair back against the wall until my back was well protected. "What brings you out tonight, BA," I recalled Anna having said that his friends called him by his initials.

"Nice hood on that sweatshirt. Can't hardly tell who you are."

"You didn't have any trouble picking me out of the crowd."

"Maybe you stand out more than you think."

I felt the pinpricks of his words. "I didn't know you were a socializer or I would have invited you out on the town. Have you been to Lenny's before?"

"Can't recall, but I was in the neighborhood, and felt like getting a beer."

I showed my teeth in a smile and tossed in a chuckle for good measure. I wanted him to know I wasn't buying his line. "Maybe next time....I'll get the tab."

"I never turn down a free drink. Let me get your phone number, and I'll call next time I'm out." We both sneered and showed toothy smiles.

Ware lifted his glass as if making a toast and took another drink. He set his mug down and went eye to eye with me. "I came across something of interest today, news to some I suppose. I thought of you."

"I can't tell you what that means to me."

"I think about you a lot, lately—."

"I'm already in a relationship with Anna."

Ware turned to look at the girl he'd kicked out of the chair and said, "Is her name Anna, too?"

I took the question to be rhetorical.

"I'd like to help you finish that article on Mona."

"I thought we talked about that—it's pointless."

"I disagree. The article you were going to write is old news, but what if your piece was made relevant by exposing her murderer?" He nodded his head.

"Cops have a collar on someone you know about?"

"It won't be that easy. Months ago, the governor's office announced it was setting six-thousand prisoners free on an early release program."

I couldn't contain the smirk, "It's a stupid move, and everyone's heard about it. The cops will be working overtime picking up the retreads."

Ware's lip curled as he shook his head. Was it possible that we'd found common ground?

I leaned forward, my hoodie falling further over my eyes. "That's what I love about the justice system. They're always looking out for the victims and society."

He finished another swallow then dipped his head low to make eye contact. "It may be stupid, but the move made sense to the State. It left them upfront money in their Department of Corrections budget and temporarily solved their over-crowding problem."

"I don't see how that helps write Mona's new and relevant story?"

"Owen Moore is one of those selected for release by the Board."

Ware had brought a tantalizing bit of news to the table, but not enough to cause a reaction. He'd questioned me before as if I were the suspect in Lott's death. Whatever he was up to I had to consider Owen "Icky" Moore was nothing more to him than bait to catch the vigilante. If he didn't think of Moore as bait, maybe he thought Moore and I were in cahoots and arranged her murder while he was locked up in jail. I didn't know his angle, but he had one, and I was sure if I waited he'd reveal his hand.

Minutes passed without either of us saying a word. He was content with the carrot he'd dangled in front of me. I was content planning a strategy to take Icky Moore out.

"So how are you going to get Moore to talk?"

"As a retired officer of the law, Moore would never consent to an interview with me. But, through you, he would get another chance to proclaim his innocence and enjoy some fleeting fame."

"You think if I ask him a few questions about Mona he'll confess. Is that the idea?"

"I'd give you questions to work into the interview. His answers might shed light on the murderer and give me the lead I'm after."

Ware finished his beer, set the glass on the table and stood, "I'll leave you to your evening. Think about it?" He looked toward Hope as he said, "I'll give you a call next time I'm out, or I can swing by your place and pick you up if that's easier?" He looked back at me with a cheesy grin. "I don't want you to get away…" After a short pause, he continued, "Without buying me that beer."

He wasn't fooling me. I was as much his target as Moore was. I mustered up a Boy Scout salute from the edge of my hoodie and said, "See you around." I was confident I hadn't misspoken.

Ware was a cop for a long time, maybe the only life he'd ever known. He wasn't going to change. When he retired, he didn't become something else. In his mind, he was still the same true-blue detective investigator he had been on the force, only without the power or authority that he once had. Being a PI was the closest life he could find to being a cop, and it made him dangerous.

Relieved that he was on his way out the door, Ware had walked only a few steps from the table when he turned back toward me. "Oh, by the way, compliments on your attire, Hunter."

"I can't tell you how much that means coming from you."

Ware sauntered out the tavern door not looking back. His parting comment was meaningful, and I took it the way he meant for me too. From his ambush visit, Ware had walked away with a new piece of personal information. He had accidentally happened upon my new alias—Hunter. Maybe he assumed I'd hidden my name from the woman at the table. He might have chocked it up to the way some guys operate. Regardless, he couldn't be underestimated. He could connect the dots. After all, he was a trained bloodhound.

CHAPTER 5

"Life is not a matter of holding good cards, but of playing a poor hand well.

—*Robert Louis Stevenson*

The door had scarcely shut behind Ware when Hope returned from the bar and pulled her chair back close to the table, sitting gracefully while smoothly crossing her legs. I needed time to process what Ware had said and solve the riddle of what he wanted from me. Questions conjured up by Ware aimed for my entrapment. Was there anything in a word or an emphasis on a syllable that shed light on his plan? The only thing that came to mind was, "I don't want you to get away."

Hope made for an appealing distraction from the whirlwind of besieging thoughts. She'd pulled her chair in front of mine, close enough for her foot to rub against the inside of my leg. It wasn't an accidental brushing but an intentional suggestive petting. Before Ware arrived, we were getting to the nitty-gritty part of her life where she laid her soul bare and likely anything else I wanted.

"How well do you know the Southeast area?" I asked.

"Parking lots and back alley's…do they count?"

"Maybe, but how about people? Who's who in the bar scene? Barfly's, hookers, pimps, pushers?

"That's a big list." Hope peeled my hood back until it fell to my shoulders and searched my eyes for understanding. "I know pimps and working girls, a few of the John's are familiar, but I don't have a lot of dealings with them or the drug dealers."

Being straight up with Hope about what I wanted, when I wasn't sure, wouldn't have made a lot of sense, but she'd given me an idea. If we palled around, she could point to the players she knows and clue me in on their game. If she could show me the ropes, she'd be a viable asset. The body snatchers might stick out amongst the usual human traffickers that she knew. All I needed from her was to point out the usual and identify the unusual.

As with all operations, I ran the risk of trespassing onto an active investigation complete with undercover cops and snitches in play. Thaman's case might not be dead at all, but part of a larger investigation. The cops might feign a cold case while going deeper in their research. Maybe they had a snitch in place, so they backed off. Street level informants were the eyes and ears for the cops and relied upon heavily for leads. They'd drop a dime on body snatcher scum because stoolies would see traffickers of organs as dangerous to people like Lance Thaman. But if the cops had the traffickers in human organs in their sights, I still wanted to intervene. If the police made their play first, it would result in a costly and time-consuming intervention that would likely end with a hitch behind bars costing the taxpayer more money, and for what? Rehabilitation? The Palatini way was much more efficient, inexpensive, and a guaranteed zero criminal recidivism.

With Hope's help, I could think like a profiler. Once I located and identified the traffickers, I'd trail them to their burrow. When it was time to feed the inner beast, Hope would have to go. Other Palatini operators had cultivated working relationships with a variety of sources that ranged from the dregs of society to the pinnacles of success. In this business, you can't afford to judge a book by its cover. If I put my time and energy into her, groom her to meet my needs, she might end up a sound investment.

Ware had shown himself to be sly and likely to stumble into my operation at precisely the worst time. I didn't figure him for a high-tech guy, but his actions warranted a close examination of my Avenger for a tracking device. The Avenger had to be the link he used to locate me at Lenny's. How else could he have known my whereabouts? The tail had to go.

My take on the encounter with Ware was Icky Moore's release date. It wasn't an artificial lure on Ware's part; it was live bait. I've never forgotten the ploy Ware had pulled before he announced his retirement from the police force. The Oregon rumor mill had it that an unknown serial killer had wreaked havoc on a small population of the state's citizenry. However, when properly reported by the news media, it caused little concern. But, the mounting body count had become an embarrassment to the Portland Police Bureau and the Multnomah County Sheriff's Department. With a task force of detectives and uniformed officers, Ware devised a plan to ensnare the vigilante. Ware had been correct in his assumption that the killer targeted sex offenders for extermination. But, his ownership of the vigilante case became his Achilles' heel. He postulated an incorrect theory that the killer wanted media attention, and Ware with all his eggs in one basket used a high-profile sex offender as bait. There was nothing artificial about the lure. Seymour Johnson a.k.a. Big Johnson was a viable target for the vigilante, and on his way to a trial that would likely go in his favor with all his money. Ware's thinking was, what more could a fame-seeking assassin want? His action to snare me was the reason that I believed Icky Moore wasn't a phony setup. In Ware's world, Moore had exposed himself, and Ware planned to capitalize on his bad luck and poorly thought out choices.

Ware's sting, codenamed Vigilant Response, flat-out failed. A little birdie chirped a warning in the vigilante's ear and told him of the setup. The killer struggled and was heartbroken that he had to let the prize walk. However, his adversary, Brandon A. Ware ended up with a big fat goose egg, and the FBI took over the investigation. As a result, Ware left police work via the back door, humiliated, with his tail tucked between his legs.

The main difference between an artificial lure and live bait was the reaction of the predator when the bait was stolen. Once the ownership had changed possession, only then did it make a difference if it was a lure or live bait. If the bait was real, it ceased to be bait once it had become a provision for the predator.

A few years ago, Mona Lott suffered a tragic death at the hands of the vigilante for her part in her daughter's torment and abuse. Mona's daughter, Vanessa, was barely out of the toddler stage when I made a promise to myself that she would have her justice. Icky Moore, who had tortured and victimized the innocent young girl, escaped my wrath at the time through incarceration. But with the promise of an early release, I intended to keep my pledge and snatch the bait from under Ware's nose.

With Big Johnson, Ware had a task force behind him; now he is but one man. With the first sting, I chose to ignore the bait. This time, I will accept the challenge. There will be no defensive measures only calculated risks. I intend to make Ware look like a sap.

Johnson was wealthy with a big name in Portland, but he was nothing in my book. News sources plastered his picture in all the local rags and covered the story on the nightly broadcasts. Who was he to the vigilante? A meaningless garden-variety perp that I didn't know. Owen "Icky" Moore, however, had taken on trophy status through injustice. Unlike the weak judicial system, Mona and Owen would pay the same price for the same crime.

Hope waved her hand in front of my face and said, "Hello… Did you forget about me?"

"I was thinking, that's all."

"Well I hope that something you were thinking about was me," she quipped as she ran her open hand down the side of her hip as she leaned back in her chair.

If Hope only knew her suggestive behavior wasn't a close second to what preoccupied my thoughts, she would have packed up and broken camp at my table. More pressing was how to juggle finding the body snatchers and double tapping Icky? Maybe it would be wise to call for another shooter? If I understood Anna, there wasn't one available.

"How about a fresh drink before you slip into la-la land again?" Hope grumbled.

I motioned to the barkeep and caught his attention to give everyone another round. The crew received it and honored me as if I were Robin Hood. I was a hero.

Hope sported an unhappy look then stood and scooted her chair alongside mine with her back to the wall. "Maybe you can pay attention to me now," she said.

"You know the streets around here, right?"

Hope squinted as if a light had shined in her eyes. "Hey, what's up with you? You're not interested in my company at all. The other guy looked like a cop, but you don't come off the same way."

"The other guy can't help the way he looks because he is a cop. He's retired, but I'll guarantee you, once a cop always a cop."

Hope smiled and snuggled next to me like we'd had a long-standing relationship.

"I have questions, and I need answers," I said. "You might be able to help." To a degree, I'd grown comfortable around Hope and believed she was at ease with me. I wasn't ready to divulge any secrets, and maybe we'd never cross that bridge—it was too early to know. Unlike with Anna, however, Hope didn't pressure me; with Anna, I always toed the mark and made a maximum effort to stay on my best behavior, to be accepted and avoid her critical eye and sarcastic barbs.

"Listen, you need to know, I'm expecting a call tonight, and need to go take care of business. I'm telling you that beforehand because I don't want you to think I'm giving you the slip."

Hope slid her hand up the inside of my thigh, "What if I made it hard for you to leave me here all alone?"

I didn't move her hand but restrained my smile. "There's no such thing as too hard."

Her response was an unconvincing pout that spread across her face and morphed into a playful smile.

"You probably hear this all the time, but you're a talented girl. Too smart to be doing what you do. I don't get it."

"Smart? Not really...usually, they say I'm pretty or sexy, but never smart." Hope fell into silence as she looked toward the darkest part of the barroom that was quiet and empty. Finally, she spoke, "It's the same old story you've heard a dozen times."

"Not likely, I'm a recluse." I thought to clarify that I meant a recluse spider but decided against it. "Enlighten me."

"Teenage girl hates home, bored in a little town, and no prospects for a life worth living. Along comes a high school dropout of twenty, with a wad of hundred dollar bills in his pocket, who promised me the world. I fell in love with him, and on my sixteenth birthday I ran away with Reggie." A sneer crept up the side of Hope's cheek as she thought about him. "Of course, he was the first man in my life; if you know what I mean."

"I got your drift."

"Reggie Koontz, I was so connected to him, and he used my love against me. He took me away from everyone I knew. He repeated things I had said about my family when I justified my reasons for running away. I was so dumb and naïve. He used everything against me, and it was my fault."

"They call that grooming, honey. Naive, yes. Your fault, no."

"Reggie didn't plan for things to work out the way they did. We made friends with people that used drugs, and Reggie fell in real deep—he blew all his money. My part-time job wasn't enough for much of anything." Hope paused.

"How was he making his money?"

"Selling drugs, but not using often."

She reflected on her past for a moment, "Well, you know what came next. I ended up turning tricks for money and drugs trying to please him."

"You use?"

"No. Reggie wouldn't let me. He was hooked, it was all I could do to keep him supplied. Drugs made him happy. So, I made him happy. I was in love with him, so…."

"As long as you brought the drug money in you made him happy."

"You know, Hunter, you don't make a girl feel any better when she tells her story."

"Yeah…sorry about that. I call 'em the way I see 'em."

"The drugs and the lifestyle became a trap for us."

"Takes a lot of strength to move on with your life after something like that."

"Reggie helped me with the decision. I got tired of supplying him with drugs and money. When I said no more, he beat me. Never in the face or where it would show in public. He was smart that way. Like I said, it's the same old story. It happens to thousands of girls every day."

She'd been duped, pimped, and finally wised up. She was right about one thing, the drugs, and the violence happens to thousands of girls. But, there was still more to her story. What she had told me so far was too shallow to be the end. She'd learned to survive on her own terms, but what they were remained a mystery for the moment—she would tell me when she was ready.

I'd given the questions a rest, after a few seconds of silence, Hope shook her head. "I went out on my own with no place to go. Guys at my part-time job would give me a place to sleep, but they were interested in only one thing. That's when I learned to use that one thing to better my situation." Again, she stared into the dark recesses of the barroom. Expressionless. Motionless. Her thoughts encapsulated for the moment. Still staring, she said, "Some like to hold it over your head forever."

"I'm not one of those guys."

Hope turned back toward me, her eyes shifted to meet mine. Maybe something in the tone of my words rang true and sparked a willingness to open up to a complete stranger. "Why the interest, Hunter? I'm nothing to you."

For a moment I stepped out of my façade and was real with her, "Because I don't make friends easily."

"Friends!" She laughed.

"Why not?"

She paused.

"Tonight, I'm not me, and you're not you. We're a couple lonely people, strangers in the night that got together for a drink."

"I like that, Hunter." Hope snuggled in tighter.

I tried to make her feel better. Her memories were painful, and I wanted to help. "You're smart, aggressive, and have strength. You broke out of the trap. It's commendable what you've been able to do."

Hope's shoulder rested on my chest as she sighed, "It feels good, to be honest with a guy. It doesn't usually work out that way."

"I'm a lot different than other guys you meet; different in more ways than you can imagine. Except for the sex and dope; I'm not much different than you."

"Hunter, you're easy to talk with."

"I enjoy listening to people—you arouse my curiosity, and you've made me interested in you."

She flashed a smile and after a moment of silence continued. "One night, I met Tommy. Like with most of the guys I climbed into his car, and we went for a ride down an alley. I was honest with him and let him know I was almost eighteen. He said he was impressed and thought I had a real talent for as young as I was. He asked me to enlist in his escort service, but he had two stipulations. No more Reggie or drugs of any kind. Tommy ran a legitimate escort business. Straight up. He set up the date and collected a small charge for the companionship. Many times, they were corporate people looking for someone to go with them to an event. Sex was up to each of us. No pressure. If it came up when we were with our client, and agreed, we negotiated the price for the service. All Tommy asked for was a percentage of the gross that was collected from each customer."

Hope respected Tommy. Maybe she had given him too much credit but was thankful that he took her in off the streets. Pointing out that Tommy pimped an underage girl was a failed argument. It was time to change the course, but she beat me to the punchline.

"What's your story, Hunter?"

"That's fair I guess. In a nutshell, honey, I was born and raised right here in Oregon. I did a hitch in the military, got out and did the next twenty years at a factory. Married once, divorced once, and never had kids. I don't own a house, quit my job, and have an old Dodge I'm running into the ground. I drink as you can see, sometimes more than I should, and never used drugs. That's probably the same kind of life you ran away from—boring as hell."

"Wow!" Hope followed with a laugh. "Are you ever guarded?"

Hope had no idea what I was saving her from hearing.

She slowly slipped her right hand across my chest and said, "Maybe I can get you to drop your guard before the night is over?"

"So what's the story with this lady friend of yours?"

"I left the escort business when I met, Samantha. We've lived together ever since. That was three years ago, and I've never regretted my decision."

I scratched my head. "I really don't get what you're doing out here if everything's as peachy as you say it is at home."

"I have a need and men fulfill it best."

"Sweetheart, try chocolate, it'll please you longer."

We laughed.

Hope said, "My needs are never met permanently, just like yours."

"What's that supposed to mean?"

"Your needs are not different from mine or the way I find satisfaction."

"You think I need some loving? All I want is to know who's who around here."

"No—I'm sure you're not interested in sex because it doesn't do anything for you."

This girl was good, I thought. Of course, I'd made the point all along that she was barking up the wrong tree,

"But your want is so strong it's a driving force in your life."

"You've known me for a couple hours, honey."

"My men are usually after a non-committal romance or what they can't find elsewhere. You're not like them. You're looking for that something that satisfies you...whatever it is. When you find it, you'll be satisfied, but the gratification won't last. It'll be a short-term fix, and then you will need again. I know."

Insightful. A good sign she read my intentions toward her. Street smart, Hope had learned to interpret her surroundings and relied on her instincts for her form of survival. Her ability to read behaviors was remarkable. Her skills were developed naturally, and I was fascinated with her. I didn't feel threatened or exposed by her psychoanalysis of my needs. It made her more desirable to be with.

"Hunter." She smiled and stroked my inner thigh. "I know I'm not what you are looking for."

I interrupted her, "Yes—you are...you're exactly the kind of girl I could use."

Stunned by my response, she quipped, "Those are not the words a girl likes to hear."

"You weren't planning on a long-term relationship with some stray you picked up tonight, right?"

"Define long term? If you mean all night...hopefully."

"I'm asking if you want to hang out with me for a while. Whatever happens, happens."

"Why? What's in it for me?"

"You can walk, honey if that's what you want to do." Hesitation punctuated her response. Maybe she didn't want to get tangled up with whatever I had cooking. But as curiosity killed the cat, it drew her to me.

"I'll stick around. I want to see what makes you tick."

"Tommy said you had talent. I believe him. I want a savvy escort that can take me to the sleaziest watering holes, strip clubs, or wherever."

Her eyes continued to probe mine for further clues. Maybe she'd grown weary of one-night stands or bored with the same old bar scene that caused her to accept my proposal. Whatever her reason, I intended to get full use out of her.

"Sounds like it could be fun." She leaned toward me, tilted her head back and exposed the soft skin of her neck next to my lips. She forced her lips to my ear pushing the hoodie aside, and whispered, "Are there to be any perks on the job?" I caught Lenny's eyes fixed on my response to Hope's behavior.

"We'll see when the jobs done. What about this joint?"

Hope settled back into her chair. Disappointment written all over her face, she answered, "Two nearby hotels refer traveling businessmen to Lenny's. That's why I come here. I'm always safe with Lenny and some of the other guys. They keep an eye out for me."

"Yeah, I see Lenny keeping an eye on us right now."

Hope smiled, "Is that what's bothering you?"

"Nothing bothers me, honey. I only noticed he was watching real close."

Hope continued, "If I like one of the businessmen, then we hook up for the night. Otherwise, I can always count on one of the men to buy me a drink and Lenny to give me a ride home."

"Hold that thought." The vibration of my cell phone interrupted our conversation. "Yeah." I shot a glance at Hope who picked up on my cue and took a walk. Her perception was perfect.

A raspy voice on the line said, "Let's meet."

"When and where?"

"Tonight at ten…"

"I'm on the south side, where do you want to meet?"

"There's a ball field at Glenwood City Park next to Kelly Elementary School. Got that?"

Thaman had complicated the scenario by not choosing a bar or diner. During the daytime, a ball field was no big deal, but at night it could draw the attention of shady characters or police. "Got it," I replied.

"Take Southeast Cooper Street to the ninety-degree bend in the road. You will see the backstop barely lit. There's curbside parking at the bend area. Park there and walk to the dugout farthest away from where you parked. I'll be waiting at ten o'clock."

"On my way," I said. I put the address for Kelly Elementary into my new GPS.

Hope had made her way to the bar and was jacking her jaw with Lenny. I motioned to Hope to return to the table. She sat in the chair as before and reached across the table for her drink.

"I need to go."

"It was the phone call, wasn't it? Hope purred, "Oooh, how mysterious—Secret-agent stuff like James Bond."

"Nothing exciting about it, and you're not old enough to remember James Bond. I'm checking out information for a friend is all."

Hope's eyes had panned the barroom before she jested, "No action here. Might as well tag along with you."

The combination of an oversized hoodie shrouded in a brown leather jacket easily concealed my handgun as I stood from my chair. Hope followed suit and rose as she handed me the black leather jacket. In gentlemanly fashion, I held her jacket out for her to slip on and cover her tightly fit frame. She glided one arm into the left sleeve then pivoted, exposing her back to me as she slid her other arm into the opposite sleeve. Flawlessly, with one continuous rotation of her body, she'd turned until we were face to face, our bodies touching sinuously. Boxed in by the wall and table, my hands awkwardly extended over her shoulders. Hope's hands quickly slipped under my leather jacket and down and around my waistline.

Her hands moved with experience and didn't stop until her fingers were stopped in their tracks. Excitedly she chirped, "Oh my God!" Her hand had met my weapon. Without thinking, I reacted and did the only thing I could; I pressed my lips against hers violating her only rule.

Quieted by force, I leaned back from her and brought my hands down from her shoulders and gently brushed her hand away from my .40-caliber. "Easy honey, it's just an insurance package that's all. That has to stay between us."

Hope's hands snaked their way to the middle of my back then pulled me tightly against her. She whispered, "Players have to pay to keep secrets silent."

"Pay?"

Still, in a whispering voice, she said, "Don't worry, I'll think of something." Hope ran her cheek playfully along the edge of my goatee, "Maybe we can take it out in trade."

I didn't ask what she had in mind she'd already made that clear. I thought I'd made myself clear too, but she was determined. I'd shown myself to be a match for Hope's persistence, but it was exciting having a good looking babe swoon over me that was half my age. Besides, I liked the attention. Maybe it was nothing more than the adage when the cat's away the mice will play, but I'd never thought that way before. The fact that sexual interaction had become nonexistent between Anna and me over the past few weeks, no doubt influenced my thinking. Whoever said, "Absence makes the heart grow fonder" assumed too much. With the possibility Anna might never return to me, since she'd stepped up to fill Max's shoes, did not make my heart grow fonder—it left me lonely. However, I didn't have time to dwell on things of the heart. I had business to take care of.

With my hand on the small of her back, I walked her to the tavern door and then on to the Avenger. I opened the passenger door and gave Hope plenty of room to be seated. As she slipped into the bucket seat, she placed her right-hand midway on my back to stabilize her balance. Her hand drifted down across my hip and down my left leg. It could have been innocent on her part. When she ran her hand back up my leg, I knew it hadn't been an accidental touching. In tavern atmospheres, Hope made for great cover and concealment. On a personal level, she was a major distraction.

I slipped in behind the steering wheel and ignited the Avenger's fire. Hope noticed the overhead light did not illuminate. She pointed and said, "The bulb must be burned out."

It hadn't been a statement which further exposed her powers of observation. Given her history, she'd likely ran across clientele with bulbs that were conveniently burned out for the same reason the dome light wasn't illuminated in the Avenger—to avoid being seen or identified. People in hiding avoid light—at all costs.

Hope didn't look surprised to see the overhead light inoperative. With her instincts awakened, however, the picture of who I was, or more accurately, what I was had taken shape. Like a tabletop puzzle, piece by piece, the image became more defined. Soon it would come together as understanding. Hope with all her primal predator drives would soon figure out the reason I dwelt on the cusp of society. I wouldn't be able to hide it.

We pulled out of Lenny's lot and followed the GPS route. Without any complications, I would arrive ten minutes before ten.

I buzzed south on the 205 Freeway then zigzagged a route through the housing area until I hit Southeast 92nd Avenue which brought me to Cooper Street. Hope was quietly observing everything I had done, and I only had to move her hand twice off my leg. I made the turn and proceeded slowly toward the ball field. Portland is known as the "City of Roses" but what it had was an abundance of trees of every imaginable size and shape. Cooper Street was no exception and hid the ball field from view. I pulled up to the first stop sign on 91st and took an extra-long wait taking in all the eye could see. The school sat to my left and the parking area stretched to the ninety-degree turn next to the ball field.

A thin crust of gravel layered on top of the asphalt in front of the backstop, crackled like popcorn until I pulled the Avenger to a stop. Thaman had been right about the lighting on the field; it barely lit the concessions trailer. He'd also been wrong. There was no dugout. The player's area was see-through chain-link fencing. A flickering street light stood at the bend in the road and directly over where I'd parked. I didn't like the conditions of our meeting or being exposed to the street light, but I assumed the risk. If Matt had the leads, a Palatini project would soon be underway.

With my gun still strapped and ready to rock-n-roll, I said to Hope, "You'll have to sit this dance out, honey. Don't get out of the car."

"Is it dangerous?"

"Maybe. Can you drive?"

"Yes."

"I'm leaving the car running for heat, but if something crazy goes down, anything that doesn't look right, I want you to take off—go to Lenny's."

Hope nodded as I stepped from the Avenger and made my way to the corner of a green concession trailer that was strategically centered behind the backstop for maximum exposure and sales. I stepped to the front side of the trailer with the chain-link fencing on my right, I was hidden in the shadow. Visible was the lone silhouette of a person sitting on the two-tier metal bleacher behind the dugout. I walked from the dark, and he startled.

"Is that you?" His voice cracked and quivered.

"Hunter," I said clearly to put Thaman at ease. "Why are you sitting under the light?"

Another shorter pole lamp that lacked the brightness of the street light, but still had illuminated his presence stood directly above where he sat. Thaman looked up and into the light then turned, so his feet touched the ground from the metal bench and walked in my direction. As he approached, he put out his hand and said, "Matt Thaman." We moved back into the darkness of the concession shed.

"I thought you were trying to stay incognito. You were lit up like a birthday cake."

"Sorry about that, I wasn't thinking I guess."

"You didn't see me pull up or get out of the car either. If this is as big a deal as you say it is and you want to live to tell about it, you're going to have to do a lot better at protecting yourself. Do you have a gun?"

"Yes."

"Can you get it quick?"

Matt bowed his head, "It's in my car."

"Okay, Matt, enough of the twenty questions. What do you have for me?"

"My older brother, Lance, was murdered. It will be three years next month."

I could see Matt was broken up. He held the tears back, but his emotions rode piggyback on his words. He struggled to speak at all. "Take your time," I said. "It's just you and me."

"It was his fault I suppose. He got himself tied up in that mess."

"What was he doing, working for them?"

"No...Lance didn't work very steady after Vietnam."

"How old was your brother when he died?"

"Fifty-one."

"Drugs? Alcohol?"

"All the above. He didn't drink often or much when he did. He said it made things worse. Self-medicated on the street, I suppose. He had VA drugs, but he didn't stay on them long."

"Hospitalized?"

"Not that I know of. He traveled coast to coast. Loved Florida, but always came back home to Kelso."

"Is that where he stayed?"

"Most of the time when he was in the area. My mom kept his room open to him. He was never a problem."

"Okay, let's get into it. What can you tell me?"

"The coroner said he died from Sepsis secondary to Post-Operative Infection. In the first operation, he had his right kidney removed."

"The first operation?"

"That's right. The coroner determined the second kidney, liver, and pancreas were taken in a later surgery."

"What you're saying is your brother volunteered to go under the knife, and likely died from the operation. That happens all the time in general hospitals."

"I was joking one morning with him at Mom's, and he said something about paying off her mortgage. I knew he didn't have the means to do it, so I didn't pay much attention to what he had said. After I had found out how he died, I racked my brain to remember what he'd talked about. He said things like, 'Do you know how much a liver is worth?' I thought it was Lance just talking foolishness."

"So he'd planned it?"

"Yeah, as much as he ever planned anything. He was running it by me seeing if I approved or something."

"You've been in contact with detectives on the case?"

"The lead detective moved on, and the case went into their cold case file."

"On the phone, you said there was a lead."

"More than one." Matt pulled from his pocket a slip of paper and handed it to me. I walked out of the darkness into the dim light shining down from the shorter light pole. Matt followed. Names and phone numbers were inscribed on the folded piece of paper. Not much to go on, I thought. I read the first name on the list out loud, "Benito Reyes." I waited for a check in the spirit. The feeling I attribute to Destiny dwelling with me. Then I asked, "Do you know who he is?"

"No. But my brother never called me, our mom, or anyone that I knew. He didn't have a phone and didn't have a use for a phone number that I can think of. I believe this guy Reyes was involved. Maybe he was the recruiter or brokered the deal with my brother. I would bet on it."

"This is third world country activity. Westerners travel to the Philippines or India all the time for these sorts of operations. I can't think of a good reason people would take a chance in the U.S. Did you give the information to the cops?"

"No. Mom found it in his fatigue jacket a few months ago, when she finally cleaned out his room. I was going to turn it over to the detective, but that's when I found out he was gone and the status of the case."

"Did you call the number?"

"It goes to the Flames Tavern. They never heard of a Benito Reyes."

"Mister Hunter…"

"Just Hunter."

"Okay…Hunter…I've spent time studying how the 'Red Market' works to try and understand what happened to Lance. I can tell you there is more than a recruiter involved. There are contractors, transporters, clinical staff, buyers, and possibly banks where organs are stored. This is not a fly-by-night operation; it is highly organized. I don't know what my brother was promised, but what he received wasn't what he was told."

"Matt, I need you to trust me…and I need some time—but I'm going to help you."

He responded reservedly, "Okay."

"I need to know anyone that knew him out on the street?"

Matt thought for a moment before he answered. "One guy, Henry, he's one of those veteran's that work a stand with flags, and signs. It's supposed to be a charity that helps vets…I guess it does. I talked to him a few times, he helped my brother some, and they were friends, but he doesn't know what happened. He works a parking lot at a strip mall of Powell. I can get you the address."

"I've seen it. They always salute you when you drive by."

"Yeah, that's them. There's more than one guy, so you have to ask for him by name."

I put my hand on Matt's shoulder; he hung his head and cried.

I've done my dead level best to stay disconnected, but Lance got a raw deal, and it wasn't right. Somebody had to answer, and it sounded like there was a long list of people responsible for what happened. They needed to pay up.

I got a good look at Matt. He looked his age of forty-six, thinning light-brown hair with blondish eyebrows. He stood close to six foot and a medium build. He pulled out a cigarette and lit up as I said my good-bye.

Hope had stayed put as I'd asked and looked eager to hear what was going on. I had nothing I could tell her and if I lied she was savvy enough to catch on. "Any idea where the Flames Tavern is located?"

"Sure." The sneer on Hope's face spoke volumes about what she thought about the joint. The Flames wasn't likely on her list of choices for a nightcap.

"What kind of place is it?"

"A dump."

"Redneck joint, biker bar, longshoremen hang out?"

"Drugs, fights, gangsters, the opposite of Lenny's place. It's not safe."

I liked places that had a reputation. The kind of people I hunt liked them too. "I need to check it out. You want to go for a ride?"

"Are you going to leave me in the car?"

"Not at all. I'll use you there."

"You're every girl's dream of a romantic date."

"Aren't I, though?"

CHAPTER 6

"Acting is behaving truthfully under imaginary circumstances."

—*Sanford Meisner*

The Flames wasn't a happening joint. Only five cars dotted the parking lot, and not a soul had entered or exited the tavern in the ten minutes we'd been parked. As we sat in the car, I commented, "Not as exciting as you thought it would be?"

"It's a nice change, Hunter. Most men have me back to Lenny's in fifteen minutes."

"They must be pretty stupid. I'd think any guy with red blood in his veins would want to spend as much time with a good-looking, sexy woman like you for as long as their money held out."

"If that's a compliment, I'll take it." She gave me a coy look as she ran her hand up the inside of my thigh and gave a gentle squeeze. I grinned wryly as I pulled her hand off my leg, mentally admonishing myself to get back to the task at hand.

The Flames was a target rich environment entertaining only the dregs of society according to Hope. First-hand knowledge trumps rumors and I wanted to check out the joint and get a look for myself.

"We're going in." Hope rolled her eyes but refrained from comment.

With the naked eye, the vehicle license plates were indistinguishable, but with the aid of 15 X 56 Lucas binoculars, I jotted down the license numbers in my little notebook.

"That's interesting," Hope commented; trolling for an explanation.

"Forget about it."

Hope was taking it all in and filing it in the back of her mind until she had enough data to fit me into a category. At the moment, she was trying to figure out why we were at the Flames.

With Hope as my escort, we strolled through the Flames main entrance, Hope slightly ahead. A woman with her looks turns heads and interrupts conversations. The eye candy didn't disappoint. I watched everyone in the place check her out. Hope still hadn't realized her value. She was more than an escort keeping me company and more than an informant showing me the ropes of who's who. She was a mobile cover and concealment platform for my movements. With Hope by my side, no one paid attention to my presence. If anyone noticed my trailing behind her their only thoughts were, how did that bum get so lucky? I'd caught the act before. Time and time again when Anna entered a room the scene repeated itself. The primal instinct of human behavior never changes—a fact I counted on.

We stopped at the curvature of the bar where it dawned on me how funny the two of us must look. I whispered in Hope's ear, "They think we're a Disney production."

She whispered, "Why?"

"Because together, we look like beauty and the beast."

Enjoying the moment with an amused smile as she scanned the room. Hope turned and snuggled close to my right side. She reached for my inner thigh, hesitated for a moment, then moved her hand up to my belt buckle. Well aware my manhood had reacted to her touch, she pressed against me and whispered in my ear, "You know what they're thinking. He's either got a lot of money or a lot of male attribute." Her eyes twinkled, and a devilish little smile touched her lips as she added, "I told you I could make it hard for you to say no."

All eyes had been upon us, but soon the patrons turned a blind eye. Maybe the gawkers thought they had neither of Hope's perceived requirements and being unable to compete, returned to their gossip and drinks.

I guided Hope to a small table that sat across the room from the entrance. Pulling out the chair that I wanted her in, I gestured for her to take the seat. Hope looked confused.

"I can't see anyone with my back to the room."

Point well taken. Hope was more than camouflage. She was working project Intel. The rectangular table allowed for both of us to sit with our backs against the wall. Rearranging the table and chairs for Hope's field-of-view observation, I took the seat to her right with my gun hand to the outside. We were a match made in the depths of hell.

Hope slipped out of her jacket and placed it on the backrest of a nearby chair, while I watched the tavern's clientele mix and move around the joint. Like Lenny's, the Flames was another one-man band. The lady bartender waited tables, poured drinks, and when she wasn't busy with customers, she handled security and bused tables.

The barkeep, wearing a sports jersey, looked like a blocker for a Roller Derby team. She stood five-foot-eight or better, stout, thirtyish with short cut hair. Impressive. My guess was she could handle herself if the need arose. Hope studied the patrons looking for familiar faces while we awaited our drink orders.

Without counting, I estimated two dozen people were inside the tavern; far more than what I would've guessed from the number of cars in the parking lot. The Flames fit the definition of a neighborhood bar to a T. With the surrounding housing area a vehicle wasn't necessary. A nearby bus station also made the Flames a convenient homeless hangout, especially when the weather turned bad.

I shared an observation with Hope, "Where's the bouncer?"

She assessed the clientele. "They don't have one."

"Do you see where the bartender is hanging out?"

"With the two men at the end of the bar?"

"Yep. I'll guarantee one of them is her backup in case there's trouble."

"How can you tell?"

"Her actions. She feels safe. Either she's packing a gun, or somebody has her back, and I don't see a bulge under her jersey. She doesn't have a gun."

"Maybe it's a boyfriend or husband?"

"Maybe—but at face value, my impression is one of those guys at the bar gets a free beer or two. Regardless, she's not as alone as she appears."

It was Hope's turn to weigh in on the action as she saw it. "The skinny, fidgety woman grinding her teeth at the table nearest the door. I know her. She's a big-time drug user."

I glanced at the Barfly. Impressed by Hope's accurate description, I asked, "Think she recognized you?"

"She knows who I am, but from what I can see, she doesn't have time to say hello. She's busy hustling the two men she's sitting with at the table."

I'd taken a moment for a quick study of the two men at the table. I estimated their age around twenty-five, give or take a year or two, and wearing similar clothing to include matching ball caps with company logos displayed. I had them pegged for a pair of construction workers. "I don't see the attraction," I said. "Chewy is twice their age."

Hope shot back, "No she's not—she's my age."

"You're kidding?" Hope was young and beautiful. Chewy was easily twice Hope's age with none of her beauty.

"She's been on the pipe. It takes a toll on the body."

Again, I was impressed by Hope's knowledge. She slipped her hand up my leg again for a quick squeeze as she leaned into me. "You should know, Hunter; all men are alike. Looks and age are not the deal-breakers. How much money they have for sex and what they get for the price are the only two factors at play."

I shook my head, "What a sad commentary on men."

Hope laughed in secret merriment. "Don't get uptight about it—men can't help the way they're wired and hookers like her count on the easy money."

Whether Hope realized it or not, she understood what all predators innately know—human behavior is predictable.

We had finished our first round of drinks when a pair of silicone implants that would've made Dolly Parton blush walked through the Flames entrance. Close behind her was an elderly gent strutting proud as a peacock. I looked away as if I hadn't noticed her, but Hope had and knew I had too.

"Her name is Faith. The old man is her sugar daddy. She had been a working girl that bar hopped in the past, but now, she's a kept woman."

I'd spent enough time in and around bars to know the score, but this was the first time I'd had a tutor and a beautiful one at that. It was eye-opening.

"Hope, Faith…who's next, Love or Charity?"

Hope patted my leg, "You're jealous of that old man."

"Not me!" Then jokingly I muttered, "Well, who wouldn't be."

I turned my attention back to Hope who continued her observations, "I don't know anyone seated at the bar, but the man standing at the curve of the counter is an EastEnders."

"EastEnders?"

"He's a gangster, pimp, and drug dealer."

"Gangster," I said. "He's nothing but a baby. Hard to believe he's twenty-one years old and allowed in the joint." Having a slimy pusher in the midst of the bar's clientele and acting smug like he owned the place was a positive sign I'd landed in a den of inequity. Drug dealers attract the worst of the worst, and obviously, he was unimpeded in his actions.

I didn't know any EastEnders but understood they were ethnically Asian and biracial. I asked Hope, "You know his name?"

"I can't recall. It's been a year since I've seen him. He's probably been in jail."

As I eyeballed the young thug, I took note of his clothing. I'd seen the same color coordination on hats and jackets in the hood on other guys. I concluded the silver and black amounted to gang affiliation. He wanted to be noticed as an EastEnders.

Hope caught my attention and gestured toward the door. The hooker whose teeth had ground to a halt, reminded me of my days growing up on the ranch in Oregon. A black quarter horse that stood fifteen and a half hands used to try and work the bridle out of his mouth when he was saddled. He rolled his tongue over the bit until I was able to focus his attention on the work. Faith stood and tossed on a denim jacket as she prepared to leave with both men in tow. "Chewy scored with one of them, huh?" I said.

Hope shook her head and smiled. "She's taking both of them to their car."

"Maybe they're going to another joint."

Hope laughed unreservedly, "She'll be back in a half hour, and both those guys will be happy campers."

I had no reason to doubt that Hope was right. She called them like she saw them and had proven her ability to flawlessly interpret behaviors. As the last man of the possible ménage à trois exited, he stopped and held the door open for a woman as she entered the Flames.

Asiatic, and in her mid-thirties, wearing a red blouse, long, dark flowing hair, her eyes searched the room. A few seconds behind her came a male, perhaps of mixed ethnic origins, fortyish, thin build, balding, with graying hair at his temples. Once inside, the man made a brief gesture with his hand to say, adios, and the two went separate ways.

"How about those two that came in together?"

"No, I don't know them."

The Asiatic woman moved along the counter and next to the first man available to her. Within a minute, she was sitting on the stool. All her actions telegraphed her predator role in the Flame's lush Serengeti. The prey, a fiftyish-year-old swag-bellied man, with a thick neck, and unshaven for the past few days, ordered a drink for his self-invited guest. I whispered to Hope, "You read Chewy's action, of course, you knew who she was and what she did. How are you with someone you don't know, like that gal at the bar? Can you tell what she's up to?"

"I can tell you this already, she entered with a man, and they went separate ways. That caught my eye right away."

I nodded. I didn't want to let on I'd seen the same thing.

Over the course of the next hour, and another glass of wine, Hope studied the woman's movements and behaviors. I expected Hope to recap the obvious that she was hustling the fat guy who was buying the booze for her. But, instead, she made a startling supposition when I asked.

"She's like you, Hunter."

"What do you mean, like me? I'm not a hustler."

Hope's eyes fastened on mine. "Neither is she. Her behavior is all wrong for a hooker. She's looking for someone—like you are."

That's one of the things I liked about Hope—her intuition. "Is she dealing?"

"I don't see that, maybe she did with the bald guy she came in with because he looks higher than a kite."

The balding man, seated alone at a table, appeared comatose, but I didn't see any drool hanging from his chin. What I saw was a man absorbed in what the woman at the bar was doing. Creepy.

The guy Hope identified as a drug-dealing pimp had begun to get obnoxiously loud. The bartender approached him twice and asked him politely to quiet down. He complied, but not for long. The lady bartender raised her voice and called him out, "Keep it together, or you gotta go!" The ugly hand gesture he tossed her was a brave response. But then again, his hand was below the top of the bar and likely meant for those of us in the table area to see and not the bartender. He cackled and laughed at himself. There was no need for me to intervene, he was a small fry and not worth the effort unless he got stupider. I kept the possibilities open.

"Oh great," Hope mumbled. "What a piece of…"

I interrupted her, "Is he getting under your skin?"

"See, it's what I told you about this place. He's a gang member, and he gets to acting crazy."

The thug and the bartender traded barbs with each other until it grew old and no longer entertaining. Soon he eyeballed Hope. Drunk or high, I didn't care. I wasn't about to let him disrespect her. That wasn't Hunter.

"I've heard he beats on his girls," Hope said.

"He's a pipsqueak, and you're not one of his girls—you're with me. If any beatin' takes place, he'll be on the receiving end of it…so don't worry." Hope didn't know me well enough to rest at ease with what I'd said. She'd have to learn to trust that what I told her—even when I lied to her—she could bank on it.

It took the tadpole all of five minutes to make his way to our table. He tossed Hope a distorted smile then focused on me. Either the booze or a mix of drugs, maybe both, caused him to grow more courageous. I, on the other hand, maintained my usual humbleness as I rose to my feet. He stopped in his tracks and looked at my nearly six-foot frame. Moving closer and into my personal space before looking upward into my eyes, he let out a screeching cackle. His putrid breath hung thick and heavy like the humidity on a hot August day in an outhouse. It caught inside my hood, so I reached up and pulled the hood off to gasp for fresh air.

"Who you be?" He roared with an Asian accent you could cut with a knife.

I thought why not dispense with the formalities of getting worked up into a frenzy, chest pounding, and yelling. Might as well get down to business and launch into fight mode. I measured his resolve and calculated that if I ignored him and his actions, we would still end up tossing blows in a matter of minutes. Having Hope by my side didn't restrain me in the slightest. If anything, she looked favorably upon me doing a dance on his head. I wasn't a shy guy, and fighting in a bar was never a problem, other than having an audience. I preferred to remain anonymous and to scrub the floor with this punk would bring attention my way, in the form of accolades. I might get a free beer from the bartender too.

"Hunter."

"What?"

"My name is Hunter?"

"Hunter!" He cried out as he annoyingly cackled louder, panting as if he were out of breath. No doubt the reaction to drugs.

"Stay out of my face," I said.

"He stood tall as he could and closed the gap between us. My eyebrows drew low on my forehead, and my eyes narrowed as I prepared for him to strike. I kept my cool. He postured moving his right foot behind him. With his left side now forward it allowed for a right-hand punch. I'd let him have the first throw, slip the punch like Joe Frazier and then introduce him to pain. But, instead, he turned toward Hope. "You got you a real man here, sweet thing."

Hope watched silently.

"His momma must not like him much...She gave him a dumb name." He cackled again before turning to address me. His eyes, bloodshot and dilated, bugged out and sweat beaded profusely across his forehead. His cackling laugh and fidgeting was nothing more than the uncontrollable impulses and tweaking from the drugs.

"Hunter—you have last name or that be first name?"

"Doesn't really matter, does it?"

Once again, he cackled uncontrollably, the sound was getting old in a hurry.

"What do they call you?"

"Chaka. I be known all around."

"I'm sure. Like I said, stay out of my face. And while you're at it learn English, you're not in a third world country anymore zipperhead."

Chaka turned pale-ish white; his mouth hung open as he stared. I expected he'd go Rambo on me then I could finish what I'd started, but he was nothing but a little punk with a big chip on his shoulder. His guttural Spanish curse didn't affect me in the least. I'd heard the words before just never from the mouth of a guy with oriental features. Slowly he stepped back from me. I prepared to draw my weapon. Why else the need for space? The tone of Chaka's voice flattened as he responded, "Okay puta, I got your number. I see you 'round."

The irritating bravado Chaka had displayed moments before my disrespect to him was gone.

Chaka continued to back away from our table and soon became reanimated at another patron's table. Hope had become tense while Chaka and I jousted our salutations, but didn't relax any with his withdrawal from our table.

"Can we split now?" Hope asked.

In response, I ordered another round of drinks. While we waited for the bartender to deliver our order, I overheard the noise of an escalating heated argument. Some words were in Spanish others in an Asian dialect. I could understand little of what they said and assumed they didn't fare much better listening to each other squawk. The Asiatic female and Chaka were at each other's throats growing increasingly more antagonistic and hostile. I guessed he'd caught on to whatever she was peddling on his turf and didn't approve.

The swag-bellied big guy that the Asiatic woman had sat with, spun around from the bar and off his stool to confront Chaka who had taken a step back from the man. Chaka opened his silver sleeved black letterman jacket slightly and lifted his T-shirt. What he had I couldn't see, but it made the big guy gesture with his hands which I interpreted as saying no to whatever Chaka showed him. The Asiatic female stepped in front of the man and with her finger waving in Chaka's face, yelled something in her native language.

The bartender ordered the verbal combatants to leave. Chaka became argumentative with her while the Asiatic woman took off without so much as a word. I wanted to tail her, but with a hostile argument fresh under her belt, she'd be watching for anyone following that might do her harm. With a last glance over her shoulder, she slipped out the exit.

I took Hope by the hand, "Come on, let's go have a cigarette."

"I don't smoke."

"Neither do I, Miss Moneypenny—come on."

"Who's that?"

"I thought you were a 007 girl?"

Outside the Flame's main entrance, I stood next to Hope and watched the woman continue walking to a white camper van. Within a minute the balding man that had entered with her walked from back of the tavern to the van, getting in on the driver's side. Hope by my side worked perfectly. No one noticed us.

Hope shivered in the brisk morning air. It dawned on me that we'd walked out without grabbing her jacket. We were engaged in surveillance, and I didn't want to break it off. The only solution was to pull my leather jacket off and offer it to her. But I'd no sooner unzipped and opened my jacket when Hope seized the moment to run her hands under my jacket and wrapped her arms tightly around me. Pressing her curvaceous body against mine, she whispered, "Hmm, now that's what I'm talking about." I closed my jacket around her for warmth. She pressed in so snugly the jacket wrapped us into a cocoon.

I couldn't deny I was enjoying her body pressed against mine and I was in a great position with her back to the van to unobtrusively maintain the surveillance. I could look past her long buttery blonde hair directly at it. A minute later, headlights from the van swept across the front of the Flames Tavern and past us as it continued to turn and exit the lot.

Hope looked into my eyes, "Did you get the license number?"

"I saw what I needed to see, we can head back in now."

Hope kept her hold, "Not yet...I'm still cold."

The body heat we'd generated made me doubt her truthfulness. I could have pressed the issue, but why? She was more than generous with her time and help. And besides, she was anything but cold. I'd call her smoking hot and her body furnace sent a flush of heat coursing through mine.

After a few minutes, Hope loosened her grip, and without saying anything, we casually walked back inside the Flames. Our drinks were still on the table, but one never knows what might have been dropped into a glass when you weren't watching. I pushed them to the front edge of the table and ordered a fresh round.

Hope had, up until now, observed my eyes when she asked a question. I knew she looked for telltale signs of truth and deception. This time she looked away when she asked, "Why are we still here?"

"Enjoying the evening with you, honey."

Still looking away, she said, "Until the phone rings again." Hope was savvy enough to have figured out I was on standby for some sort of action and it wasn't all above board. Soon she'd put the whole picture together. I'd have to decide on how to handle her.

"Sweetheart, it's almost closing time. Where would you like to go?"

"Your place is fine." Her seductive smile and eye contact returned.

"What's your second choice?"

It was back to pouting in a flash as she said glumly, "Lenny's, I suppose. I'll get a ride home from him."

The streets had emptied along our route to Lenny's bar. Hope sat quietly looking out the passenger window. From where I sat any future together looked grim. She was a tough read and as phony as I was. Given her history, and her stated reason for our encounter, my shot at a one-night stand was about over. I'd likely not see her again.

The end of the trail was in sight. I gave the steering wheel a hard crank to the left. We crossed an empty traffic lane into Lenny's parking lot and pulled the Avenger to a stop by the front door.

Still looking out the passenger side window, the tone of her voice was soft. "Are we done?"

"For the night."

For the umpteenth time, Hope turned toward me and searched my eyes for more answers. I looked away. Slipping the car door open, I walked around the vehicle and opened the passenger door, but Hope remained seated. The parking lot was poorly lit, and the lack of an interior dome light made the night appear that much darker. I bent down close to her and asked, "You want me to walk you to the door?"

"No...I'm waiting for you to ask me for my phone number."

I took Hope by the hand and helped her to her feet. She removed from her jacket a folded slip of paper that she'd written her phone number on then pushed it down deep into the bottom of the left front pocket of my pants. "Don't lose it."

"I can't promise you anything, but I might need more orientation."

Half-heartedly she responded, "I might be busy."

"I know."

Hope reached out in what I interpreted as a customary farewell handshake. Oddly, I felt we'd grown closer than that, but I wanted to get rid of the feeling. She leaned into me and kissed my cheek. "I've never met a man quite like you. No one has ever turned me on by turning me down."

She was powerfully seductive and visually persuasive. I believed she was telling the truth.

A minute or more passed then Hope's hand slipped from mine as she walked into Lenny's.

On the drive to Anna's condo, I called Matt.

At three in the morning, I expected to wake him from a sound sleep, and I had. "This is Hunter. What are you doing around noon later today?"

"What do you have?"

"Let's go find Henry, your brother's veteran friend."

"I've talked to him, he doesn't know anything, but I'll meet you. Where?"

"No sense in complicating the simple things that don't have to be made difficult. Let's get a cup of Joe in the strip mall on Powell where Henry works the corner."

"The end store is a coffee shop."

"Okay, noon then."

I lay in Anna's bed and waited to fall asleep, but any restful slumber eluded me. Bothersome thoughts of Brandon Ware cycled through my mind. How could he be tracking the Avenger? It was my car he said he'd seen in the tavern parking lot. If he'd used a LoJack system, he was able to locate the Avenger at any location or time, and likely had found my spider hole at Anna's place. In a few short hours, I'd give the vehicle a good going over and would know where he'd hidden the locator. Maybe I could attach the tracking unit to a long-haul rig and send Ware running cross country on a wild goose chase and out of my hair.

The day had put a lot on my mind, and the only answer was pleasurable fantasizing of the hunt. But rather than lull me to sleep, it worked against me, stimulating my alertness, not quelling my desires. I thought how badly I wanted Chaka. I forced my dream world to comply, and my thoughts surrounded Chaka's imaginary return to the Flames

Tavern to settle the score. How beautiful the scene, the opportunity to rectify our differences and my envisioned actions. Each time, our encounter brought an ensuing gun battle and justifiable self-defense as I blew his guts out. In my mind's eye, I watched as life pulsated from his body. Sure, it was a dream, but now and then dreams come true. Then there was Hope, an altogether different kind of dream.

CHAPTER 7

"Give me six hours to chop down a tree,
and I will spend the first four sharpening the axe."

—*Abraham Lincoln*

It was common to check in with Max from time to time, a Palatini practice when engaged in an operation. If the current project wasn't reason to call Anna then the sense of loneliness that had set in, stimulated by Hope, was enough motivation. I let the phone ring a long time before Anna answered. Even so, I was happy to hear her voice.

"Hey, it's me."

"Walter, I'm glad you called. Any news on the project?"

"Moving forward, but I wish you were here. We could do it together."

"I do too. Is there anything you need?"

"Just you baby."

A lengthy and uncomfortable pause followed—it didn't feel right. Did Anna feel the same icy chill in our conversation as I had or was it only me? Gone from her response was the warm fuzzies I'd felt so many times in the past. "The operation Thomas initiated needs my attention. I'm sure you understand, you've been in that circumstance."

"Gotcha. Just wanted to say that I miss you, and not to worry about me or the project."

"Miss you too, Walter."

While I sipped my first cup of Joe, I dug through the small stack of instructions Anna had left on the kitchen counter. She wasn't one to leave her house messy, but she knew I wouldn't search for her notes unless they were kept in one pile in plain sight. Anna promised to leave the contact information for her mechanic friend. A set of typed notes held the key. In bold print, the name Bernard was at the top of page two—parenthetically the word mechanic followed by a phone number. Anna and I had discussed plans to divest my interest in the Avenger; she thought Bernard could help.

I placed the call. When Bernard answered, I introduced myself and chatted for a few seconds about Anna. Bernard provided his address and an invitation to drop in anytime, no appointment necessary. Following his directions, I headed south out of Portland on Interstate 5, through Wilsonville. Crossing the Willamette River, I continued south before turning onto Northeast Miley Road. From there I held right on Northeast Butteville Road and followed the tree-lined road through a series of curves. With thirty-five-mile-an-hour safe-speed warning signs posted I couldn't resist. I sped through them not only for the fun of it but to keep my driving edges sharp as well. A mile or more down the road, farmland became the prominent feature of the landscape—the sense of freedom from the city was extraordinarily comforting.

Shortly after noon, I came upon the turn off to Bernard's place. I crossed over the bridge which was made from a flatbed trailer spanning a drainage ditch, paralleling the paved road in front of his shop.

Bernard was what I referred to as a shade tree mechanic; others might call him an entrepreneur. It was evident from the looks of his place he bought fixer-uppers and flipped them for cash. If the Internal Revenue Service caught up with him, they'd likely call him a tax evader and the county sheriff might consider him the owner of a chop shop. To me, it was his life, and he could live it any way he wanted. Far be it for me, an assassin, to be judgmental about such things.

A large gravel pad connected a three-bay garage to a dated farmhouse. I braked to a stop, threw the Avenger in park, killed the ignition, and waited until I saw a man emerge from the unattached garage, walking in my direction. I stepped from my car as he drew near and extended my hand. I played the role of a feature writer like Anna had suggested facilitating our meeting.

With salt and pepper hair, Bernard looked to be in his late fifties, but without the distinguished look of a suit and tie guy. His grip was calloused and firm, but he wasn't trying to prove anything with his handshake. In fact, I didn't get the impression it mattered to him whether we did or didn't exchange the customary greeting. He was a man that had worked hard with his hands most of his life. There were smudges of grease on the back of his knuckles and embedded in the wrinkles of his hands. Light brown dirt covered his wrists to the cuffs of his shirt sleeves. Immediately I was comfortable with him. Honesty was his hallmark whether the IRS would have thought so or not.

"Like we discussed on the phone, I'm concerned someone may have attached a tracking device to my car."

"Cops?"

"Not likely, just a nosey dude that keeps showing up at places where I happen to be. Yesterday, he mentioned he saw my car in a bar's parking lot and stopped in to visit.

"I take it you don't want him around."

"He's a pest, and it's unnerving to be stalked. He asks questions that are none of his business."

Bernard said, "Okay Boss, give me a few minutes, and I'll see if I can rid you of that stalker."

I looked around the shop while Bernard backed a vehicle out of a stall and ran the Avenger onto the shop's lift and up in the air.

With a keen interest in his findings, I watched and waited as he combed through what he believed to be the common hiding places. Thirty minutes later he said, "It's clean as a whistle, Boss. I don't see a thing. You sure he's following with a tracking device and not just following you?"

"Suspicion is all I have to go on. To ease my mind I should get rid of the old girl, but I don't like paperwork or the government knowing my business."

I had Bernard pegged and knew we were on the same sheet of music. "Boss, you ever see a demolition derby."

"Yeah, years ago on TV."

"Well, they still do 'em. I've got a friend that races, he's always on the lookout for a screaming deal. Mechanically, your car is in good shape. Might even be a winner. But if not, they'll haul it off for scrap metal."

"Give your friend a call and see if he's interested. Get back to me when you find out. I'll leave you my number. Now, what do I owe you for your time?"

"On the house, Boss. Maybe I'll make a buck on the flip."

Surprised and pleased at the unexpected perk, I gave him a thumbs-up as I cranked up the Avenger and headed north. I'd made a good contact and I had a feeling I might be availing myself of his services in the near future.

The afternoon was young so I gave Matt Thaman a call. With a quick apology, I let him know my car had been giving me problems, and that I'd spent the morning with a mechanic. Matt was gracious and happy that I hadn't stood him up. We decided to meet at the coffee shop as planned.

Putting boots on the ground without Ware in my rear-view mirror was an important step. When I spoke with Henry, I didn't want Ware to interrupt us or have a subsequent conversation with him. I kept an eye out for the obvious. I couldn't overlook the idea that Ware might have employed a surrogate. Traffic was heavy and played to my advantage. When I pulled into the Mall's parking lot, I swung the Avenger to the opposite end of the lot from the coffee shop and parked. I walked in through the anchor store's east entrance and directly to the west doors, and back out onto a sidewalk. I stepped into an electronics store and looked in the direction of the window display watching for a tail. A couple of minutes later I was outside the store making my way to a hot cup of java.

The coffee shop had a specialty blackboard at the entrance with blends of coffee, unique foo-foo ingredients, and special prices that were outrageous. I ordered a cup of regular coffee, black. The pimply faced teenager behind the register wasn't sure if they had a blend called Regular, so I settled for a triple shot of espresso. It almost passed for coffee.

Matt hadn't arrived, and the coffee needed a place to land. It wasn't difficult to choose between the five tall tables or the bar stools that dotted the little shop. The setting was comfortable without a customer in the place. I took a corner position.

Matt parked directly in front of the shop and flew in through the door as if his hair was on fire. "I'm sorry I'm late," he said while waving his hand in my direction. Without breaking his stride, he approached the barista and placed an order.

When Matt joined me at the table, he whispered, "Did you see him?"

"I haven't seen anyone."

"Henry is out there at the vet's setup."

"Okay, then I need your help."

"Sure, sure, no problem, anything."

"I need you to let me ask the questions. If you think I'm missing something, we can talk afterward. I will intentionally leave off some issues which will give me a reason to follow up with a second interview."

"Okay, okay, I got it."

"Matt, you're looking awful excited about this. It's preliminary, that's all."

"Yeah, yeah, I'll be okay. I'm just excited to get something going—for Lance."

"Listen, I'm not working your brother's case, I'm researching the validity of your claim for Anna. She's a feature writer, not a detective."

"Oh, ah, yeah, yeah, I know, no problem."

"Okay, let's finish up here, and then you can introduce me to Henry."

Matt and I walked the seventy-five yards or so to where the turn lane emptied into the parking lot. The vets had an area roped off with the various branches of the military represented by flags all in a row. The United States Colors appeared larger than the others and had a prominent position centered amongst the branch flags.

Two men stood with brochures in hand, saluting and waving at cars that drove past their stand. Both men wore ball caps with military insignia and leather vests over their jackets that were strewn with various military patches and medals.

"Henry?" Matt called out to the man standing nearest us.

Henry, a man who looked to be in his mid-fifties, smiled from ear to ear and rendered a snappy salute.

"I'm Matt…Lance's brother. Do you remember me?"

Henry cocked his head to one side then smiled again, "I sure do, Mister Matt."

A friendly handshake ensued. Matt took the lead and introduced me. Following the customary greetings and handshake, I told Henry the reason I was there. "We are writing a feature article on what happened to Lance. I've read the coroner's report, but it's filled with technical jargon and not very useful to tell the story. I'm hoping you can shed some light on what transpired three years ago."

"Well, sir, I am heartbroken over what happened to my fellow Army veteran. The truth is, I don't know how it happened. Only what Mister Matt had told me."

Henry had chosen heartfelt words and looked me in the eyes while he professed to lack knowledge of the incident, but his words were hollow sounding. That impression became my first red flag.

I played twenty questions with Henry to get him relaxed and coax him into talking. "How long did you know Lance?" "How often did you guys get together?" Questions that didn't require him to be guarded with his answers. When I saw him loosening up, I popped a tougher question into the mix. "How much did Lance get for his kidney?"

"Four-thousand dollars."

"How did you know how much he was getting if you didn't know anything about it?"

With his best salesman smile, he responded, "Well sir, Mister Matt told me. I think he did anyway."

Matt immediately bellowed, "I've never heard that figure before."

Henry gathered his thoughts. "I'm losing money here, Mister Hunter. Maybe we can talk some other time?"

I gathered at that point that he didn't have an answer that he wanted to share, so I kept after him. Walking the few steps to where a thirty-two-ounce canning jar with a slotted lid sat squarely on a three-foot table stand and looked inside. A ten-dollar bill stuck out among the fives and ones. All told he'd collected less than thirty dollars in donations. Without saying anything, I looked back at Henry. He was no longer smiling.

"Mister Hunter, it's been really slow today. It's cold and people just don't like to stop when the weather's like that. It's why I need to get back to work. You understand, don't you?"

"I do." I removed a fifty-dollar bill from a wad of bills that I pulled from my front pocket and dropped it into his donation fund. Henry's partner stopped working the display closest to the turn lane off Powell Boulevard and focused his attention on Henry.

I said to Henry's partner, "I need to borrow your friend to buy him a cup of coffee." I pulled another fifty from the wad I had in my hand and put the bill in his donation jar. At that, Henry conceded. I'd given them more money than they'd get for an entire day handing out their brochures.

Matt, Henry, and I made our way back to the coffee shop where I placed the order, "Four large cups, regular coffee, black." Remembering the clerk's inability to understand terms like regular and black, I held up four fingers and said, "Quad-shot espresso, four times, you understand?" The clerk nodded.

When the kid finished brewing the second cup, I motioned to Matt, "Take these outside, one's for you, the other one goes to the Vet." Matt nodded. He understood I wanted to talk with Henry alone.

I brought the two remaining cups to the table Henry had chosen. He had made himself comfortable near the entrance, his jacket, vest, and ball cap already was on the chairs drying out. Contrary to my usual preference, I sat with my back to the entrance. Henry wore a thick grey sweatshirt with one word emblazoned across the chest—"Army." Henry was proud to be a veteran of the Armed Forces which made him a man with whom I could relate. Abruptly I asked, "Why are you holding out? You said Lance was your friend. He was a Vietnam Veteran just like you. You shared camaraderie and experiences beyond a civilians understanding. You may be black, and Lance was white, but my friend, he was your brother, and you know it."

Henry's head hung low.

"I have a problem with what happened to Lance. And I'm going to get to the bottom of what went wrong."

Henry slowly nodded. I pressed him by lowering my head and stared him in the eyes. A tear welled up and streaked down his face. Henry didn't strike me as a criminal type, and he didn't have a callused personality. He appeared to love his fellow Vet's and was sincere in his service to our country. It gave me leverage.

"You're holding out...I'm not a cop. I'm a journalist and sworn to confidentiality."

"Yes, sir."

Henry wanted to talk, but he was high-centered on something stuck in his craw. "Did you hook him up with the people who did the operation?"

"No sir," Henry said. He glanced up at the two customers who had entered the shop and made their way to the counter. Henry abruptly stood and lifted the right side of his sweatshirt nearly to his armpit. Visible was an angled scar on his abdomen that ran from the back side of the bottom rib toward his front a few inches to the right of his navel and disappeared under the waistband of his pants.

"How long ago?"

Henry let his shirt drop and sat back down in the chair. "Mister Hunter, it was the same time my brother had his taken."

"Lance?"

"Yes, sir."

"They paid you four-grand too?

Henry nodded.

"For what...a kidney?"

"That's right. I have a daughter and son-in-law that I stayed with after the operation. They took good care of me until I mended. Lance was supposed to recover at their facility..." At this point, Henry had begun to weep.

Trying to stay focused and unmoved I asked, "When did you see Lance last?"

"Day of the surgery. Never saw him again after that." Henry's eyes glistened as another tear slipped down his cheek. He paused for several seconds and then forced himself to speak, "The next thing I heard was Lance was dead."

"What can you tell me about their operation? How did they contact you? Where did you have the operation? When did they give you the money? Was it cash?"

"Lance met this lady at the bar—."

"What bar?"

"The Flames, it's a hangout for some of us vets. Lance didn't drink, but the bartenders gave him free coffee. Anyhow, this lady offered him a solution to his money problems."

"Did you meet with this lady too?"

"Just once, she turned us over to the guy who set it up."

"The lady's name was what?"

"She was a Mexican lady...pretty...I think her name was Carmen. The guy who made the deal's name was Ramone. I saw him four or five times."

"At the bar?"

"Yes, sir...I couldn't say nothing when Lance died. I was afraid I'd get in trouble. Lance and I both knew it was on the down low. But, it was fast and easy money...we both needed it."

Henry and Lance bore the responsibilities of their decisions and actions, but they'd been conned into an illegal and unsafe procedure. The Red Market traffickers owned the aftermath. Lance's death was on them. "Anyone else you know who had an operation like yours?"

Henry's mouth twitched as he mused on my question. "One of the guys went to see them about six months ago..." Henry's eyes dropped to the floor and his lips pressed together into a thin, hard line. "I should've watched out for my men...I didn't...look what's happened to them."

"What's this guy's name and where can I find him?"

"Robert's a Desert Storm vet. He's screwed up in the head, but I don't think it's related to the war. I imagine he took the money and lit out."

"You haven't seen him since the operation?"

"Not sure."

Henry's answer was guarded. He was hiding something. "Do you know where he made his recovery?"

"He was going to stay at their place."

"Do you know where they do their operations?"

"If it's the same as Lance and I had, it was in an ambulance."

"A mobile surgery?"

"Yes, sir."

"After the surgery, we were taken to a trailer house."

"You and Lance had your operations on the same day?"

"One day apart...I was first."

"Day...you mean night."

"No, it was the middle of the day when they picked me up, and when Lance arrived, it was still daylight. About three days after the surgery, they gave me a ride to my daughter's house in a camper van."

"Any markings on the van you remember?"

"I'm sure there weren't any. I know the ride to my daughter's place took an hour and a half—maybe two."

"How about the money?"

"They gave me the money when they dropped me off in the van."

"They?" I pressed him for the details. "How many people did you see in total?"

Henry counted the people out loud. The two at the bar who gave me a ride in the back of their van. In the ambulance, I want to say, three men, one of them was the doc. The other two men, maybe white guys, helped the doc. At the recovery trailer, I think they were Chinese or Vietnamese. So, what was that—six or seven altogether?"

"At least. Doc had a funny name that sounded like Coyote. The men in the ambulance didn't call him doctor, just Coyote."

"When you were in the trailer were there windows?"

"Yes, sir. I could see trees, like a forested area. When they transported me back to town, they brought the van to a side door in the back of the trailer and took me straight out of the bedroom, into a short hallway, and out the door. It was evening time and dark. I didn't see anything out front."

"Tell me about the room, anything you remember?"

"Small, wood-paneled, drawers built into the closet. The bathroom was down the hall. I could hear them flush, and occasionally a shower would run, but they gave me a bedpan and a handheld urinal."

"Thanks Henry, I believe Matt will finally get the answers he's looking for."

Henry nodded. His smile faded. I hadn't made him feel any better about what had happened to Lance, and I had one final request of him, "If you see any of these guys around, you get a hold of me, okay?" He nodded. "Don't say anything to them about any of this, savvy?" I wrote "Hunter" on a sheet of paper from my memo pad and scrawled the phone number I'd assigned to the Thaman project for Henry. "Call me if you see or hear anything."

We stood and walked out the exit and into the chilly weather. Matt saw Henry and me as we walked in his direction. Henry, with head, hung low, avoided eye contact with Matt as he passed him on the way to the vet's stand on the six-foot-wide median that separated the inbound and outbound parking lot traffic.

"What happened?"

"Sorry, I can't say. You can respect the confidential nature of what we are dealing with I'm sure."

Matt scrunched his face into a frown.

"We had a good discussion, and I'm sure we'll get mileage from what Henry has given me. He too was a victim. Next, I'll dig into histories, names, and places and see what I can come up with. Can you give me the time I need to blaze a trail?"

"Blaze away...I want you to know in the end I'm going to be there."

Matt left unhappy but agreeable for the time being. I dodged in and out of the buildings until I reached the Avenger, fired her up and was on the road.

I was a half hour drive from my favorite shooting range. The forecasted cold front continued its move into the Pacific Northwest bringing increasingly chilly winds. The winding road dropped down onto the valley floor where a field sprawled and on which the range was located.

The range was quiet with only a pair of shooting enthusiasts braving the menacing weather. It wasn't my first time plunking holes in a target with less than ideal conditions. Being seasoned as I was, I remained in the Avenger with the heater running while I loaded my magazines.

A three-sided shooting canopy, twenty feet in length, was a welcome sight for winter range users looking for a windbreak. The shed's siding, a mix of plywood and Plexiglas, allowed sunlight to enter, brighten, and warm the bench area. The only down-side to the structure was a blocked view of the parking area.

After I had placed a man-sized silhouette target on the seven-yard mark, I blew through a magazine firing head shots. As I stripped the empty mag, I watched the other two shooters head for the parking area. What caught my attention was a dark-colored sedan parked alongside the gravel road that led down onto the range. I walked to the shooting bench a few yards behind the line of fire and placed my .40-caliber on a table. Gradually, the sedan made a three-point turn and drove out of view. I had no way to confirm my gut instincts, and the sedan was too far away to identify, but the car looked like Ware's Impala. Had he used a more sophisticated tracking device than a Lojack? How else could he have known I was at the range? The sooner the Avenger became history, the better for me and the operation I'd embarked on. The project was in jeopardy with a blue nose nipping at my heels.

Uneasy, I cut my shooting engagement short and swung into a fast-food place to grab a bite to eat. With a hamburger in hand, I made my way to the cockroach motel on Southeast Insley where I'd planned to clean the alleyway and back my vehicle into hiding. I swung through the parking lot looking for the kind of activity I didn't want to find. Last time I'd paid the motel a visit, two EastEnders were sitting on the steps. The clouds had rolled in with the storm front, and darkness prevailed early in this unlit area. It was unlikely anyone would be on the street with the weather getting worse. I expected to be alone for the cleanup party.

My headlights cast a beam across the motel parking lot. No movement. Good. I had plenty of time to tackle the cleaning task before my meeting with Hope.

Using my headlights wasn't the safest way to get the job done but time was critically short. I braked the Avenger to a stop in front of the alley where it narrowed and circled behind the building. I planned to dig out a small area and see if the setting was comfortable before I backed completely behind the building.

My foot rested on the brake pedal, as I slipped the tranny into park and unsnapped my seatbelt. At the range, when I finished shooting, I'd stuffed the .40-Cal into an unzipped pocket on my bug out bag rather than strapping it on. The alley wasn't the kind of place I wanted to be without my weapon. So I removed it from the pouch and prepared to put it in my holster as I set foot on the hardtop to work.

No sooner had I cleared the top of the bag with my weapon than a man's face appeared at my passenger window. He was an Asian man, short in stature, twentyish-looking with an EastEnders silver and shiny black jacket. With only the dash lights slightly illuminating my face, the gangster couldn't see the Walther in my hand. I press-checked the weapon to ensure I felt brass in the chamber. Locked and loaded. The Asian man pulled at the door handle and shouted, but the door locks were engaged as they usually were when I traveled. He pounded on my passenger side window with an open palm.

I didn't see the other guy until I was startled by a loud crack and a tinny sound on the driver side window. As I spun my head to look, I saw two more figures with silver and black jackets shining in the headlight beams approaching the front of my car. It wasn't a social call.

The Asian guy at the driver's side window was about the same age and size of the first man who tried to open the passenger door, only he didn't have the matching jacket. He did, however, have a gang colored ball cap and brandished a small caliber automatic as he shouted orders to unlock the car door.

The two Asian guys in front of the Avenger drew closer. Out of courtesy, I revved the RPM's on the engine, but the response was all wrong. One man moved in front of my car, leaned forward and placed one hand on the hood, and with his other hand reached for something inside his left coat pocket.

They'd given me a clear signal that I wasn't going anywhere, but at the same time, I'd given them a clear warning I wasn't planning to leave. They had the upper hand it seemed, but I remembered a story about Marine Corps General, Chesty Puller, and the address he gave his troops in Korea. "All right, they're on our left, they're on our right, they're in front of us, they're behind us…they can't get away this time." I never compared myself to the Leatherneck, but I did take motivation from his words. With my foot resting on the brake and the heel of my hand on the shifter, I pulled it back into drive.

In a matter of seconds, I was surrounded by hoods as they closed in as tightly as they could and escalated their intentions to do me harm. One guy near the front of the Avenger moved off to my left and out of the headlight beams. He looked like he was searching the ground for something. The alley's debris field had plenty of brick, broken concrete, and other implements one could use to smash a car window with, and I wasn't planning to wait around to see what he found.

The man at the driver's window pounded the butt of his pistol on my window and continued to shout commands salted with obscenities. I didn't find what he had to say to be particularly interesting and no one in their right mind would relinquish the security of a locked vehicle in an attempt to verbally mitigate the circumstances. However, foolish victims, motivated by fear, have been known to fall into the mindset they can talk their way out of the predicament.

The gang worked themselves into a screaming frenzy and jumped around like apes. They were foolish young men who tried to outdo each another. Maybe they interpreted my calmness as shock and fear, or maybe they didn't give a damn because the odds were on their side. They were in the prime of their life, and their threats had to be taken seriously. Their quick escalation left me with little recourse. No further incentive was necessary to act, and their mistake came to fruition before their eyes.

The man standing at the front of the Avenger with a small caliber wheel gun pointed it in my direction. Reflexively, I blew out my passenger window with the first round striking one young man square in the face. Half a second later I punched the throttle, and the car lurched forward six or seven feet trapping the man in front somewhere under the Avenger. I popped the driver's side door open and dropped the gun-wielding man with two quick taps to the chest. He'd had his chance to shoot first, but never took it. That was his fault. If you're in a gunfight, you should always shoot and do so often.

The last man of the group who noticeably had frozen in his tracks dropped a metal pipe to the ground and took off running. I poised to shoot, but the best marksman would have only burned powder. He disappeared into the darkness. After a quick threat scan noting the world had become a safe place again, I moved from man to man ensuring there were no survivors. I'd expected to see Chaka in their midst, but I'd never laid eyes on these guys before. I backed off the body that had been pinned under the Avenger and drove off the lot with no intention of returning. What had been a promising hideaway had been made useless through their utter foolishness. The most unfortunate part of the evening that deeply saddened me was the loss of my passenger window. I was in for a cold, wet night. I headed to Lenny's for a stiff drink and an uncertain rendezvous with Hope.

When I parked the Avenger, I stored my bug out bag in the trunk and wore my Walther concealed. I strode into Lenny's and to the table that Hope and I had occupied the previous night. When Lenny came for my order, he had two beverages in his hands. He sat a brew in front of me and a concoction that Hope drank on a second place setting.

"She'll be here soon."

I reached into my pants pocket to pull out my wad of dough, but Lenny stopped me.

"On the house."

Ravishing and radiant, Hope made her entry on cue. Single-handedly she had transformed the gloomy dark wood paneled environment of Lenny's bar into a place of beauty. Hope hadn't bothered saying hello to the grasses of the Serengeti bellied up to the bar. Rather, she walked directly toward my table. Or, was it our table? I stood and slid a chair next to mine and moved her drink where she could reach it.

Hope had poor personal boundaries which was refreshing. At least, that's the way I saw it when she embraced me and squeezed my butt cheek.

"Glad you could make it tonight, honey."

In a pouty voice, she cooed, "I'm happy you didn't stand me up. I would have been crushed."

Hope was a fast learner and had dressed more appropriately for what I had in mind. Her soft blonde hair flowed over the collar of her belted dark blue windbreaker. Dark jeans, sweatshirt, and tennis shoes completed her wardrobe. Nothing revealing, and just as well, a guy can only withstand so much temptation, and she had plenty of what lures a man.

"Drink up honey, we have to make tracks."

"Where to?"

"Let's start at the Flames."

We downed our drinks and beat feet out of Lenny's. I had to sweet talk Hope into riding in the Avenger as it was missing the window on her side. With a wink and a look at me sideways she said, "You owe me sweetie."

Twenty minutes later we pulled into the parking lot of the Flames Tavern. Like the previous night, there were only a few vehicles aligned close to the entrance. I backed the Avenger between two of the cars near the front doors and killed the engine.

"You need to warm me up." Her smile, which was subtly seductive, telegraphed the meaning. She slipped her right hand onto my leg with a light caress. But at that moment a set of headlights swept through the parking lot and lit the Avenger's cabin for a brief second. The vehicle cruised slowly toward the front of the Flames and parked on the opposite side of the entrance from where we'd parked. Hope watched the car and remarked, "Isn't that your friend from last night?"

"Yeah." I shook my head while muttering under my breath, "Ware…"

A choice had to be made. Drive away or deal with him inside. With Hope by my side, we walked through the entrance. I didn't want to expose Hope to further antagonism, I let her hand go free by a bar stool.

"This chair taken?" I gestured at the chair opposite Ware.

"I was saving it for you."

I put in my order with the heavyset bartender and asked him to run a tab for my lady friend and me. He returned a few minutes later with a mug of beer from the tap and placed it on a coaster. "Your lady friend said she'll cover it, but you owe her."

She had one-upped me again. "I know," I said with a resigned shrug. "So, what's this all about, B.A. Why the stalking behavior?"

His face formed a slight sneer as he responded, "Mister Goe, only my closest friends call me B.A."

I sipped the froth off the top of my beer. "Since you've decided we're going to be close, I figured we were friends."

"I know my friend's names, but you...I doubt I know your real name. Walter one day...Hunter the next. That disqualifies you as a friend—whatever your name is today."

"Why are you following me?"

Ware swept the room with his eyes. After a long pause, he whispered, "I'm wondering who you're target is this time?"

I laughed. "Target...you're being accusatory. I don't own a gun. You can check the registry if you like."

"I have. Nothing found in your name—but I didn't say anything about shooting someone. I was talking about who you're doing the article on."

I had to slow my game. "I'm out on the town having fun. So, I'd say you're wasting your time following me around."

"Walter, if you don't mind me saying, you're a fascinating man. I checked into your background and came up with a complete zero." Ware paused as his eyebrows became one long furrow. "You don't look surprised by the lack of what I turned up?"

Treading lightly I responded, "Not at all."

"What's the bottom line here Walter, Hunter—whoever you are?"

For the next few minutes, we sat sipping our beers and not saying a word. I studied his facial expressions and body posture. I assumed he sized me up the same way.

"I've got to go, B.A., thanks for the entertainment."

"Did a judge seal your personal records? Is that why you aren't talking?"

That was a possibility I hadn't considered. Anna had taken care of the legwork on my identity, and the Palatini had "friends" in high places. His guess was correct.

"You tell me, you're the private snoop?"

I stood and pulled out a dollar, placed it on the table for a tip, and sat my empty glass on top the bill.

"He got away with it—"

"What?"

"Owen Moore was released today from prison. The governor made good his promise."

"Why would that concern me?"

"Because Mona's daughter was robbed of justice. Maybe because Moore hasn't paid for his crime. I think that eats at you, and that's what drives you to expose people like him."

"I told you, the story's old news."

"I'm sure of two things, Walter. You are unquestionably interested in Moore, and the story's not old—because it's never been told. My offer's still good. I'll provide you with the questions, tape recorder, and then you interview him. I'll take it from there."

Once the badge goes on it never comes off. Sure, I knew what he was doing, but how could I resist. Icky Moore deserved my consideration. After all, his crime warranted absolute justice. But rather than engaging Ware any further, I turned to leave.

"The story doesn't have an ending, not yet," he declared loud enough to draw the attention of the bar's clientele.

Ware was correct, Icky owed more than he'd paid. However, the Owen Moore project would be less complicated without Ware's assistance. As for the end story, there would be plenty of writers to complete the article when I was done with my part.

As I leaned my left side against the bar, Hope turned on the barstool to face me. With my back to a local she'd been talking with on the stool to her left. I wasn't concerned about my back, especially with my gun hand free. "Did you find out what he wanted?" She asked.

"He's lonely, that's all."

I could watch Ware from where I stood. He finished his beer and walked toward the exit. Hope caught my eyes following his movement and uttered, "Uh-oh. We're in for a threesome tonight."

Frustrated with Ware riding my tail my retort was crisp, "Yes, well, not likely, but I appreciate your spin on the situation."

Ware might follow us when we left the Flames, if for no other reason than to be a thorn in my side. I could try and lose him, but he had the ability to locate my car. An issue I had to address, convenient or not.

Most of the people seated at the tables were in pairs, and only two men straddled barstools. Out of the corner of my eye, a small Asiatic female walked from the hallway to an empty barstool between the two men and seated herself. I didn't get a good look at her, but the size and shape fit the woman from the previous night.

I watched the Asiatic woman as she cozied up to the sweat-drenched, reddish-faced bartender, with a thinning hairline and thinner ponytail. I couldn't help but wonder at the moisture that accumulated on his brow and streaked down his neck, and hoped it hadn't dropped into the head on my beer as he poured it from the tap.

More than once the bartender spoke to the lady calling her by the name, Carmelita. I questioned whether she was the woman described by Henry as Carmen and Mexican.

I'd directed Hope to focus on Carmelita as well. She'd said little about what had transpired. "What do you think she's up too?" I asked.

"She doesn't care about the bartender. That's all a sham. Her sights are set on the man seated closest to her."

Hookers are notorious for chumming johns, and that's what it looked like to me. But Hope was insistent that Carmelita wasn't hooking. However, Hope couldn't rule out she was a pusher.

"You are infatuated with her. I wished you showed me half as much attention as you show her."

"I have my limitations."

Hope cupped her hand and delicately brushed my cheek, "Self-imposed."

"Come on, get your jacket on, and we'll cruise."

Ware's Impala was gone from the Flames parking lot giving me some breathing room. I hurriedly loaded Hope into the passenger's side and fired up the Avenger. Idling the car forward twenty yards I pulled to a stop next to the main drag, tossed it in reverse and swung a semi-circle and put it in park. I didn't have to tell Hope what we're doing, she could read the signs.

Carmelita and the fiftyish-year-old man she had sat next to stood outside the club's main door and shared a cigarette. Ten minutes later she started walking toward the main drag and turned west along Powell Boulevard.

"Where's she's going?" Hope asked.

I didn't interpret her statement as a question, but before I could make an educated guess, Carmelita turned into the Lents Garden Villa. The old two-story motel with the room doors facing east was visible from where we'd parked. Carmelita walked to the bottom end unit, looked about then knocked on the door. Seconds later she entered the motel room. In the parking area was a white camper van. It was starting to add up.

"Did you get what you needed?" Hope asked.

"Maybe...it's just the beginning."

Hope decided she wanted to meet for the third night of exploration. "I haven't spent this many nights with one man in a long time."

More pressing than what to do with Hope was what to do with Ware. I had to resolve the problem and get under his radar, or the project was dead in the water. If Carmelita was the tip of the iceberg, her whereabouts had become known. If nothing spooked her, she was the key to others in her network.

The only viable way to get rid of Ware was to unload the Avenger. A task that proved difficult since we had grown together in an unusual murderous relationship. We had been on many kills, and she played an integral part of my success. She deserved to be treated right.

CHAPTER 8

"Deceits favorite role is playing the victim"

—*Paul E. Galindo*

At Bernard's Garage, it was time to make a deal. "You said you had a friend who was looking for a car, did you get a hold of him? I need to move the Avenger out of my inventory."

"Boss man, he said he can't do it right now. But, I'd like to take the car off your hands for the right price. There's a demolition derby in Tennessee this spring I'd like to run in."

"She's yours under one condition. I'd like to see you doll her up. Put some makeup on her and let me see what she looks like before the derby."

"That's a deal, Boss."

"Bernard, have you seen a roly-poly old guy with a blue Impala hanging around?"

"Can't say that I have. Is he the guy following you?"

"Yeah. Don't trust him if you run into him."

Bernard dropped me at a local mall where I took a cab to within a block of Anna's condo and then hoofed it the rest of the way. Ware would likely continue his use of techno-gizmos to gain the upper hand on my whereabouts. Eventually, he'd locate the Avenger in Bernard's Garage if he hadn't already. When Ware realized my car had found a new home, he'd question Bernard. The less Bernard knew, the better for him and me.

Anna's Lexus wasn't a good fit for the Lents district and if parked in a lot and left would be subject to vandalism or theft. But I needed transportation, and until I found another ride, it had to do. Checking the classified advertisements and Craigslist, a few rigs caught my eye, but none were remarkable. There were plenty of used car lots in the area, but I only purchased with cash and from individuals. The beauty of private car sales was the title. As long as the tags hadn't expired, there wasn't a rush to put the title into my name and thereby extend my anonymity a while longer.

I'd dumped the Glock at a murder scene with hopes of tying Boe to my past infamy. Likewise, the Avenger had to go away. I needed to adopt a lifestyle change that would return my anonymity. With my new persona, I was on the right track. Avoiding predictable patterns required forethought. The simplest change in a few of my habits would aid in my disappearance and drastically shield me from Ware who had become a particular speed bump in my quest.

Investigators are akin to spies, and in a free society like America, we were subject to being tracked by everyone from government Intelligence agencies and local law enforcement to banks, credit card companies, utilities, and corporate businesses. Anna paid for the services of a company that specialized in tracking electronic records from tax returns, and past residences, to professional and business licenses when she researched projects. Ware had access to these same services and more. You can't be a cop over thirty years and not have built a vast network of resources from cop buddies to street level informants.

For the past few years, I'd used cash only. Credit and bank cards made for easy tracking that could be accessed quickly and efficiently. The electronic trail worked like radar. I first realized how important cash was when I saw a true crime story on television where police back-tracked the movement of a killer through his gas card. The ten-percent he saved on his loyalty card for a fill-up sunk his alibi which resulted in his conviction.

Retail establishments employ teams of investigators, called customer service agents, who track purchases on loyalty and discount membership cards. They have years of records on members at their fingertips that not only showed purchases but what locations were used for the transactions.

Then there are the surveillance cameras. Major metro regions have hundreds of traffic monitoring cameras set up. In some areas, you can connect to the live feeds and determine the speed and flow of traffic. They also have the capability of being used to zoom in on license plates and faces. Ergo I needed to sidestep the areas where known cameras are located such as toll booths on bridges and roads. Avoid parking garages, large retail markets, and high crime areas. Most are protected with surveillance monitoring.

Higher qualities Smartphones have GPS, a primary reason I use the cheap throwaway phones on a project. When I no longer need the communication device, the phone is destroyed and tossed into a remote body of water or landfill.

It's impossible to avoid all tracking. But through employing stealthy practices and maintaining that mindset, it can be made difficult for investigators like Ware.

I packed my gear into the Lexus and drove to the gun range. On shooting days early afternoons worked well, and I planned my arrival for after one o'clock. Most of the other shooters arrived later in the day. I avoided the crowds whenever possible. Practice makes perfect, and I needed to work my long rifle. I prefer up close and personal, but, if the unknown arose, I had to be at the top of my game. I might have to clean up something foul at a distance.

After leaving the range, I cruised the strip mall to see if Henry was working the Veteran's stand. I had a question that needed an answer. I used the heavy traffic to obscure my route and took a couple side jaunts rather than a direct route to my destination. If I was tailed to the mall, it had to be the old "cat and mouse" surveillance.

I watched Henry showing big toothy smiles and salutes as vehicles pulled off Powell Boulevard into the shopping market. When I was comfortable with exposing my position, I stepped from the Lexus and walked to where Henry stood. At twenty yards away I watched his countenance take a nose dive. Seeing me didn't excite him the way I hoped it would. Maybe it did.

"How are you today, Mister Hunter?"

"I'm good, Henry, and you?"

"Couldn't be better."

"Sure you could, if I hadn't shown up, you'd still be smiling."

"Don't be like that, Mister Hunter." Henry shook his head. His mouth grimaced.

"I'm not going to beat around the bush. I need you to go with me to help identify the recruiter. Better yet, introduce us."

"Well…see…uh," Henry stammered then inhaled deeply. "Mister Hunter, I don't think I should get mixed up in anything like that."

Maintaining a calm manner, I tried to appeal to his better senses. "Nobody wants to get involved, Henry, but here's the deal. You've been mixed up in it ever since you sold your kidney to them. It was illegal. Maybe you thought out of the kindness of your heart you were helping some other soul regain his or her life from a death sentence. Maybe you did it because you needed the money. I'm not here to judge you. What you did is none of my business. But there is a reason why the practice is illegal worldwide, and Lance was a victim of that criminality."

"I told you all I know. That's all I can do."

It was my turn to shake my head. "Do you think if you had told the cops the names, places, how they operated, it would have been helpful to their case?"

"Maybe, I suppose it might have."

I stared into his eyes until he broke eye contact. I pounced on the opportunity, "We're in luck, brother because there's still time to tell the cops everything."

"Mister, Hunter, I don't mean to be disrespectful, but—"

"Then don't be! Lance's case is not dead, it's in the cold cases which indicate all the police need is a hot lead. Then you'll really be involved. You'll end up as the star witness for the prosecution. You'll be on television and in the newspapers. You'll be famous for a day then forgotten by almost everyone. These butchers you're protecting—they won't forget you. They will probably take exception to you ratting them out. They represent organized crime, and they'll make you a target—"

"Why are you doing this to me?"

"Doing to you? I don't think so. Get in the car, Henry."

Anna's Lexus accelerated quickly and purred toward my destination. At five-fifteen in the evening, I arrived at the Flames

Tavern accompanied by Henry. With a casual head turn, I swept the width of the barroom from the entryway and didn't see the Asiatic woman, Carmelita, in the joint.

The burly lady bartender was serving, and I was buying for the two of us. We wet our whistles with a big gulp of the brew. The night was young, and we had time to shoot the breeze if Henry wanted to, but he remained silent and introspective. Henry's nerves must have gotten the best of him and showed through his veneer in animated expressions. I thought I would have to tie him to his chair. Finally, he erupted with concern. "What if she doesn't show up today? What then? Are you talking to the cops?"

"Then we'll be back tomorrow." Then I beat him to the punchline, "And the day after that, and the day after that, for as long as it takes. All I want from you is an introduction. After that, I don't want to see you around anymore."

He nodded.

When the mission was tied off, I'd be responsible for an after-action report. It was going to take a dash of creative writing when it came to Henry's treatment. Society Palatini would not look favorably on the mistreatment of a victim like Henry. Threatening leverage against the innocent was wrong. The situation could be handled by telling them what they wanted to hear and not with all the gritty details of what makes an operation successful. Why spoil their happiness and cause them to question my commitment to the Palatini standard?

Shift change for the bartenders was at seven, and Henry had grown increasingly nervous. The new bartender was the same reddish-faced bartender from the previous night only this time he wasn't drenched with sweat. Shortly after seven he made a round and checked on patron's drinks. When he came to our table, he called Henry by name. I jumped in, "Henry, introduce me?"

Henry gestured toward me and said, "Phil, this is Mister Hunter."

"I stood and extended my hand. "Hi, Phil."

He responded, "Good to meet you…what can I get for you, gentlemen?"

"Another round from the tap for my friend and me."

At seven-thirty Carmelita arrived. She too made a round and apparently was on a first name basis with a few of the clientele in the tavern. Henry, more nervous than before, turned his head away from Carmelita. She'd already made eye contact. I whispered to Henry, "Too late, she saw you."

I questioned whether she would recall my presence from the previous night, so I pulled the hood off my head.

"Senor Henry," she giggled. "I come back see you, okay baby?"

Carmelita moved toward the bar. I wanted to ensure she couldn't hear the discussion Henry and I were about to have. Henry sat perched on the edge of his chair. He knew what was in store. "You want to tell me about it, Henry?"

His response was word salad; a mixture of gibberish and stammering.

I looked in the direction of Carmelita then back to Henry, "You're a liar. You can't think fast enough to get out of this. She knows you by name. I'll give you one chance to level with me. If you can't do that, I'll take it to the next step." Henry might have thought I was threatening him with the police again, but he would be wrong.

"Next step?"

Motivation, who couldn't use it? I gave Henry one, "I'll beat the truth out of you."

"It's her…she's the contact."

"When she comes back, introduce me just like you would anybody else. You have introduced others, haven't you?"

Henry's head drooped.

"Thought so…after you introduce us, make yourself scarce. When I'm done talking with her, I'll give you a ride back to your stand."

Carmelita had fluttered amongst the locals for fifteen minutes before returning to our table where she promptly hugged Henry and said, "You don't look good, honey, you sick?"

"Miss Carmelita, I've been under a lot of stress lately."

With a glance at me, She smiled and asked, "Who is your friend?"

Henry buzzed through an introduction. I followed up by presenting my hand as a courtesy. Carmelita placed her hand softly on mine and said, "Nice to meet you, senor."

It was the first time I had a chance to get a good look into Carmelita's face. At forty-plus years old she had neither age nor beauty on her side. Her naturally wavy coal black hair hung to her mid back and was brushed neatly but not styled. Without makeup, her face carried the unmistakable pock marks from acne scarring or smallpox along her jawline. Her clothes were the latest K-Mart fashion and covered her petite body a little too snuggly. She fit into the bar scene at the Flames inconspicuously and could just as easily at a factory setting like the old aluminum plant where I'd worked. Only she wasn't cleaning slurry tanks or handling flash in the foundry; she was securing body parts for her peddlers. That's the behavior Hope saw but was unable to identify.

Carmelita's eyes drew my attention. They were lifeless eyes; big, black, empty holes that went nowhere.

"How about a beer?" I asked.

"No, Senor, no drink. I will like to talk with my friends."

Henry stood, "I'm going to talk with Phil at the bar for a minute."

Carmelita put her hand on Henry's forearm and guided him back into the chair. Her facial expressions had given no sign that she recognized me from the previous night. Her lips pulled back into a thin smile as if she was clenching her jaws at the back of her mouth. She drew in a deep breath and exhaled. "Are you a veteran too?"

"Yeah, I tail-ended the 'Nam."

Criminal empires must have loyalty from their followers. That was a given. Carmelita, however, fell into a different category. She was more than a follower; she was a recruiter. I failed to see how her Pidgin English made her the right choice as their representative.

"You go to VA for medical?"

"Nah, I don't need doctors for nothing."

Carmelita had a clipped business-like quality to her voice. "Where are your dog tags?"

"Don't need them for nothing. Uncle Sam gave me a set once, chiseled with my name, service number, and blood type, but they're useless to me for anything."

Henry spoke up, "He might be interested donating."

Carmelita nodded and told Henry, "We will see." She turned her attention back to me, "You live in Portland?"

"I live in the U.S. of A. I live anywhere I damn well, please. Right now, I'm passing through here en route to there."

"Where you stay at here?"

"Around."

When we left, Henry and I were going to hoof it out of there. I couldn't let her see me getting into the Lexus. I'd never pull off being a dejected homeless Vet. I'd have to give her the slip, circle around, and come back for the car. Carmelita's questions were the beginning of two simultaneous assessments. One from a medical perspective where she was getting a general impression of my health and the second was my need to donate. If she thought I was a good candidate, she'd wiggle the bait in front of me and wait for the strike. Until then I couldn't move the operation forward.

"A good looking lady like you must have a lot of admirers?"

She didn't smile or blush. Carmelita was all business and all about the deal.

"What about—"

Carmelita saw my attention divert. She turned in her chair to look. I wasn't sure how to interpret Ware's arrival at the tavern's entrance. It would put the skids on any progress I hoped to make. "Henry, buy Carmelita a drink. I'm going to be busy for a couple minutes."

Ware picked up a cup of coffee from the bartender and tossed a greenback on the bar. When Ware approached our table, he didn't look happy. Eye contact with Carmelita and Henry led to a gruff order, "Beat it."

Prearranged, Henry and Carmelita responded immediately and slipped away without saying a word. Ware sat in a vacated seat and quietly stared into my eyes.

"Coffee and no beer—must mean business," I said. "You didn't drop in just because you saw my Avenger in the lot, did you?"

"Why are you driving Sasins' car? Something wrong with your Dodge?"

"Nothing wrong with my car and it's none of your business."

"I tried to contact Sasins at her listed number. Her phone service said she's taken a hiatus and is unavailable."

"Yes."

"I would like to speak to her."

"I'll pass that on. She'll be delighted to hear you're looking for her."

The problem with Ware was he looked and acted like a cop. His presence would likely burn the bridge I'd built with Carmelita.

I figured he'd used the LoJack on the Avenger to find the condo. It wasn't rocket science; the digital system kept track of location records. When he reviewed the printouts, he likely saw it led to Anna's place. But how did he locate me at the Flames? Maybe a hunch since he'd found me there in the past.

Ware interrupted my thoughts when he asked, "What's your angle with the hookers?" He leaned slightly forward until his jaw rested on a closed fist. "The woman I saw you with the past couple nights and now this one tonight. What's your deal?"

"I don't know how to say this, but women find me irresistibly handsome and fascinating. I don't imagine you've had that problem. But, if that's the reason for the visit—"

Ware interrupted, "Not at all. I wanted you to know your pal, Moore, is restricted to a halfway house."

"He's not my pal, and I told you, I don't care. A halfway house is the same as sitting behind bars."

"He may not be your pal, but you care more than you're letting on. I don't know why, maybe it's the story you didn't get to complete, or you just got scared off when Mona died. Maybe Moore ordered her death from prison, and you had an angle on it, but you didn't finish the story for a reason. You know damn well the story would have made a name for you. Few journalists get lucky enough to have someone they interviewed get killed. You could have spun that story a hundred ways. You chickened out, and I want to know why?"

"You sound delusional. There is no story, and the reason I didn't publish the first article was that, with her death, my angle was over. Listen, you seem like a smart guy. You know as well as I do, Mona was all bad. She aided and abetted Moore as he committed criminal acts on their daughter. Yeah, I wanted the world to know she was guilty. But, more than that, I wanted the world to know the state was guilty. They failed to prosecute her through a flimsy excuse of mental incapacitation."

Ware stared for a minute then nodded as if he understood my passion. "Moore's in violation of his parole. He's in a bar and hanging around a bunch of felons. If you call it in, you'll send him back to a locked facility."

"Why are you keeping such close tabs on Moore? You could rat him out on your own. You don't need me for that."

Ware shrugged and sipped his coffee then finally made his point, "Because I need you to end the story. If they throw him back in prison, you will never finish, and I believe the story is the cornerstone to solving a complex murder."

There was nothing complicated or elaborate about Mona's death. I shot and killed her because she deserved it. I planned to do the same for Icky. Ware wants me to recreate the scenario he thinks got Mona killed. Maybe he'd find the clue to her killer.

"Like I said, Mona is dead and so is the story. It doesn't concern me."

Ware finished his coffee with one long gulp, smiled and said, "Check out the Lucky Strike Saloon sometime. It's a great place to meet people."

Ware's visit had cost me time and opportunity. I'd try again with Carmelita tomorrow evening. Whether I'm baiting for Icky or he's the bait for me, Ware's angle was unclear. He name-dropped the Lucky Strike Saloon for a reason, and I figured I'd find Icky Moore and his criminal buddies hanging out at the joint. But, before I checked it out, I wanted my cover and concealment with me.

Carmelita was busy jacking her jaw with the bartender. I whispered to Henry to start walking, and I'd pick him up. We walked out toward Powell where I doubled back and picked up the Lexus. I grabbed Henry alongside the road where he'd waited and dropped him at a supermarket that was close to his daughter's home. I handed him a Franklin for good measure. Henry looked worried. I questioned, why?

"You should know Carmelita and her man Ramone, both carry pistols in their belts. They might be dangerous if they find out you've got your nose in their business and plan to expose them in the newspapers."

"Thanks for the tip. You've strung me along like you didn't know anything and all along you haven't been quite truthful. I hope I don't find out you're knee deep in this mess."

"No sir, Mister Hunter."

"You're not a victim, and I don't want you to become one now. No one can make decisions for you—but you. Make the right one and stick with it."

"Yes sir, nobody else." With that, he saluted and closed the passenger door.

It was late when I arrived at Lenny's place. Hope was antsy and ready to hit the town. I escorted her to the Lexus.

"Ooh, a beautiful new car. Classy. What happened, a friend die?"

"Get in."

"Where to tonight?"

"Ever hear of the Lucky Strike Saloon?"

"Oh, God…didn't James Bond go to any decent places?"

Rhetorical, I'm sure, but I couldn't resist. "What I'm looking for doesn't hang out in nice places."

With a newly acquired GPS finder, we drove straight to the tavern's doorstep. The place was creepy. Wedged between the shadows of an abandoned, eight-story brick hotel and a no-tell motel on the corner of Powell Boulevard the joint looked eerie. Someone must have greased the skids for the fire marshal, and building inspector or the joint would've been condemned long ago.

The Lexus didn't fit into the neighborhood. The Lucky Strike had a rear parking lot that wasn't well lit. Ideal under normal conditions but I opted to park curbside and under a light pole right in front of the rat trap. Hope didn't fit the environment any better than the Lexus did. For a quasi-hooker, she had too much style for the likes of this seedy, downtrodden bar. Fortunately, my brown leather jacket and hoodie balanced out our deception.

I opened the front door to the place to let Hope enter first, but she said, "You first." All situations cannot be led from behind, so I did the manly thing, I stepped in first. For more than a minute my eyes struggled to grasp the setting of the bar. The joint was as creepy inside as it had been on the outside and reminded me of an illegal after-hours club more than a tavern.

A pudgy, bald bartender busied himself behind the dimly lit counter and apparently hadn't seen Hope and me. Above the counter was a shelf that held dozens of various liquor bottles. A man and woman sat at the bar with their backs toward the front entrance, and another man sat three stools away and carried on a conversation with the bartender.

The dreary atmosphere was supplemented by a dozen dark tables and chairs. Too many for the tavern's relatively small floor area. Two patrons, a man, and woman sat at a table near the entrance snuggled together. They had the look of lovebirds nestled on a tree limb. Seating was widely available in the joint and I took advantage of the emptiness by choosing a table that allowed for my back to rest against a wall. Hope slid her chair close to mine.

Drying his hands on a multi-colored towel, the bartender tossed it on the counter and waddled his way to our table. "What'll it be for you and the little lady, Mac?"

"Couple of beers from the tap?"

"You got it."

The bartender returned with two frosted mugs sporting a two inch head on both beers, a stack of napkins, and a small bowl of roasted peanuts in the shell.

"Where's all the action?" I asked.

"First time here?"

I grinned and put the words in his mouth, "It's this way all the time?"

"Just about always," he said.

Vaguely, I remembered Icky's face from a newspaper clipping. I assumed he hadn't changed much over the past two years of incarceration. If I had a problem identifying Moore, all I had to do was call in a favor from my buddy Ware. He'd gladly point him out. What surprised me the most was Ware wasn't in the joint—yet.

"Who are we waiting for tonight?" Hope asked.

"Just an opportunity, that's all."

"You must be blind then," she quipped.

"Why's that?"

"Opportunity knocks every night, and you're not hearing her." Hope's seductive smile was back.

"What I'm looking for is the scum of the earth."

"What a sad commentary on the life of a man. A girl throws herself into your arms, and all you want is to play games with some guy. Sad. Sad. Sad."

Hope was first to taste her beer. She spat the mouthful back into her mug. With a "Yuk" Hope picked up a napkin and wiped her mouth, inside and out. "That's the nastiest beer I've ever tasted."

In my preoccupation, I'd forgotten Hope wasn't a beer drinker. "Sorry," I said, "Next time I'll order you a glass of wine." Hope slid the mug toward the middle of the table and let it sit.

I snapped open the shell of a peanut and emptied the contents into my mouth followed by a swig from my mug. Vapid beer and stale peanuts weren't a winning combination to attract customers.

"When is your cop friend getting here so I can go sit at another table alone?"

"Funny girl." I was getting used to Hope's sarcasm.

"Did you change cars to throw him off?"

"You're getting too smart for your britches."

"I can take them off—if you like?"

I liked a lot. Tempting as the offer was, I had to decline. I had more pressing business to take care of.

I nursed the rotgut in the mug and bought Hope a glass of wine on the second round. The bartender left Hope's beer sitting on the table. Maybe he thought I was going to knock it down since I'd paid for it but, warmed to room temperature, I couldn't bring myself to touch it. The bartender opened up the jukebox and flipped a switch for free play then programmed a series of country-western hits by David Allen Coe, Merle Haggard, and Hank Williams, Junior. Nothing in the bar looked cowboy-ish, it must have been his personal choice of music. The bartender cranked the music loud but not loud enough to cover the noise three guys made when they entered through an alley entrance. I detected the unmistakable stench of trouble. When premonition alerts you to a foul situation, I've found it valuable to use all your senses for survival.

The men ranged in age from early thirties to early forties and were old enough to behave better than the immaturity they displayed.

It was times like these that having eye candy wasn't a benefit and it didn't take long before their rude behavior got under my skin. They made their way to a table opposite of where Hope and I were seated and continued their loud, boisterous behavior. A couple of them rubbernecked and ogled Hope.

By one in the morning, I was convinced I was spinning my wheels waiting for Moore to show his face. My mind focused on a thought—nocturnal. The body snatchers were night dwellers. Like all nocturnal creatures, they foraged at night. By day, nocturnal creatures crawled into their dens and found respite while hidden from view. Carmelita referred candidates to a man Henry called Ramone, the contractor for recruitment. Intervention at their level would circumvent the organization's human trafficking activity—but not permanently. I had to go deep into their structure and destroy the main players. The van I'd seen at Lents Villa was the vehicle I believed transported Henry to his daughter's house and the key to their nest. From there I'd track them to the recovery trailer Henry spoke of, and continue up the ladder until I took care of business from the top down over their entire operation.

Two more men, rowdy and boorish, entered the bar's alley entrance. Someone from the table across from us called out, "Icky" and a man that had stopped at the bar's counter waved toward the table. I awaited my opportunity to identify my target. Soon the two men joined forces with the three loudmouths at the table. A minute later the barkeep brought two pitchers of beer and a handful of mugs to their table.

A few moments passed when I noted the talking heads had grown quieter and their focus had shifted. The very texture of the air seemed to shift. Uneasiness loomed. In the midst of the pervading gloom and sense of threatening danger my inner beast awakened. My mouth watered in anticipation and with thumb and forefinger, I slowly wiped the secretion from my lips, enjoying every second of the instinctual arousal.

I leaned back in my chair and pushed the back of my head deep into my hoodie as if I were the Grim Reaper himself. Hope sat forward, vulnerable, and exposed like bait. The men's eyes took on the look of pack hunters. Killers.

Had they been able to see my eyes they might have thought twice about their scheming.

CHAPTER 9

"How long do we have to stay here, Hunter?"

Fair question, I thought. The table opposite us had created a nefarious atmosphere and an imminent cause for concern. I presumed it would be particularly so for a beautiful young woman.

"This place gives me the creeps," Hope murmured under her breath.

A reaction experienced by any sane person no doubt. However, it didn't bother me in the least. Sure, Hope felt their eyes undress her. She sensed the violations they committed in their thoughts. Evil burned deep in their wicked desires. Hope represented all the pleasures they knew they couldn't have, not the way they wanted her, and not while I stood in their way.

Their eyes roved over me, not in the same way they looked upon Hope of course, but rather with red embers of hatred. Passively I watched. They couldn't feel Destiny as she stirred deep in my soul, urgent in need for a reckoning. I'd been given fair warning about their intentions. I stood motionless with my right hand dropped close to my side. I stared in their direction. I'd had enough.

Hope had drunk only a portion of her wine but was prepared to leave with her jacket belted, and Gucci cross-body bag pulled onto one shoulder. She had no clue the greater danger lies outside the bar's doors in the darkened lot. We would be followed.

I caught the bartender watching the drama play out until he seemingly grew wise to my intention to leave and do bodily harm to his friends. He intervened.

"Ain't no sense rushing off." His pretentious attempt at customer service dripped like the drool from Pavlov's salivating dog. "The night's still young—how about a beer on us?"

"Depends on who the 'us' is that's buying?"

The pudgy bartender had come from behind the bar and hurriedly made a beeline to our table. Despite his pudginess, he stood all of five-foot-six and looked to be forty-five or close to it. His belly rolled over the front of his beltline, and his blubbery sides jiggled with each step.

He extended his right hand, "I'm Chuck, owner of the Lucky Strike."

I understood business. A man in his position didn't want to lose a paying customer. After all, he hadn't rung the register for the loudmouths, and he'd served each of them drinks. Freeloaders were bad business, but finances were the owner's problem, not mine.

"Hunter," I said and shook his hand.

Chuck reached toward Hope to share his greeting with her, but she avoided his conciliatory gesture. Had Hope looked him in the eye she would have seen his glee as I had from under my hoodie.

"Sure, I'll take a free one."

"Ugh," Hope huffed.

Chuck turned and hurried back behind the bar to fetch my libation. It doesn't take a lot of time to pick up an empty mug and pull the handle on a tap. But Chuck took too long, and my distrust kicked into overdrive. Slipping someone a Mickey Finn was common trickery at nightclubs and bars. I couldn't chance it. To make it look right to my hoodlum audience, I had to play it smart.

Chuck placed a beer on a new coaster directly in front of me, but as I sat back down, I pushed it toward the middle of the table. Chuck continued to stand between me and the felony faction table. That's when I noticed the pasty white pigmentation of his hands. They looked like he'd hidden them inside a set of rubber gloves and the flesh was ready to fall off. The only notable color to his hands was at his thick yellow fingernails.

"You can go," I motioned to Chuck to leave. I didn't like him standing so close to me. He distracted my focus and partially blocked my view of the boisterous ensemble.

I let the beer sit on the table which seemed to be a sore point with the gawkers. One man in the group, tall and lanky, was seated center of the group, stood looking in my direction. Leaning toward Hope I asked, "Do you know lanky over there?"

With a quick glance at their table she shook her head no.

Lanky raised his glass in my direction, proclaiming, "Here's to the two of you." The room grew quiet as he awaited my response. Wasn't that special? His actions solidified my concern. Why would Lanky be interested in me downing my beer? Hope leaned in close and whispered, "I don't have a good feeling about this."

"The hand's been dealt; it has to be played." It wasn't what she wanted to hear. I stood, picked up a mug full of beer and answered, "And to you my friend." I followed by emptying the mug in four or five gulps. The baboons were so excited you would have thought I'd tossed a bunch of bananas on their table rather than setting the empty beer glass back on our table. Chuck rushed over with his tray in hand and picked up Hope's unfinished wine, the mug of beer in the center of the table, and the mug I'd emptied.

As Chuck moved toward the bar, Hope whispered softly, "Very smooth."

"Hang on, the hand's not over."

In their excitement, they failed to see the bigger picture. With all eyes fastened on the prize, they hadn't watched the minute details of our game. Having kept my fingers on the table, I'd slowly pushed Chuck's free beer next to the one Hope had left sitting on the table. None were the wiser, when I slurped the nasty warm beer down, except for Hope.

Nestled snuggly in close to her, as if we were lovers, I spoke softly into her ear, "Look at all the smiles on their faces and ol' Lanky standing there beaming from ear to ear. He's so proud of himself. If we'd left earlier, these poor boys would have felt robbed of the exhilaration we're giving them."

"They do look pleased," she sighed as her lips grazed along my jawline. Then in an abruptly bold move, she pulled my hood back and off my head, tightly gripping it as if she had a handful of long hair. She pressed her lips against my ear and as she slightly nibbled on my earlobe I heard her breathe the words, "This is all a game?"

"A deadly game."

She continued her play, "How so?"

"You don't want to know."

Hope was a natural. She had the game down pat and made a fast read of the cards. All she needed was to know the rules, but I wasn't ready to share the details. It wouldn't be long, and she'd figure out my role too and then she'd possess the keys to the entire game.

After a few moments, Hope sat back as comprehension dawned in her eyes. She casually scanned the barroom and took a long minute before she spoke. "They are the reason we're here, aren't they?"

"Maybe."

"Hey," Lanky bellowed interrupting what I thought was a pivotal moment between Hope and me. "You're not very friendly. The man bought you a beer."

Since Lanky had drawn the audience's attention, I decided only an alpha response would do. I stood, tossed my hood back on top my head, and walked to his table. The room grew quiet. Lanky stood six-foot-four inches or more in his broken-down cowboy boots and was skinny as a rail. I didn't feel threatened. Another guy at the table stood too. These guys may have been friends, but if they were, it was superficial. He moved out of my way while Lanky moved from behind the table. The man identified as Icky Moore stayed seated but kept his eye trained in my direction. Lanky might have thought I was confrontational, but it allowed me to move closer and get a good look at him. He was a cruel, brutal, and violent man that looked the part.

Focusing on Lanky, we went eye to eye. "Never said I was a friendly guy." I said this softly but with sufficient menace that there was no mistaking my meaning. Lanky tried to keep up the hostile stare but, if one were watching closely as I was, the fearful quiver in his hands gave him away.

Message delivered, the tension broke as I laughed out loud, enough for everyone in the bar to hear and extended my hand. "Hunter is the name."

Lanky relaxed and reached forward to shake my hand. I introduced myself to each of the five men. No one had a last name and Icky identified himself only as Owen. There was no mistaking I had eyes on the target.

I turned toward Hope, "You're right."

Lanky smiled and gave Hope a thumb up sign. She smiled back in return. I jawed with the guys for a minute then returned to the table with Hope.

She said, "I was right? They don't know, do they?"

"No, and neither do you."

"I know more than anyone at their table. You are looking for satisfaction, and they fulfill your needs. They don't know that...yet."

I had to give her credit. Her assessment was spot on.

"When we leave, we'll go out the back door. I want you to write down every license plate in the lot. I'll keep an eye out for trouble following us."

Giddy, Hope clung onto my arm. "Finally, 007 action. Tell you the truth Hunter; I was getting bored with the undercover routine."

"Let's get some."

Hope stood and smiled lasciviously as she hooked my arm with hers and said, "Hmm, I can't tell you how long I've waited to hear those words," then snuggled tighter.

I was digging the flirty stuff but I needed to get her attention. Dramatically I pulled her face to face. She melted into my arms. I whispered, "Never stand on my right side." I didn't have to explain further. She instantly understood I wanted my gun hand free. "Go to the bathroom and wait for me." She acknowledged with an extra tight squeeze on my arm.

Lanky stood to his feet, "Hey, why are you leaving so soon—" but was cut short as Chuck grabbed his arm and set him back down in his chair. Chuck played it off with a wry head shake and a laugh. The gawkers tightened their circle and lowered the tone of their conversation as Hope and I approached the bar's counter. Owen Moore, who had continued to sit with his back to our table, didn't express concern for our leaving, which suited me fine. The less he was aware of my interest in him; the easier the kill would be.

No clear-cut alpha leadership had emerged in the little pack of thugs. They were a hodge-podge of criminal elements, convicted or maybe lucky so far, but they had been brought together with nothing in common other than criminality. It was time to create space and disrupt their thought process allowing Hope to carry out her task.

The alley exit was at the end of a hallway that housed two bathrooms and a storage room. I stood by the end of the bar and waited while Hope slipped into the first bathroom. The miscreant's table was out of view of the hallway, but where I'd taken up position, it kept them at bay.

Chuck rubbed the top of his head, "How was everything?"

"I'm glad I found this place. I'll be back." I turned toward the table of lowlifes and said, "Catch you next time."

"Are you driving?" Chuck asked. "You're looking a little woozy."

I laughed. "Only had two beers."

Chuck slumped at the shoulders, his face slackened, and his eyes grew dull. Maybe he was bummed out because he thought his Ruffie was a dud.

"I need to use the head. Entertain my girl when she comes out."

"My pleasure." The idea made him smile.

I walked down the hallway and eased the first bathroom door open. Hope was waiting and ready to go. I put my index finger up to my lips, and she nodded. Quietly we headed for the exit. As I opened the alley door, I momentarily stopped to listen to the hinges. Hope asked, "What are you looking at?"

"Just admiring the old woodwork."

"No, you're not."

"The hinges, honey, don't make any noise. The door opens, and there are no bells or buzzers to alert Chuck that someone entered. He's a sitting duck."

"Is there a reason that's important or should I not ask."

"Don't ask."

The eight-story abandoned brick hotel that overshadowed the Lucky Strike Saloon kept the main drag's streetlamps from shining across the parking lot. The pale illumination of our surroundings came from a single light above the back door of the tavern. I motioned for Hope to start and then took a position next to the door.

Anticipating an interruption, my attention focused on the back door. Time stood still until the moment I heard Hope say, "Let's go." Amazed by how calmly and quickly she'd finished her task; we walked down the dark alleyway to the front of the tavern. Passing the bar's windows, I stopped Hope in her tracks to peer inside. "What do you see?" I asked.

Hope described what she saw, "The bartender looks nervous and has walked to the hallway twice in the last minute. He must be looking for us. One man is still sitting at the table with his back to the other tables; the tall man is talking to the other three men. His eyes are shifty, and he gives me the creeps. The other people are into themselves. It doesn't look like they notice the men acting strangely."

"Spot on."

Once at the car, any threat that haunted us in the back lot and our subsequent walk through the alley had diminished. The potential for action had brought a noticeable adrenaline rush that energized Hope and gave me a bump too. Hormonal effects of the adrenal reaction once the danger passed are not easily controlled. Fresh and vibrant, Hope said, "Whew, my heart is pounding so fast. I want to release it."

Opening the car door for her, I said, "It'll go away in fifteen minutes."

"I don't want it to go away. I want to use it." As she started to step into the car, she turned, moved her body close to mine putting her arms above my shoulders and pulled me into her embrace. The scent of lavender teased my nostrils. The same alluring fragrance she'd worn the night we'd met.

Hope tilted her head, a sign she wanted me to read. Vulnerable to my advance, she broke her one rule. Her lips opened softly and met mine. Electricity flowed. I fought off the urge to take what I wanted. Hope was more than willing to meet me halfway. I never considered myself a strong moral man and I was close to proving it. I was playing with fire and wanted to feel the burn.

Hope had come to Lenny's bar looking for a fast, fun time. Her goal had been another one-night fling with a man of her choosing. She set her sights on me. I told her straight up that I wasn't that guy, but she developed an imaginary journey that made her life more thrilling. So to her, I had become a mysterious secret-agent man. A dream-like fantasy that was suited for her purpose. If she'd known, I was a deadly assassin, she might not have so willingly entered my sinister world of reckoning and retribution. She trusted me to act out a part that she'd imagined. Up until now I had only let her down in one way. She found my persona, and the action we'd encountered, exhilarating and wanted to consummate the excitement of the night with a climactic ending.

Violating her only rule—the kiss, she had embarked on the beginning to an end she desired. Where was it leading?

I kissed her neck and pulled at her jacket loosening it from her shoulders then continued with my lips, breathing life into what had become our fantasy. Hope and I could travel the road together, exploring each curve to the mountaintop and navigate the deep valleys below, but in the end, it would ruin everything. Daydreams play out every day in real time but rarely along the paths sojourners intend. In Hope's world, I had no doubt our journey would end when we reached its finale. She would snap back to reality and once again be on the hunt for a new adventure. Much to my chagrin, and physical frustration, to sustain our relationship, I had to maintain a firm boundary of restraint.

Her eyes probed mine looking for answers why I didn't wade into the warmer water. From her expression I could see she sensed something was wrong and slowly relinquished her hold. Perhaps she was waiting for me to pull her back into my arms and ravish her like I wanted.

A slight nod, acknowledgment, and Hope accepted what was never verbalized. Did she understand that a sexual interlude would destroy our association? The enjoyment we shared came from living on the edge of romance, adventure, and mystery. To continue the relationship, we had to maintain the ambiance that had brought us this far.

Once in the car, I feared she would withdraw and end our caper for good. But I was comforted when she asked what was on the agenda for the following night.

"Do you venture out earlier than nine or ten at night?" I asked.

"Afternoon shopping is fun."

"Can you shoot a gun?"

"Ooh, I'd love to."

"I've got your number. We'll see what the weather is doing, and I'll give you a call if it's a go."

I dropped Hope at Lenny's then cruised by the Flames Tavern to look for the body snatchers white camper van. Henry had said he was transported to and from the surgery recovery trailer in a similar van. Knowing where to look was half the battle, so I started my search at the watering hole. When I didn't see the rig parked at the tavern, I slipped across the street and checked Lent's Garden Villa. No van.

However, on my memo pad, I copied the number of the motel room Carmelita entered.

Lent's Garden Villa wasn't the sleaziest looking motel on Powell Boulevard, but it was close. To get to the Flames, Carmelita was either transported or hoofed it across the street. Once across Powell, she had an option of going east on the boulevard then walk north on the access road to the parking lot and continue across the lot to the Flames entrance, or she could use a path that cut through an overgrown row of rhododendron and a five-foot concrete block retaining wall. She'd been transported the day we'd observed her in the white camper van. I had to set the stage for a meeting. Carmelita was a recruiter according to Henry, but that's all. She didn't head up the organization, and she wasn't the money maker. She was a low-level underling and part of the path I wanted to follow.

No lights on in the motel room and no van in the lot equaled no activity on the recon and time to head to Anna's condo.

Early the next morning, I called Anna with a request. After we had spoken casually for a moment, I asked for help from one of her resources. "I need you to run a few plate numbers, I'm interested in the registered owner's histories and backgrounds."

"I'll get to it as soon as possible, Walter. I have a challenging situation, Thomas dropped off the grid."

"He doesn't get into anything he can't get out of."

Silence followed. Anna cared greatly for Kuhl. He was more than a Palatini, he was her friend.

I tried to be optimistic, "You know how he is. He's a shadow warrior. He's missing because that's the way he operates."

"It's not like him to not communicate before he vanishes. I am the only one he was in contact with during this operation."

"If you looked for him, where would you start?"

Again, I was greeted with silence. Anna's Palatini responsibility was to facilitate the operator's requests. No one expected her to be a knight in shining armor to the operators—except her. The call disconnected. From the tone and tenor of the conversation, I guessed it wasn't a dropped call. She wasn't upset with me, just angry at the situation. It also revealed another side of her.

Before the noon traffic rush, I swung into Bernard's Garage. After a few minutes of shooting the breeze, Bernard pulled out a computer graphic of the paint pattern he planned to apply to the Avenger. Emblazoned across the hood and trunk was the word 'Vigilante' in blood red. Applied over the car's black paint, it made for a sinister appearance. Immediately, I wanted to keep her with the new paint job.

"Why vigilante?"

"Sounds bad! Demolition derbies are built around names like that. Besides, it goes with the model of car, don't you think?"

"Yeah. Killer. Looks good too."

The Avenger had earned her recognition as part of our team, and the new paint validated her worth. After all, she had faithfully discharged her duties, and if she went down creating havoc and ended in a blaze of glory—it was fitting. That's the way I wanted to go.

As we continued our friendly chat, I let him know I was in the market for a new ride. Bernard opened one of the overhead garage doors, pointed at the vehicle in the stall and said, "Right there. I've got a clean title for it."

"What's wrong with it?"

"It's in need of TLC—oil changes and maintenance keep vehicles in top shape."

"What is it?"

"A 2000 Jeep Wrangler Sport."

"Wrangler," I said. "When I was a youngster my dad had a Willys Jeep that was incredibly uncomfortable to ride in and great fun at the same time."

After a lengthy discussion about dollars and cents, we settled on a price. Cash on the barrelhead without a bill of sale, only the title.

Bernard had been wrenching on the vehicle, I asked for a few additional upgrades.

"I'd like run-flat tires installed. Can you do that?"

"Boss, if you're footin' the bill and don't care they're a little pricey, I can get 'em."

"I'd like unbreakable glass for the windows."

"If someone's shooting at you, you probably need bulletproof, and that's both pricey and hard to get. But, if it's your typical radical protester with a brick, you can get by with window armor. It won't make 'em bulletproof, but the shielding can keep people from smashing out your windows. I'll talk to a friend who has a window-tint business. He can get it done. What else?"

"I'd like a sunroof in that hardtop. It needs to open all the way so I can stand up through it."

"Done."

"When will it be ready?"

"Another week, maybe."

"Let's plan on it. I'll get the cash together and give you a call when I'm coming by, okay?"

Bernard extended his hand to seal the deal, and I waved good-bye one last time to the Avenger before climbing into Anna's Lexus.

I called Hope to pick her up and give the shooting range a visit. She was waiting at Lenny's. At three o'clock I picked her up and headed for the range. Thick rain clouds had moved into the area. The only good news was the drizzle brought a warming trend to the Portland area.

"You ever shoot a gun?"

"I shot my dad's shotgun once."

"Did you like it?"

"What I remember was the pain it caused and my father laughing at me."

"Okay, maybe it wasn't a great experience. You can watch and see what you think?"

I turned off the highway onto the frontage road that led to the range. As I approached the northbound turn onto the access road that led to the range, a blue sedan heading southbound pulled to a stop at the access road's stop sign. I braked, made the corner, and continued down to the range.

"Wasn't that your friend?" Hope asked.

"He's not my friend." Anna's Lexus had tinted windows. With some luck, my identity was concealed. Why would Ware be at the range? Only one reason came to mind—me.

Once the targets were up, safety glasses on and earplugs in place I was ready to see what she could do.

"Think you're ready to shoot?"

"A vulnerable girl needs to know how to protect herself," she cooed in a teasing voice. "There's not always going to be a big, strong man like you around to keep me safe."

She had a point. My core belief was all women should arm up and know how to deploy their weapon in time of need. Too many handguns were brandished by people who didn't know how to use them effectively and ended in a worse scenario with their weapon in the bad guy's hands.

"Handling a handgun is like a love affair."

Hope was all ears.

"You want to find the right one, the one you want to spend time with, hold, and become more than comfortable with—become as one with it."

"You know how to sweet talk a girl, don't you?"

Maybe a love affair wasn't the right analogy to use. With her history, and orientation to life and love, a cheap, use once and toss aside was more understandable.

At the base of the canyon, the shooting range sat at the end of a gravel road. With its close proximity to the Portland metro complex, you would think the gun range would be packed with people. As usual, only a handful of shooters were there.

On a shooting bench, I displayed a small arsenal that I'd loaded into the Lexus. Hope felt each of the handguns until she settled on the one that fit nicely into her hand. I thought a wheel gun would be more to her liking, but she had her eye on an automatic. The beautiful old Beretta she had chosen was shapely with curves rather than corners and smooth to the touch. I had picked it up at a Hood River flea market, in the event a situation arose that warranted a throw down. For the price of a couple crisp Franklin's, I'd purchased an insurance package.

"I like this, it's cute."

I sighed. "Weapons are not cute or any of that jargon. It might be sleek or shapely, but not cute."

Hope smiled. Not seductively, but a genuine smile and quipped, "I think it's cute."

"In one ear and out the other," I said hoping she listened better when we went hot with weapons on the range, or I might end up a statistic.

"And wow! It looks like it's been written on with gold." Hope pointed to the caliber and inscription on the barrel.

"Good call, that's gold inlay. A previous owner must have had that added. They don't come that way from the factory."

Hope smiled and nodded. She liked being right about her observations.

After we had operated the slide on the .380-caliber and practiced by inserting an empty magazine, we went hot. I walked Hope to within three yards of the man-sized silhouette target and helped her into a relaxed stance and made sure her ear protection fit properly. Next, I drew my .40-caliber, shot, then asked her to do the same. She held the Beretta at the ready as I had instructed and at my command, fired a pair into the target, center of mass. Rather than continuing to shoot, I assisted her. She finished a couple magazines shooting pairs. We tried a little more distance then changed the drill. In quick succession, she shot two rounds to the body and one to the head. It was obvious she was a natural and the fat grin on her face made me think she was fairly pleased with herself.

Hope became more and more comfortable with the weapon's report, the motion of the slide, and the loading of a fresh magazine. She understood that once engaged in self-defense, she'd stay in the fight until it ended.

I entertained the thought that Hope might be Palatini material, but the weapons training I'd provided wasn't intended to put her on a path to be a killer. It was slightly more than an orientation to self-preservation.

I handed her the Beretta and said, "Why don't you take it home and see how you feel about it in a day or two."

Excitedly, Hope responded, "Thank you. You're so wonderful. How can I repay you? Oh, I know—"

"Save it, honey. We don't have the time."

I wanted to show Hope what practice could do, but I had trouble focusing on my aim and trigger control. Ware's presence at the range didn't sit easy with me.

The night was perfect for hunting predators with the evening darkness aided by a winter cloud cover. Hope and I stopped by Lenny's to wash down the taste of gunpowder. She was excited to tell Lenny about her day at the range. While she yakked, I made a call to Matt Thaman.

"Hey bud, I wanted you to know I'm still working on the scenario. Henry spilled the beans on their operation, but there is more truth to be had."

Matt was silent for a few seconds before he responded, "I want to help. I don't feel right about sitting this out."

"You said they know who you are. I don't see how you can be involved."

"My mom's sister has a son, and we look remarkably alike in photographs. I never thought much about it, but people say we do."

"Your point?"

"I can borrow his driver's license and use it."

"To do what, Matt? What are you thinking?"

"To infiltrate or whatever you call it. Undercover. I'll volunteer to donate a kidney."

"That's a bad idea."

"I've got to try. I won't go through with it. Just up to the point where you get your story."

The slow speed at which he spoke and his tone left me with the impression he wasn't sincere. "You're planning something. You were a cop once. I think you want to take the law into your own hands."

Quietly he said, "Wouldn't you? They took advantage of a disabled man. Weakened by the war, PTSD, and then they took what they wanted and discarded him like an animal carcass."

Hope returned to the table, but before she was seated, she pointed to an empty section of the bar. I shook my head. There was no need for her to go away.

"Don't do anything stupid, Matt. Let's talk about it tomorrow."

Matt agreed, and we disconnected.

"More secret-agent stuff?" Hope asked.

"Yep. Drink up, and we'll ride."

The Flames set sixty yards or more from the boulevard, standing alone, at the end of a large parking area. At one time, a building bordered the entrance to the large crumbling parking pad where an access road passed by and dead-ended at the Flames. Covered by weeds and mounds of dirt were the visible signs of a concrete foundation as it peeked through the vegetation overgrowth.

Surveillance was the key to gathering Intel. By parking, on the west side of the Flames, I could maintain a visual on the van across the street at the Lent's Garden Villa. If Carmelita and her driver went mobile, I could run a tail and intercept her action.

Hope and I parked alongside the Flames and set up watch. It was all fun and games for Hope. She watched the van with the field glasses and talked incessantly about everything she could see from cars to people's movement, having nothing to do with the van or the end unit. I didn't need the binoculars I could see the van hadn't moved.

After an hour, Hope settled down and leaned back in the seat. "Why are we watching that stupid old van?"

"Because it's a link to a mystery I want to solve."

"Really? What kind of mystery?"

"Serious business. I solve puzzles, resolve conflicts, and remove obstacles."

Content that she'd embarked on an exciting and worthwhile project Hope returned to watching the van and calling out the action.

A short time later she slipped into the Flames to use the restroom. When she returned, she said, "That woman you've been watching is in the bar."

"What was she doing?"

"Sitting at a table with a big man."

The Flames door opened, and a silhouette of a woman came into view. Trailing a few seconds behind her was a large-framed man who filled the width of the doorway. Carmelita fired up a smoke, and the two of them meandered out into the darkened parking area. The idea that she had more than one iron in the fire crossed my mind, although, Hope didn't see it in Carmelita's behavior.

The two made their way toward the pathway along the retaining wall, the last vestige of the property's border, and into the rhododendron grove along the outside edge of the wall. With my eyes adjusted to the dark, it was difficult to see Carmelita no more than twenty yards away.

"Stay here and watch the van. I won't be long." With that, I reached into the back seat and pulled out my silencer and slipped it into the Kangaroo pocket of my hoodie. I didn't anticipate using it but there was something in the air that was making me edgy. Once out of Hope's view and after a quick press check of my weapon to ensure it had a round in the pipe, I attached the silencer.

I worked my way down the wall remnant, stopping to listen for sounds, every other step. I came upon a section of wall that had broken down to less than a foot in height and followed the scarcely visible path in the dark as it crossed into the rhododendron thicket. Blending into the shadows of the overgrowth I was invisible to the naked eye.

An ear-piercing shriek ripped through the darkness. I froze in my steps, the hairs standing up on the back of my neck. The sound had come from the direction I was moving and not far from me. The .40-caliber I had carried alongside my right leg instinctively came up to the ready position, and firmly gripped now in both my hands.

There wouldn't have been many people that heard the sound. The clouds hung heavy, moisture and wetness added to the darkness; a spangle of light here and there glistened—otherwise impenetrable.

All senses alert now, I continued forward, slowly, step by step, in the direction of the scream. A male voice could be heard. Harsh. Labored. Rustling noises. Muffled. In the grove, I could see an ill-defined mass. I slipped closer, squatted and listened. Not many feet away from the man, his voice rang out with threatening demands.

Another step closer I could see the fat man that had accompanied Carmelita into the thicket sat perched on top of her, his left hand covered her mouth, his right hand pressed her hair to the ground. Through spells of labored breathing, he told her what he wanted, or she would pay with her life. His loud gasping for air kept him from hearing the movement of a predator from behind.

He removed his left hand from her mouth, leaned back through great effort, continuing to hold a big glob of her hair. "What the…what the hell is this?" Fatso demanded as he shook Carmelita by her hair. "You gonna roll me with this little thing?" Fatso ranted as he held a small pistol he'd taken from her. Unable to hold the gun and his weight up he tossed the gun over his shoulder with no inkling I was so close the weapon nearly struck my foot.

Carmelita had made it to her knees while Fatso struggled with unbuckling his pants but quickly jerked her to the ground, face first. He pinned her under his weight and moved like a slug up her legs. He yanked at her pants and underwear to pull them lower. As clearly as if she had tapped me on my shoulder, Destiny awoke within me and begged me to act. With the thickness of the foliage and the muted moisture-laden air, and only intent on his brutality, the soft pop from my silenced weapon went unnoticed. Once struck, Fatso gasped heavier followed by a nose dive alongside Carmelita, but still pinning her legs. She couldn't see, she was face down in the dirt and had no way of knowing what had happened, only that something wet and warm had splattered on her bare buttocks as Fatso's grip went slack and he collapsed.

Immediately acting on the opportunity, she scrambled to get away as Fatso continued to struggle with his breathing. Finally, she broke free, pulled her pants up and, without a backward glance, ran frantically toward the motel. I stepped closer to watch Fatso squirm, a perplexed look in his eyes as he tried to speak. Left alone his lungs would eventually fill with blood and drown him, but my time was too valuable to waste waiting on him to die, I had other business on my agenda. Double tap was this would-be rapist's reward.

It was doubtful that Carmelita would contact police or anonymously report the incident. She'd gotten out alive, and that would be sufficient. No thanks were necessary, doing good was its own reward. Who was Fatso? Who cared.

My only concern was Carmelita might blow town and set my project back on its heels. Maybe a barfly saw Carmelita and Fatso together in the Flames, and for a couple bucks would spill the beans to investigators—maybe not.

I'd leave Anna out of the loop on this kill. Not that she's all that interested in what I'm doing to save the world, but she doesn't understand vigilante justice from my perspective. Convoluted moral ambiguities exist, and sometimes I've found the need to step over the line for justice sake.

On my return route to the Lexus, I breathed deep and slow to shake off the momentary rush. I reached the car with a renewed sense of calm and satisfaction. I pulled the silencer off and stuck it back in the Kangaroo pocket of my hoodie and strapped my Walther. No sooner had I popped the car door open I heard, "What's happened?"

Without waiting for an answer, Hope continued, "I thought I saw that woman going into the motel room, but I'm not sure. I had the glasses on the van most of the time. What about you?"

"Nothing," I said with a slight shrug.

Hope's expression was saddened by my lackluster report. She laid her head on my shoulder and slipped her left hand on the inside of my thigh. "Now what?" She sighed.

"We watch the van."

Hope responded by moving her hand as if stroking an animal's fur. I'd been on many boring surveillances but this wasn't going to be one of them.

CHAPTER 10

"It is only by choice that our true nature is revealed."

—J.D Netto

We continued our surveillance of the motel room. Carmelita would likely hunker down for the night. It would be the smart move. Once Fatso's carcass was discovered a full-blown investigation would follow. Shaking the neighborhood down for clues was standard procedure for police. Carmelita checking out of the Villa in an unexplained rush during the middle of the night would be a red flag the police were likely to follow up on. Motel employees wouldn't go out of their way to call the police, but when questioned, the desk clerk more than likely would recall the odd event and pass it on to the investigator. There was no best course of action for Carmelita, but to lay low until morning and then if she felt the need, check out and run would be her best plan. However, people who are traumatized and scared behave irrationally. If she ran at this hour, I wanted to be in a position to follow.

Lance had died three years ago at the hands of a criminal organization. There wasn't any reason to consider them anything less than seasoned offenders of the law. But, like all criminals, their weaknesses were learnable.

Carmelita's room door burst open, and she ran out to the passenger side of the camper van. Close on her heels was a man who stopped by the driver's side. By the time I had the field glasses dialed in, the van's headlights had switched on. Seconds later the rig pulled out onto the boulevard.

"Are we going to follow them?" Hope asked.

"Why not?" They hadn't checked out. Where were they rushing off to?

Over the next thirty minutes, we followed the van through Portland, gradually shifting northbound and onto Interstate 5 North. Hope was delighted, bouncing around in the front seat like the energizer bunny. Trying to be helpful, she called out lane changes and turns that the van made.

At the Marquam Bridge, I backed off the tail which sent Hope into a tizzy. "You're losing them!" She cried.

"Maybe, but the traffic traveling northbound is thinning out. We'd be taking a chance of being seen if we ride their bumper."

Hope looked puzzled, "You've followed people before?"

"Part of what I do. You can help by keeping an eye out for police cruisers."

Baffled she responded, "Why? Are we doing something illegal by watching them?

"I want to know who they associate with and how widespread their influence has become? Illegal? Maybe."

We crossed into Washington and continued our journey north. Shortly after we passed Castle Rock, we came to a rest stop at Toutle River. The van took the exit. We continued our tail.

A half dozen eighteen-wheelers were parked on the long stretch of hardtop, and a handful of cars had parked near the bathrooms. The van parked at the south end of the lot where it was least conspicuous, poorly lit, with plenty of trees and shrubbery. It looked like a great place to tuck in for the night without having trucks and headlights harassing them in their sleep.

It had been an hour's drive from Vancouver to the rest stop. The rain had let up, but a dense fog was rolling in, wet and cold.

We pulled the Lexus to a stop alongside the line-haulers. Our target was fewer than twenty-five yards away. With their headlights off the van was barely visible at our distance. A door of the vehicle opened, an overhead light illuminated the interior.

Carmelita and the male driver both made their way along the sidewalk to the truck stop's restrooms about fifteen yards from where we'd parked. The driver was the same balding man that had driven the van from the Flames parking lot the first night we'd visited the bar. From what I could see the thinly built man walked with a slight limp. He waited outside the women's restroom while Carmelita was inside.

"Who are they?" Hope asked.

"Small time actors. Leads…maybe."

"Leads to what?"

I knew that was coming. I would have been surprised if it hadn't. "Traffickers, people who benefit from weak, poor, and disadvantaged people. It's not right, and I aim to stop it."

"I hate people like that."

"I don't."

"What?"

"I don't hate the people; I hate what they do." Without addressing the specifics of my project, I answered her back to back questions. When Carmelita came out of the restroom, she was talking on a cell phone. As they walked away from my position, I dropped my window to eavesdrop and raised my hand gesturing to Hope to stop the chatter. The tone of Carmelita's voice was angry, loud, and her words indistinguishable. She gave the phone to Baldy who appeared to listen more than talk. Twice more they passed the cell between each other before she put it in her pocket and they trekked back to the van.

"What do you make of that, Hunter?"

"My guess is they were getting instructions."

Moments later, the van's headlights came on as it rolled slowly out of the truck stop, accelerated on the ramp, and was up to speed when it pulled onto Interstate 5. We held back. With little traffic on the road, a tight tail was risky.

We kept the van's taillights in sight. To our surprise, the van traveled only as far as the next freeway exit. We followed and crossed the overpass on Rogers Road before we lost our visual. We scoped out Gee Cee's Truck Stop, and Restaurant didn't see any sign of their rig and took a chance by heading south on Barnes Drive. Long straightaways that seemingly led nowhere and no taillights to follow spelled doom for our surveillance. One of the multiple turnoffs leading to rural houses covered by heavy foliage hid the van from discovery, but which one? We had no way of knowing. Following Barnes Drive, we came upon the Old Pacific Highway by the Cowlitz River. "I'm pulling the plug on the observation for the night."

"If we keep searching we'll find them."

"They're close by, or they wouldn't have exited off the interstate, but we won't find them tonight, honey."

It was evident Hope enjoyed playing cat and mouse. Her facial expression turned from excitement to disappointment and her bubbly conversation to silence the moment I told her we were packing it in.

"It's too late to go back to Lenny's, he'll be long gone."

"You did that so I would have to spend the night with you. All you had to do was say you wanted me." Her frown turned into a smile, and the disappointment vanished.

"I was asking how you want to get home."

She cooed the words every man wanted to hear, "You are amazing."

I smiled, "I do my best to keep you happy, honey."

"You are not right in the head, Hunter."

"If I had a dollar for every time I've heard that I'd—"

Cut off in mid-sentence, Hope replied, "You'll have to give me a ride to my house or take me to your place."

Taking Hope to Anna's place was wrong on many levels, and I couldn't guarantee my strength and endurance would hold out against opportunity and desire. I opted to avoid the situation and take her home. Following her directions, I drove to Forest Grove, a sleepy little town that had been swallowed up by Portland's sprawl. I pulled the Lexus to a stop in front of a large, well lit, white Virginia foursquare home, with a classic symmetrical porch and four stone pedestals.

"This is Sammie's? She must make bank on her nine to five."

"She's a Psych nurse and excellent at her job."

"Yeah, has she helped you adjust?"

"What makes you think I need adjusting?"

"Just sayin' you're kind of screwed up with your love life and all?"

Hope shook her head adamantly in disagreement. "She helped me with coping skills and taught me to journal, and—"

"Whoa, girl, you're not making a written record of what we're doing, are you?"

"Don't be silly. Of course I am."

"Uh…"

Her deadpan stare turned into a laugh. "Stop acting like I'm an idiot. No, I'm not writing anything down. I'd probably get in trouble with you if I did."

"Hey, I don't want you to think of what we're doing as illegal."

Hope grinned. She was toying with me, but I didn't know what part she was joking about. Still smiling, she leaned across the seat almost touching nose to nose and stared into my eyes. "Of course we're doing something illegal. I told you I'm not an idiot."

She reached her hand around the back of my neck and pulled me the few inches that separated us. Her eyes closed, her lips opened, our tongues met. One kiss. That was all, and the door closed behind her.

I watched to see if she looked back. Volumes have been written on a person's frame of mind by their behavior when saying good-bye. It wasn't until she opened the front door that she stopped and waved. Hope and I had traveled a long way from a one-night stand.

As odd as it might seem, we had formed a relationship. It wasn't a romantic bonding, but one of camaraderie, nonetheless a relationship I could accept. Hope's actions had never been truly passionate. We both knew it was a mere game she played to break the monotony of her humdrum life. Men to her were easy entertainment, and no bonding could ever occur with that foundation.

Much later, my Palatini phone rang and cut into my sleep. "Yeah." My raspy voice barely choked out the word.

"I have the information you asked for. I will encrypt and send," Anna said.

"Gotcha. I have another request. I need the background on a guy named Benito Reyes? I have a phone number to go with it."

"When do you need it?"

"Yesterday."

Short, sweet and to the point. Not really. Nothing sweet about it—just business. I realize she'd taken on a weighty responsibility, but there should have been the time in the conversation for at least one, "I miss you." I suppose I could have said it first, but it felt awkward. Crawling out of bed, I dusted off my attitude and waited for the email.

I wasn't surprised when three of the license plate numbers Hope had collected came back registered to felons. It was time to set up a war room. I'd stumbled into a hornet's nest of bad guys, and there was only one way to deal with it. Total destruction.

Wiping out a nest of hornets wasn't foreign to me. Growing up on a ranch I was in my early teenage years when I came across a hornet's nest built on a barbed wire fence. Knowing the menace hornets caused to livestock and passersby I assembled a handful of large dirt clods, backed away as far as I could, and chucked the clods at the nest expecting to knock it to the ground. Unsuccessful at hitting the target I drew close enough to strike the nest and put a hole in it which cost me six painful stings. The hornets massed and constructed a new nest. Ultimately, I had failed.

My father took me under his wing and pointed out the futility of scattering hornets. The best course of action was to catch the hornets in their nest and kill every one of them at the same time. One night after dark when coolness had filled the air, my father, using a blowtorch, set fire to the nest. None escaped. Lesson learned.

Chuck's Lucky Strike Saloon was a nest. If I struck Icky, it would be like hitting the nest with a dirt clod. Bad guys would scatter and build new nests. Although burning the nest wasn't the end-all solution, it served its purpose of total annihilation—a concept I would remember. When I destroyed the nest I didn't want to miss anyone who'd earned their fate.

I contacted Hope on her cell phone, "You ready?"

Hope responded enthusiastically, "Finally."

Perhaps the question was too vague, leading, or easily misunderstood. It was Hope after all, and she interrupted what she saw and heard in a uniquely different manner than what was often intended.

"I want to spread some ideas out and get your input."

"I'd love to help you spread out the ideas."

Words carry many meanings, and the sound of her voice caused me to clarify what I wanted from her. "You're sharp and intuitive. I'd like to get your impression on information I'm assembling."

"Like secretarial work?"

"More like Tarot card reading."

"Sounds like fun. Pick me up at my house."

I couldn't bring her to Anna's condo. Even with the purest of intentions, I wouldn't feel right about having her there. Besides, I didn't want to reveal my spider hole to anyone. I drove the Lexus to the storage yard where my '57 Chevy pickup was parked and switched vehicles. The Lexus was a nice ride, but it didn't fit in the rundown neighborhood.

I drove the loop through Lent's business district looking for a place to establish a permanent headquarters for my project. When nothing stuck out, I expanded my search. Lenny's place that I'd used for the past few days had been only temporary from the beginning. I drove west on Southeast Powell until the road intersected with Southeast Foster. I swung left to follow Foster back into Lents when I saw the sign for an extended stay hotel that read, "Collins Best Apartments." A second sign flashed the words, "Rates—nightly, weekly, and monthly." Sounded right. I stopped to check on availability.

I pushed the entry door open that set off a single bell tone at the desk. One camera was visible with its lens focused on the outside door. A second camera was located in the hallway and yet another over the register area. Places like Collins Best handled cash on a regular basis. Credit card transactions were too easy to trace.

An elderly woman sat in a room behind the desk glued to a portable television. Slowly, she responded to the counter where I stood.

"I'm working a construction job in the area and need a place to hang my hat until the project wraps up."

She motioned for me to follow her and we walked the hallway of the first floor. She opened two rooms which were similar with kitchenettes. The first room was an efficiency apartment the second, a two-bedroom. She quoted a weekly price of seventy-nine dollars on the efficiency and one hundred and forty-nine dollars for the two-bedroom. I didn't need the extra room, but the larger apartment was close to the keyed entrance at the end of the building. I handed her the cash she required, filled out the renter's agreement under the name Jon Smyth, and received keys to the apartment and back door. She finished off with a receipt for the month's rent and an equal amount for a security deposit.

From there I stopped by a local general merchandiser for supplies to build a visual layout of the two projects I had in mind. It gave me time to reflect on my goals. Palatini operatives pride themselves in developing confidential informants and assets. I saw potential in Hope, but couldn't identify what role fit her best. Bringing her in closer to the project would result in either furthering her latent talent or being the biggest mistake of my life.

What I wanted Hope to see was in part learned from courtroom proceedings and from studying law enforcement techniques. Used books from criminal justice courses I'd bought in second-hand bookstores dotted my personal library. Found within the pages of these books was the basis of graphic organizing. I'd used forms of visual display long before I donned the Palatini mantel. However, larger scale operations called for improving the method to clearly identify targets in what would otherwise be a jumbled, chaotic mess.

In the case of Lance Thaman, a diagrammatic approach made good sense. There were a lot of unknowns to process. Details were easily muddled or lost without a clear understanding of who's who and at this point of the game I didn't have much to go on. What I did know was the traffickers had an organization comprised of positions from recruiters to surgeons, and I had to piece it together. There was no better way than a visually memorable way.

Hope quietly rode to my new apartment where we entered through the back door on the first floor. Once inside, Hope walked through each chamber giving close examination to the décor. After pushing firmly on the bedroom mattress, she stated, "I'm satisfied."

I figured I knew where she was going with that, "Satisfied."

"You've never lived here."

"It's still my place whether I've stayed here or not."

Hope shrugged.

Using scotch tape and copy paper we went to work. I listed all the available information on the sheet to include positions that I expected to encounter and hung them on the wall in the smaller bedroom. A photo of Lance served as the focal point, with his newspaper clipping, and all known associations fanned out in a circle. Next, I stretched lengths of colored yarn between the actors and positions to show their relationships—with a color-coding key to the far right. The link analysis looked promising.

Laid out neatly on the wall were the fundamental problems I intended to resolve. The short blurb on Benito Reyes indicated Anna hadn't spent much time researching him. Even so, it was helpful with the connection to Lance.

The phone number I'd provided paid dividends because it was connected to his personal account. Reyes background consisted of low-level information, but it was something to work with. Benito was a natural born Filipino shy of forty-five years old. He'd been an Oregon resident for the past decade with no criminal history. He held a Pharmacy Technicians license employed by PI Medikal Klinika. Not much to go on.

I had Hope prepare another diagram with Icky Moore as the central figure, his group of friends stretched with yarn like spokes of a wheel. Hope stopped mid-way to ask, "Who is Icky Moore to you?"

"Never met him."

"Not good enough, Hunter, not if we are going to be partners."

"Partners?"

"You've had me partnering with you from the start—remember? I didn't ask to be used—you asked to use me. So, we're partners."

She had a point. Not about being partners but about who had initiated the working relationship. I decided at that moment to level with her as the need arose. "Icky violated the most sacred of trusts and badly abused his daughter. In my book that is unforgivable."

Hope stood silently studying my eyes. Was she going to press the issue for more information or was she content to leave it alone?

"I don't see how someone can do such a thing. He should be hung!"

I liked her enthusiasm. "It just might happen," I jested.

Again, she studied my eyes then nodded. Icky owed a debt he could not pay in one lifetime. The judicial system had incarcerated him for two short years before the governor decided to ease the burden of the overcrowded correctional facilities and commuted his sentence. When I killed Mona for aiding and abetting Icky in his abuse, I swore then Icky would pay. I was closing in on that promise.

I gave Hope the Intel from Anna. I waited to see what conclusions she drew. Her facial expression changed as she began reading. The more she read, the more her face hardened, and her eyes narrowed.

The eighties model Grand Prix was registered to Cecil James. His legal problems started in 1995 with a plea deal for Lewd and Lascivious behavior netting him zero time in jail, and two years' probation, deemed just payment to society. Subsequently, James violated his probation in 1996. He was caught with child pornography. He had learned the ropes well enough to cop a plea deal in exchange for less than one year in jail. From his history, he hadn't met Icky in prison. His driver's license was recently renewed and photo updated.

Alvin "Sonny" Links was the registered owner of a late nineties model Ford Contour. In 1984, he was convicted of sexual abuse of a minor in the first degree. He netted an eight-year sentence and served all eight years. The circumstances of the case were not clear, but it must have been a horrendously violent type of crime. In '84 they didn't hand out long sentences for sexual abuse. He registered with the State as a Class III sex offender on Oregon's registry. In other words, there was a high probability he would sexually offend again. Sonny lived at the same address as Cecil James. His driver's license picture had been recently updated.

The third car, a 1999 Dodge Caravan, belonged to Teddy Simms. He'd taken a run of the mill plea deal in the mid-eighties for kidnapping and sexual abuse of a minor in the second degree. He was also listed as a Class III sex offender on Oregon's registry. He was paroled after serving five years. His driver's license picture was included. His registered address was the same as Sonny Links and Cecil James.

Hope looked over the diagrammatical design and said, "They are all horrible men—horrible!"

I put Hope on the spot, "Were any of them at the table the night we were at the Lucky Strike?"

"The tall guy you called Lanky was there, and one man looked like the picture of James."

"Good, that's the best I could do too. What else in the Intel was helpful?"

"According to car registrations, all three live in either an apartment building or together at their Canby address."

"What's the best way to resolve where they live?"

She responded quickly, "See it."

"That's right—Reconnaissance."

"Anything else meaningful in the Intel?"

Hope hemmed and hawed. She wasn't looking at what the Intel said. Her sights were on the wrong question, and she stumbled trying to find the answer. To get her back on track I asked, "How about Sonny Link's time served?"

She looked back through the note then it registered. "He served his entire sentence." Hope's puzzled look begged an answer.

"Corrections didn't shave any time off for good behavior. My guess, Sonny Links had acted poorly when in state custody and didn't earn any. That's something to keep in mind when we deal with him."

These were Icky's people. Like any assassination, there were matters that complicated predator extermination. Chuck was the odd man out. I'd run his background and couldn't find a thing. No criminal history and no apparent reason to form friendships with a pack of felons. But, the adage serves the purpose, if it walks like a duck and quacks like a duck, it's probably a duck. I put Chuck's name on the board. Chances were, he wasn't clean. There were also two other men seated at the table that I didn't have leads on. As Palatini went, I was more willing to stomp out parasites than Anna had been. I did have standards. I didn't kill innocent people.

As I looked at the link analysis spread out across the wall, both projects had grown and taken the shape of an octopus. The smart move was to concentrate on one project at a time, but that wasn't my style. Juggling the challenges of a multi-headed hydra only served to spur my determination to succeed. With Icky, I felt pressed to hurry. With his history of trouble, I was concerned he'd get his ticket punched and sent back to jail.

Troubled that Matt Thaman had grown antsy and might initiate an action that he'd be sorry for later I attempted to contact him. The assurance we were moving forward with the quest might pacify his needs to act and keep him from striking out on his own.

Thaman didn't answer.

We left the diagram on the wall and slipped out the back door at Collins Best. The skies lifted long enough to catch the fleeting rays of sunlight. With her hair highlighted, Hope was strikingly beautiful. The darkened bar scene didn't do her justice. Long-legged and slender, she had an incredible smile that brightened up my day. Her stylish off-the-shoulder sweatshirt, skinny jeans, and tennis shoes reminded me of a runway model, balanced and graceful, moving quickly down a catwalk. Sleek. Powerful. Determined.

My hesitation to mention Anna had bothered me initially but vanished in the presence of Hope's eye-twinkling smile. I wasn't married, and Anna's recent attitude change pressed on my thoughts. Hope and I weren't romantic. There were overtones of suggestive and sexualized horseplay on Hope's part, she enjoyed playing the aggressor role to the hilt. The big turn-on for her seemed to be when I told her to stop, no, or don't. All I could do was ignore, avoid, and sidestep to keep out of her provocative grasp.

Before we scouted Icky's residence in Canby, we cruised south on Powell. As we approached Lent's Garden Villa, I directed Hope's attention to the parking area. "Do you see the van?"

"Nothing," Hope said.

"Keep looking, they may have parked nearby."

Hope wasn't aware I'd offed Fatso, but if she had looked across the street toward the Tavern, she would have seen an Evidence Collection Team vehicle parked at the edge of the lot. Police cars and crime scene tape indicated the officers were in full investigative mode.

Canby was the epitome of small-town America. With just under fifteen thousand population it was quaint and quiet. Unsuspecting communities were frequent dumping grounds for trash like Icky. Halfway houses were cheaper and the population less vocal.

Following my GPS heading, we entered town on First Avenue and hooked a right on Cedar Street. The Manor house, a two-story converted motel was clearly government subsidized housing. All three of the cars we'd run the plates on were neatly parked together in a row. Further confirmation we had the right place.

"Are we going to set up a watch?" Hope asked.

"Not tonight…Let's go to the Lucky Strike and see if these guys show again."

We pulled my old Chevy pickup into the lot behind the Lucky Strike and moseyed in through the back door. Hope stepped into the hallway restroom while I continued to the bar. Chuck was behind the counter serving four guys, locals, all seated together at the bar. I eavesdropped on the action and waited for Chuck to break loose from the conversation and take my order. The locals were expressing their concern to Chuck about someone getting mugged in the parking area. I said, "It's Portland." They stopped to look.

"What'll it be, Mac?" Chuck asked.

"Coffee."

He poured a cup and charged me two bucks. One sip told me it was as rotgut as the booze he served.

The guys at the bar who had their eye on me were quickly distracted by Hope as she joined me at the counter. Chuck motioned with his hand and asked, "What can I get for you, honey?"

Hope shook her head. When Chuck turned back to the group of guys Hope whispered, "I wouldn't drink water in this place."

She had a point. If the health department stepped foot in this joint, they'd shut it down in a heartbeat. I figured the hot coffee was okay. Whatever bacteria or bugs that had climbed in had died long ago. We took a table with a view of the counter and out of sight of the back door.

"Why were those men at the bar all looking at you when I came out?"

"I heard someone was rolled out back. I guess they're concerned."

"Wow! They must be scared."

"Their kind—yeah."

"What's their kind?"

"Sheep. But listen, if you want to find out what happened, slip yourself onto that empty stool between those two big guys. They'll tell you everything they know and don't know. It'll all be facts, too." The locals wouldn't be so willing to open up if they thought they were being interrogated, but a good looking girl who showed interest in what they had to say could get an ear full.

Hope had a gift for gab and fit in seamlessly.

For the better part of an hour, I watched Hope interact with the patrons. This bunch wasn't anything like the felons from the first night we'd visited. Hope gave up the gossip session regurgitating the high points of the conversation.

"A man was robbed at gunpoint next door in back of the brick hotel," she said.

"Does anyone at the bar know the guy?"

"Chuck said, although he'd never seen the man before, he'd been drinking in the bar earlier in the evening."

I was intrigued by Hope's response to the incident. She appeared to enjoy the fact-finding and listening. "He didn't have a friend in the place, I'll bet."

"Chuck said none of the other patron's knew him either. Supposedly, they'd learned of it from police."

The felony faction that met nightly at the Lucky Strike might lie low while the heat was on around the joint. To me it meant delay. I suspected Chuck had warned his buddy's that police were investigating the crime so they wouldn't get pinched for being in the wrong place at the wrong time. I also suspected one of the felons fingered the guy to get rolled. It was a gut-reaction, but my sixth sense is never wrong.

"Chuck said he laughed when the cops asked about a camera system in the bar. He doesn't have one. Did you notice that too?"

Hope was referring to my educating her on the lack of alarms on the back door on our first visit. She was wrapping her mind around the whole picture.

"I didn't see any evidence of a system."

Other than Chuck, the bar atmosphere seemed less criminal during the early shift. However, once the night crew showed up, it would change to a den of iniquity. Evil ran deep with the felony faction, and now that I had a lead on the players the game would move forward.

"Hunter, are we going to get involved?"

I could see she was putting the scenario together in her mind. Without saying, she questioned whether the names on the wall were tied to the mugging. But, before I could answer she started to beg, "Please, please, please?"

"I don't know what there is to get involved with—sounds like the dude got smacked around and rolled. It's over, and he's lucky he got out alive."

Hope sat back in her chair and frowned. "I suppose we have to look for that stupid van and the ugly chick again?"

"I had to prod you to come in this sleazy bar, and now I have to drag you out!"

Hope merely grinned.

The old '57 Chevy pickup was okay to run around in, but it was my personal vehicle, and I didn't want it at a crime scene. I called Bernard to check on the status of my Jeep. After we had spoken casually for a minute, Bernard mentioned the Wrangler would be ready for pick up in the morning. I closed the cell phone and turned toward Hope with a proposition, "Can you drive the pickup?" Hope had never mentioned if she drove and to complicate matters, the pickup was a clutch.

"I don't have a license."

"Yeah, but can you drive it?"

"I learned to drive on a stick shift."

"Okay, I need a favor. I bought a new rig and need to pick it up tomorrow. I'll need you to shuttle the pickup back to my apartment."

Hope turned on the seductive smile and slipped her hand onto my leg. I'd grown at ease with her ways. She was a better choice than Bernard to have involved in my business. Her lavender scent was far more pleasing than his grease monkey bouquet.

We slipped out the back door of the Lucky Strike. Hope wanted to find where the heist had taken place behind the hotel. After ten minutes of searching and questioning out loud what might have happened, we climbed into the pickup and swung out onto the main drag.

It was a slow crawl to her home in Forest Grove, but by nine o'clock I'd made it to her driveway. I pulled to a stop and said, "Tomorrow, we need to pick up my new ride."

Hope nodded then smiled. "Do you want to come inside? I'd like you to meet Sammie."

"Tell you the truth, honey; it took me a while to get used to the idea you're bisexual. I don't know if I'm ready to meet your life partner."

"Is that what's keeping you from being my lover?"

"Yeah, that and a dozen other reasons, like you being half my age."

She reached for my forearm and slowly caressed. "Walk me to the front door at least."

The more she asked, the more I found myself doing. I was a sucker for a pretty face and a sparkling smile. I walked with her to the front door. "Thanks," she whispered.

"Listen, I'll say, hi and bye, but that's all."

Hope smiled broadly as she opened the door. A short, heavy-set woman appeared, but stood motionless. "Sammie, I want you to meet Hunter." The stocky, fiftyish-year-old woman ambled in my direction. I reached out to greet her.

"Hope doesn't usually bring her toys home."

"I'm not a toy, Ma'am. The names Hunter."

Our hands still clenched in our greeting, she back peddled. "Samantha. Everyone calls me Sammie."

"Nice to meet you, Sammie. Well, I have to run."

"See you tomorrow, Hunter."

Back in the pickup, I had time to think about the relationship Hope had with Sammie. I didn't doubt Hope loved her, but more as a parent figure than a romantic connection. Maybe that was why Hope sought the temporary company and enjoyment of men. They filled a hole in her heart that wasn't being met. Sammie likewise filled a void in her heart for a mother figure that she'd somehow missed in her earlier life. Then it struck me like a ton of bricks. My head was filled with too much psychobabble. I needed a drink to stabilize my mood.

I buzzed past Lent's Garden Villa and checked out the Flames Tavern parking lots—no sign of the van. Leaving the Flames I hadn't paid attention to the vehicle behind me, but it closed in tight, so I decided to lose it. At the next city block, I made three right-hand turns, and the tail dropped off.

Another mile and I pulled into the back lot of the boarded-up brick hotel that overshadowed the Lucky Strike. Using my headlights, I swung through the lot in a three-hundred-sixty-degree turn lighting up the dark. Satisfied, I was the lone vehicle in the lot I let the Chevy coast to a stop facing in the direction of the tavern. Cyclone fencing had separated the two parking lots in the past, but now it was barely hanging in some areas and missing completely in others. I thought I'd take a short hike and have a drink. In the event a mugger decided I was an opportunistic prey and followed me to my '57, I would make it his last rodeo.

I armed up as always and made my way to the fence line. I stopped short of stepping over a jumbled mess of wire while a car pulled into the Lucky Strike back lot and parked next to the old hotel. There was no mistaking the sedan or the silhouette of the man that got out of the rig. Brandon A. Ware had arrived. It had been a few days since he'd harassed me in public. I thought I'd make it a couple more and stayed my position.

There was no doubt he would remember my Chevy from his visit to my trailer house, and he was likely the tail I'd lost earlier. I climbed back into the pickup, sat back and waited to see how long it took him to leave. I planned to run a loose tail, and if he spotted my '57, I'd buy him a drink. Professional courtesy.

Ware remained in the bar for more than an hour, and the feeling of being robbed of my drink had grown. A few people had come and gone from the back lot since I'd set up on the surveillance. One man had walked from the back door and through the parking area to the edge of the lot with a cell phone held to his ear. I didn't see anything out of the ordinary. The man talking on the phone lit up a smoke, finished it, and lit up again. Watching the man in the lot, who I dubbed, Smokey, distracted me to the point I almost missed Ware as he walked from the bar toward his Impala. Smokey caught my attention as he crouched low and moved quickly in Ware's direction. Another man stepped out the back door of the Lucky Strike and called out to Ware, "Hey can you give me a hand?" I'd lost sight of Smokey after he'd hunkered down by the cars and moved in Ware's direction.

I slipped silently from the cab of my pickup pulling a large guitar case from behind the bench seat. Quickly, I assembled the AR-15 for action with my GemTech Halo Suppressor and new military-grade thermal night vision scope. I leaned over the driver's side front fender and watched.

Ware was standing near the tail of his rig as the man who had called to him moved closer. Soon, Ware was within arm's reach of him. I panned the scope to the right and spotted Smokey hunched down near the front of the car next to the Impala. The man facing Ware pulled a handgun from his waistline and loudly demanded, "Give me your keys and your wallet." The assailant didn't know the man he had at the end of the muzzle was a retired cop who was likely armed and dangerous.

Smokey emerged from the shadows of the old brick hotel approaching Ware slowly from behind. My weapon spoke twice, Shuup . . . Shuup and Smokey collapsed almost into Ware, startling him. The other assailant, confused by what had happened and the chaotic scene that developed, momentarily stared at his partner as if waiting for the guy to get up. Shuup...he took a round dead center. I hated to not pull off another shot, but wisdom told me I should stealthily sneak away.

With two men down, Ware knew they had been shot, but he didn't have a clue where the shooter was hiding. He also knew he wasn't the target or he'd be down too.

Ware looked in my direction as if he had a visual then pulled his cell phone from his coat pocket. I cranked the Chevy up and quietly drove from the hotel parking lot turning left on the side road and hastened down side streets. From the scene of the shooting, it was a two-mile jaunt to Collins Best and the security of my apartment.

With some luck, Ware would be tied up for weeks with the investigation into the killings allowing some freelance time on my part.

CHAPTER 11

"There is nothing as deceptive as an obvious fact."

—*Arthur Conan Doyle*

By ten in the morning, I'd finished two cups of coffee and called Hope. She sounded eager to get started and was already waiting at Lenny's. Ten minutes later I strode through the front door of the tavern.

Lenny smiled and waved. He'd become friendlier over the past few days which I credited to Hope for having his ear and speaking respectfully of me. Hope hopped off the bar seat, reached around the small of my back and pulled me into her embrace. Casually dressed for the day, she wore her farm girl attire like a model. With hair pulled back into a ponytail she took on a tomboyish look. She tightened the firm grip of her hand pulling my body next to hers. I was content to stand in front of the bar with her arm wrapped around my waist if that's what she wanted to do, but she didn't. She'd found something more enjoyable and thrilling than what her past had brought her. Hope picked up a small duffle style athletic bag and said, "Ready."

"For what?"

She lifted the bag, "It's my bug out bag."

I nodded. Hope had picked up the jargon fast. We walked toward my rig and angled off to the driver's side door. Hope stopped by the passenger door and placed her bug out bag into the bed of the pickup. "You're on the wrong side," I said.

Hope, thrilled with the idea of driving, hurried to get behind the steering wheel.

Pointing at the bag, I asked, "What do you have in there."

"Clothes, food bars, bottled water, toothbrush and stuff like that."

I nodded, "Good start."

As I showed her the starting sequence, she was intrigued having never seen a floor starter. "Move the seat forward," I said. "You'll need to comfortably reach the pedals." I explained the gear pattern, and then had her shift through a couple of times to ensure she was clear on how and when to shift and whether to shift up or down. Satisfied, I took my place on the passenger side bench seat.

Her coordination with the clutch and gas was jumpy at first, but she soon had the rhythm down and went up through the gears on Powell Boulevard. I turned my hand-held GPS on and entered Bernard's address. We headed south on Interstate 5 ten miles an hour under the speed limit which contrasted with other traffic traveling over the speed limit. Once off the Interstate and onto the access roads, Hope took the corners a lot slower than I had in the Lexus. She didn't have any problems behind the wheel and made the turn-off over the makeshift bridge safely. As we entered the parking area in front of the garage, one overhead bay door opened, and Bernard made his way to meet us. Hope turned the key off but missed her timing on the clutch causing the vehicle to lurch forward. Bernard held his hands in the air as if he had a weapon pointed at his gut but gave Hope a big grin so she'd know he was joking.

After a quick introduction between Hope and Bernard, he fetched the Wrangler from the bay. The gray, overcast skies didn't bring out the gloss black paint as I'd hoped but mirrored the gloominess of the day's weather.

"Let's kick the tires." Bernard motioned for me to lead the way. After a quick trip around the Jeep, I kicked a rear tire and asked, "Run-flat tires?"

"Yes sir, Boss."

I opened the cab from the passenger door then tried it from the driver's side. No dome light illuminated as I had requested. Next, I tapped the window and asked, "Unbreakable?"

"All the windows have the shielding," Bernard said. "Remember now Boss, it ain't bullet-proof, technically. Like I told you, the glass has a laminate shield added that's effective window armor. It'll give you plenty of defense from someone trying to smash it. Maybe even a small caliber pistol."

Hope stuck close to my side, not saying a word, but taking it all in. Climbing into the cab, I slipped the sunroof open and stood up through the opening. It was tight, but in a pinch, it would work.

"One more thing Boss, I made a modification in the rear compartment." Bernard rolled the rubberized covering aside and unlatched a storage area. "Not real large but you might have the need for the hidden space."

Within a few minutes, our transaction was finished, and Hope was prepared to follow behind the Wrangler to my apartment. I snagged the guitar case containing my AR 15 from behind the pickup's seat and stored it in the Jeep. Next, I moved my bug out and shooting bag into the back seat of the new rig.

"Don't forget my bag," Hope said. "I have my gun in there."

I placed my finger in front of my lips and whispered, Ssssh." When Bernard hadn't noticed what she'd said, I whispered, "We don't have anything to hide, but it's never smart to let your trap flap." I wanted her to always keep in mind that privacy was of the utmost importance.

We made our way back to Collins Best slowly to not draw unwanted attention. Hope parked the pickup near the front entrance of the apartment complex for increased security on my rig. Then climbed into the Jeep and buckled up.

Hope studied the window glass with her eyes and fingers. Something was on her mind. I could wait out the inevitable question or simply ask.

"What's troubling you, sweetheart?"

"Are there more like you?"

"Like what?"

"Secret-agents or whatever you are…an organization?"

"You want the down and dirty version?"

"Try me, I like it that way."

I paused a beat then took a deep breath to begin. "There are consequences to actions. Criminals think they can commit offenses without paying the price. I'm no secret-agent, and you know that. What I am is—a consequence. Just so you understand, it hasn't slipped my mind that there's a price to be paid for what I do, but I've counted the costs, and am willing to pay."

Hope turned toward me. Her body posture indicated she was listening.

I made my sales pitch, "I make a difference in people's lives—good and bad people alike. To some, I'm a Godsend, to others, the Angel of Death. I'm both a lone wolf and a loyal pack animal. I'm equally friend and foe, but my behavior is based on their behavior. I am not a respecter of persons."

"I don't know what all that means, Hunter, but I like you. You have a strange way about you, and I find the quality attractive."

"What quality?"

"Mysterious."

I'd withheld from Hope the whole Palatini story or having been in league with other like-minded operators. It wasn't her business.

Hope had been distracted by our conversation and hadn't paid attention to our travels. As we headed toward the countryside, she asked, "What's on our agenda today?"

"Target practice…I can't think of anything more fun?"

"I can," Hope murmured.

At the end of an hour plinking holes in the target, Hope had proven she had a steady hand and sharp eye. She was nowhere ready to undertake my line of work, but she had laid a good foundation to build on. Removing my AR's scope, I looked over the terrain of the access road in the event Ware had set up an observation on the range. Hope stored the gear in the Wrangler while I kept watch. I needed to know how Ware tracked me.

We pulled out onto the gravel drive that leads to the access road and the hill out of the valley. "You still think you want to do my kind of work?"

"I want to help victims. Maybe rescue young people from the kind of hell I fell into."

"You'd have to know something about the business."

Solemnly she said, "I know the business…from the inside out."

Hope had me on that one. She'd seen things from the other side of the fence I likely wouldn't understand. She didn't seem bitter about her life but realized how easily manipulated a person could be caught unaware.

"No two child molesters, kidnappers, or pimps are alike. File that away because it will help you to know who's who. You don't look at people in poverty more than you do people living in mansions. It doesn't matter if they're young adults, middle-aged, or old; or if they're male or female. Sex offenders run the gamut."

"Fascinating," She said. "But, you're working the sleaziest downtrodden bars in the poorest part of town."

"That's not true. I'm working a target not a section of town. There are poorer sections of town like Albina. But I'm in Lent's because the evidence pointed me in that direction. If Icky Moore happened to be hanging out in a ritzy district, I'd be there too."

"You have a one size fits all solution."

"That's right. If the shoe fits, wear it. People who exploit children or can't resist the urge to abuse them will pay the price. They manipulate parents, and in particular single parents, to gain access to the kids. Sometimes, they will marry someone with children so they can get to them. You'll find perps grooming and luring children into their grasps everywhere from churches to foster parents. I treat them all the same."

"Have you gotten some children out?"

"I haven't done enough."

"What did you do with your handgun?"

"In my bag."

"Keep it there."

At the top of the hill, I pulled into the turnout and behind Ware's sedan. He was getting smarter. Instead of parking in the overlook, he'd parked near the stop sign to the main road.

Ware was standing by the driver side door with binoculars in hand. I stopped and ran the passenger window down.

"Car troubles?" I asked.

"Sightseeing. It's a beautiful day for bird watching."

"Seen any birds that grabbed your attention?"

"Oh man, the longer I watch, the more interesting it becomes." Ware smiled like he held something clenched in his teeth. "Every time I see you, you're in a new vehicle. It is new isn't it?"

"Have a good day."

Ware nodded.

As we rolled onto the hardtop toward Portland, Hope, commented, "That's a weird game you're playing with him."

"It's all cat and mouse. Ware should thank me, but he doesn't understand the bigger picture." What I'd said begged another question and rather than field the "why's" I interjected a question. "Do you remember the name of the clinic we put on the wall?"

Hope thought for a moment then tried to articulate the words, "PI Medikal Klinika."

"Maybe it'll be easier to find than to say."

"Do you have a secret-agent way of finding it?"

"A well-kept secret. However, since we are partners…I'll show you the ropes. Prepare to be amazed."

When I pulled into the Multnomah branch library on Holgate, Hope didn't look amazed at all. I led her to the public computer and typed in my version of spelling the name of the clinic. "Voila!" I pointed to the screen.

"That's it," she said disappointedly.

"Yep. Right there in Lent's."

"No, I mean is that all there is to your secret method?"

"Nothing, my dear, is more deceptive than the obvious."

Hope scribbled down the address, and we were back on the road in minutes. A short drive from Holgate stood the small complex where PI Medikal Klinika was housed amidst a dental office, childcare facility, and a community outreach office. The walk-in clinic clearly catered to low-income. Benito Reyes supposedly worked in the pharmacy.

"This is where you come in, honey. I want you to recon the pharmacy. It's a small place and doubtful if more than a few people work there." I pulled a twenty from my pants pocket and handed it to her. "Buy something and get a good look at the place. A head count would be helpful too."

"Do you want your money spent on anything particular?"

"It's just a ruse. Buy whatever."

Hope smiled, climbed out of the Wrangler, and headed for the main entrance. Minutes passed slowly as I questioned whether it was a smart move to send her scouting without knowing how critical the Intel was I sought. I trusted Hope's ability to correctly describe the pharmacy. Whether she delivered anything of value or not, she needed to see I had unwavering confidence in her talents.

Ten minutes had passed before Hope exited. I sat back in the driver's seat and put on my look of confidence. When she was settled into the passenger seat, I asked for a debrief.

"Small pharmacy with products from humidifiers to crutches stacked along the walls. Two short aisles with over-the-counter medications stacked full. The register counter is short. There may be room for two people side by side behind the one register. Only one man worked behind the counter, but he wasn't the pharmacist. Probably a floor clerk."

"You did well. Did you buy something you needed with the Money I gave you?"

Hope handed me the little bag and said, "No, something for you."

I opened the bag and looked in. "Why do I need condoms?"

"You'll have to figure that out for yourself, Hunter."

Hope leaned close to my ear and whispered, "Benny."

"What?"

Again, she whispered sensually, "Benny?"

"Benny?"

"The nametag on the clerk in the pharmacy is Benny. He's about fifty, five-foot-four, and very polite."

"You think it's our boy?"

She handed me three business cards. Benito "Benny" Reyes was one of the three. "Where did you get these?"

"They have a display next to the register. He won't think twice about it."

"We'll have to set up on him and watch his travels. Chances are he'll lead us in the right direction."

"Do it."

I looked at my watch and read it out loud, "Six-fifty."

Hope responded, "The pharmacy closes at seven."

By driving around the building, I got a good look at the parking in back.

The car park was well lit with large pole mounted vapor lamps. Six cars were lined up side by side, and two vehicles were at the front of the building. The walk-in clinic was available throughout the night, but the other offices in the facility had closed for the evening. I backed the Wrangler into a parking space a short distance from the rear exit and dug out the field glasses handing them to Hope. "Watch for him."

First to exit were two females who made their way to an SUV parked near the door. Our boy, Benny, was next. Hope didn't have to tell me it was him, her body language screamed it. I remembered my father's comment whenever I exhibited such excitement, "You're fit to be tied." That's the way she was, but I refused to mention it. She'd take me up on the offer.

Benito climbed behind the wheel of a silver colored PT Cruiser, kicked the engine over, and waited a couple minutes before pulling out on the road. Hope and I were close behind.

The city's rush hour traffic thinned as we made our way north from Lent's. Once we'd crossed the Marquam Bridge I pulled into the right lane and picked up the speed passing Benny's PT. "You're going to lose him," Hope said.

"I've got a hunch."

"What if you're wrong?"

"This is recon, honey. I count on there being a tomorrow."

Exiting Interstate 5 at Rogers Road, I swung across the freeway and into Gee Cee's Truck Stop and Restaurant. With the Wrangler pointed in the direction of the three-way intersection, we waited.

Benny's Cruiser wasn't far behind and hooked a left at the intersection. We gave him a little distance, but not like we had Carmelita's van. We traveled about a mile and through a long sweeping bend and then into a straightaway. Benny's brakes came on, and he crossed Barnes Drive to the left onto a dirt topped road.

Looking at Hope, I said, "I need to get a closer look, and I need to do it alone."

Her face showed she was unhappy about being left in the Jeep, but she wasn't ready for the undertaking. After a quick U-turn on the blacktop, I cut the lights and pulled the Jeep to a stop on the shoulder of the road.

"Get behind the wheel. There's not a lot of traffic out here, but if someone stops to help, tell them you're okay. And if it's a guy, give him one of your come-hither smiles, bat those baby blues, and let him glimpse a little cleavage, but not too much. Then follow-up with whatever song and dance you think he's buying."

Quoting me, she said, "Not too much? You sound jealous."

"Maybe I am."

She gave me a little performance of what I'd suggested, "Is this what you had in mind?"

I smiled, "Don't overdo it."

"You are jealous!"

I winked as I pulled on gloves, flipped my hood up, and repositioned the .40-caliber on my hip. I removed three GPS trackers with magnetic frames and put them into my jacket. If I encountered vehicles, I could place a tracker on them and monitor their movements from my laptop.

Stepping from the Jeep, I held the door open for Hope to climb in behind the wheel.

My trek through the wet roadside overgrowth of tall grasses and weeds lasted for ten yards where I stopped and pulled my Walther from its holster to attach the silencer. Killings weren't on the agenda but better safe than sorry. If I had to shoot a silencer was the best option.

Twenty yards further through the nearly impenetrable interlocking brush brought me into a clearing and what appeared to be structures illuminated by incandescent interior lighting. Crossing the long neglected field out in the open for one-hundred yards or more wasn't my idea of sneaking up on the place. I held to the brush line and worked my way around closer to the buildings. The winter had taken its toll on the field's foliage which made for easier walking. Moist ground aided my stealthy approach leaving each step quietly behind me.

The first structure was a 1950s-style cracker box house with a single porch light. I listened and looked; a dog was my chief concern. Hearing nothing, I moved behind the house where Benito's PT Cruiser was parked in the driveway. I bent down beside the rig and placed a GPS unit inside the rear wheel well.

Creeping across to the next building my eyes had become oriented to the shadowy darkness. Visible was the shallow lighting of three structures. With my hand against a barn-like building, I felt the post and beam construction.

To the right of the barn set a travel trailer with the light on inside. The dim glow shining through the window barely illuminated the ground. I listened with my ear against the metal skin of the trailer. The only discernible noise was a television in the forward portion of the living quarters. I stepped off the distance and estimated the length of the trailer.

A beater of an old Ford pickup set next to the trailer. I slipped a tracker deep down inside a middle stake pocket on the truck bed.

From there, I made my way to the last illuminated structure. Oddly, the house, barn, and travel trailer each had doors opening northwesterly. The mobile home entry sat in the opposite direction toward the southeast. I estimated the mobile home to be fifty feet in length with two access doors, both located on the same side. A makeshift three-step landing constructed of two-by-fours and plywood was at the front end with a single light over the door. The back door was without steps or lighting. It was a three-foot drop straight to the ground. Bending down I felt the deep ruts made from tires pulling up to and away from the mobile home. The winter months had brought a steady stream of moisture to the area and made it impossible to determine how frequently the rear door was used.

Backtracking to the barn, I entered a man door into total darkness. Carefully, I put a thumb over the lens of an incandescent Mini-Maglite I'd removed from my coat pocket and twisted the head of the flashlight to switch it on. By slipping my thumb ever-so-slightly to one side, I was able to limit the amount of light escaping the lens. Having been raised on a ranch around hay sheds, outbuildings, and barns nothing looked unusual except for the red and white ambulance parked in front of the sliding barn door. No city, county, or service markings identified the vehicle's origin only the six-pointed Star of Life was painted on the double back door. A flashing red light on the dash indicated the ambulance had an alarm system and it was armed. There was no way to look inside. If I tried to enter the sirens and flashing lights would sound an alert and compromise the project. It wasn't worth taking the chance. I softly attached the last GPS tracker underneath the metal rear bumper. Satisfied this was the place Henry had spoken of, and that Benny was a major player—my reconnaissance was sufficient.

It took only a few minutes to cross the field and reach the road. To avoid surprising and most likely scaring Hope out of her wits, I tapped on the rear fender of the Jeep as I approached the driver's side. She threw open the door and launched herself into my arms. "I was so scared for you. I thought something had happened."

"Something did happen."

Hope clung tightly with her arms around my neck. Her heart pounded against my chest as she whispered, "It's the right place, isn't it?"

I patted her on the back, "The yarn that stretched to nowhere now has a location."

Hope nodded her understanding.

"Let's go back to my apartment, put the details on paper, and get it on the wall."

For a long minute, Hope held me in her embrace. The scent of lavender pervaded the surrounding space and encompassed us as one. To say my mind was flashing delightful and exciting scenes in front of my eyes would be an understatement.

I pointed the Jeep toward Interstate 5 and wasn't surprised at all when Hope's left hand slipped across my leg and rested on the inside of my thigh. No stroking, no squeezing, no seductive behaviors. It was a milestone in our relationship. Care and concern for camaraderie had trumped the light-hearted mischievous teasing I'd become accustomed to.

At Collins Best, I brought the AR inside while Hope copied my actions bringing in the bag containing her handgun. She needed to find a way to conceal the weapon on her person, but I was without a suggestion to help her.

We dropped the gear in the living room and filled in the wall diagram from the Intel I'd collected then laid out our next step. We needed to locate the camper van and run a tail. We hadn't seen it since the night I offed Fatso, and I'd intentionally avoided the Flames Tavern where Carmelita worked the clientele.

Hope sat quietly on the bed in front of the wall studying the diagram while I placed a call to Thaman. I surmised with the lateness of the hour he'd likely be home and available. After the tenth ring, I disconnected.

"No answer?" Hope asked.

I could feel the consternation in my face, "He's up to something."

"I thought he was the reason you're involved?"

"Matt's the cornerstone of the operation." What I didn't say was the importance of keeping him on a short leash. Thaman had expressed an idea that would've put him in the center of the action. It was a bad idea, and without contact, I couldn't be assured he'd given my advice serious consideration. If he engaged the body snatchers without my knowledge, he could threaten the safety and security of everyone involved in the project. It went without saying, his life would be in jeopardy and so would mine—I had no doubt the people running the Red Market had ways to extract data from victims.

"You don't have to tell me, but what does your friend Ware have to do with all of this?"

Another sore point. "Nothing. His issue is with a guy from his past." Remarkably, Ware hadn't barraged into any watering holes recently. He was still on my tail and more dangerous now that the Thaman project had become active.

"What now?"

"Let's meet at Lenny's when the doors open."

She nodded and leaned back on the bed for a moment without saying a word then left the diagram bedroom. It wasn't like Hope not to be perky about our next day plans. I questioned whether her excitement was wearing thin from the lack of action. Maybe the trip to Washington had taken an unexpected toll on her enthusiasm.

The bathroom door latched which gave me time to look at Icky Moore's diagram. I hadn't placed as much emphasis on Moore as I had on the body snatchers, but when I wrapped up the Thaman project, I would assassinate Moore and fulfill my promise to his victim, the little girl that I'd never met, seen, and whose name I could not recall. With my focus on Moore, I didn't hear the bathroom door open, but Hope stood in the bedroom doorway dressed only in one of my favorite tee shirts. It was my turn to not say a word.

"I thought it would be easier if I spent the night?" Hope moved closer. Her eyes focused on mine.

"You are a lovely young lady, half my age—"

Hope's finger touched my lips silencing my words. "You're not twice my age."

I considered myself a strong-willed man. I'd over-estimated my resolve. It seemed I was closer to average than I wanted to be with all the weaknesses of the typical guy.

"One night stands are not—"

Hope silenced me as she leaned forward, her lips touched softly against mine. Flooding my thoughts was her heretofore rule for flings, no kissing on the lips. Her actions telegraphed a new and different rule for me. One I was inclined to follow. Drawn into the void, I kissed her back.

CHAPTER 12

"Never believe that a few caring people can't change the world.
For, indeed, that's all who ever have."

—*Margaret Mead*

In the morning we lingered lazily, finally rising Hope showered while I cranked out a pot of coffee. With fresh java in hand, I leaned back on the apartment's ratty sofa. My eyes closed as I rested. Usually, I woke refreshed, but I hadn't gotten much sleep during the night.

At first, I thought the slight tremor under my feet was a small magnitude earthquake, but a shaker nonetheless. Then a strange spinning sensation came over me that launched my consciousness into a simultaneous existence—I'd experienced it before. Hovering in the air, I could see me as I sat, leaned back with my eyes closed. Cognizant that I was undergoing an out-of-body experience I drifted further from the couch continuing to look down at my body. Destiny's voice rang out with power and authority, shattering the peaceful mood I had sought.

"Let not your heart be troubled, Warrior. You do not stand alone."

Being alone hadn't crossed my mind. Hope had been more than accommodating, keeping me company all night. Connecting through our thoughts rather than our voices Destiny and I had found a universal language. "I know I can count on you to be with me. There are so many who need to be killed that the goal seems unrealistic and unachievable."

"With leadership, the people will rise up."

"Meanwhile, the numbers of the depraved, driven by greed and lust, quadruple."

"You are not alone."

"Thought we covered that. The people are indifferent."

"Not so Warrior. Some wait for the sounding of a trumpet announcing that their salvation draws nigh, while others, dedicated to bringing salvation, make implements of warfare and stand forward to do battle. He who has Called you has likewise provided for your every need. Rise up, Warrior, and lead; His Will be done."

"Someday we'll have a talk about "who" Called and what this "will" thing is all about. I accept the supernatural because I can't explain you any other way, but I've never believed in the Divine."

"Your feelings are yours alone to bear. Master them and find the understanding you seek."

The natural light that had streamed through the windows dimmed. Against one apartment wall flashed an image like that of a vintage sixteen-millimeter movie projector showing a black-and-white film. Without sound, hundreds of faces, some infants, others elderly, both men and women, smiled as if posing for the camera. Unknown or unrecognized, inquisitively, I asked, "Who are they?"

"These are the faces of would-be victims spared through your intervention."

"There are so many."

I wondered how each one was connected and through whom. Then came the second series of faces against the wall all of which I recognized, brutal incestuous rapists, child pornographers, and human traffickers. A rush of pride came over me as I viewed the face of Toronto Mobster, Giuseppe Pelosi aka The Pimp. Rich but morally bankrupt he looked so happy for the photo op hidden in time. But like the light that had dimmed so did Pelosi's smile fading into a shadowy Buffalo, New

York alley, and his lifeless body, face down, oozing blood. I'm not a sentimental guy, usually, but Pelosi would forever hold a special place in my heart and gun sights.

There were more, all dead. I recalled each one as their faces appeared.

"Evil evolves, Warrior. The fate of many hangs by your actions. Be violent, ruthless, and without rest. Awaken the beast within and let him feast on the blood of the wicked."

My eyes opened as if from a hypnotic trance, my coffee still hot. Air in the water lines squealed and drew my attention toward the bathroom as the sound of water ceased. I presumed that only a few minutes, perhaps only seconds or no time at all had passed during my vision.

Hope wrapped herself in a skimpy bath towel that barely covered top and bottom at the same time. Her hair hung tangled and wet.

"Want a cup?" I asked.

"Of course!"

I pointed toward the cups and said, "Knock yourself out."

With Anna, I'd felt the pressure to try to please her with every movement. With Hope, I could relax and be me. Only, neither was me. Living life alongside other people was an uncomfortable necessity.

Hope sat sipping her coffee as the towel slid slowly to her lap—no doubt for my benefit.

I found it a pleasure to view perfection. She knew it and was eager to please.

After a moment, she asked for the day's agenda.

"Put an eye on Benny, find the white van, and research who owns PI Medikal Klinika. Get dressed and we'll get after it."

Hope stood with coffee cup in hand allowing the towel to drop to the floor. "Oops," she cooed. With a smile, she bent down, picked up her towel and turned toward the bathroom.

"Or we could give it another hour or so."

With a wicked grin she tossed the towel on the chair, sat her coffee cup on the table, and came to me slowly, teasing— she was comfortable in her nakedness.

It was afternoon by the time Hope and I were cruising the district. The van couldn't hide forever. I swung through the Garden Villa. No sign of the van or any activity at room 109 where Carmelita frequented.

Across the boulevard at the Flames, police barricades had been removed, and the Evidence Collection Team had vacated the crime scene. We stopped in for a drink and to see if Carmelita was working the joint.

When we entered, I spotted Henry, foolishly with his back to the door and drinking alone. "Henry," I called out. He turned in our direction and sported a big smile from ear to ear. It didn't last when he got a look at who had called his name. With a half-hearted wave of his hand, Henry turned back toward his drink and chugged a nearly full beer. I took it as a sign he planned to leave. "Hold up, Brother."

His eyes dropped to the table in front of him, and his head hung low. Hope and I made our way to the table. "Who is he?" Hope whispered.

"A puzzle piece."

After a quick introduction, we took our places on either side of Henry. I ordered a round of drinks.

"Everything going well, Henry?"

"Oh, yes sir. Everything is just fine."

"Seen Carmelita?"

Henry wouldn't make eye contact. Seconds had passed before he answered. "Can't say that I have."

"How about Matt, has he been around?"

The bartender had arrived with our drinks before Henry answered. With the drinks distributed and paid for, Henry still hadn't answered. I pulled out my phone and dialed Matt's number. The phone rang; I tapped the speaker button and waited. On the fifth ring, the answering machine picked up. "This is Matt. You know how these things work so leave a message and I'll get back to you." I disconnected the call.

"So, have you seen Matt?"

Fidgeting with the napkin under his drink he shook his head. Hope sat back and murmured, "Shhhh" at Henry's answer. "He's lying," she said under her breath.

"No sir, I don't know where Mister Matt is."

"That's not what I asked. Have you seen Matt? You better be straight up with me."

Henry didn't answer. He was either too afraid to tell the truth or too scared to lie. Not answering was an answer and less than cooperative in my book. "You're a Veteran," I said pointedly. "Let that sink in, Henry, because it's the only reason I'm giving you leeway to answer." I leaned forward to make eye contact. I whispered, "Otherwise, I'd take you for a ride and put you out of your misery."

"Okay, okay, I ain't lookin' for no trouble. Matt come by yesterday to see me. He asked a bunch of questions just like you always do."

"What happened when he ran out of questions? Did you tell him something he could act on?"

"No sir, Mister Hunter. We talked until Carmelita came into the bar. They moved to another table and talked for a spell."

"They leave together?"

"No, but Ramone come in too."

"Ramone's the driver?"

Henry hem-hawed and guarded against saying too much, "He's the deal maker."

"Let's take a walk outside."

"I told you Mister Hunter, I don't want no problems. Can you understand that?"

"I'll tell you what I understand. You have no honor or integrity. And for that, you will have to answer."

Henry's head drooped. "You don't know what it's like."

"How much did you get?"

"For what?"

"For hooking Matt up with Carmelita."

Henry shook his head vehemently denying my accusation. I clarified my position, "If I find out something has happened to Matt we're going to have one last talk." I tempered my voice for emphasis on my promise. It wasn't to be understood as an idle threat.

"He came to me," Henry admitted, "Why is that my fault?"

"If you had honor you wouldn't have to ask." I looked over at Hope who sat back with arms folded tightly across her breasts. "Drink up, Honey, we have business to take care of."

We weaved through traffic until we reached the small Filipino clinic where Pharmacy Tech, Benito Reyes worked. Benny's car was parked in the same spot as before. I pulled to a stop in front of an adjacent building. Hope excitedly pointed, "There it is! The van."

I'd been so focused on Benny's vehicle and where to park for surveillance that I hadn't scanned the entire lot. Hope's observation was spot on. Wedged alongside a metal fabricated building that sat at the rear of the complex was a white van. The structure, a utility or maintenance shop, matched the office complex's color scheme. Its single rolling overhead door stood open. The way the van was parked gave me the impression it was intentionally hidden from view.

Hope and I hunkered down and waited for Benny or the van to move. Less than an hour had passed when Carmelita exited the clinic's back door. Sashaying toward the parked van, her eyes systematically scanned for hidden danger around her.

Surprisingly, Carmelita climbed behind the steering wheel and started the engine. My theory that she needed a driver to get around went out the window. First impressions and supposition can easily fool a person and lead to errors in judgment.

The greyish-blue exhaust dissipated into the frigid air as Carmelita edged the vehicle forward. When she pulled out of the lot, I was within eyeshot behind her.

"Have you thought about how I should resolve the red meat marketers?"

Continuing to watch the van, Hope uttered, "We."

"We?"

Hope smiled, "We."

We followed for only a few blocks from the clinic when Carmelita pulled onto an access road and next to a small, dumpy tavern, called Sid's. I thought she'd caught on to our presence and tried to ditch us, but my fears soon abated.

Neither Hope nor I had been in the joint, but judging by the rundown exterior, it wasn't the kind of joint she wanted to set foot into. Carmelita braked to a stop twenty yards from the entrance and shut off the van's engine. I drove past her rig and parked on a side street that ran behind the tavern.

"We can't see very well from here," Hope said. She was right. The problem wasn't that we'd staged the Wrangler too far away from the camper van. Field glasses easily overcame the distance between vehicles. It was the angle of our view. Carmelita blocked our line of sight to the tavern's front door with the van. Moving the Wrangler wasn't a good option. Doing so would ultimately expose my vehicle. Carmelita's watchfulness in the clinic's parking lot told me she kept a good eye out for potential danger which signified a change in her demeanor. Maybe it was Fatso's attack and his subsequent demise that changed her behavior. My vehicle was within eyeshot at the clinic, at times during the tail, and driving past her rig in the parking lot. I'd have to hoof it to get another angle on the front door.

"You haven't answered what you think I should do to dismantle this slaughterhouse."

"Cops are out of the question, I'm sure of that. I guess we do what comes natural."

"Define natural. Your version and mine may not be the same."

"We do whatever it takes when the time comes. I imagine that's why we have guns, isn't it?"

"Smart girl." I didn't feel like I was out on a limb with her.

"Lady," she said playfully.

I played along, ready to advance on the van as I agreed, "Lady indeed," then added, "May I take a temporary leave of thee, M' Lady?" Hope reached and took my hand in hers. "What a rush," she said. "I've never felt anything so rousing."

"It's only a shot of adrenaline. Just roll with it. It'll settle down in a few minutes."

"It's more than being wired and so much deeper."

"Feed it then—whatever it wants."

"It? Feed it what?"

"When you get hungry enough you'll know what it wants."

Connecting with Hope on a different level caused me to ponder how two people from such diverse walks of life could be drawn to each other like Bonnie and Clyde. Outlaws, who, together, committed horrendous acts of violence and killed without remorse. What kind of insanity comes over two people that cause them to act in unison? Somewhere in the recesses of the human psyche, an element of barbarism exists that is common to all generations of mankind. It is in our nature. I for one, stand firm in my convictions and unapologetic for the active roll I play in vigilante killings. My targets are the vilest of creatures and deserved killing. For those that cannot defend themselves from the evil, I welcomed more fighters, like Hope, into the gladiatorial arena of death.

With one foot on the ground, I froze in place as the camper van driver's door swung open.

"Hand me the binoculars."

Reluctantly, she passed the field glasses to me. An older model station wagon entered the parking lot and braked to a stop near the van. Ramone popped out of the old car's driver's side like a Jack-in-the-box. The passenger side door opened and one leg came out, but no one emerged. Was it another player to add to my wall?

Carmelita and Ramone moved away from the wagon and to the far side of the camper out of view of Ramone's passenger. While I watched the two known targets, the passenger stepped from the car and moved in the direction of the camper interrupting what appeared to be a lively disagreement between the two traffickers.

Wearing an olive drab Boonie hat pulled down tightly onto his eyebrows, the male passenger stopped short of joining the conversation.

"Does he look familiar to you? I asked.

"Who?"

"The guy with the hat and aviator sunglasses."

"Without the field glasses, I can't get a good look."

The new addition, decked out in an M65 military style jacket, fashionably matched his olive drab backpack that he had slung over his left shoulder. Most vets are proud of their time served and continue their association with their military past, others, handicapped by post-traumatic stress can never move past it.

"He's another victim."

The rider climbed into the camper van through the side door that closed behind him.

Carmelita pointed her finger at Ramone's face and shook it.

"They're fighting about something," I said to draw Hope's attention to the action. She didn't appear engaged.

"Maybe she's upset with the man because he took her binoculars away?"

"What?"

"I don't have any either, but I know I would be mad if I had a pair and someone took them away."

"Priorities honey."

"I am only saying that men...some men...fly off the handle if they are challenged for dominance."

I handed Hope the field glasses, "Here...you're not going to shut up until you get them back."

Hope jerked forward, "Oh, oh no! He just slapped her."

178

I'd been distracted by Hope, but saw the argument abruptly end when Ramone threw his hands in the air and stomped away toward the old wagon like a pouting child.

Carmelita jumped into the van with her passenger on board and pulled out of the parking lot. A combination of deteriorating weather conditions and the onset of sundown ushered in an early nightfall. We shortened our leash on the van.

For fifteen minutes we drove stop sign to streetlight without leaving the district. Hope had picked up on it too, "We're driving in circles."

"Yeah, either Carmelita is buying time or making sure she doesn't have a tail."

"Maybe she's trying to confuse her passenger as to where he's been, how far he's traveled or where he's at."

"Good call."

After an hour's drive in scenic downtown Lent's, we arrived back at the clinic. She had avoided the main drag to get there relying on side roads until she turned into the lot. The passenger, likely another homeless vet or pretending to be, was probably unfamiliar with the town and easily disoriented. Hope was likely right, why else the long way to the clinic?

"The clinic is open all night for walk-ins," Hope said. "The only thing that has changed from an hour ago is it's darker now, and the passenger might think he's traveled a long way to get here."

Her thoughts were trending in the right direction. The more she related her observations, the more comfortable I became with her involvement. I gave her something else to consider. "Maybe Carmelita was waiting for the other offices in the building to close for the night. Makes for fewer possible witnesses."

"Certainly would make sense."

Carmelita nosed her rig into a parking space next to Benny's car and parked. The van's sliding side door was hidden from our view. The van headlights went dark. Hope dialed in binoculars while I pulled out my night scope.

Carmelita was already standing at the front of the rig when I put my scope on her. Promptly, the man in the Boonie hat walked from the passenger side to Carmelita then proceeded into the clinic through the back door.

Hope and I settled back in the Jeep to ride out the wait. Fifteen minutes later the passenger and Carmelita were back in the van and had pulled out of the clinic's parking lot.

The return route was as long and non-specific as our original trip crisscrossing Powell and Holgate. Finally, Carmelita pulled into the Flames Tavern and parked twenty yards from the entrance. I circled the block before swinging into a parking spot near the bar's door. Hope leaned over the Jeep's seat to get a good look with the field glasses.

"The man is out of the van. He's leaning into the passenger-side window." Hope unintentionally mimicked a play by play sports announcer on a radio show. "His backpack is over his shoulder. He's walking our way."

"Good, it'll be a chance to get a visual on this guy's face."

From behind tinted windows, I watched the man. His head bent slightly forward as if his backpack weighted him down. At the entrance, he glanced back toward the van, took off his Boonie hat and shook off the moisture that had accumulated. "It's a ploy," I said.

"What is?"

"He's not concerned with a little rain on his hat. He's looking at the van."

The man continued into the bar. Hope asked, "Are we going in?"

"Nope."

Surprised, she replied, "The van again?"

"That was Matt Thaman…he's in way over his head."

I dialed Matt's number. His failure to answer was a growing error in judgment, and I wanted him to know it. Forced to leave a recorded message I made it short and sweet. "You're making a big mistake. You're getting in over your head in something you don't understand. Give me a call."

"Do you really think Matt will call?"

"No…but I appease my conscience that I've done what I can do."

Hope nodded. "Now what?"

"My hand is being forced. If I don't make a play, Thaman will end up missing a kidney or worse. Maybe you should sit this round out. It's liable to be dangerous. Rumor has it they are armed."

"Not a chance!"

"Suit yourself. We'll tail the van when it pulls out."

Another vehicle pulled into Flames parking lot, cut its headlights, and inched its way toward the van. Hope put the binoculars to use. The arriving vehicle was the old station wagon from earlier in the day when Thaman was transported to the van at Sid's. The taillights brightened as it came to a stop. In the moments that followed I could see movement around the van, but it was a blur at best.

"Change of plans, honey, we're following the ratty car when it pulls out."

With my night scope, I could see the exhaust vapor on the old wagon and a dim light emitting from its interior. At nine-thirty-five the van pulled out of the Flames lot and turned right onto the main drag followed by an immediate left into Lent's Garden Villa. The wagon made the same right hand turn but continued straight. Carmelita was low on the totem pole and could be caught whenever the mood struck. What I was compelled to do was intervene and disrupt the action before Thaman got hurt.

The driver of the wagon continued another mile before turning into an all-night café. Few cars dotted the lot, but Hope was quick to spot a possible connection. "Isn't that Benny's car?" She pointed out her side window to the silver colored PT Cruiser parked against the outer edge of the blacktop. We pulled past the vehicle to get a look at the license plate. Hope confirmed, "That's it!"

"I'm going to park near the window and see if we can spot him inside the café."

Late night diner's and all-night cafés provided as much safety as bright lighting, and multiple windows would allow. Seeing inside from the outside was the design goal and suited my surveillance strategy equally well.

Dozens of patrons and staff were visible through the window directly in front of us. The corners of the joint were hidden from view, but the open floor plan aided our visual. Ramone and Benny had taken few if any precautions for their meeting. The men sat at a table in public view just inside the main entrance.

We watched the men converse, laugh, and slurp coffee. When they stood to leave, they shook hands. Benny was first to exit while Ramone took care of the bill at the cashier counter.

I smiled at Hope, "We need to talk to little Benny."

"How do you plan to make that happen?"

"Kidnap him." With Hope, I wasn't free to be as callous as I liked, but she had to be introduced to the interview process. Thaman had made a deadline for us by his involvement.

Benny fired up his Cruiser, and over the next thirty minutes, we followed him through Portland shifting northbound and onto Interstate 5 North. We crossed into Washington and continued our journey for nearly an hour.

"Are we going to Benny's place?" Hope asked.

"That's where he thinks he's going."

"Do you have a plan?"

"Unless something occurs that makes us alter our course, yes."

Hope sighed, then asked. "Are you incapable of giving straight answers?"

"I'm still working the idea out, but you'll love it."

At the Freeway mileage sign near Castle Rock, we buzzed passed Benny's Cruiser.

"We are going to get on Barnes Drive, pull off and wait. You'll play the bait. All he'll see is a damsel in distress. He'll cast himself as the white knight. It never fails."

"Preaching to the choir, Hunter, all men are the same."

We pulled through the three-way intersection in front of Gee Cee's Truck Stop and a quarter-mile south on Barnes Drive to set up the ambush. Hurriedly, I slipped my black facemask on followed by my leather police-style search gloves. The clouds had opened to a star-spangled sky as we'd traveled. The moon, half-full, illuminated the darkness.

"Do I get a mask?"

"I want him to see you and stop his car, not accelerate. You know the game…you play it all the time." The idea resonated with Hope as she settled into her role.

"If someone else stops first, I'll tell them to beat it."

"You got the picture. Approach Benny's car from the front unless he pulls past the Jeep. Either way, keep him in the headlights so I can get close without him seeing me. Remember, surprise is the element."

Hope nodded, "Got it."

The wait for headlights was over in less than a minute. Hope stepped into the roadway and frantically waved. The PT Cruiser's brakes screeched as it slid to a stop on the wet pavement in the middle of the road. I would have preferred his vehicle was either in front of my Wrangler or behind and not alongside in the roadway. But the hand was dealt and had to be played.

Hope showed her talent and had Benny out of his car and walking toward the Wrangler. Hope, who was taller than Benny, stayed to his left side drawing his eyes toward her as she walked him to the Jeep. The moment he knew he wasn't alone with Hope was when he bent into the cab of the Wrangler to look at the shifter, and the cold steel of a silencer touched the side of his bare neck. I could only imagine the rush of goosebumps up, and down his spine, that my .40-caliber automatic must have given him.

"Don't move! Don't even breathe!" My voice carried the emphasis loud and clear.

From his silence, I took that he fully grasped my meaning. With Benny, the language barrier wasn't in play. There wasn't any reason to repeat my questions, he'd learned English well enough for us to have a productive interview.

"Put a bead on the back of this guy's skull and pull the trigger if he acts up in the slightest."

Hope drew her .380 auto and racked a round into the pipe like I'd shown her on the range. I had questioned whether she would pull the trigger if things got out of hand but by the same token, Benny didn't know that she wouldn't shoot. He was a model captive while being cuffed. Plastic cable ties behind his back and the second set of zip ties hooked through his belt loops to anchor his hands. Still standing by the Jeep's door, I leaned Benny against the driver's seat and slapped a piece of duct tape over his mouth, finishing the touches needed for transport. Being a polite sort of guy, I helped Benny into the back of my Jeep.

"Put your gloves on and pull his Cruiser onto the shoulder," I told Hope. "Make sure you turn the ignition off, lock it up, and bring the keys with you. He might have need of them when we are done."

Thugs get the cart before the horse and beat their victims senseless to get what they wanted. Benny had heard my directions to Hope. If he listened, he understood there was a chance he could walk out alive. I wanted Benny to cooperate, compelled by his own thoughts of survival.

Once Hope climbed into the passenger side we were off looking for a destination with a more private setting than alongside the road. We traveled south four miles to where the Old Pacific Highway and the Cowlitz River intersected. We pulled into a boat launch area and swung the headlights in an arc to ensure we were alone. Then I backed the Jeep into a makeshift camping area and turned off the lights. After a moment of silence, Hope asked, "What are we waiting for?"

"Our eyes honey. They need time to adjust to the darkness."

With the clouds breaking up our eyes made a quick transition, and we got down to business, ripping the tape from Benny's mouth with one hard pull.

"I have you right where I want you, Mister Reyes."

"I don't know what you're talking about."

"I want names, places, dates, everything you know or remember about the harvesting of body parts?"

He shrugged, "Can't remember."

"I assume you recall you have a car down the road that's waiting for you?"

Benny nodded slightly.

"If you want to see it again, you better talk. Who was the bald guy you were with at the diner?"

"Ramone."

"Is his last name, Mendoza?"

"You already know him?"

Benny didn't know what I knew. In my line of work, it helped keep people truthful or expose their lies if they are in the dark. Benny thought I knew more than I did and that I was playing him. "How long has Ramone been a recruiter?"

"He doesn't recruit. He's a gofer."

"What's a gofer?"

"Ramone takes care of the deals."

"Is Carmelita the recruiter?"

"She plays a part. Why do you want to know? We provide people a medical service."

I laughed scornfully.

"Our organization helps those who need transplants. Too many laws keep people from getting the ones they need. Lawmakers are the ones responsible for thousands of deaths by putting people on waiting lists. There aren't enough donors to save them all. We find volunteers who are ready to exchange organs for money. It's their body and they should be able to do what they want with it."

"Sounds like you've practiced that line."

"The law doesn't let them. That's why organ sales go underground. We solve their problems and save lives."

"Sounds almost noble, Benny, but I have a problem how the selection works. Your organization, as you call it, exploits the poor and vulnerable members of society who sell their organs to make ends meet. The only ones buying your service to be saved are the wealthy."

Benny looked off into the darkness, he knew I was right.

"It's a for-profit business. How much do you pay for a kidney?" Quietly, he said, "It varies."

"On?"

"Ramone makes those arrangements."

"Ballpark a price for me?"

"Five or six thousand, I guess."

"Let me suggest it's less…And yet, those getting a kidney will pay what? A hundred thousand or more for the body part?"

"Carmelita brought a guy to the clinic tonight, why?"

"Probably a volunteer."

"Why the clinic?"

"Blood work, pre-surgical evaluation, and general medical assessment."

"When's his big day?"

"Always on the weekend."

"Why the meeting with Ramone tonight?"

"Why do you ask what you already know?"

I waited.

"Yes, yes, yes, like always before an operation. I bring the drugs to Ramone."

"How do you get around the watchdogs on the pharmacy?"

"DEA agents watch narcs, not the medications we need to perform the operations. I over order the drugs which end up expired and have to be discarded."

"You use out-of-date medications?"

"They're still good," he insisted.

"What was the volunteer's name that came in tonight?"

"I'll look when I get to the office tomorrow, but I don't remember."

"You do a lot of these operations."

"One or two every weekend…when we have volunteers."

"That's a lot of money coming through. Who's the doctor?"

"No doctor. One of the physician's assistants at the clinic."

"Are they all in it together?"

"No…just one."

"What about the clinic owner or doctor?"

"We don't have a resident doctor only a couple PA's that are licensed under the owner who's a physician."

"He's not around?"

"He stops in, but he owns other clinics."

"So who did the workup on the volunteer tonight?"

"The PA."

"Name?"

"Albert Tomas."

At first, Hope watched the interview process but at some point had begun to write down Benny's statements.

"Give me the names of everyone involved."

"Too many. I don't know the name of the transporter or who the security men are? Two men who work at the clinic help the PA with the surgery."

"In the ambulance?"

"Why are you asking if you know everything?"

"Carmelita drove around in circles before and after she picked up her volunteer. Why do you think she did that?"

"We never let anyone know how close the clinic is."

"Does that sound like an honest business, Benny? You mislead your victims. They have no idea where the clinic is or where the services are performed?"

He shrugged.

"Do you remember if any of the patients died from their operations?"

"I've heard of complications with surgery that had resulted in death. But it happens in hospitals too—all the time!"

"I've heard that before, but if there were complications, would the patient be transferred to a hospital to save their life?"

"We would take care of them."

"And the ones that died. How do you handle the dead?"

"I don't know."

"You're lying! Like you said Benny, I already know the answer. You dump the bodies."

Benny shook his head.

"Three years ago you dumped a body?"

"Like I said, people die after operations."

"But your victims die because of inadequate aftercare and substandard medical treatment. I've seen the mobile home you use for patient recovery. It's filthy. It's a wonder anyone lives. Tell me, Benny, if the victim dies do they harvest more body parts?"

"No, never."

"Yeah, you do. In fact, it's a smart business move. The more body parts, the more lucrative the profit margin."

"I suppose...but they know what we are doing and the risk they are taking."

"You and your people benefit from homeless vets, illegal immigrants, or anybody that's landed on tough economic times. You buy cheap and sell high. You don't care about the victims in the slightest, and I have a problem with that."

"It was their choice."

"You're going to stick with that line and not accept responsibility for the deaths of your victims? Let's stretch our legs."

Pulling Benny out of the car door was like handling a hundred-pound bag of mash on the farm; dead weight. Unwillingly, but given no alternative, Benny joined me at the river's edge. I halfway expected Hope to go with us, but was relieved that she stayed in the Jeep.

Benny vigorously protested this treatment but it fell on unsympathetic ears. A well-placed sidekick to his leg buckled the knee and sent him rolling on the ground. "You're a scumbag, Benny. You have no decency or respect for human life."

Begging for his life and calling on the name of God would do him no good. Why would a godless man expect to be spared by God? It never made sense.

He lived without respect and mercy in his life, and I didn't show him any in his death. Two well-placed rounds from my .40-caliber put any debate on Benny mending his ways to rest.

Removing Benny's watch, two dollars from his front pocket, and his wallet, I'd set the stage for the police investigation—the motive—robbery.

I kicked his body into the river and prepared for the onslaught of questions and possibly opposition that might come my way from Hope.

We pulled out of the boat launch and onto the highway that led to Interstate 5. Hope recounted details from what we'd learned from the interview but didn't seem fazed by his assassination. Was she that hardened?

She never asked why I killed him. Maybe she knew it was the logical outcome all along.

Hope's voice was upbeat, and the familiar twinkle in her eye had nothing to do with sex but everything to do with satisfaction. She derived enjoyment from being Miss Moneypenny.

CHAPTER 13

*"The greatest way to live with honor in this world
is to be what we pretend to be."*

—*Socrates*

I'm a killer, and I'd proven to Hope how lethal her 007 could be and is. The ball was now in her court and up to her to handle what she'd learned.

We rolled into Portland metro a few minutes past midnight. Hope had become a chatterbox. I attributed her new-found excitement to the rush she'd felt at the caper with Benny and his ultimate demise. Her assessment of the Intel collected through Benny's interview was impressive. Sensitive materials we couldn't afford to be wrong about deserved a second look before we worked it into our diagrammatic chart.

Hearing a lull in her unrelenting jabber, I interjected a question, "What's your plan for tonight, Lenny's or home?"

Hope pondered the question before responding with a question, "How much time do we have?"

"Tonight?"

"No silly...until they find out Benny is missing?"

"Not long. Maybe this weekend. Losing Benny will be a major glitch in their operation. But they have the drugs for the upcoming surgery, and they're driven by greed. They'll likely chance it even if Benny's body is found."

"Finding Benny's body might make them dangerous."

"Honey, we are the dangerous ones. We'll take them like dominoes. And if they do get spooked, it won't be because Benny's body was found, but because the place is crawling with cops. The body snatchers have no reason to think someone is coming after them. Maybe the back story on ol' Benny is he saw a beautiful woman hitchhiking alongside the road and got killed for being a Good Samaritan or maybe he had a bad gambling debt. The possibilities are endless. However, I doubt vigilantism is high on their whodunit list. It won't be until a second kill is made before they want to run and hide."

Hope leaned across to softly nuzzle my earlobe and coo into my ear. "It's the right thing to do."

"You understand then?"

"Yes…and you can take me to your place for the night."

"What about Sammie?"

"I'll call her and let her know I'm safe and with you."

If Sammie wasn't questioning what was going on in Hope's head, I was. In my book their relationship was weird, but people carve out what suits them best, and one size doesn't fit all. If Hope was unsure of how she felt about Sammie, I was equally confused. My thoughts weren't only about Hope's professed love for Sammie, but I'd kept Anna tucked away like a guilty secret.

At my Collins Best apartment, we immediately went to work stringing yarn and copying our Intel onto small sheets of paper to place on the diagram. Without a schedule to keep we didn't set an alarm clock. The thought of sleeping in late was nice, but I doubted the morning would end up that way.

Hope had a strong drive and couldn't stop rehashing the interview with Benny. It took a lot of attention to satisfy her, and she knew I had the answers to her, "what if's."

Hope had finished her shower and was drying her hair when I took my turn under the water. I wasn't alone for long. Hope slid in next to me and handed me a sudsy washcloth, turning her back in my direction, "I think I missed a spot."

A couple of hours later we were dressed and ready for action, a different kind of action, as I checked my bug out bag for supplies. Hope asked, "What's our agenda today?"

"Disruption. And when we're done, we're going to disrupt some more."

"Sounds detailed."

"Yeah. I thought it through...blow by blow. It's like steering a boat in the current of a river. We have to navigate quicker than the action around us, or we won't have control over our course."

Hope checked her weapon and bug out bag. We tossed the gear in the Jeep and drove to the most popular local greasy spoon. I held up my cup of coffee and said, "Here's to success." Hope clicked her mug against mine. I flashed her a smile and watched her eyes sparkle as I signaled the waitress that we were ready to order. Hope had ordered light—I stopped her. "You have to watch your figure, I get it. But, the day might get long. Eat like there is no tomorrow because there's no guarantee we'll see another meal until late."

Hope took it all in then abruptly flagged the waitress down. Her second order included yogurt and whole wheat toast to go with the fruit bowl she'd previously ordered. I stuck with the bacon and eggs.

"We'll locate the van when we're finished with breakfast. If we're lucky, we'll conduct another interview before the day runs out."

"You like interviewing."

"It beats sifting through mounds of paperwork to put a puzzle together without all the pieces."

"Why weren't the cops able to discover what had gone on with Lance Thaman? You said they investigated and came up with nothing."

"We don't know how many stones they turned over or what they ended up with. We only know it wasn't enough to make a case."

"It doesn't seem like it was hard to come up with what basically happened."

"Henry, our primary lead, never talked to the cops and wouldn't have willingly. He's more involved than he says and that's the main reason he's guarded. When we spoke, Henry lied more than once and what he did give up was because I put pressure on him. Even then, it was like pulling teeth. The reason we can't turn it over to the cops is their hands are bound by the law they enforce. The criminals know that and use their rights under the law to protect their criminal enterprises."

"What about Matt?"

"I'll put in another call to him and see if I can get him to cooperate by lying low until we've finished. But, I'm not wasting any more time trying to find him. I'm going after the players and interrupt the game. We'll plan to have a chat with Henry after we find the van."

First stop was Lent's Garden Villa. Traveling southbound on Powell, I turned into the back side of the Villa's parking lot and crept along the motel until I reached the west end. The rain had poured throughout the early morning hours and what had accumulated on the ground hadn't dissipated. I pulled to a stop at the motel's end where room 109 was located and rolled the driver's window down halfway. Vehicles on the main street splattered rainwater against a concrete barrier in front of the Villa. Otherwise only the dull day to day noises of the city hummed unobtrusively like background music.

It was a stroke of luck seeing the van as it pulled into the parking lot by way of the south entrance. Hope and I hunkered down in our seats so not to be detected.

Instead of the van pulling into a parking space, it stopped in front of room 109. Carmelita opened the passenger door while at the same time leaned toward Ramone. Ramone followed suit, leaned in her direction, and the two kissed. "Did you see that?" I asked Hope.

"Wasn't very passionate."

"Exactly. Remember, actions speak louder than words. What did the behavior say to you?"

"It was formal, like saying, I'll see you later or bye."

"Okay. What about the two of them sharing loyalty and commitment?"

"Probably."

"When the interview goes down, I can spend the knowledge of their relationship like currency. Hostages always buckle under their concern for someone they love."

Carmelita shut the van's door and entered her hotel room while Ramone pulled away toward the main drag.

"Will we ever know what happened to Lance?"

"He died, and they caused it. That's enough."

"Seems sort of black and white."

"To the world, the facts will remain a mystery. But, we'll know, or the best rendition of what happened because we'll do what the cops can't—extract it."

Carmelita stepped out of room 109 carrying an empty laundry basket and walked toward the front of the motel. Her actions prompted an idea. I grabbed for my bug out bag, slipped on the leather search gloves, and gave Hope a little smile.

Her eyebrows rose.

"Follow me." Stepping from the Wrangler, I quietly latched the door. Hope followed suit. We walked together, arm in arm, the few steps it took to reach room 109. With Bump keys in my bag, I was assured entry, but Carmelita made it easy and had foolishly left the room door ajar. We stepped through the doorway and closed the door like she had left it. "Now what?" Hope asked.

"We ambush her."

Almost immediately I was sorry I'd made the decision to move on Carmelita. The room stunk like a dirty diaper pail. Maybe two pails. Having never smelled one it might have been an overreach, but it was bad. Hope looked around and commented rhetorically, "We are going to catch some kind of disease in here." She paused before adding, "Disgusting! Someone lives like this?"

I fastened my silencer to the barrel of my .40-caliber and tried not to breathe in too deeply. Hope offered, "I'll keep watch for her return at the door."

"I want you safely behind me. Put on some gloves and look around for tale-tell evidence of their crimes. Maybe Carmelita kept a journal of who they've transported, a log of money transactions, letters, and letterheads, anything that might be useful as a lead." Hope walked the short distance into a bedroom while I leaned against the hall wall with my focus on the entryway. I didn't care which one got back first, Ramone or Carmelita. I was poised for a conversation with either of them.

Five minutes had passed before Hope emerged from the bedroom area. "There isn't much to the bedroom besides a queen size bed, nightstand, and a TV. I flipped the beds up on one side and pulled out the drawer on the nightstand out. It was empty. No books. No magazines. She missed a few grungy pieces of clothing on the floor. The rancid odor is from the carpet in the bedroom. Maybe something spilled, and they didn't clean it up. I can't imagine living with it."

Slowly the entry door opened exposing Carmelita's back to the room. Her manner of entrance through the doorway delayed what would have been a startling moment. As she turned toward the living room, her attention was drawn to a piece of clothing that had fallen from the basket she carried. The door closed behind her as she bent down to retrieve the item. It was then, stepping from the short hallway, I made my presence known; my silencer leading the surprise.

Still squatting by the basket, her eyes flared to saucer size. A gasp from down deep inside rushed to the surface.

"Ssssh," I whispered.

Carmelita stood leaving the basket on the floor in front of her.

Pointing the silencer toward the heavily stained blue sofa, I said, "Sit."

Carmelita interlaced her fingers as she clasped her hands together at her waist. In a moment of defiance, she shook her head.

"The gun doesn't scare you. I get it. But if you don't do what I say I'll take you apart piece by piece with a butter knife."

Carmelita hesitated until I reached for my bug out bag. At that moment, she took four short steps to the couch without further drama. Her hands folded in her lap she sat staring at me. I motioned for Hope to join us.

"Put a set of pretty bracelets on our guest," I said to Hope who pulled zip ties from my bug out bag.

"On your face," I said to Carmelita.

Hope grimaced at the thought, but, after all, it was their nasty stained furniture. They were used to their living conditions.

Carmelita responded in broken pigeon English, "I not think so."

I looked toward Hope and quipped, "Sometimes an ounce of prevention is better than a pound of cure."

Hope looked perplexed. If she had a shortcoming, it was her inability to understand the colloquial adages I often spewed.

I elected to explain it differently as I responded to my prisoner, "I know so," followed by a quick love tap with my Walther upside her right ear as she sat facing me. I looked toward Hope, "That's called applying the ounce so I won't have to hit her with the whole pound."

Hope nodded her understanding.

Carmelita lay face down on the sofa as I'd directed. "Put your hands behind your back." Quicker to comply this time, I asked Hope to do the honors with the plastic ties on her wrists. Once they were in place, I helped her to a more comfortable sitting position.

Hope pulled the duct tape out and tore a four-inch strip from the roll. "Hold on," I said. "I want her to talk." I turned my attention to Carmelita, "I'm going to cut to the chase. What's your name?

"Carmelita Flores."

"American, Hispanic, Filipino, what?"

"I'm an American citizen."

"Since when?"

"My parents brought me here when I was fourteen."

"Carmelita, it's not by chance we're talking with you. You're part of a criminal ring that deals in human organs. Don't waste my time denying your involvement. Got it?"

"Yes."

"Okay, your job has been to make the connections, right?"

"Yes."

"How long have you been doing this work for the organization?"

"Five years."

"The ring's method is to target the disadvantaged like the poor or homeless, yes?"

"If you say."

"I want you to confirm or clarify, that's all."

She nodded. "The donors help others and themselves too."

"That's very noble of them. They need the money so they sell a body part, I get it. Do you and Ramone work together? You recruit, and he follows up with the deal?"

"I don't have to talk to you, you no cop."

"You're wrong. You don't have to talk to the cops, but you do have to talk to me."

Carmelita sat without showing a trace of emotion. Her coldness, disturbing. A pathological sign that she was a cold-blooded killer. I should know.

"We work together. Why you want to know?"

"Call it a vested interest in the outcome. You're careful. You look around and hide your comings and goings. I watched you work the floor at the bar, and I tailed you through the rhododendron grove to this very motel room. You remember the fat guy, don't you?"

Unresponsive, only Carmelita's eyes reacted to the mention of Fatso. She remembered. Hope's eyes squinted. She remembered too.

"What do you pay for this crappy room?"

Carmelita sighed, "Ramone covers expenses."

"Yeah, Ramone, what's his last name?"

"Mendoza."

"I thought it might be Flores." I wanted her to know I'd done my homework. "Besides Mendoza, how many people are involved in the organization?"

"I don't know."

"Doctors, nurses maybe. One person, you can name?"

She shrugged, "Can't help you."

Hope interjected, "Can't or won't?"

Carmelita shrugged off the question.

"You took someone to the clinic yesterday. What was his name?"

"He was a poor man that bummed a ride."

"You don't know the guy's name and don't know anyone's name at the clinic. Maybe I can help fill in the blanks for you. The pharmacy guy, Benny, Benito Reyes, does that ring a bell?"

Carmelita pondered the name I'd tossed out before giving her answer. Casually she said, "No," as if my question was no big deal.

I made it relevant. "Benny's dead."

Her eyes widened as she gasped in surprise. No shock there, hardened criminals react the same way when sideswiped by such news. "But you're lucky, Benny's death doesn't bother you any since you didn't know the guy and all."

Hope looked in my direction as Carmelita reacted to word of Benny's untimely death. I winked to let her know I was fully aware she had lied.

"What magic does the Flames Tavern play in this organization? You and the bartender have a thing going on behind Ramone's back?"

"He's nothing..."

Letting Carmelita in on my secret about Benito Reyes had softened her up. She seemed willing if not eager to respond. She understood I meant business and took me seriously. I took the advantage and pressed her, "Why the Tavern?"

"The homeless look for handouts and free drinks there. Some of them stay in the rescue mission down the road."

"A target rich environment?"

She curled her lip into a sneer, "If I can help them I will."

"Henry helped you make the connections in the veteran community, right?"

"No."

Hope, seemingly disgusted with the answers Carmelita had given, slipped across the room and next to the metal framed window at the center of the room. Taking up a position at the corner of the shade she kept an eye out for Ramone.

"How many of the poor and homeless have you helped?"

Carmelita drew silent.

Hope looked my way—and winked. "Maybe a better question is how many of them died?"

Carmelita squirmed as she sat perched on the edge of the sofa. Wrestling with the lies she'd already told, she asked, "When did Benny die?"

My question had likely sparked her memory that she'd seen Benny late the previous night. Maybe she'd caught me in a lie, and Benny wasn't dead after all. But if that was her notion, I put it to an end. "Not long after you left the clinic with your new victim. The guy you don't know."

"Henry helped him get hold of me."

"What's Henry get out of all this?"

"Fifty dollars."

Hope spoke up suddenly, her tone urgent. "The white van is back."

Glancing at Carmelita, I detected a slight smile creeping up the side of her mouth. I grabbed the duct tape Hope had ripped off the roll earlier and pressed it firmly against Carmelita's lips. "Don't move."

Hope reported, "He's getting out."

"Targets?"

"Just one."

"Okay, down the hallway." I stepped behind the entry door as Ramone opened the door and stepped over the threshold. Seeing Carmelita bound and gagged he startled, stepping back against the door causing it to slam shut. I couldn't resist compounding his reaction as I presented my weapon at eye level.

"Couch," I commanded.

"Secure him." Hope opened my bag and removed three plastic ties and strapped a set on Ramone. When she had cinched the extra strap through the cuffs and onto his belt, she returned to her position at the corner of the shade. I threw the bolt lock on the door to ensure our privacy then introduced myself, "My name is Hunter."

Ramone was short, scrawny, and nearly bald with only a wreath of hair remaining in the back and sides of his scalp.

"Let me guess, you're Filipino too," I asked.

"What of it?" He snapped in clear English.

It was beginning to look like the French Connection with Filipino's at the root. Ramone and I had gotten off to a bad start, and his attitude needed adjusting. I reached over and pulled the tape from Carmelita's mouth. Perhaps if they were able to converse, he'd become more reasonable. She immediately started to speak to Ramone in her native tongue. I suppose it was rude of me when I interrupted, "Do you like wearing tape on your lips?" Neither of my hostages acknowledged my question. Carmelita continued to speak the Filipino dialect. "Knock off the gibberish and speak only when you are spoken to, and it better be in English."

Having acquired their attention, I continued my interview. "Ramone, you've joined us late, so I'll recap the highlights for you. Your game is up. I've been tracking your movements, and the deals you've brokered and the murders in which you've participated in. It's over. Before you ask, I'll tell you this upfront; I'm not a cop. I killed Benito Reyes and I'll kill you too if I don't get better cooperation."

"Don't hurt her." Ramone looked toward Carmelita, "She didn't have anything to do with it."

"That bothers me, Ramone. I know she is as involved as you are. However, I do respect your attempt to protect her. Tell me where they cut up the people?

"The clinical staff uses an ambulance for their operations."

"That's the one hidden in the barn at Benny's place?"

Ramone tried to wipe a tear from his eye using his shoulder. I intervened and pulled a clean t-shirt from the laundry basket and patted his face off. "Yes," he answered.

"Kind of like meals-on-wheels, they go different places and harvest body parts."

"No, that's not it. They operate right there on the Bunga."

"A what?"

"That's what we call the place. The recovery is made there too."

"How do the victims get there?"

"I take the patients to the Bunga, usually on the morning of the operation."

"How many people have you taken out to be cut on? Ballpark it for me."

"A hundred, maybe more."

"Do you give the rides both ways?"

"Always. They spend a week or so in recovery."

"Then you'd have a pretty good idea of how many people you took out but didn't give a ride back, right?"

Stammering, he said, "Well I wouldn't know. Some get rides in other ways."

"No—you said—always! You always give them a lift back."

Ramone stared silently into my eyes.

"What was the guy's name Carmelita hauled to the clinic yesterday?"

"He said his name was Frank."

"If I wanted to talk with Frank, maybe persuade him from making a donation, how would I get in touch with him?"

"Too late for him. I took him out last night."

Hope made a throaty noise that caught my attention. She'd understood the revelation correctly. While Hope and I were having a friendly chat with Benny, Ramone had transported Thaman to the Bunga. I focused on the words Ramone had spoken, "Too late." They sounded wrong and carried an air of wickedness. "You know who Frank is, don't you?"

"Henry told us who he was. Matt Thaman has been a problem for years. His brother died during an operation, and he couldn't accept the consequences."

It didn't take a Rhodes Scholar to figure out that if they were wise to his identity that he was in mortal danger. They were going to cut him from stem to stern and make a few hundred thousand dollars in the process. "When's Thaman's operation scheduled?"

Ramone shrugged, "Maybe today. We drugged him real good and took him out to the Undertaker."

"Undertaker?"

"He runs the recovery center."

"That's a lousy name for a guy who takes care of patients. Sounds like survival is unlikely, don't you think?"

Neither Ramone nor Carmelita answered. I turned up the pressure by pointing my gun at her.

"You already plan to kill us," Carmelita said.

"You are so negative," I said. "There are things worse than dying from a gunshot wound. Death can be quick and painless or be extended for weeks with pain you can't imagine."

Her lips pressed tight as she stared defiantly at the muzzle. I placed the tape back over her mouth and turned my attention to Ramone. "How do you put up with her?" I asked. Carmelita had a bad effect on Ramone. He had drawn on her strength to be a tougher cookie to break. In a harsh tone, he blurted, "Danny Carabeo, he transports the donations to California. That's who you want. Go see him."

"Tomas is the doctor's name?"

He nodded.

"Where does he work when he's not moonlighting as a butcher?"

"You know. Why are you tormenting us with questions you know the answers to?"

"What do you do with the dead bodies?"

Ramone answered with silence, but it was silence with an attitude that was written across his face. He burst out angrily, "I have nothing more to say. Threaten me all you want, I'm done."

"If that's the way you want to play, I'll oblige." I tore a new piece of duct tape off the roll and pulled it tight across Ramone's mouth. Reaching into my bag, I laid my Walther inside, and removed my KaBar knife. Hope looked out the window. She didn't seem to have the stomach for what might come next.

"I'm going to play fair with you two. You answer the questions as I ask them or I'll take both of you apart piece by piece."

Ramone stood and squirmed trying to work the tape loose from his mouth. I kicked him between the legs and dropped him to the floor. Hope tried not to watch but was drawn to the action as it unfolded.

I grabbed Carmelita and shoved my forearm under her throat pushing her back against the sofa. She choked, and with her mouth taped shut she struggled all the harder. Finally, I let up and pulled off the tape that held her lips closed. She rolled off the sofa collapsing to the floor, coughing and gasping for air.

"Is this what you wanted for your woman, Ramone? It doesn't have to be this way."

With the tape in place and his hands secured behind him, he needed to find a way to signal me he was ready to talk. "Your turn Carmelita, give me a name and make it count."

Still recovering from her brush with death she was slow to respond. I put a fresh piece of tape over her mouth and went to work on Ramone's ear with my KaBar. One slice and his left ear lay on the floor, blood pooling. "All this cutting off of body parts is a typical day in the hood for you two," I said. "Ramone, I'm passing the baton back to you. You can continue your lame act or run with what you have. It's your decision?" Without hesitation, I reached down and pulled the tape from his mouth and pulled Carmelita by the hair to a sitting position. "Which ear, Ramone? What happens to her is your doing."

"Let her go, I'll tell you everything I know."

"You're not in a position to negotiate. You answer, or I cut. That's the only deal on the table."

"The organ bank is in Redding, California. That's where Danny takes the tissue."

"When does he make the trip?"

"Every Monday?"

"Benny said the operations were on the weekend?"

"Saturday's usually. Your friend Matt was an exception."

"What's the Undertaker's name?"

"I only know his last name—Aquino. We make the deals, take people out and bring them back. We are never there for the operations. I've told you all I know."

I put tape across his mouth and put the few items I had pulled out back into my bag. I said to Hope, "Get your stuff...we're going."

"Are you leaving them here?" Hope asked.

"Yes. I picked up my handgun and fired a round directly into Ramone's torso. Carmelita closed her eyes, and for a moment she looked like she was in church, or in prayer, or something. Maybe she was. Shuup...the force of the .40-caliber knocked her back against the sofa.

Her body doubled over next to Ramone's. I prepared for the next round to enter her skull when I noticed that she'd reached to touch her lover's hand. I put my foot on her wrist and watched as her dying gesture was denied. Shuup!

"That was cold," Hope said.

"Life's cold, honey, and she got what she deserved. She was far worse to those she sent to be butchered."

We quickly made our exit, slipped around the corner of the building where the Jeep was parked, and a minute later we'd pulled out onto the main drag en route to Collins Best. There were adjustments to be made with the yarn, new players to be added, and some removed who were no longer active in the game.

Hope had watched as I dispatched Flores and Mendoza. She appeared emotionless, and was either in shock or overwhelmed by what she'd seen. A block north of the Villa, Hope opened up with what had been pressing on her mind. "We're too late for Matt, aren't we?"

"We tried to warn him to stay out of it. He got in way over his head, and now he's bought it. He didn't have a clue that Henry had sold him out and set him up."

"Henry had to know they'd kill Matt if they had a chance," Hope surmised.

"He'll have to answer for what he's done."

Hope hesitated before stammering out another pressing question, maybe the most important one to her. "Do you enjoy hurting people, causing pain, and killing?"

"The hurt and pain is a means to an end. I don't like it...or dislike it. It's just a thing."

"The killing?"

"It's not a popular belief, honey, but there are criminals so morally reprehensible that the only appropriate punishment is death. Do I enjoy killing? Yes. Do you remember we talked the first night at the bar about looking for satisfaction?"

"Yes. I could tell it wasn't sex you were after."

"It's not in the act of killing that brings gratification; it's in the eradication of a predator that's my passion."

"I know you think of me as a child sometimes, but I've been around some very bad people and places. You are fighting a losing battle."

"What happened to 'we'?"

"It's hopeless."

"I disrupt criminal activity. When I take players out of the game, it is a one-hundred percent guarantee they won't ever offend again. Zero. There are others that seep out of the dark to fill the void. I'm not naive. There are always others. But, the ones I assassinate never return to harm another person, and that is the point of my work."

At my apartment I let Hope enjoy the honor of removing the yarn and taking the player's names from the diagram. Without asking she took the initiative to change Henry's status from stooge to hustler. Hope studied the wall hanging while I placed a call to Anna. She answered on the first ring.

"How is Island life?" I asked.

"Hawaii would be better."

"I need you to run some names and a couple of addresses through your sources. With the Intel, I believe I'll wrap up the project. Three packages are in the basket already."

I gave her what I had on the Undertaker and the physician's assistant plus the properties of the clinic and Castle Rock area where the Bunga sets. She also had news, "Thomas is back in play. No injuries were sustained."

"Great...he's a MVP."

"He has more innings to play, but he drove a few players deep into the turf. He knocked it out of the park with a bang and burn home run."

Bang and Burn were code amongst Palatini operators for a demolition and sabotage mission. An area of Kuhl's expertise thanks to Uncle Sam teaching him the tricks of the trades. The drug cartel didn't fare well if he'd knocked it out of the park.

"How's Max?"

"I don't want to speculate. His mind is sharp, but his body is frail."

"Sorry to hear that, tell him Scythian said, 'Mission First.'"

"He'll appreciate that."

Hope had overheard the conversation and joined me at the kitchenette table. "You do work with others?"

"It's convoluted. We are independent operators. Occasionally, we join forces, but when we do, we do so by our own choice. More frequently we work alone on a project."

"But you called someone and asked for information on the people we're working on?"

"It's a resource. We'll have to leave it there for now."
"Do you trust me, Hunter?"
I didn't have time not to trust her. "Emphatically," I said.
Hope flashed her prettiest smile and reached for my hand.

CHAPTER 14

"In union there is strength."

—*Aesop*

"It's time to rock and roll, honey." Sweeping through the room, I gathered extra clothing items for an extended engagement.

Hope looked at me askance, a false smile pulled at the corner of her lips. "Are you going alone?"

"Only if you want to sit this one out."

"I want to be with you, Hunter." Hope slipped her windbreaker on and prepared to leave.

"The Undertaker is top on my list." I saved Hope from asking the question.

"Why is he so special?"

"Ramone was clear that they were medicating Matt. If he's still alive, I have to spring him."

I preferred a different strategy than rescue. Anna insisted freeing victims was the primary focus of our mission, but for me, not so much. Sure, it felt good to save a life, but I thought in terms of preventive measures more than reactive. Unfortunately, that's the scenario that had unfolded with Matt. If I hadn't felt compelled to intervene, I would have gone after the butcher next and toppled the whole organization. "It's going to get bloody. I intend to dismantle their business all the way to the core."

"Understood," Hope said as she accompanied me out the door. No longer caught off guard by my sudden decisions she seemed excited to further our goals.

We swung into Lenny's during Happy Hour. Watering holes like his tavern had my future written all over them. As much as I disdained the atmosphere, I realized my clientele frequented such places, and I had to be in tune with my surroundings.

"Long time no see," Lenny smiled ear to ear as he addressed Hope. "The first round is on me." I presumed it was only right to take advantage of his mood. Doing otherwise might offend him.

We found our favorite table empty, pulled up chairs, and ordered a plate of Nachos to chase down our drinks. Lenny nuked a plate of chips and cheese and delivered them to our table then took a seat.

"It's been days since you stopped in, what have you been doing?" Lenny directed his question to Hope.

My interest piqued. How would Hope explain our time together with a trusted friend?

"Hunter was so kind. We took an incredible ride out of the city and into the countryside. The weather wasn't cooperative, but the scenery was, uh, just a killer."

Their interaction was absorbing. Lenny now, more than ever, treated Hope like she was the daughter he'd never had. "I'm glad you had fun," he declared enthusiastically.

"We really did have some fun all right." Hope winked and squeezed the back of my hand. "We met new people and had an interesting time getting to know them!"

Oblivious to Hope's real meaning Lenny said, "Ah, that's good" then with a head tilt toward the bar he said, "Gotta go."

Hope had proven to be an asset. Her background and experience coupled with a heartfelt interest in the type of projects for which the Palatini were known were the beginnings of a superb killer. Hope's ravishing appearance and the sorted behaviors she'd mastered in Life, allowed her to walk straight into a den of iniquity and straightforwardly slaughter every last predator if she had the moxie. A sexy good look was an advantage most Palatini operators didn't have.

The thought of Hope as a potential candidate for the Society Palatini was intriguing. Although still early in the process of self-discovery, I wanted to explore her attributes. Whether she decided to follow in my footsteps or make her own path was yet to be seen, but I could feel her instinct to kill. She had a passion for justice and accepted that the end justified the means. That criterion was a hard pill for even some seasoned Palatini veterans to swallow. Some used our code of ethics to avoid making a decision on their own while others measured right and wrong by it. I didn't have the same restraints. The code we lived by established parameters of guilt and was, at best, a guideline, not a black and white rule to which I'd sworn allegiance. I was a Palatini, a Freelancer, and willing to take care of business without fear or favor.

Hope started to ask a question then backed off. What surfaced was sheer nervousness and I wanted to quell her indecision. "I know what's on your mind, so here it is. In a day or two, I'll get the Intel back from my source, but we don't have that much time. We've been put in a position that we didn't ask for, and maybe we're too late already. I plan to strike tonight."

"Okay."

I'd anticipated more excitement. Something else weighed on her mind.

"Thank you, Hunter...I'm serious when I tell you, the past few days have been amazing. I mean that. I haven't felt the need to find anyone to entertain me."

"I've done what Sammie couldn't...being with me cured you."

"See, you're laughing it off, and I'm serious."

"Yeah, sorry, go ahead."

"Hope fiddled with the coaster under the edge of her wine glass for a moment and then floored me. "I want to move in with you, Hunter.'

I felt a swallow of beer catch in my throat.

"I want to be your Moneypenny."

This was no joking matter, and I wasn't going to crack wise. This was a bullet aimed straight at me. The problem with dodging a bullet is that it's a matter of luck, not skill. I questioned why Hope had quit going to Sammie's every night like she had when we first started to hang out together. Now I knew why. Maybe I'd always known the direction we were headed. I doubted it was possible to stalk our prey and kill together and not form a deeper union than the camaraderie of co-workers. I had to think through how to tell her that she's the right girl, but I'm the wrong guy. "Let's put this project to rest and then lay it all out on the table and see if it's the right thing to do."

Lenny had picked up the television remote from behind the bar's counter and switched to the local news. Hope pulled her chair close to mine for a better view of the bar. She wasn't practicing observation skills but rather the natural response of a predator. Whether she realized it or not, her modus operandi was methodical.

Patrons yakked all the louder in competition with the television and each other but stopped abruptly to watch a live report as it aired on the primetime broadcast. "Homicide detectives are working an active murder scene on Powell Boulevard," the reporter commented. Visible behind the newscaster was Lent's Garden Villa barricaded by yellow police tape. "Names of the victims have not been released pending notification of next of kin."

I tapped Hope's arm to get her attention. I wanted her to catch the broadcast, but she had been distracted by a visitor's arrival.

"Looks like something the vigilante might do." I knew the voice.

My attention had been focused on the people's reaction to the broadcast when Ware had slipped through the tavern entrance. He couldn't have planned his timing better if he'd tried.

"You're just in time," as I motioned to Lenny. "Whatever he wants, Lenny."

"Coffee," Ware said, "And the girl can beat it."

"Don't be rude, she's my guest and can stay if she wants. Anything you have to say can be said in front of her."

Ware shrugged indifferently then slid into a chair, partially hiding his plump midsection under the table's edge.

I followed with introductions, "Sweetheart, this is Brandon A. Ware, retired MCSD Detective." As Hope reached her hand toward Ware I said, "Mister Ware, this is Miss Moneypenny."

He responded cordially, shook her hand, and said jokingly, "I'd like to see that on your driver's license."

"I don't have a driver's license," she countered.

"Of, course you don't."

Hope was quick with her response and had schooled Ware. She'd told the truth and lied all in the same breath. She didn't have a license, not one that had Miss Moneypenny on it.

"It's been a while since you've interrupted one of my evenings, Ware, what's on your mind?"

"Are you going to interview Moore like I asked?"

"What's the difference if he had someone kill her or it was due to her lifestyle? I fail to see how that brings closure to the Lott family."

"It would confirm what they've believed all along about Moore."

"You mean they could blame him…like that makes her a different person. I don't think so. She was responsible for what happened to her daughter as much as Icky was. If she died because of what she did or because of who she knew doesn't alter my feelings toward her in the least."

Ware leaned to the side and faced me, "I'd like to have seen that article you were going to write. It would have been a doozy."

"I try to be more objective when I write. But, just so you know, this story is water under the bridge."

Ware sat back. A look of frustration crept over his face. "Moore is running around out here free, and the Lott girl is dead. I don't see the happy ending to the story."

"It's life…real life doesn't have happy endings, not when degenerate's like Icky are involved."

"You're a tough guy, Walter."

"I've written too many articles that all turn out the same. Two crappy people come together and make a crappy life. Into that life, they bring an innocent child and commit atrocities upon him or her. Neglect their responsibilities, fail to protect and provide for their children until eventually, they are busted. Once the child is taken by the State they get a minimum sentence in the slammer that barely amounts to nothing more than a slap on the wrist. Subsequently, the child bounces around the system with their mind polluted with what they've seen and what happened to them and perhaps become the same way, a worthless piece of humanity perpetuating the same atrocities. The parents go on to find two more people of the same caliber to make another crappy union and bring more misery into the world and so it goes. Do you know what I do?"

Ware shrugged.

"I change the names of the players and publish the article as new, and the reading audience is astonished as if they had read this account of life for the first time. Mona got what she had coming to her and Icky will too."

"Are you going to write the article after something happens with Moore?"

"Like what?"

"When he hurts another child."

"I'll tell you what, for you, I'll write a piece after someone off's him. At least it will be different than the others I've written."

"I think you should get ready to write." Ware sipped the last of his coffee and then grimaced. "Cold, ugh...never understood how anyone drank it iced."

I nodded distractedly. I had unintentionally shown my hand almost forecasting Moore's future tragedy. It wasn't a wise move to make with a skilled player like Ware.

"Why do you want me to write the article?"

"It would make a good read?"

"Nah, that's not it at all. You want me to flush the vigilante out of hiding by writing about Moore. Do you think he was the one that killed the Lott woman?"

Ware studied my eyes. That was it. I could see the answer. Ware stood and threw a couple bucks on the table for Lenny then asked, "Is Moore still hanging out at the Lucky Strike?"

"No clue, I haven't been there to check."

Ware nodded and casually drifted to the exit. When the door shut behind him, Hope asked, "Walter?"

"I'm known by many names to different people. One person knows me as James Bond the next as 007."

"James Bond and 007 are one and the same."

"So is Walter and Hunter."

It didn't satisfy Hope's question of who was who, but she brushed it aside and dealt with a more pressing issue. "What if Ware waits in the parking lot for us to leave?"

"Then we'll lose him. We have business to take care of."

Traveling north across the Columbia River toward the Bunga we ran into a dense fog bank that slowed our progress. As we drew near Castle Rock, Hope asked, "What's my job tonight?"

I found it difficult to answer. The last thing she needed to know was that I didn't have a plan—for her or me. Killing everyone in sight wasn't a plan, just an outcome of how I envisioned it would go down. "I need you to stay with the Jeep and keep your phone on. You're my lifeline if something goes wrong."

Hope pouted, "How am I supposed to learn?"

"In an operation where you are planned into it and after months of working that .380, until then, you're my back-up."

We pulled the Jeep close to where we'd parked the first time, cut the lights, and went through my spiel a second time. "Jump in the driver's seat when I get out, let it run with the defroster blowing, and keep the rig ready to go. If something goes wrong and you don't hear from me, don't call, but head to Gee Cee's Truck Stop and have a cup of coffee. If I have to, I'll hoof it there."

I gathered my gear and prepared to exit when Hope held my arm. For the first time in a few days, Hope pulled me into her embrace. Her lips were moist and welcoming; her kiss tender and passionate. She wasn't pleading to come along; she was saying hurry back. I turned to go.

Gloves, ski mask, and coat weren't a match for the layer of moisture that soon engulfed me. The fog, heavily laden with condensation, dripped from the tip of my nose. I moved through the brush and onto the field's edge then made my way along the tree-lined perimeter toward the group of buildings. I held fast at the closest point to the trailer and watched for movement.

Benny's place was pitch black, the travel trailer and the mobile home each had lights on inside. My choice of weapons for a night operation was my AR15 equipped with a night scope. I'd strapped on my tactical vest that held my KaBar and extra magazines and a tactical leg holster for my .40-caliber.

Through the fog, my scope would detect heat images if I came upon someone. But, I'd likely move in close to make the shot. Still, I'd have eyes on before they knew I was there unless they were likewise equipped. The darkness coupled with fog played to my advantage.

Making my advance on the mobile home where I anticipated my primary target would be found, was a fifty-yard trek from the wood line that I'd been following. According to Henry, if he could be believed at all, the trailer was where they housed surgical patients for their recovery. If there was any chance of finding Thaman, it would be in one of the two bedrooms. In all likelihood, they'd harvested what they wanted and dumped what was left in the nearest burn pile. Whether Thaman was alive or not was secondary, my target was the Undertaker.

Moving alongside the trailer, vigilant and listening for the slightest sound, I didn't pick up on any noise, human or otherwise. To my left, Benny's house sat dark and as lifeless as he was. Moving toward the front of the mobile home the travel trailer came into view. Nothing new or notable, except the single light that appeared to have been on inside the trailer was now off. Stepping back to the mobile home I worked my way to the front door and up the wood steps, each level groaning with my arrival.

My AR15 moved into position, tight into my shoulder, and at the ready, as if it had a mind of its own to engage. I reached for the door handle. It opened with ease having been left unlocked. The element of surprise was in my favor as I made entry into the living room of the recovery center. I swept the room from side to side with my night scope.

The living room had been transformed into an office with a bulky desktop computer, combination phone and fax machine, and file cabinet that sat next to the desk. A row of metal folding chairs lined the wall to my right that separated the kitchen from the office.

Prepared to move down the hallway and clear the remaining rooms a metallic clanking noise interrupted the night time ambiance followed by the sound of a vehicle engine. Quickly, I closed the front door and stepped into the kitchen. Through the window, I could see headlights appear as they came around the back corner of the mobile home and pulled to a stop behind the travel trailer. A moment later came the sound of a single car door opening and closing. I waited to see what good fortune had brought me.

Distinctly, as when I climbed the steps, each level moaned the visitor's ascent. The door opened, and a single light flicked on above the desk. I molded into a dark kitchen corner.

Only glimpses could be seen of the man that entered. First, a hand as he laid keys on the desk followed by his shoulder. Then his back was in view through a reflection from a diamond-shaped mirror that hung on the wall across from the main entrance.

A few short steps and the man had made his way to the first door. Opening it, he said, "You need anything?"

I couldn't hear the response if there was one, but the man's retort was clear. "I'm going to give you another shot. You're less of a problem when you sleep through the night."

He shut the door and walked back into the office to be met by my AR15. Startled, he followed with an indiscernible term bellowed at the top of his lungs.

I spoke quietly, "Sssh."

I motioned with the barrel of the AR for the man to have a seat in a folding chair. Moving carefully, he opened the first chair, sat down and asked tremulously, "Mind if I smoke?"

"Yes...it's bad for your health. What's your position here...house mouse for this place?"

He didn't answer. I tried an easier question, "What's your name?"

"Aquino."

"You're the one they call the Undertaker?"

The stockily built fortyish-year-old Filipino with hair cropped tight to the scalp like a new military troop lit up a cigarette and sucked in a deep lungful. "What's this all about?"

"Who were you talking to down the hall?"

"If I tell you, is it going to make a difference? You don't know him."

His cool and calm exterior gave way to a nervous tic. Aquino's eyes repeatedly shifted from one side of the room to the other. "Why don't we take a walk and you can introduce us?"

Once again, I was put in a situation I wasn't prepared for. What to do with a rescue? I'd have to make an anonymous call to the Emergency Medical Services and have them handle the victims in pre- or post-op status.

Aquino slowly stood and started down the hall. I gave him the lead with three steps in front of my AR's silencer. Aquino stopped outside the first door and looked back at me. I told him to open it.

Aquino turned the door handle slowly and pushed it open. Immediately, I heard muffled noises as if someone was trying to yell and a racket reminiscent of people scuffling. Aquino moved forward into the dimly lit room. I embedded my foot into his back and shoved him into a recliner.

Before me, sitting on the edge of an old, metal framed, military hospital style bed sat Matt Thaman. "Do you still have all your body parts?" I asked. "If not I can come back later."

Thaman, barely able to contain himself, bounced up and down like a monkey in a zoo who wanted to be fed. Calming him with my hand on his shoulder I reached for the gag that covered his mouth and gave it a quick jerk. "They planned to kill me."

"I thought about it a couple times myself."

Matt's wrists had been individually secured to the metal bedposts with handcuffs. I didn't waste my time asking Aquino for his key to unlock the cuffs, I had my own.

With the first hand I freed, Matt pointed at Aquino, "He said he was going to gut me like a fish, the same as he did my brother!"

"We talked about it, Matt. I told you, you're in way over your head. Your pal, Henry, sold you out. They knew who you were all along."

"How did you find me and why do you have a rifle?"

"You can be thankful I did and do. We don't have time for 'Twenty questions.'"

Using the muzzle of my weapon I pointed Matt toward Aquino and gave directions on how I wanted this to play out. "Handcuff him behind his back."

Thaman shoved the Undertaker to one side of the chair and pulled his hands together. Matt was former law enforcement and knew well how to cuff a guy with a whack on the wrist.

"Do you have any bags or clothing here that can identify you if we left it?"

"Just my coat." Matt pointed to a light brown Carhart jacket hanging on a rack behind me. I reached for the jacket and gave it a toss to Thaman. Something fell from the pocket onto the floor with a solid thump. Matt's eyes locked on mine.

"What's that about?" I asked.

"They weren't the only ones planning to do some killing." Matt reached down and picked up the revolver from the floor.

"You're not thinking straight. Why don't you give me the pistol to hold?"

Matt's face surged with pain as if a levy that held back his emotions had burst. Abruptly and without warning he turned and fired three shots into Aquino. For a long moment in the silence that followed, it appeared that Matt couldn't break away from the almost trance-like stare at his would-be murderer. Slowly he dropped the gun to his side as the Undertaker's corpse drooled blood from his mouth. Still dazed, Matt asked, "Now what?"

"Now you live with it."

His lips pulled back tight clenching his teeth. I interrupted his thoughts, "Set this place on fire. Your fingerprints and DNA are all over."

Matt nodded. "Are you helping me?"

"I've been helping you all along. You didn't see it, that's all."

Matt soaked the bed linen in rubbing alcohol and lit it on fire while I rummaged through the filing cabinet collecting all paperwork into a plastic garbage bag next to the desk.

From outside the flames lit up the house. "Pocket your gun." Matt quietly complied. The last thing I wanted to have happen was an accidental discharge when we went through the brush to the roadway. I handed Matt the garbage bag. It gave him something to do and kept his hands busy.

I made a quick call to Hope and let her know that Matt and I were on our way out.

"There's someone else involved?" Matt asked.

"Hope."

Thaman, still holding the plastic bag, climbed into the back seat of the Jeep while I rode shotgun. It made Hope's day, she liked to drive.

We had turned onto Interstate 5 heading south before the atmosphere eased up enough to talk freely. Aided by the darkness of the Wrangler's cab, Matt asked, "How did you know I was there?"

"I didn't."

"But you came in with a rifle to get me out?"

"I was armed because I wanted to question Aquino about their organization and felt he'd be more cooperative with a muzzle in his face."

Matt sat silently as the growl of the Jeep's tires against the asphalt seemed to grow louder. "He let my brother die," Matt said. "He joked about it and said I was going to join him in the same way. I didn't believe for a moment that Lance had died accidentally. Now I know they purposely killed him because they thought they could get away with it and sell body parts."

"Maybe you're right, but we'll never know because you killed the guy who could have given you the answer as well as the answer to many other questions."

Hope gasped, "Matt killed the Undertaker?"

"That's right, honey, Matt's a natural born killer."

"What's that mean?" She asked.

"Instinct...the natural law of all mankind."

"If Henry sold me out like you say then I have a score to settle with him."

"There's no "If's" to it. Henry's more of a player than he claims to be. Don't believe anything he tells you."

Crossing back into Oregon, I asked Matt where he wanted to be dropped off. He gave directions to an IHOP diner on 82nd Street that he said stayed open all night. I shook Matt's hand and said, "I think we're done. You've gotten your revenge, and that's likely as close to justice as you're going to get."

"Thank you. I know it's not enough, but it's all I have."

Matt was still in shock from his near-death experience. He'd dodged a bullet but returned the favor on the Undertaker. Revenge. Both scenarios wreak havoc on a person's psyche when they haven't mentally prepared to accept the end results-ending a life.

Once Matt entered the diner, it was my turn to drive. I rehashed the evening's events with Hope. "Do you think Matt will continue to be a vigilante?" She questioned.

"He's not a vigilante. He's a guy who sought revenge for his brother, that's all."

After a long silence, Hope, teary-eyed said, "There are times I'd like to talk to Reggie again."

"Reggie who?"

"Koontz, I told you about him. My first boyfriend."

"Reggie Koontz, where did that come from?"

She wiped the tears from her cheek as she said, "He needs to be brought to justice."

"Vigilantes don't do personal."

Disappointment canvassed her expression. "Can you drop me off at home tonight? I have to talk with Sammie about the future."

"Sure, I need time to go over the materials I picked up at the recovery trailer. Given the right leads this project isn't over yet."

"I want to sift through the paperwork and see what I can find too," Hope said.

"How about I pick you up at noon?"

"I'll catch a ride with Lenny to the bar, and we can go from there."

I was relieved Hope wasn't sore over the tough love I'd shown her about Reggie and responded, "Sounds like a plan."

CHAPTER 15

"Hell is empty. All the devils are here."

—*William Shakespeare*

Shortly after nine in the morning, I drove toward Lenny's for my rendezvous with Hope. Eager to get the day started I skipped breakfast and planned to treat Hope to brunch. She'd had time to digest Matt's killing of the Undertaker, and I anticipated a slew of questions.

The Wrangler's run-flat tires sprayed gravel under the wheel wells in the taverns parking lot. It was doubtful I could stealthily approach a target with the noise it made, and I questioned whether they had been a sound investment.

I pulled to a stop near the front door and killed the engine. Lenny's pickup wasn't in the parking area as I expected. I looked at my watch. Lenny was a businessman and had found the mornings easier to complete paperwork and make orders uninterrupted. Whatever had caused the delay was likely due to Lenny. Hope was reliable.

The bar was due to open at eleven and with five minutes to spare Lenny's pickup sped into the parking lot grinding the brakes to a stop near the side entrance. Lenny jumped out from the driver's side and entered the building. Seeing only Lenny, I followed him to the side-door entrance. I tried to open the door, but it was locked. After I'd knocked twice, Lenny cracked the door about two inches and stared.

"Where's Hope? She was catching a ride with you."

Lenny responded, "Do you know Sammie?"

"What happened? Don't tell me something happened to Sammie?" It would devastate Hope if Sammie reacted badly to their conversation. Hope had planned to break the news to Sammie that she wanted to spend more time with me and less with her which might not have sat well.

Lenny closed the door, and the sound of the bolt latch slid into place. The weird vibes from Lenny lingered in the air like a foul odor. He was passing the buck. He knew what was going on, but he wasn't willing to tell or trust me with the information.

I'd walked only a few feet from the door when Lenny called out, "Try Holy Cross Hospital."

My heart sunk.

It was a half hour's drive to Holy Cross that I made in twenty-two minutes flat. At the reception desk, I asked the portly man lodged behind a computer screen in a small cubicle if he could help with locating a patient. He sat a white bread sandwich aside and said, "Name?"

"Samantha Ebert."

He brushed breadcrumbs from his whitish Van Dyke goatee and entered the name into the computer.

"No sir, nothing under Ebert."

"How about Hope Lockwood?"

"Yes, I have that name. Check with the fourth-floor nursing station. Take the elevator in tower one."

If Sammie had been severely injured or otherwise incapacitated, it made sense Hope might have the room listed in her name. I feared that wasn't the case.

On the fourth floor, the elevator opened into a foyer with a counter that spanned nearly the width of the reception area. On either side of the nurse's station were brightly lit hallways leading to patient rooms. The staff was busy working with charts and talking on phones. Catching the attention of a nurse who had placed a chart into a rolling rack I asked, "Hope Lockwood's room please."

She looked over at a whiteboard and read, "Room 465," then added, "The hall to your left."

The door was ajar when I pushed it open far enough to get a good look. Sammie sat in a metal framed chair with her back toward the entrance, hunched over the edge of the bed, and holding the hand of a person lying supine.

Silently, I slipped through the doorway to draw closer. Heavily bandaged about her head, Hope's delicate jawline was visible. I was staggered by what I saw and was unaware that Sammie had noticed my entry. She reached and took my hand. Our eyes met, she looked at me helplessly then pulled me in the direction of where Hope lay. Only the slight hum of the electronic medical machinery rose over the haunting silence.

"Was it a car accident?"

Distraught, Sammie shook her head.

"Don't make me guess."

"Someone…" Sammie whispered, "An animal." The tone of her voice sharpened as she spoke once more, louder this time. "Some…thing…did this to her!"

I lifted Sammie's chin until our eyes met, "Tell me everything."

Fresh tears rolled down her cheeks as she spoke. Her voice trembling, "We talked last night before she went back out. She had gotten this crazy idea that she was going to save the world from all the horrible, nasty people that were in it. Just crazy talk."

"What else did she say?"

"She said there were ways to help children escape the vile things that she'd seen and been put through as an under-aged prostitute." Sammie paused to regain her composure before continuing, "She was adamant, Mister Hunter, that you were in that line of work. Is that true? Do you rescue children?"

"I have."

Sammie looked back at Hope lying motionless with tubes running in and out of her body. "She told me that she needed to be more aggressive and that she found her niche in life. I believe she left last night to pursue that idea."

"Did she say where she was going or whether she was meeting anyone?"

"No, I don't think so."

"How did she get to the hospital?"

"I asked the same question of the officers. A man found her in a park about midnight. She was unconscious and beaten. He called the police and stayed with her until they arrived."

"Where?"

"Lent's Park."

My gut wrenched with an awkward and ill feeling. I wondered if she'd gone to find Icky at the Lucky Strike Saloon. She knew my intentions of cleaning out that den of iniquity and Lent's Park sat only a block from the tavern.

I shared in the responsibility for what had happened to Hope. I'd purposely planted thoughts about my missions to persuade her to join me but didn't realize the ramifications the invitation carried.

Hope was a babe in the woods when it came to understanding the dangers that lurked on the dark side of reconnaissance. Maybe I bore the responsibility for this error in judgment having encouraged her participation in my vigilante quest too quickly.

I moved up next to the head of the bed and softly stroked Hope's cheek. "If she wakes, tell her I was here and that I'm sorry."

Turning, I walked toward the exit then stopped. "When Hope was transported to the hospital did you see a gun with her clothing and purse?"

"No, she was naked and her clothes taken. Besides, Hope knew I didn't allow guns in my house. They do not serve a useful purpose."

I nodded. "I'll bet she wished she'd had one when whoever it was beat the hell out of her."

I took a few more steps toward the door when Sammie said, "The police want to speak to you, Mister Hunter."

I stopped in my tracks. After a moment's pause, I shrugged it off. I had vermin to kill.

I climbed behind the wheel of the Wrangler and placed a call to Anna. After a minute's worth of casual chat, I asked if she'd dug deeper into the Castle Rock properties owned by the PI Clinic doctor.

"The clinic's owner is not the same person as the Washington property's owner. A physician's assistant, Albert Tomas, is the owner. He is listed as employed at the clinic."

"That's helpful."

"I was thinking, if we can work out the details, maybe you would like to see the Isle of Mann when you tie off your operation?"

"Sure, I'd like that. But first, I have some Icky business to take care of. After that, I'd be happy to visit."

"Great, I will hold you to the date."

Back at my apartment, I realized there was no way to think through what happened to Hope. I had to get back on point. I fired up the Jeep and cruised the main drag in Lent's. I reached back in time to my military days where I walked point on a fire team. Often, we encountered enemy combatants who would lie in wait to ambush. The point man was the easiest target in the fire team. However, the enemy allowed the point to walk past their hidden positions to attack the main body. On point, I was positioned approximately fifteen meters in front of the team as we worked our way through the jungle terrain. My responsibility was to detect booby-traps and engage enemies before they had an opportunity to launch an attack. Walking behind the M-60 gunner weighted down with bandoleers of ammo wasn't all that exciting. But on point with a government issued M-16 gave me the feeling of hunting rather than being a pack mule. Point was where I was most comfortable.

Less than an hour passed and I found myself back in Lenny's bar. I wasn't interested in a drink. Sitting with my back against the wall at the table where Hope and I had met I waited for Lenny to take my order. After a twenty minute wait where we exchanged glances, he realized I wasn't leaving and called out from behind the counter, "What are you having?"

"Coffee."

I could tell Lenny wasn't himself and I wasn't me. I surmised we had both suffered from the tragedy that befell Hope.

When Lenny arrived with the coffee, I said, "Have a seat."

In a curt tone, he said, "Don't think I will."

I kicked the chair out from the table and said, "Sit."

Lenny would have been a lot to handle, but I could see he wasn't looking for trouble. He pulled the chair back a little further from the table and sat down. "Make it fast," he said.

"I went and saw Hope at Holy Cross."

"Anybody see you at the hospital?"

"You can ask Sammie if you want, but how does that make any difference? Do you know what happened?"

"No, do you?"

Lenny left the impression he thought I was involved or somehow responsible for what happened to Hope.

"I know she was beaten. I don't know why and I don't know who, but I intend to find out, and when I do, there will be a reckoning. I don't have any leads or much to go on to find who is responsible, so I'm looking for help. It's the only way I can piece together what happened. Tell me what you know of her movements last night?"

Lenny's eyes flared with anger, his words lashed out, "Last time I saw her, she was with you." He wanted to do something, anything, to avenge Hope. "She didn't come in last night. I wished she would have. I would never let anything happen to her."

Lenny remained suspicious and tried to find out if I had anything to do with Hope's brutal attack. I understood. I probed him with the same intention. His anger was too genuine to have hidden any dark secrets. I turned my attention to information. "I'm afraid Sammie wasn't any help either. She didn't know where Hope had gone."

Lenny fighting back the tears said, "Hope called late last night and asked for a ride home. She never showed." He rose from the table and motioned with his hand toward the bar's counter, "I need to get back to business."

As the caffeine hit my system, my mental acuity sharpened. Was Icky to blame for what happened to Hope? I didn't have a gut sense that he was responsible. But I wanted it to be him, Lanky or even Chuck. Somebody in the circle at the Lucky Strike knew what happened. All I needed was proof to act. That left me with no choice but to recon the Lucky Strike. Afterward, I would conduct a targeted follow up with Chuck and felons. Vigilantism has its perks. Likely one of the faction would drop a dime on those responsible for Hope's injuries.

I'd no sooner walked from the counter toward my table when I heard the entry door slap shut. Brandon A. Ware dressed in a new suit and tie and with the grin of a Cheshire Cat, looked the part of a hard-boiled detective. I didn't have time for his foolishness. His stay or mine would be short.

Ware stopped by the bar and asked for a cup of coffee then made his way to where I sat.

In a humorous Irish flat-foot manner Ware quipped, "Mister Goe, I hope I'm not interrupting your plans for today?"

Sarcasm and a smile, he was on his game. I retorted, "You are, but that won't change anything."

"You wouldn't mind if I had a seat, would you? Perhaps I can buy you a drink?"

"Sorry buddy, I'm spoken for already." I looked around the barroom and said, "Maybe you can find another guy in here that will suit your needs."

Ware laughed. "It will only take a minute of your time. I am surprised to see you out and about."

Here we go again. Didn't this guy have anything better to do than shadow me? "Yeah, I work the late shift, usually."

"I meant alone, but since you brought it up, what work would that be?"

He waited for an answer that he wasn't entitled to, but I threw him a bone, "Public relations."

Ware's broad smile reflected he had something up his sleeve and didn't want to spring it too early in our chat. He wanted me to know what it was so I could play along.

"Your friend Anna is as mysterious as you are. People have histories that can be researched. But just like your background, she's a blank page. How do you explain that?"

"You know it's odd you brought her up. I was talking to her earlier. Just so you don't worry, she's doing fine, but it completely slipped my mind you wanted to talk with her."

"Don't let that bother you too much. I'm sure we'll have a chance to visit one of these days."

"Maybe your researchers missed what's there. I can't explain what you or others have done in your searches."

"Sasins appears in the records when she is an adult."

"That ought to be enough for an investigation."

"It's odd she doesn't have a mother, father, schools attended, or birth record on file."

"From a journalistic perspective, I've noted government records are often corrupted and usually inefficient sources."

"Your files are the same. You have a birth record on file in the state, but the origin doesn't have a trail. Can you explain that?"

"I thought I just did."

"I'm sure you can do better than blame the government."

"No clue. I don't know about Anna's past. I assumed what she'd said about herself to be true. You're asking me to explain some mystery that isn't a mystery to me."

"You're not surprised?"

"At what?"

"That you and Sasins are blank pages."

"Hey, you said yourself you found history on both of us. I think you're sore because you want our backgrounds to tell you something that's not there. That's not my fault or hers. I can't speak for Anna, but I don't have a rap sheet and have never been involved in a crime. Maybe there's not much to find on a law-abiding citizen."

Still coming at me with the smiles, Ware said, "I tell you what I believe Mister Goe."

"I can't wait to hear it."

"You and Sasins have powerful and influential friends within government agencies who have manipulated your profiles to suit their needs."

I shrugged, "Yeah, buddy, I'm a high roller."

"I ran your names with a contact at the Witness Protection Program."

"He didn't find anything, did he?"

Ware confidently said, "I think he did." Then with a nod, he continued, "He called and told me to back off—its government business."

Surprised by what Ware had recounted, I wondered what error his contact had made that he wasn't able to search for records. Anna's Palatini Cobbler had created an outstanding false passport, visa, and other related documents when I went to Thailand. I assume she used the same Cobbler for my driver's license and inserted my false identity into the Oregon State data system. To my way of thinking, Ware still didn't have the answers that he'd come for and would continue to shadow my movements.

"Where is that lovely blonde girlfriend of yours?"

"Search me."

Ware's cartoonish expression set the stage for his response. "Strange, she spent all those late nights with you, and suddenly she disappears?"

"I don't have time for your nonsense Ware. Cut to the chase."

"I know your girl is in serious condition at the hospital." Ware nodded with his comment. "I'm just wondering how that tragedy occurred."

"So am I."

He paused and glanced over his shoulder then spoke in a low tone, "I think people turn up missing or dead when they cross your path."

I had to laugh. "Well, I guess you better be careful because you never leave my side. According to your theory that could be deadly."

It was Ware's turn to laugh. "I'm not worried. But I would like to know who I'm spending my time with, Hunter one day and Walter the next. I have my doubts that either of them is your true identity."

We stared at each other, neither of us breaking the focus. It was threatening behavior, full of intimidation and provocation, on both our parts.

"You're a real player, Walter. I'll give you that. You live with one respectable lady, use her expensive car, turn around and pick up hookers, and now you're out on the town looking for another lady companion."

"Jealous?"

"Not in the least."

"That's a shame. I might've been able to hook you up." I had to give Ware credit, he'd been a damn good cop in his day, and it showed. As a competitive and skilled adversary that kept continual pressure on my movements, he'd earned the respect I had for him.

As Ware continued his discourse, it dawned on me, if he kept me jacking my jaw one of his technician buddies could plant a sophisticated tracking device on my Wrangler. If I hurried, I might catch them in the act. Abruptly I said, "Gotta go!"

"I heard your girl was found in the park next to where your friend Moore hangs out. Maybe it's a coincidence, maybe it's not."

As I turned toward the exit, I said, "Maybe? What have you heard?"

"Something...maybe nothing."

"Yeah, well, you and I both know that maybe is never right."

Ware's big, toothy smile reappeared. "I'll be around," he said, his voice forceful enough to ensure he could be heard.

Once outside I was alone in the parking lot. Behind the wheel of the Wrangler, I drove circles around the park, stopped and looked at what might be a crime scene or possible evidence. Unable to locate where Hope was found I cruised the streets around the Lucky Strike Saloon. I was coming up empty. I didn't have a lead to go on. It was too early to interview the bar crowd that I was interested in. There wasn't a vehicle parked outside the saloon I recognized. Chuck was likely tending bar, and as much as I would have liked to beat some answers out of him, I fought off the urge.

It was one of those days when I welcomed the phone call that interrupted my thoughts. I wasn't disappointed. "Is this Mister Hunter?"

"Yeah, shoot."

"Shortly after you left the nurse ushered me out of Hope's room. It scared me so bad I didn't know what was going on. The doctors took her off that intubation tube."

"I'm sorry to hear that, Sammie. Hope was a good person and—"

"She's still a good person. The doctors had her sedated and intubated but brought her back to consciousness. I talked with her. I wouldn't call her lucid, but she mumbled something about Reggie. Do you know the story about him?"

"Hope mentioned him in an unfavorable light."

"Yes, that would be him."

"Do you think he had something to do with what happened to Hope?"

She paused. I gave her time to think her answer through clearly. "She repeated the words, 'motions,' 'Reggie,' and 'Pearl.' Does that mean anything to you?"

I thought out loud in the hope Sammie might hear me say something that rang a bell. "Pearls, in motion, swirling, floating in the air, pearls on the move—"

Sammie cut me off, "I wasn't counting, but four or five times she said the same thing, motions in Pearl, not the other way around."

"Okay, thanks, Sammie, I'll think about it and see what I come up with. How is Hope doing?"

"The doctor says she's resting comfortably, but they'll have to run tests when she's recovered consciousness fully. She's still groggy."

"That sounds positive. By the way, how did you get my number?"

"Hope has always journaled. She makes notes about everything."

Sammie had no way of knowing that the word Pearl had struck a chord, and she didn't need to know. Like Lents, Pearl was a district in downtown Portland. It was a long shot, but Destiny stirred in my soul. From my earliest vigilante quest Destiny dwelt with me and within my heart. People wouldn't believe me or understand, but her spirit has guided me as an Angel of Light and now inspires me to explore Pearl.

Portland like many other cities have an online Yellow Pages available twenty-four seven. I rushed to my Collins Best apartment and used my laptop to get online. Marveling at the speed of the Internet to produce results with the simplest of terms placed in the browser. Motions in Pearl was a winning ticket. The advertisement called it a gentlemen's club with adult entertainment. In other words, a strip joint.

Like most adult clubs, Motions didn't open its doors until late afternoon. Taking advantage of the time I used the power of the Internet to explore the name, Reggie Koontz. I didn't have the time to have Anna's source run the name in depth. I had to shoot from the hip.

Reggie or Reginald Koontz was an uncommon name in the Portland area having only a few listings available through the browser. There was the usual Facebook reference to a Koontz in Portland, but the first name wasn't Reggie. A couple more references appeared to prominent people with the same last name which I doubted had any connection with him. There were also fifty-three public records advertised and available for a small fee. Not a wise place to leave your credit card number like a fingerprint that can be traced.

By six in the evening, I'd finished three more cups of coffee and my online search. It occurred to me that if, Hope's purse and clothing had been taken by the perp who assaulted her and not by some passersby who saw opportunity in the late-night situation to better their own prosperity, the perp might have her cell phone. I gave Hope's number a call.

It rang only twice and the line connected. I waited for a greeting. "Hello," I said. Although the person who answered didn't speak, the music in the background came across the receiver clear and distinct, a Carlos Santana tune that I recognized.

Whoever had the phone made no attempt to muffle the background noise. When the music stopped the receiver picked up what sounded like more than two people talking and more than one conversation. Unfortunately, the words came across fuzzy like word salad. Just before the call disconnected, a women's voice came across clearly as if she was close to the phone's receiver, saying, "Hey honey." She wasn't talking to me.

I was wrong when I told Hope that vigilantes didn't do personal vendettas. I wanted her to stay focused because other fish had to be fried first. But, as a special favor to myself, I determined to take as much time out of my schedule as needed to track down the people responsible for Hope's condition.

With the lead Sammie had given me, the Pearl District in downtown Portland was the right place to start. There wasn't much to like in that part of town, and subsequently, I wasn't familiar with the inner city. The area seemed miserably cold, having less to do with the weather and more by the city's design. A chill that crept up from inside the body, not a penetrating cold that entered a person through the skin's barrier. The assemblage of towering steel and glass structures interwoven with concrete sidewalks that laid dormant during the night. A cold, cold area for life to be lived.

When I reached Motions in Pearl my first impression of the dark and seedy club was that I'd arrived in a holding pen for the Hellbound. Drug infested lowlifes without redeeming qualities lined the meat rack with their chairs scooted close to the edge of the dance floor for the best view of what their money could buy. I shrugged off the distraction and continued past the pool table to the bar. I didn't get many looks from the locals until I tossed a sawbuck on the countertop for a five-dollar beer. Even then there was no big commotion, but I knew the girls wouldn't be far behind. Word travels fast when there is money to be had.

I watched to see if my next move caused a stir when I took a seat at a corner table with my back to the wall. From my vantage point, I could see the patrons as they entered and exited the joint. Better than that, I had a good view of the bar and table area. I didn't feel lonely sitting alone, not with a three-hundred-pound bouncer seated nearby at the entryway. I figured he was only doing his job when he approached where I'd taken refuge and quietly said, "Take the hood off when you're in here." Lowering my hood prompted a smile through his burly black beard. He shuffled back to his stool by the doors and sat, glancing only occasionally in my direction.

Dancers, when not on the stage, made their rounds taking drink orders and hustling lap dances. It was a helluva distraction to my recon.

It wasn't long before an angel-like creature floated near my table and exchanged a brief eye-twinkling smile. I acknowledged her with a nod. That's all it took, she was in the chair next to me in an instant, her auburn hair falling in thick waves onto her shoulders. One eye peeked out from under a thick curtain of bangs.

"What's your poison?" I asked.

"Champagne babe, its hot in here tonight."

Gesturing to the barkeep, he nodded in response.

She continued, "Where are you from, honey?"

"Born and bred right here in Oregon."

"A real globetrotter, huh?"

"I took a trip once, before your time. It wasn't all that it was cracked up to be."

"Where was that?"

It was all routine jabber that went hand-in-hand with the game she played, but she wasn't the only one holding cards. It suited me too. Continuing I said, "A little Asian country you've probably never heard of. I spent a year there and didn't care for it, so I made tracks back to Oregon and been here ever since. What's your name?"

"Sherry."

Before I had a chance to finish our introductions another dancer brought Sherry's champagne. I paid up front and gave her a healthy tip so she'd remember where I was sitting and come by often. Lifting my beer to touch her glass I said, "My name's Hunter."

While we sipped our drinks, I remembered Hope saying, young dancers, like this one, picked up a few bucks on the side turning tricks.

I didn't want to have that conversation. I wasn't buying her off-duty services, only her time.

She fired up a cigarette and let a perfectly formed smoke ring lazily drift from her lips. "Have you been here before Hunter?"

"First time."

"What do you think?"

"I don't see how you make money in a place like this."

"Don't kid yourself, there's money here. It's not always in the suit and tie crowd. What brings you out tonight?"

"What brings any man out?"

"You're funny, Hunter. I like you already."

We toasted again touching glasses and took a drink. Sherry flipped her hair over one shoulder while casually shifting her eyes to mine. "Did you see me dance earlier?"

"No, I would have remembered. Probably wasn't here yet."

"You like what you see?"

"Sure."

"Well, there's more."

"I'll be watching you for sure."

Fifteen minutes passed while we made small talk about her career. What followed our exchange was predictable. There was money to be made. If we spoke long enough, Sherry probably had the same type of story as Hope. "I have to get around the floor to other tables, but I'll be looking for you when I dance."

"I'll be looking too. Before you go, is this the usual crowd?"

She scanned the room before she answered, "For a Tuesday night, yeah, pretty much."

It paid dividends to remember that bars operated to make a profit. Strip joints were no different. If it seemed like a game, play it, everybody does. Money talks, but you can't be stupid with it, or you'll attract too much attention and seem phony to the hustlers. If you are generous and thankful for the attention, you'll be treated with respect.

I waited for Sherry to dance, moved up on the meat rack, smiled and showed my appreciation with a steady flow of Washington's. I made sure she saw me encourage the two jokers seated nearby to contribute to her college fund the same way. They thought it was a competition and shelled out more. Sherry let me slide a Lincoln into the back of her panties. When I hooted, the boys next to me couldn't let me get away with that and matched my contribution. Sherry was well worth the wait and as good as they came at Motions Gentlemen Club.

After Sherry's three-song performance, I returned to my table. She'd be back soon, and I had business to take care of before her return. The entertainment had a lull in the action between dancers to accommodate the patron's needs. I sat my cell phone on the table and pressed the numbers for Hope's phone. When the call connected, I muted the microphone and watched the movement and behaviors of the clientele.

One man, a thirty-five-ish-year-old who looked like a bad copy of Vanilla Ice, put a phone to his ear. With as many calls that are placed and received it could merely be a coincidence, but if he stayed on the line long enough, I'd know for sure. The next dancer had made it to the stage. Foghat's Slow Ride started to play as the new dancer walked toward the pole at the forward section of the stage. It echoed in my phone's receiver clear as a bell. He disconnected the call, stood, and walked to the bar. He sported a big smile when he turned toward the pool table and drank from a fresh beer. I wondered if, in his thoughts when the phone call came in, that he relived some aspect of what had happened to Hope, which made him grin ear to ear.

He removed his ball cap then repositioned it using the mirror behind the bar. Finally, he pulled it down tight to finish off the look of cool. The flat bill of the Pittsburgh Pirates baseball cap sat cockeyed off one side of his closely cropped haircut.

I heard him call out to someone he knew, "Yo-Yo my maaaan," then step from the bar to greet them with a fist bump. Another guy stood up from a table and likewise *daped* with the new arrival. My newly acquired target tossed his arm around one of the dancers who was walking past the trio, she shrugged him off. His cool stopped there.

CHAPTER 16

"Revenge, the sweetest morsel to the mouth
that ever was cooked in hell."

—*Sir Walter Scott*

"Last call," the bartender announced across the scratchy PA system. A moment later he flipped on the extra lighting above the bar signaling the dancer to cut the stage show short. Sherry was long gone having slipped out the back door earlier without saying goodbye. A paltry four customers remained in the show house. Vanilla was one of them.

Squeaky and high pitched, Vanilla's voice grated on my last nerve. He needed a dose of testosterone. The barkeep called him to the counter, addressing him by the name, "Reggie." His cocky walk fresh off the MTV channel betrayed him as an actor and a bad one at that. He came off superficial like he didn't know who he really was. One minute he talked like a hipster, the next, he thought he was a gangster. I'd engaged and killed Mafioso and street hoods. Vanilla didn't even measure up to wannabe status.

What was he? Punk came to mind. He was a common hood rat with cheap bling. A Nobody. I'd sized Reggie up quick because there wasn't much to him. He was all about ego. You didn't have to stroke his sense of self-worth he did that without any help. All he needed was a platform to crow from, and this little rooster would find his head lopped off. He might have been tough with the young girls, but I'm surprised he'd survived this long.

A free drink was my preferred method of breaking the ice and gaining a target's trust, but it was too late for the formalities. There was a stirring deep inside. Destiny had awakened the beast within me.

Shaking hands with the bouncer at the door I made my way to the Wrangler that was parked near the entrance. My wristwatch showed it was past two in the morning and the streets reflected the time—deserted. Reggie stepped through the doorway alone and be-bopped south on Northwest Lovejoy Street. I figured he had a hike ahead of him. As far as I could see it looked like an industrial complex.

I swung alongside Reggie, hit the passenger power window, and called to him, "Hey, you just left the club, right? Jump in, and I'll give you a ride."

"Cool, cool, my brother, that is way cool of you to do."

Vanilla hopped into the passenger seat, "What's your name, m'man?"

"Hunter."

"Thanks, Yo, I'm Reggie."

"No problem, just call out the directions and I'll get you home."

We continued south for two blocks. Reggie carried the conversation, although I wished he'd kept his mouth shut. All the yo, yo, and maaaan stuff in his squeaky voice was driving me crazy.

"Haven't seen you around, Yo."

"New to the area...thought I'd check the club out."

"Hell yeah, that's what I'm talkin' 'bout. Plenty of girls and I've had most of 'em."

"That's why I'm there...can't beat the action." Reggie put his fist up, and we bounced knuckles in a fist bump.

"Take a left at the stop sign, and it's on the right side of the street. You can pull up beside the house if you want to."

The flat driveway circled around behind the house. An old faded blue beater set three-quarters of the way into the drive blocking the route next to the house. I pulled to a stop, curbside, in front of the cement walk that led to the house. "How about a beer, man? It's on me for the ride."

Tapping my finger against my lips, I gave it a minute before answering, "Sure, why not. The bars close too early 'round here anyhow."

Similar to the Lent's District, Pearl had suffered from a subsidized housing project years earlier. What was left of a downturned local economy resembled what I'd seen in a dozen other inner cities. Urban renovations rarely ease the conditions of the poor. It only made the bleeding hearts that had raised tax money for the project feel better about their surroundings.

The 1950s, small ranch style house Reggie was calling home wasn't any larger than eleven hundred square feet and no garage.

Reggie led the way across a patch of grass and onto a broken concrete walkway that led to the entrance. On either side of Reggie's place were similar cookie-cutter single units. As best I could tell the nearby homes all had their lights off, which wouldn't be unusual for two-thirty in the morning.

"Yo, cop a seat," Reggie said, pointing to a badly worn sofa.

"Hey, don't toss the word cop around so loosely."

Reggie responded with a grin and a high-five then took off down the short hallway. I put my hand on the handle of my .40-caliber in the event I needed it to respond quickly. He unbolted the door at the end of the hall and stepped into the room.

Behind the closed door, I could hear Reggie's voice grow louder and stern. The distinct sound of a slap followed by a woman crying was disturbing. When Reggie reappeared, he made a beeline for the refrigerator, pulled a couple beers out, and handed me one before sitting on a wooden chair.

"Where you from, yo?"

"Florida."

"No way. That's why you were at the club tonight," he exclaimed.

"Why's that?"

"You a lonely man. But it's your lucky day my man cause the doctor is in the house. I can hook you up with a sweet young thing tonight, what you think, man?"

"You talkin' about a girl, right?"

"Hell yeah. I don't do no flippin' pretty boys. She's the kind of girl that'll treat you right."

Again, I faked serious contemplation. "So that's why you had more than one cell phone. You're a businessman."

Reggie was quick on the uptake. "That's right, my man, too much action to handle on only one phone, yo." Like a parakeet on a perch bobbing his head, he displayed three phones. "I'm your genie in the bottle, yo. Man, if you can dream it—I can deliver."

Reggie had no idea that he'd landed square in the middle of my dreams, and when it escaped my control, it would be his nightmare.

"Listen, man, she's cheap tonight. I'll let her go for thirty-five bucks." He waited for my response. When I didn't bite right away he said, "Com'on man, you looked at it all night, you might as well get some."

"I've never paid for sex, I don't know if it'll feel right."

"It feels the same, maybe better, cause you don't have to cuddle her when you're done. Just come back out when you want another beer."

"Yeah, but paying for it—."

Reggie interrupted, "You think a married man don't pay for it. Yo, it's a lot more than thirty-five dollars a throw. It costs those dudes their whole stinking paycheck and for what? The same old thing once a week, and that's if they're lucky. Thirty-five bucks a bargain for some strange. I'll set it up with the girl and make it happen. All you got to do is enjoy the ride, yo."

"What's the girl's name? I ought to know her name. Otherwise, it'll be too awkward."

"Rachel…but yo, you can call her whatever you want if it makes you more comfortable. She'll do whatever you tell her to."

"Are there other people in the house?" I unzipped my brown leather jacket giving Reggie the idea I was planning to take him up on his offer. He laughed loudly, "You afraid of a little audience?" He sniggered again. "You don't have to worry it's going to be just you and her—alone." Reggie extended his hand palm up, "Where's the money, brother?"

I pulled out the exact amount letting Reggie see there was more where that came from and handed it to him. He responded with, "Cha-ching. Hang right here, and I'll introduce you two lovebirds."

Reggie walked to the room at the end of the hall and talked at the doorway with a young girl who looked to be maybe fifteen years old.

I didn't like the cards I was dealt, but dictates of the game forced me to play the hand or fold. I wasn't leaving. I'd made a vow to the weak, innocent, young, elderly, sick, distraught and downtrodden, to deliver them from evil. I'd always kept my promises and intended to play.

Rachel's head hung low as Reggie led her out of the room by the hand. With her hair pulled back in a ponytail and dressed in a matching T-shirt and gym shorts, she appeared to be about twelve-years-old. Briefly, she looked up at me when being introduced and just as quickly dropped her eyes to the floor. I motioned to her to have a seat next to me on the nasty sofa while I finished my beer.

In the process of standing to meet Rachel and sitting down again, Reggie caught a glimpse of my gun. Immediately, he reacted, but not in the way I'd expected.

"Yo, what's that," he shouted, pointing in the direction of my weapon.

"What, my pistol?"

"Hell, yeah!" Reggie pulled up his untucked shirt displaying the butt of a handgun stuffed into the waistband of his pants. The way they sagged below the top of his underwear, I wondered how the gun stayed wedged in there.

Reggie had given up his trump card and evened the playing field when he displayed his weapon. A surprise attack was the only element to victory left to be discovered. Reggie's low self-esteem kicked into high gear with story after story he rattled off, each ending with him capping some thug or putting a gang to flight. "Yo, man, did you hear about those EastEnders in South Portland?"

"Something recent?"

Reggie smirked, "Like two weeks ago, maaaan, I had to fight my way through a mess of them."

Easily, I could have trapped him in his lies. I was the one who eliminated the EastEnders threat that night, but instead, I played along. "That's pretty impressive."

When I acted like I was losing interest Reggie upped the ante. Leaning forward and with a convincing serious tone, he said, "It's all about street rule...and I know how to do it right." Reggie backed up his words with a hard, cold stare that he'd practiced in a mirror. His eye's narrowed and his eyebrows knit together forming wrinkles across his forehead. He scanned the room as if engaged in a criminal act. He reached under his shirt and pulled out the handgun and waved it around like an amateur with his finger on the trigger. "Yo, I'll tell you, m'man, I keep it close by just in case. Sweet, huh?"

Reggie held up his hand to display the small automatic.

"What kind of gun is it?" I asked.

Reggie, unfamiliar with the weapon, read the gold inlay inscription. "Beretta .380-caliber." He didn't know what a .380 was and likely had never heard of a Beretta.

The handgun with the gold inlay was, however, familiar to me. The weapon that I'd given to Hope. I'd had questions initially, but now I didn't care to hear his lying answers. His fate was sealed. "What did it run you?"

"I don't know what they cost, but if you're tough enough to beat some sucker down and take it from him, then you can have one too."

"Wow, that's what you had to do?"

"Yo, m'man, beat the dude unconscious and took it and his money. I owned him. Now why don't you use the back room and do your business? Rachel will take you there."

The young girl stood as if in a trance reminiscent of the Eloi from H.G. Wells' The Time Machine. Subterranean hells are alike. Morlock's or John's—no real difference. Rachel, without uttering a peep, led the way. Once inside her room, she shut and locked the door from the inside. I turned slowly, my eyes swept the breadth of the dimly lit room. Nothing more than a box spring and mattress that had seen better days sat below the boarded up window and pushed against the wall. It wasn't a homey atmosphere.

I took her by the hand and led her to the bed. Her countenance changed as she sat on the edge of the bed and waited for my command. It was as if she had disengaged reality and had slipped into an alternate existence to escape.

"Reggie said you were a good girl and will do whatever I tell you to do."

Rachel, holding back the tears, said, "Please don't hurt me."

"I can't promise you won't feel pain, but I'll do my best to make it quick." Rachel nodded.

"Don't lie to me, tell me your age?"

"Sixteen."

"You look younger than sixteen."

"If you're worried about my age just say I'm legal."

"Slavery isn't legal. You're not old enough to make it legal and that pimp you call a boyfriend, isn't legal."

"Please, I don't want to make you mad. I'm just trying to make Reggie happy."

"This is going to come as a surprise to you, but you're not the first girl to believe Reggie's lies. Where's your phone?"

"I don't have one. Why? Please don't call the cops, that'll only make things worse."

For a moment I had a glimpse into the life Hope lived when she was with Reggie. "Do you know how to drive a car, Reggie's car?"

"I guess."

"Collect your stuff, anything you want to keep. You're leaving for good."

"I can't go. I don't have any place to go."

"This is the part that's going to hurt. Reggie is a parasite. He lives, pays the rent, and buys his drugs and alcohol by selling you. I'm not the first guy he's brought here, but I will be the last. Get your stuff now."

Rachel picked out clothing from two cardboard boxes at the foot of the bed and placed them in a garbage bag. She put on the warmest clothing she had for the outdoors and slipped on a heavy windbreaker. Hope's windbreaker. "The jacket looks new."

"Reggie gave it to me this morning." Rachel stared into my eyes. Maybe for the first time, she questioned what Reggie had told her. "I shouldn't have it, should I?"

"It looks good on you."

Rachel hung her head in silence, reluctant or afraid to take the steps to freedom.

"You can have friends, talk to family, or have a phone. Wise up. I'm giving you a chance to get out. If you want to stay, you can, but Reggie's world is ending."

Rachel nodded.

"Good… Stay here until I call your name to come out."

"Okay."

I slipped on my tight black leather police gloves, and pulled my .40-caliber from its holster, attaching the silencer with a twist. Rachel's eyes widened. She understood I was serious and this was happening.

Reggie yelled from the front room, "Awful quiet in there."

Cracking the door I complained, "What are you trying to sell me here? I want my money back." Rachel stood next to me shaking.

"You tryin' to cost me money, girl?" He tossed something aside, and continued to yell obscenities as he stomped down the short hallway. "When you're told to do something, you better do it, or your ass will be out on the street."

His rant came to an abrupt halt at the door. Admittedly, my .40-caliber with the silencer in place looked like a howitzer when it's up close and personal.

"Hey, yo, it don't have to go down like that. It's not your fault, brother. I'm feelin' your pain. That girl's just a young thing and untrained. If you want to leave, I'm cool with that. You can have your money back, too. Where is she, I'll get her taught up right."

"You're misunderstanding me, Reggie, she's going with me."

"Yo, m'man, you can't take my property for thirty-five dollars. That just ain't right. You can find your own girl, or we can renegotiate the money, and you can take her."

I laughed. "You really are dumber than the day is long. Turnaround." For the first time since he'd stepped into my Jeep, he was silent. It didn't last long.

"Oh, maaaan! You're a cop! Am I busted for this?" Obviously he'd done this before and with no further argument Reggie spun around in disgust, slapping the palms of his hands against the wall.

"Lay your face against the wall looking away from me and put both hands behind your back." After cinching tight the plastic ties, I stood him off the wall and gave him a solid push in the direction of the sofa.

Planting Reggie face first into the couch, I said, "Don't move." I closed the front room blinds and turned the bolt lock. I didn't want any interruptions while Reggie and I hashed out our differences. Rachel joined us with her belongings ready to go. Reggie rolled onto his side and watched while I took something away from him as he had from me. "Is Reggie's car drivable?"

"I think so."

"Okay, Reggie where are the keys to that nice ride of yours."

"She can't take my car." Reggie glanced at his jacket that hung on the back of the wood chair. Betrayed by his own eyes, I directed Rachel to look in the pockets of his coat. Voila!

Reggie continued to lie on the couch. With his eyes full of hate he muttered curses and a few choice words.

"You owe me thirty-five dollars, buddy." I patted him down and by the time he'd stopped squirming I'd recovered more than one hundred forty dollars. "Thanks, my man. You're financing this young lady's new lease on life."

Folding the money into Rachel's hand, I said, "Put it in your pocket, I'm sure you've earned it. Do you know where Denny's Café is located by the Interstate entrance?"

"I think so."

"Go and have a piece of pie. Don't go anywhere else or talk to anyone until I tell you, got it?"

"Don't listen to him Rachel," Reggie bellowed. "He's just going to use you as a sex slave."

"You're free. You don't have to go to Denny's. I'm trying to lend you a hand up onto your own two feet." I looked at Reggie, as I continued to address Rachel, "I'll call you after Reggie and I have caught up on old times."

"What phone number?"

"Denny's. If you're not there when I call then that's the way it is."

I turned the bolt latch and opened the door. Rachel stepped part way across the door's threshold, then turned to me, "You're not doing this because of me, are you?"

"Because of you? Yes...and the girl that came before you...and the one that would come afterward. Reggie has to be stopped."

"You've got a kind heart, Sir. I'm sorry I've forgotten your name."

"That'll work, now do what I asked and get out of here."

It had slipped my mind how nasty the house smelled until I watched Rachel take a deep whiff of the cool, fresh air. I let the door stand open until she was safely behind the wheel of the old faded blue Comet. Backing out the driveway, she narrowly missed the rear of my Jeep.

When her taillights had disappeared, my thoughts lingered for a moment on what Rachel had said about a kind heart. Reggie violated my contemplation spouting out, "She's a loser" at the top of his lungs. I responded by closing the door and re-engaged the bolt latch. Reggie didn't know, but the illusion of caring and kindness had come from a sense of righteousness that would not be wasted on him. Hidden behind a veneer of human flesh was an assassin and people like Reggie served to fuel my vicious insanity.

"Yo, I got it now, man, you one of those religious, right-wing do-gooders. M'man, I got a deep respect for that. We should pray together."

I shook my head. "I'm sure there will be prayers offered up before we're done."

"You seem like a reasonable man—"

Interrupting, I said, "Save it. I can't be bargained with, and I can't be bribed. You have nothing to offer."

What Reggie had discarded earlier that had caught my eye was Hope's Beretta. I leaned over and picked it up from the floor stuffing it in my back pocket.

"That's mine," Reggie said. Then it dawned on him the gun had something to do with why we were here. "Is it about what I said about taking the gun. Yo, you've won. You can have it. No need to beat me down, maaan."

"It does have to do with the gun, and you own this one."

"You talk in riddles, man. I don't understand." Reggie stared as a grim puzzled look came over his face. "What do you want from me?

"Hope is a friend of mine." I heard his breath catch in the silence. I continued, "The gun belongs to her."

"I don't know no Hope. I told you how I got it."

"The cell phone, the one I called, the one you answered, is Hope's too."

"I'm telling you the god-awful truth."

"The windbreaker you gave Rachel, the one she wore out of here, was Hope's."

With a tirade of brash and ugly words, he lambasted Hope. While he worked himself into a frenzy, I took my coat off and pulled my gloves on tight. Pulling him from the couch, he landed on the floor on his knees. Handcuffed he couldn't stop his fall. A well-placed kick to the chest toppled him to his back. As he lay stunned by my assault, I straddled his chest and said, "I want you to remember the last time you saw Hope." Blow after blow I struck him. Reggie had thugged on Hope. His size and strength didn't impress me, but to someone like Hope, she would have been helpless and utterly defenseless when he beat her repeatedly and without mercy. I wanted Reggie to feel what it was like to be in a similar predicament. Destiny stirred and swelled within me.

But I didn't want a quick kill. I stopped punching and began to choke him. Instinctively he struggled, squirmed, and gasped for breath. Nothing but fear registered in his eyes. With a determined viciousness, I savagely beat his ribs with hammer fists over and over I pounded on them. I continued to hit his rib cage with as much brutal force as I could muster. Reggie barely moved when I stopped. Signs of shock had set in. Standing to my feet, I stomped on his chest repeatedly. The sound of ribs breaking each time I thrust my heel into him was music to my ears. Blood oozed from his mouth. Bright red. Fresh.

He gurgled as blood filled his lungs. He had screamed in agony at the beginning, but only remnants of breaths could be heard in his feeble wheezes. I beat him into unconsciousness then crushed his larynx with a wooden table leg that I'd disassembled with a swift kick. When I was done the only thing moving was the river of blood that oozed slowly and silently across the floor. Justice had been served.

The drive to the diner took only minutes. Rachel was tucked away in a corner booth. I pulled my address book from my bug out bag and called the women's resource shelter hotline with one of my throw away phones. I explained I was a concerned citizen and knew the whereabouts of a teenage girl, vulnerable, and homeless that was in crisis and in need of an immediate intervention. After describing the girl by her clothing and name, I let them know her location.

As promised, I made the call to Denny's. The manager agreed to put Rachel on the phone after I had explained she was a lost teen and there were people en route to contact her. Most people want to be helpful and part of the solution, not part of the problem.

"This is Rachel."

"You know who this is?"

"Yes."

"Some good folks are on the way to help you. I don't know if you have a home to go to or if you want to go home, but you won't find what you need on the street. I'm no good at pep talks, I'm only asking you to give it a try."

"I'll try," she said. I could discern something akin to a new hopefulness in her voice.

I knocked off a couple energy drinks while I waited for shelter folks to arrive. Thankfully, they dealt the Portland Police Bureau out of this hand. Two women responded and sat with Rachel. I had to go.

I'd crawled into bed in my Collins Best apartment, daylight bled in around the borders of the bedroom shade. Dawn had the wrong address. While I'd waited for the crisis intervention team, a disturbing thought worked its way to the forefront of my consciousness. The Thaman project was far from over. There were two loose ends of concern. Henry, the man who had received monetary gain from the recruiters for the victims he'd sent their way. Secondly was Albert Tomas, the chief butcher and man at the helm. Matt may have found satisfaction, but I struggled with a job half done.

I slept on and off until noon then rolled out of the sack. A check of my phone indicated that I'd missed a call, but the voicemail box was empty. The likelihood of it being anyone other than Anna was remote.

The Isle of Mann had a ten-hour jump on us in Oregon, and I hoped to catch her before it was too late. As it turned out, Anna was wide-awake and office bound working to supply the needs of the operators. She cut to the chase. "Not receiving a report on your project doesn't translate into good news, Walter. I was concerned that something had happened."

"I was chasing a rabbit all night."

"Whatever you say. I was thinking about sending assistance your way to help wrap up your project. Thomas has a need for a small army of operators to join him south of the border.

"I don't need any help. I've been developing a local asset."

"How exciting, what's his name and how did you two meet?"

"Her name...is Hope, and we met at a watering hole."

Anna's silence was dicey.

To ease the tension, I asked, "How's Max?"

"Maximillian is recovering, and should be back in the position soon. Has Ware continued his harassment?"

"You know how he is, honey. I think he has a man-crush on me."

"Put your ego in check, Fabio, and be careful. He is the same police officer he has always been, only with more latitude as a private investigator. Twice, in the past week, I received calls that he made inquiries on our backgrounds."

"Usually, law enforcement is content if they can't find anything negative. He's taken it a step further. The mysterious lack of history galls him."

"I'll have the Cobbler borrow a few files and slip them into our data. That should take care of his curiosity. Have you told your asset about us?"

"I've kept the Palatini a secret."

"When you do, let her know I look forward to our meeting. Be careful, rabbits are notorious breeders."

"The joke was on her. Chasing rabbits had nothing to do with a female and everything to do with getting off my course of action. But I humored her, "Thanks for the tip."

We whispered our goodbyes.

Around three in the afternoon, I was in Lents and close to Lenny's Tavern. If my money was still good in the joint, I'd buy Lenny a drink, and see where his head was at. I pulled into the lot and braked to a stop near the entrance. It was déjà vu for a moment, only Hope didn't come running out and jump in my rig. Without her, it was just another tavern parking lot.

Lenny was cordial. I offered to buy him a round.

"Not necessary."

"Yeah, but I'd like to."

He picked up two tumblers, filled them with ice, and poured the glasses almost to the brim. I was getting my money's worth in this one. He handed me one glass and armed himself with the other. As we both took a swallow neither of us broke eye contact. I sat my drink on the edge of the bar, pulled out a Hamilton, and said, "Thanks, I needed that."

"You're here for a reason. Let's have it." Lenny had been around the bar scene a long time and had acquired the ability to read people fast. He was correct, I had come for a reason, but how to articulate it was the question.

"I don't get the connection between you and Hope," I said.

"A connection?"

"Yeah, you're what sixty-plus years old?"

"I love her if that's what you're driving at, Mister Hunter...not romantically... Never. As you well know, she is incredibly attractive, and yes, I have fantasized about her in my dreams. But I'm not foolish enough to think she has any interest in me outside of a father figure. I doubt if she knows what true love is."

"What about Sammie, the gal she lives with?"

"That's what she does ... survives with her. Don't misunderstand, she adores Sammie, and maybe, in her own way loves her. But, on more than one occasion we've talked about their relationship. She always came up short of describing it as love. Sammie is more like a mother figure than a lover.

You're barking up the wrong tree, Hunter. I'm not a suspect in what happened to her. I'm not a jilted lover. I don't agree with what she does but since I can't change her path I look after her the best I can. Maybe you're the one that should be answering questions?"

"I know you didn't have anything to do with the assault, I'm just shooting from the hip as to why you pick her up or take her home all the time."

"There doesn't have to be something in it for someone to act kindly to another person. I live a few blocks from Sammie's house. It's convenient, and she's been a friend. I'm happy to give her rides."

"Have you been to the hospital to see her, Lenny?"

"I'm going tomorrow, early."

"That's good. Sammie will appreciate that... I need to ask a favor. Can you tell Hope I asked about her?

"You're too busy to pay her a visit?"

"If you'll do me that favor and I will see her soon. Like you said, there doesn't have to be something in it for you to be kind to someone."

Lenny nodded and finished his drink before moving down the bar's counter to where the two locals had bellied up. I stepped away from the counter and placed a call to Thaman.

He answered, "Matt."

"I need you to be available tonight." He didn't have to ask who was calling.

CHAPTER 17

"Are people born wicked or do they have wickedness thrust upon them?"

—*Gregory Maguire*

"You said it was over." Matt snapped angrily.

"I changed my mind...now get over it. I don't want a lecture from a guy that goes off half-cocked and caps a guy before we have a chance to talk with him."

"Don't remind me."

"Well, I'm going to repeat it—everyday if I have to. You were a lawman once. Maybe you should have stuck with that. I don't know what your problem is, maybe a bad experience behind the badge, but you got your wires crossed. This ain't Law and Order, and you're not a cop. You're a killer plain and simple. Nothing special about what you did with the Undertaker, except you didn't use your head. You pulled the trigger out of anger. All you thought about was your brother and vengeance."

"I reacted…it was a bad situation."

"That's a lie, Matt. You didn't react except to fulfill a premeditated act. You planned to kill. I understand how it is, but you have to face the facts, and stop struggling with who you think you are and accept who you are."

"I'm not a cold-blooded killer if that's what you're saying."

"Yeah…well, you lost your white cowboy hat somewhere along the way. You killed a guy that needed killing. You've crossed over the edge, and there's no going back. You wanted revenge, and you got it. But, you're not satisfied, and you don't know why?"

Matt was silent. Dropping his self-pity and defensive posture was a step in the right direction. I needed Matt to be the killer that I'd seen in action.

"The Undertaker was only one of those responsible for your brother's death. You won't be satisfied until they all die. We need to move on together, or I'm dealing you out. What's it going to be?"

"I want them all. I owe my brother that much."

"Okay. I went through the paperwork from the Undertaker's office, and I came upon an interesting ledger filled with banking memos and check copies. Names of people that played a part in the body snatchers organization and had a hand in your brother's death."

"Who, how many?"

"Memos refer to them as security and clinical staff. I've sent it forward for analysis. We have a chance to make this thing right."

"Right," he repeated slowly. "How does any of this make it right?"

"Justice doesn't change what happened. Justice brings closure."

"I thought you were a journalist?"

"You knew I wasn't the minute I sprung you at the trailer. As long as we are revealing truth what you wanted Anna to do was uncover the identity of those involved so you could kill them. That was your plan all along."

Matt withheld comment.

"That's what I thought. So let's get started."

"Where?"

"Henry had talked about some others involved. Let's pay him a visit."

Matt, again, was silent. His attention diverted. "Henry won't work."

"He's a good source. He doesn't give truth up easy, but he's in the know, and it can be pried out of him."

"I saw Henry yesterday." Matt drew silent again.

"No...tell me you didn't."

"I asked him how many people he had sent to the doctor. He couldn't give me a straight answer. He guesstimated more than two dozen."

"That's more than he had admitted to before."

"He said they were all Veterans, part of his community, and friends of his. I asked him to show me, one survivor, but he never saw any of them again.

"If there are no other survivors why haven't they found bodies strewn all over like they found Lance?"

"Henry can't tell us."

"How do you know?"

"He's dead. He set me up to be killed. He told them who I was, remember?"

I waited for further details of the kill. With Matt's attitude, it was likely Henry's death was neither fast nor easy. "Do me a favor Matt. Stop killing off the leads before I'm finished with them."

"You said it was over. You pulled out as far as I was concerned. I wasn't ready to give up."

He had me there. I wasn't comfortable working with a newbie, and my lack of communication showed. Matt agreed to meet at a local mom and pop store. The '50s soda shop arrangement in the back of the place had four low cut booths. It wasn't the burgers and sandwiches they served that I found attractive. It was an old-timey place that lacked a camera system.

I arrived for our meeting on the northern edge of Lent's only blocks from the clinic. By the time Matt pulled into the store's lot I had a cup of Java on the table.

Before we'd be able to work together, our relationship had to be sorted and roles clarified. Considering Matt for a Palatini recruitment would be an error. He was a man on a mission that had one issue to resolve. When the project was over, I figured he would drift into society with his lips tightly sealed like a man returning from a battlefield.

It was a coin toss on how successful we'd be at disassembling the trafficker's organization. Matt grabbed a drink and took a seat. "We know there are security, transporters, and additional clinical staff involved."

"How do we know?"

"Carmelita, the recruiter, spilled the beans, as did Benny and Ramone. But, complications have sprung up, namely police investigations. The traffickers likely had a line of outstanding contracts to fill, but can't go to the Bunga to deliver on them.

"Where to then?"

"We take the butcher, Albert Tomas. The organization can fill lower level positions much easier than they can a guy with the extraordinary skills of a surgeon."

What I hadn't told Matt was the GPS tracker that I installed on my earlier recon showed the ambulance had moved to PI Medikal Klinka. The Bunga had become useless for their purposes, so they pulled the ambulance out and hid it in plain sight at the clinic. Who would be the wiser?

The police investigation would be in full swing and the heat all over Tomas for answers. The cops had camped out at the Bunga as they completed their forensics. If the cops didn't have much to go on, they would poke and prod Tomas as the owner until they found something. Maybe he was able to deflect their inquiries telling them the dead man was only a renter and otherwise didn't know him. Tomas, being a smart guy, might have laid a line on them as old as the hills; wasn't there, didn't see anything, don't know anything. Unless the police had incriminating evidence, the story was a tough nut to crack. Besides, he had a legitimate alibi. He wasn't at the Bunga and didn't have anything to do with the murder or arson.

"I'll take the lead, you follow. We stay together until this is over."

"I'll do my part."

We took my Jeep and cruised the short distance to the clinic where we spotted the ambulance parked in the same spot Carmelita's van had been. I figured Tomas was at work in the clinic which gave me time to check out the ambulance. I geared up with my tactical vest, gloves, and weaponry.

"Stay put while I recon the meat wagon. Keep your phone handy. Plans are fluid."

Matt pulled a compact .45-caliber from a concealed shoulder holster prompting me to add, "And don't kill anyone that I might want to interview."

Thaman smiled, "While you are in the ambulance I could walk in and kidnap the doc."

"Your face will be on the nightly news, pal. There are cameras all over the place." The thought crossed my mind as my feet hit the pavement that I should hurry since he hadn't agreed.

Moving briskly across the parking area I slipped in behind the metal building that housed a maintenance shop for the facility. My advance on the ambulance was interrupted when I caught a glimpse of two men approaching from the clinic on a beeline for the ambulance. Neither of the men appeared to be Tomas.

Leaning against the rear of the structure I felt the vibration of my Palatini phone against my chest. I took the call.

"I'm tied up right now, what do you have?"

"Background on the names you sent. I'll encrypt and send."

"Real quick, do you have names for anyone identified as security?"

"Yes, Carlo Bautista, a Philippine National here on a work visa, and Chrisanto de Rosales, a U.S. born citizen."

"Gotcha. You're a sweetheart."

The men had entered the ambulance through a side door and re-emerged with their jackets removed. Visible were their revolvers holstered and strapped to their belts. Both men moved behind the ambulance, stopped and talked. After a long moment, the shorter of the two with short cropped hair continued to the driver's door. He opened the door and with an outstretched hand, started the vehicle. The man at the rear, slender and standing less than six-foot, had turned his back and lit a cigarette. He coughed and hacked then sucked in a deep lungful of smoke.

The shorter man stopped in his tracks when he saw my silencer pointed at his face. Taken by surprise, the man with the cigarette turned, reaching for his weapon. He never made it. Drilled with two chunks of hot lead he slammed into the asphalt flat on his back. My gun quickly repositioned on Shorty's face. Shocked and uncomprehending, I directed him slowly.

"Give me your name."

"De Rosales."

"Unbuckle your belt and pull it out of the pant loops. Let the weapon and holster fall to the ground."

He complied.

"Who is that?" Jerking my head toward the man that hadn't moved since he hit the blacktop.

"Carlo."

"Pick him up. I'll get the door."

De Rosales struggled to balance the dead weight in a fireman's carry while I picked up both weapons, popped the latch on the ambulance's double back door then deposited the guns in one of the interior drawers. "Inside," I commanded.

With Bautista face down on the gurney, I closed the doors and directed de Rosales to one of the bench seats. I sat opposite him.

"I'm going to ask and you're going to answer. Failure to be truthful or not answer will cost you pain. Do you understand?"

"Okay."

"Your first name is?"

"My Christian name is Chrisanto."

"Good. Where were you and your security partner going?"

"You know who we are?"

"I let you know that when I said security. I know your organization and all the dirt on what you do."

Chrisanto cocked his head to one side as if trying to figure out what I meant.

"Your crew butcher people and harvest body parts to sell on the Red Market. I know that's not you—not your part—you're a guard." Lessening tensions and minimizing an actor's role during an interview usually paid dividends. "Now that the formalities are out of the way answer the question."

"We were moving the ambulance to Danny's place for safe keeping."

"Is Danny there now?"

"Around five this evening he'll be home. That's when Carlo and I were to drive him where he needed to go."

"Where?"

Reluctantly, he spoke, "Terminal 6 at the Port."

"Explain."

"Danny and two or three of the others are going to the Philippines. Carlo and I were going to housesit at Danny's until they came back."

"What's in it for you?"

"Continued employment."

"The heat got too much for them?"

"Coyote wanted a break and had made the arrangements."

"Is Coyote Albert Tomas?"

"We only call Albert, Coyote."

"Who is in charge of the enterprise?"

"Coyote takes care of everything...I guess he is."

Over the next few minutes, Chrisanto explained how Tomas was the ringleader who paid their salaries. He insisted that he and Carlo were employees and not part of a criminal organization as I'd implied. It was a case of semantics and not a misunderstanding. Chrisanto knew that he was involved in criminal behavior. With every question, he tried to avoid personal responsibility. He gave up Danilo Carabeo, the man he called Danny, as the organ transporter and owner of the house where they were to stay. "Danny couldn't tell us how long he would be gone. He said it was for an unspecified time. The only thing he told me about the transplant organs was their destination—California. A clinic I think."

It was at Danny's house that Tomas and two of his clinical assistants, Amado Gozar and Efren Pumupula had arranged to meet. From there, Chrisanto and Carlo were to transport them to the Port where they would hop a ride on a cargo vessel. It was a revelation that freighters carried passengers. According to Chrisanto, it was a common practice.

I placed a call to Matt.

"When we pull out in the ambulance I want you to follow."

"Where to?"

"We have a break. Tomas and his crew plan to catch a cargo ship to the Philippines tonight."

Matt, itching for action asked, "From the Port?"

"Terminal 6 at the Port, do you know where it is?"

"Not a clue, but the Port is well marked. GPS can get us there."

"Our intervention will be at Danny's home. I'd rather take my chances at the house. Ports have armed security, cameras, and a lot of eyes to see us. When we get to the house, I want you gloved up, understand?"

"Copy."

Chrisanto slipped into the passenger side of the ambulance and climbed across the console into the driver's seat.

"Any thoughts of doing something courageous or stupid will result in your death. My driver is right behind us." Without further persuasion, Chrisanto looked convinced. I stepped up into the passenger side of the cab and strapped on the seat belt. Holding my weapon low on my lap I said, "Let's go."

A concern surfaced with the distance we were traveling to Danny's house. The lack of designation on the emergency vehicle made me fidgety. Citizens might not notice an unmarked rig, but it could draw the attention of law enforcement.

We beat the traffic across Portland to the north side and pulled up into a driveway that had a large fabric shed set up in the backyard. The front flap was open. Chrisanto pulled the nose of the rig through the gaping doorway to the back of the shelter and killed the engine. Matt pulled up behind us.

I stepped from the vehicle followed by Chrisanto who maneuvered over the console of the meat wagon and landed both feet on the ground. Signaling to Matt with a wave, Matt brought the Wrangler into the shelter. At gunpoint, Chrisanto dropped the flap on the shed before leading the way into Danny's house through the back door.

Matt held Chrisanto at bay while I cleared the three bedroom ranch style home. Modestly furnished the only attention grabber was that one of the bedrooms had been converted into a medical supply cache. Outside of the drugs that Benito had provided through the pharmacy for their operations the rest of their supplies, gauze, tape, needles, bandages, and tubing appeared to be stored in the room.

Chrisanto was seated at the dining table when I walked back into the kitchen area. "The same rules apply," I said to Chrisanto. "What did you do with the dead bodies?"

He stammered and became tongue-tied.

"I had half a mind to be kind and gentle with you if you continued to be truthful. Don't force me to reconsider. Where are the bodies of the people who died?"

"An incinerator on the Bunga."

"I didn't see it. It would have to be good sized?"

"It's on a trailer. I would guess twelve feet long. It's commercial grade and designed for—." He paused then laughed.

Matt took exception, "What's so funny?"

He shook his head declining to comment. Matt angrily hauled him up out of the chair, "I want to laugh too funny boy so tell me what the hell there is to laugh about?"

"It wasn't designed to be a crematory, but it was adequate."

Matt slammed Chrisanto back into his chair then with arms crossed, he leaned against a row of cabinets.

Continuing, I asked, "If you had to guess, how many people have you burned to ashes?"

"That wasn't my job. I never handled a dead person."

"But you saw them—how many times?"

"I don't know. I heard the talk. Not numbers but one of the ways they decide who leaves and who stays. If they had family or contacts they were more likely to receive post-op medical attention and be able to leave after a few days, otherwise….Coyote made the decision."

"Matt, keep an eye out the front windows while Chrisanto and I fetch supplies from the ambulance."

Matt moved to a corner of the drapes where he could see the driveway. Chrisanto and I stepped out the back and made our way to the shed and into the ambulance. "Help me find the needles."

Chrisanto opened the Plexiglas faced door to one of the overhead bins and started to remove a box when he crashed to the floor dead. Double tap to his head was for good measure. Before returning to the house, I grabbed my bug out bag from the Jeep, removed Benito Reyes wallet and wristwatch, and placed them inside of the ambulance.

Matt saw that I'd returned alone and irately asked, "Where's he at?"

"Chill. He's dead."

"I was worried you had let him go."

"Alive? That wouldn't make much sense."

"You led him on that you planned to let him walk out alive? He was just as guilty as the rest."

"Is that why you're upset?"

"It's enough of a reason."

"I did what I said. I was kind and gentle. A man of his character couldn't ask for anything more. He didn't see it coming, and in an instant he was dead. He never knew what hit him. If assassination is not enough you won't find any satisfaction in the process."

Matt thought before he responded, "Dead works for me."

"Okay. You stay on the front I'll take the back door."

At five-thirty a maroon minivan pulled into the driveway and drove to the back of the house. "If they go toward the shed we have to take them," I whispered to Matt who had joined me at the back door.

Matt nodded.

Three men piled out of the vehicle, stopped and looked at the shed, then proceeded to the back entrance. Matt and I stepped into the living room and hid behind the walls on either side of the kitchen entryway. Any noise the door made opening was masked by laughter as the men entered the house. The sound of glass clinking and the refrigerator door closing told me they were occupied with personal matters and comfortable in their surroundings. It was time to further our investigation.

I stepped around the corner, my silencer leading the way, and my weapon at the ready. All three men were seated at the table in clear view. Matt was right behind me, yelling freeze, and swinging his .45-caliber back and forth from person to person like the novice assassin he was. Matt reined himself in, and said, "You take the lead."

"Thanks."

A thirtyish-year-old man, panicky, bellowed, "We don't have any money!"

"Relax...take a deep breath," I said. The advice went for Matt too. "Now...how do you know you don't have what we want?" The men looked across the table at each other bewildered. I interrupted their questioning appearance, "You don't know who we are or why we're here. Let's start out with introductions. "Call me, Hunter. Now, around the table."

An older man in his late fifties or early sixties, with thinning black hair and a hint of gray at his temples, responded first, "Doctor Tomas, and these men work for me at my clinic."

"Okay, Doc...next man?"

The man, still frightened, hadn't taken my advice and barely choked out his name, "Efren Pumupula, paramedic, I'm a paramedic. Paramedic is what I do."

I put my hand up signaling for Efren to stop, "Got it...now you," I said pointing at the stocky built man nearest me. With resound he replied, "Amado Gozar, certified nurse's assistant."

"Thank you, let's get down to business."

Tomas asked, "What's his name?" His eyes fixed on Matt.

Matt responded by aiming the muzzle at Tomas' head. It was a fifty-fifty chance Matt was going to cap him. I waited to see. Tomas had identified himself as the butcher, maybe not in so many words, but Matt could read between the lines.

"I don't play well with others," Matt said.

"Tomas!" I cut through the tension. "Who runs your body parts racket?"

"I take offense to your language." His response was terse.

I looked at Matt, "See, that's what happens when you carry a big stick and don't use it. No respect."

The fidgety man at the center of the table, Efren, looked ready to crack. He wasn't a threat and was willing to confess to anything I asked him. Amado, however, flexed his bulky frame and added a degree of strength to Tomas by his presence. Slowly panning the table from one side to the other, and without notice, in one smooth movement, I unloaded a round into Amado's temple. Blowback filled the air with brain bits and a pink mist. Matt stepped back from the table dabbing his face with his sleeve.

Efren's mouth gaped and gasped for air as he cowered in his chair. Tomas jumped to his feet shouting, "Holy Mother of God!"

"Sit down," I demanded. "You've been running an illegal organ trafficking ring..."

Tomas stuttered, "But there is a need. Laws have pushed the organ trade underground. People in America, rich people, refuse to wait on a list with other less fortunate than they."

"Where do you take the organs?"

Before Tomas could answer, the jangle of keys attempting entry at the front room door interrupted our gathering. Matt was on it.

At gunpoint, Danny was invited to join us at the table. Once in the kitchen, I said, "Take a seat."

"Where?"

I put my foot on Amado's carcass and gave it a push. "Here. Your pal was keeping the seat warm just for you." Danny, reluctant to sit, reconsidered after I pressed the silencer to his head. "Is that going to be okay for you?" I asked.

Danny nodded. He didn't mind sitting in the sticky, coagulating blood after all.

Tomas was right back on his soapbox, but when he got to the part where he described himself as a respectable physician, and not a shady criminal the way I'd portrayed him, I had to laugh.

"Your perception of reality is flawed," I replied. "You're a scum-sucking parasite. You take advantage of people with economic hardships. In some cases, you pay them a fraction of what you'll make on a kidney or other body part that you take from them...and you only pay the ones that live to tell about it. Why don't you tell me about the people you've killed? Butchered? The Veterans and the homeless you've murdered?"

"There is no proof of these allegations," Tomas asserted.

"Not since you bought that incinerator. You learned after Lance's body was found that reducing what was left to a pile of ashes was a smart idea."

Tomas casually shrugged, "You are blinded by your ignorance. You only think it's wrong because the laws are poorly written."

I turned my attention to Danny, "What's your claim to fame in this trafficking ring?"

"I don't understand what you mean?"

"I'm not going to fool around all day, scumbag. You'll either sing like a canary or I'm going to rip your throat out." Matt perked up. He liked the sound of that.

Danny looked at the body on the floor next to him and said, "I run medical supplies to California and back."

"Where in Cali?"

"Stockton."

"Stockton's a city. I want to know where?"

"A clinic called Good Sam's. It's where I drop my shipment off each week."

Tomas interrupted again, loud and angrily, "You've said enough!"

"Hey, I'm the one who says when it's enough. I was enjoying what he had to say."

Matt interjected, "I've heard about all I care to hear."

Tomas was exercising too much pressure on the others and inhibiting their freedom of speech. To get to the bottom of their organization I needed to separate them. "Keep an eye on Danny and Tomas, and don't let that canon your holding go off."

Matt maintained an intense stare at Tomas, enough to unnerve a guy, although Tomas didn't look worried. I pointed to Efren and said, "Come on." Efren jumped to his feet kicking his chair over, shouting gibberish or his native language, I couldn't tell. I don't speak Tagalog. It was possible he'd flipped his lid from the pressure and was nuttier than a fruitcake.

I reached for Efren to get control and unexpectedly, Danny grabbed Matt's weapon. The two of them struggled away from the table toward the stove. Tomas immediately stood and looked toward the back door that was only a few feet away. If he thought he could make the door, he'd be a runner.

I'd gotten a handle on Efren's collar and pinned him against the wall with my forearm. He was digging into his front pocket trying to get his hand in; I figured he had a weapon of some sorts. I put more compression on his throat causing his hands to come up and pull down on my arm. Tomas kept his eyes peeled on the skirmishes. The wheels were turning.

The shrieking noise Efren made got on my last nerve. Matt lost control of his gun, and it struck the floor with a loud thud. To his credit, he kept Danny from making a dive for the weapon by pinning him against the sink. Tomas looked at the .45-caliber on the floor then back at me. My control of the situation was razor thin; I needed to change the odds before someone else found a way.

Without looking at Efren, I placed the muzzle of my Walther under my forearm and against his chest and fired. Shuup! Barely a sound emitted from my silencer. I let him drop and aimed my weapon on Tomas.

A blunt, thumping noise caught my attention as I turned to watch Matt swinging an old-fashioned cast iron skillet, landing blow after blow on Danny's skull. He hammered Danny to the floor and continued relentlessly until his head took on a jelly-like appearance. Each hit splattered fresh blood.

Finally, Matt stopped, stood, blood-spattered, out of breath, worn and haggard.

"Done?" I asked.

"I get the feeling I'll never be done."

"California?"

He nodded then asked, "You want to take a trip?"

"The offer's appealing, my friend, but no can do. I have business to attend to right here."

"That cute blonde? He asked playfully.

Tomas rudely interrupted, "How much?"

Matt asked, "For what?"

"You want money, I see that or I would be dead. What is it going to cost?"

Matt looked at me, apparently for approval. I shrugged, turned, and went into the living room to watch through the window blinds.

Tomas yelled once just before the first loud thud. The beating went on for a long time, although I doubt it was necessary. Tomas was frail in comparison to Danny who had been bludgeoned far less. Who could have guessed that Matt had a culinary skill set?

Matt dropped the skillet, and a peaceful quietness drifted through the house. To see if any of the body snatchers had life left in them required either Matt or me to remove our gloves. I showed him the easier way. I put a slug in each one's skull.

We cleaned the blood off us as best we could, and set a trash can fire in the medical supply room. There were plenty of flammables on the shelves. The wood structure would be engulfed quickly.

"That's not going to mask the murders," Matt said.

"Not trying to, but it will destroy our DNA."

We high-tailed it to the Wrangler and made our way back to the little convenience store where we'd left Matt's rig.

At his car, he asked, "You think we'll see each other again?"

"Contact Anna with a message number, and I'll give you a call. I want to hear what you find out in California at that organ bank."

"You got it, Hunter." He paused, he had something else on his mind. I hoped it wasn't a hug. "You know...finally...I feel like I'm fighting crime. When I was a law officer, it was all about enforcement just like the name implies, but it feels good to make a difference. When I was a cop, the courts let the criminals walk. It wasn't right, and we all knew it, but an officer's hands are tied. This felt right. They will never kill again."

"Good luck, Matt." With that, he stepped from my Jeep and climbed behind the wheel of his ride. As he drove from the parking lot, I questioned whether I'd see him again. Maybe. He'd found his path. Our trails might cross one day again—one never knows.

CHAPTER 18

"Distrust and caution are the parents of security."

—*Benjamin Franklin*

Stirring in my thoughts of Hope were the words Sammie had left me with, "The police want to speak to you, Mister Hunter." Visiting Hope at the hospital would compound my mistake of visiting her the first time. Beating my gums with detectives adversely affected my anonymity. Concerned that the cops would pull the security camera footage at the hospital and run my mug through their facial recognition technology.

Portland had enjoyed a twenty-four-hour reprieve from the usual cold, damp drizzle. Temperatures warmed as another cloud layer rolled in on top of us. Tiring of the Pacific Northwest winter weather was easy for most Portlanders. For me, it was a Godsend. Sun filled days and beautiful moonlit nights inspired love and romance; conversely, enraged stormy skies and howling winds complemented the shadowy darkness of my domain. I sat back on my sofa waiting for twilight. Being a social guy, I wanted to visit with my friend Chuck at the Lucky Strike Tavern.

At seven in the evening, I stepped outside my Collins Best apartment building and greeted the fresh scent of rain in the air that a strong breeze had ushered in. My thoughts wandered to Icky Moore. I wondered if he was standing on a street corner, a free man, and taking in perfectly good oxygen that was meant for decent human beings. I had a remedy in store.

I stopped by Lenny's to see if there was any news on Hope's condition and to wet my whistle while I waited for darkness to engulf the horizon. I bellied up to the bar and called out to a gal mixing drinks, "Jameson's on ice."

With a fresh drink in hand, I made my way across the floor to the table that afforded the best security in the house. It was slow in the joint, and the bartender was making her rounds with a wet rag cleaning table tops. "Where's Lenny?" I asked.

"He had another commitment. He practically begged me to fill in."

On the heels of her words my gut twisted. "Must have been important?"

"Very." She moved away from my table and avoided eye contact. She wasn't offering up answers. Maybe she didn't know. Concern overwhelmed my thoughts that Hope's status had changed for the worse. She had regained consciousness two days ago. Her prognosis looked good. But injuries, like she had suffered, presented an uncertainty for her recovery.

I'd downed a half glass of water when I noticed a portly form filling the entryway. Brandon A. Ware was back spreading his brand of bad luck around.

"Hello, Walter." Ware slid a chair out from under the table where I was seated and sat uncomfortably close. "Or, would you prefer I call you Hunter tonight?"

"Whatever...What can I do for you?"

"Anna Sasins...I'd sure like to meet her. I'm still mystified by her shadowy existence."

I shrugged, "Nothing to do with me." Straightforward statements were easy to remember and hard to break down. The key was not to say too much. Ware wasn't looking for history, he was looking for evidence of wrongdoing. As long as she was moonlighting on the Isle of Mann, there wasn't going to be any contact or evidence. But, his inquiry gave me an idea.

Ware would drown himself in paperwork searching for Anna and further history on me. He'd be off the playing field and out of my way while I took care of business with Icky Moore. "You won't find anything…ever…" The bait was cast. If my guess was right, it had slapped him across the face.

Ware groaned, "You're saying you have friends in high places."

"Not what I said…and I'm not going to say anything."

Ware leaned closer and looked about the room before whispering his message. "My source reported that both you and Sasins are government assets…and I was to back off my inquiries."

Jokingly I said, "Nah, he didn't say that."

"I didn't say my source was a he." Ware looked intently into my face as he strategized where to go with the conversation. "Look, I don't know what sort of man you are. Maybe your job is clandestine acts or political dissent. My source says the agency you and Sasins are attached to have the initials T.C.O.B. If I had to speculate, I'd guess the B stood for Bureau?"

"You should think before you speak. You shouldn't be talking about it, and if it were true, I couldn't discuss it with you."

"I don't want to burn my source, but he says the hierarchy you report to is the Federal Intelligence Bureau."

"Your source talks too much. You're looking for confirmation. I get it. There are criminal elements that must be dealt with, and law enforcement can't get it done. The judicial system is too political to get anything meaningful done to protect citizens. That's where I come in. I'm a consequence that cannot be bargained with and cannot be bought."

Ware was eating it up. Anna's Cobbler had made documents available that were leaked to Ware in record-setting time.

Ware was as excited as a little kid with a decoder ring that he'd gotten from a cereal box in the '60s. He'd found big stuff and hadn't taken the time to check out what his source had given him, not yet. But, when he does, he'll discover the new information is a hoax, and be back on my tail. Federal Intelligence Bureau or F.I.B., I laughed. It was all right there, but he wanted badly to believe he'd found a hidden truth.

I wasn't going to burst his bubble. A wild goose chase for Ware suited me fine.

"Trying to catch up with you I went by to see your girl at the hospital."

"Yeah."

"Gone…but you knew that. You are one strange character; always trying to throw me off the trail. You knew she was gone."

My gut wrenched. I kept my cool and forced a tight-lipped smile with my response. "Yeah…heard."

Ware stood and put out his hand. I rose from my chair and accepted the offer. With a look of concern he said, "Let your other girl know I'll be by soon. I've got her home address. Perhaps I can help with her case."

"I'm sure she would appreciate any help she can get."

"One more thing, I'm sorry to have pushed you to write that story on Owen Moore. Now that I better understand your affiliation."

"No harm."

Ware had barely cleared the doorway, and I was on the phone to Sammie.

"This is Hunter. I'd like to talk with Hope."

"She's not feeling well enough…"

I interrupted, "Ask her!" Silence followed my demand. I had made my point.

"Hi."

"Hey, are you feeling up to a visit from a good-looking guy?"

"Who'd you have in mind," she whispered.

Her sense of humor was intact and hadn't been damaged by Reggie's attack. "I'll be there soon. Tell Sammie, so she'll answer the door. I don't think she'd let me in otherwise."

I tossed her a kiss over the phone and was in the Jeep flying across Portland to Sammie's house. Ten minutes away from my arrival I called to have Sammie catch the door. I swung into the driveway and could see the door was cracked open. I stuffed Hope's Beretta in the back of my pants and let my vest cover it. I remembered Sammie was anti-gun, especially in her house. I entered without knocking.

Sammie caught me at the door, "Mister Hunter, please don't upset her. She's fragile, and I'm afraid…"

I wrapped my arms around Sammie and gave her a long hug. "I'll be careful. I want her to recover same as you." She broke down in tears, so I held her a minute longer.

Sammie led the way. We cut through the formal dining room and entered a long hallway before stopping in front of a door. Sammie spoke softly, "This is Hope's room." Opening the door, I braced myself for what I would see. Centered in the room, propped up on the king sized bed, was a badly bruised blonde that had been beaten bloody by a sadistic psychopath.

"You look pretty good...considering."

"Thanks, I guess."

"You've got room enough in that bed for two people."

"Want to join me?"

"If you feel that spunky, you need to get your clothes on and get back to work."

"Maybe tomorrow."

I took her by the hand and cupped it into mine. I had to exhibit strength in Hope's presence and react with compassion. What I felt was a whole array of anger toward Reggie for his violent criminal act. What didn't make sense was I'd already taken care of the problem. Why the anger?

I was about to confess what I felt when Hope said, "I had to try."

"Try what, honey. You're healing really well."

Hope shook her head gently, "I wanted to change the past, but he wouldn't let me."

There was no reason to intervene in the story. It had to come out.

"Reggie, my one-time boyfriend that I told you about. Remember?" I nodded.

"He manipulated me into prostitution for his drug needs. He pimped me out, and I became a drug seeker like him, but I was never an addict. Drugs were the only way I could cope with that life...my only escape."

I reached out and touched her delicate jawline. "It's okay...water under the bridge."

In frustration, she wailed, "All I wanted to hear him say was that he was sorry for what he put me through. But...he's not sorry."

I gave her space to let it all out without interference. I didn't like listening to her cry, but she had to do it. Trying to stop her would only prolong her pain.

When she regained her composure, she picked up from where she'd left off. "I knew where Reggie hung out, and I went to see him. He was nice to me, but not apologetic. I told him I was living in Lent's and he offered to give me a ride home. I was going to come to your apartment after Reggie, and I talked. He gave me a ride to the park where he said we could talk. It was chilly, but I said okay—He hasn't changed at all. He belittled me and spoke ugly to me."

"Did you take your gun for protection?"

"Yes. It was in my handbag. I shouldn't have argued with him, it only served to make him angrier. He grabbed the bag not knowing the gun was in there."

"His lack of control is not your fault."

"But I made it worse. I knew better. He beat and kicked me like he used to do. Worse. Violent. I couldn't tell you that at first. I buried it and didn't ever want to think about it again."

"I understand."

"Are you afraid to die, Hunter?"

"Not really. I've learned more about death than I have life."

"I'm not like you. Fear immobilized me. I was terrified he would kill me."

"If you had the opportunity to confront him again, would you?"

"No." She paused. She came to grips with a fact of her life. "I can't mend my soul in the past. It's inside me, and it's dead. I have to live in the present and look to my future."

"Were you delirious or were you trying to send me a message when you said, "Motions and Pearl.""

She stared deep into my eyes. She didn't have a clue how to answer.

"What are you planning, Hunter?" Her swollen eyes widened, and the tone of her voice sharpened as she asked the question again. I'd forgotten how well she read behavior.

"I never tolerate evil to exist. If I find it, I pull it out by the roots."

"I wish—"

I cut her off quick, "Reggie was a vile criminal that would have repeated his violent predatory behavior over and over until someone stopped him. He wasn't going to have a life-altering epiphany." From her expression, I surmised she'd caught my past tense reference. I continued, "Do you want to hear about some young girl Reggie beat, raped, and sold to every drunk that came along? You wanted to know if he cared about you as much as you had for him—now you know. Your quest is over, honey. He didn't give a damn about you. Sure, I know it's hard to accept, but Reggie is the only thing he ever cared about." Harsh words and to the point, but she needed to hear them.

Hope sat silently looking at her hand in mine. She whispered, "I'm sorry, Hunter, you're right."

"You've got nothing to be sorry about. I only wish you'd talked with me first. We could have worked as a team and made sure you were covered while you spoke with that clown. But, I understand why you didn't. The thing with you and Reggie was personal."

"You said we don't do personal."

"I stand corrected."

She wiped her bloodshot eyes, "Are you disappointed in me?"

"Not a chance. You are missing the action, so you need to recover. I want you back out there with me."

Hope smiled and squeezed my hand.

"Matt and I made an opportunity to clean house on the organ traffickers. It turned out to be bigger than a local problem. Matt's planning a road trip to take care of business."

Hope shook her head, "Do you think he has what it takes to finish what he'd started?"

"Matt is driven by revenge; there isn't much that can stop him now that he's crossed over the edge."

"Has your friend been keeping tabs on you?"

"Ware is a shadow that is hard to shake."

"Sammie said he tried to contact me at the hospital. Left his name and a callback number."

"Yeah, he told me. I wouldn't go out of my way to return the call. Let sleeping dogs lie. He will be by to see you soon enough. But listen, speaking of Ware, I'm going to pay the Lucky Strike Tavern a visit tonight and begin my wrap-up on Icky Moore."

"Hunter, I wanted to be with you...but I'm more of a hindrance than a help."

"The time will come when we can continue." We'd skimmed over the Reggie event earlier. She should have had more of a reaction. "I have something that'll make you feel better." Reaching behind my back and under my vest where the Beretta was stashed, I took it by the grip.

Smiling she said, "You are so thoughtful."

Then it was in my hand, the gold-inlay displayed in front of her. Shocked, she asked, "Did you buy me another one?"

"It's the one and only."

"Reggie took it from me… How did you get it?"

"He was good enough to bequeath it to you."

"Bequeath…You found him?"

"Found? Reggie was looking out for my best interests and took me to his place to have a go at his young girlfriend…real cheap too. Helluva a guy."

Despondency infused her words, "Did you kill him?

"When I told you, we don't do personal…I admitted I was wrong."

Hope became louder and angrily bit the words off, "It wasn't your place to take care of…I didn't ask you to step in. You don't get it, Hunter. I didn't want him dead…I wanted an apology. Now, thanks to you, I'll never hear him say he's sorry."

"I have a revelation for you, honey. He was never going to apologize no matter what. You're sore at me, but you know my standards, he beat you and left you to die in that park. Anything could have happened to you, and you're damn lucky it didn't. As far as he was concerned when he left you there—you were dead."

"Killing everyone isn't the answer, it can't be."

"An eye for an eye, honey, that's the reality of what I do. You know that."

"But I didn't die."

"He killed something in you a long time ago—called innocence. That's right. Then he beat you and left you to die. So, I beat him. Tit for tat as far as I'm concerned."

"I want you to leave, Hunter. I can't even look at you right now."

"Okay, but so you know, it's all black and white when it's someone else…but when its personal it's different. Gray areas are feelings, and I don't have feelings. You've got my number if you want to talk."

Hope buried her face in her hands as I turned and left. Was she angry because I killed her first love or because it was her circus and she wanted the Ringmaster's spot? Only she knew the answer. Thaman was planning a road trip to Stockton or was on his way. My gut instinct said Ware was satisfied with the conclusions he'd drawn. I turned my focus to Moore.

Hope's status had changed from asset to liability. Distrust and caution collided in my thoughts. My concern was not unfounded. If she shared our activities with Sammie, those details might make their way to the cops. I couldn't chance it and took preventive measures.

At the Collins Best apartment, I washed up, changed clothes, and cleaned out the few items I owned, making sure there was not a trace of yarn, notes on the wall of the second bedroom. Hope knew where I lived. I had no choice. I had to vacate. I paid with cash through the end of the month and dropped a Franklin on the old lady at the desk that handled my check-out paperwork.

"What's this for?" She asked.

"For you to conveniently lose my contract."

"Where should I send your cleaning deposit if your room checks out okay."

"You take it. But as a favor, I'd like my pickup to stay parked out front until I come get it. If anyone asks, you don't know anything about it."

"What pickup?" She'd caught my drift.

"Exactly." The $100-dollar bill she pocketed sealed the deal.

An hour's drive north through Portland and I was back at Anna's place. I changed license plates on the Wrangler and prepared to set out for the Lucky Strike Tavern. The events of the day had put me in a sullen mood. All I could do was hope that Icky Moore was out on the town and a target of opportunity.

CHAPTER 19

"Lightning makes no sound until it strikes"

—*Sun Tzu*

Owen "Icky" Moore was the kind of target every assassin dreams of—hated and of no use to anyone. He didn't have family support, and from court records, they didn't want to have anything to do with him. No one cared if Icky lived or died. In some sense, it could be said he was already dead to the world. His life made him an easy kill. As far as friends went, he didn't have any of those either. What he did have exemplified the meaning of "birds of a feather flock together," and Icky had surrounded himself with the worst of the worst. All of them were targets in my book.

At ten-fifteen in the evening, I was sitting outside the Southeast Flavel apartment complex where the felonious targets resided at taxpayers' expense. Parked across the street, I could monitor the parking lot with ease. However, none of the vehicles Anna had run through her source were in the lot. I intended to annihilate the nest, much like I'd learned to deal with hornets while growing up on the ranch.

Darker than usual due to the thick cloud cover, and with more rain expected I anticipated a cozy scene with the child molesters all nestled around a fire in a living room telling and retelling stories of abuse. But, without the presence of the cars that I'd hoped to find there, I concluded they were at the Lucky Strike Tavern raising their brand of hell—the worst imaginable type of hell—plotting or participating in the sexual abuse of another victim.

Over an hour into my watch, Sonny Links pulled up to a ground floor unit in his Contour and unloaded a couple of shopping bags. I made preparations to take him out, but before I could execute the plan, Links climbed back into his vehicle and pulled out on the numbered side street. He was unaware he'd picked up a shadow. I tailed loosely.

It was close to midnight when Links and I arrived at the Lucky Strike. Not surprising, he parked next to the Grand Prix registered to Cecil James. I pulled to a stop and backed into the darkest area of the lot. Opposite of where Links had parked, was the '99 Caravan that Simms drove. In most cases, I considered a tavern too public to conduct business, but this project had extenuating factors that made the bar a better choice than the assigned government paid residence on Flavel. The tavern didn't have a working camera system like the halfway house which was also staffed by facilitators that pulled security duties. My goal of a clean sweep required a gathering of the felony faction in one place. The tavern, late at night, seemed the most likely place.

With the headlights on and the Wrangler idling, Links looked in my direction and watched for a long minute. How well he could see me in the poorly lit lot was questionable. Maybe not at all. He moved toward the back door shooting glances my direction. I wondered if he felt my eyes boring into him? Did the hairs on the back of his neck rise? Did his sixth sense detect some impending doom?

The barroom door closed behind Links. No movement. Quiet. I waited to see if he came back out with reinforcements. A skirmish against the faction in the parking lot was to my advantage. Poor lighting coupled with plentiful cover and concealment benefitted a single attacker over a multi-pronged disorganized attack. When they didn't materialize, I strapped on my Kabar fighting knife to go with my .40-caliber. I didn't bother with the silencer. It was much too cumbersome for close quarters combat. Press checking the weapon ensured a round was chambered. I slipped my Walther into the Kydex holster on my belt and popped the magazine out of the weapon, loading another round that brought the magazine back to capacity. With two magazines already loaded and in the pocket of my leather jacket, I was ready to keep a promise to Vanessa.

I pulled my hood up high and tucked the bottom of my sweatshirt into my beltline. With my leather jacket hanging loosely over my Walther its presence was concealed, unobstructed, but easily accessible.

A total of five cars were in the lot, three of which were known members of the felony faction. A fourth rig belonged to Chuck, the saloon's owner. The fifth vehicle I hoped belonged to Icky. Moving from car to car I looked inside each one. Confident they were empty I moved alongside the building to the first set of windows and looked inside. Cecil James, Sonny Links, and Teddy Simms were at a front table nearest to the bar. Chuck was ten feet from the faction talking with a couple at a second table. No Icky.

My first thought after noting Icky was missing from the picture was that he'd been picked up for a parole violation and incarcerated. Bad luck if that were the case. But, rather than go home empty handed I'd let his friends start his party without him. I had no qualms extracting a level of revenge that I had held in reserve for the nastiest sorts that I hunted. Each of them, James, Links, and Simms, were sex offenders and in my book, had gotten off easy. Chuck was the only man I didn't have a beef with. By the same token, however, I wanted to know why the fellowship? What was in it for him?

At the entrance from the parking lot, I opened the door slightly and looked down the hallway into the barroom. As expected the hinges didn't squeak or moan. Pulling the door closed, I adjusted my hood to hide my identity from the visitors and provide concealment for my eye movement. I edged past the hallway bathrooms stopping to listen at each door for activity. No sounds. No surprises. I didn't need to be blindsided by an additional player.

Continuing forward the dark hall hid all shadows from existence. The jukebox came alive with a 70s tune, "Stairway to Heaven." Ironic. There was no such stairway in their futures. "Highway to Hell" would have been a better choice. Maybe for all of us.

Scanning the room from side to side as I stepped into the barroom it looked different from when Hope and I had visited last. The chatty light-hearted dayshift crew was gone for the night, and a dark presence loomed. Maybe it was only me. Lanky was seated at a small table eyeing the visiting couple, and Sonny had unwisely taken a position with his back exposed to the open floor and both entry doors. Lanky used Links to cover his predatory observance and hadn't paid attention to my quiet arrival. Chuck was behind the counter with his back to me, likely fixing a Mickey Finn for the young couple at the table. James had his head down looking at the song menu on the Jukebox.

Chuck had turned, preparing to deliver drinks to the couple when we locked eyes. I bellied up to the empty bar counter. Chuck grimaced. He wasn't excited to see me. I assumed I'd interrupted their plans. Spooked by my arrival, Chuck immediately turned back to the well and dumped one of the drinks.

I angled my lean on the bar counter and waited for service. Chuck remade the drink he'd dropped and said, "Be with you in a minute." I didn't acknowledge. Using the depth of my hood, I saw that Lanky and Links had become acutely aware of my presence.

"What can I get you?" Chuck asked as he passed by on the outside of the bar's counter. When he was back behind the bar, I answered, "Beer."

Chuck picked up a mug, but before he poured, I added, "Bottle." I was tired of his rotgut. Chuck reached into a cooler and pulled out a Miller, and charged me up front. I didn't look up or let Chuck read my expression. I threw a C-note on the counter.

Chuck went into a back room and came back with change. "Thanks," I said and dropped a buck on the counter. Before touching the bottle, I slipped on my gloves in front of the onlookers. Except for the couple absorbed with each other, I had everyone's riveted and silent attention. There was only one reason to wear gloves—to hide fingerprints. I let a smile creep out. The tension thickened and hung heavy in the air.

I strode across the main floor to a table where my back was against the wall and a clear visual on the barroom. I drank my beer in silence.

Twice in fifteen minutes, Chuck passed my table without saying a word. A regular customer would not have considered him friendly. His focus was split between the young couple and my bothersome appearance.

Destiny stirred bringing to mind what Ware had said, "Everyone has a history." Anna had found nothing to indicate Chuck was a criminal, but here he was, engaging in predatory behavior. Chuck was either leading the felony faction in their nightly activities, or was he being led?

Drugs and alcohol—the bottomless well of wickedness that so many in society point to as the source of all woes, was a ruse. Evil dwells in the heart. Predators are opportunists. The stories that people tell in court blaming a substance for what was inside them was a joke. "I would never have done that if..." Stop right there liar. Accept what you are. Hundreds of thousands use alcohol and illegal drugs every day and do not commit atrocities. If I believed in the two energies of God and the Devil I could imagine the battle taking place in the spiritual arena of the Lucky Strike Saloon. Angels and demons locked in battle inspired me. Dark forces that drifted like the haze in a smoky room were about to have a light shine brightly and force them to flee.

The lateness of the hour brought a hand wave between Chuck and the visiting couple as they headed out the back door. I caught Chuck's head and eye movement as he called Lanky off. The felony faction had been stymied in their pursuit. A moment later the crew had refocused their attention on me.

As far as I was concerned, the faction had their names inscribed in my judgment book. I entered the realm of darkness to take on the mantle of death personified, the Grim Reaper. The faction deserved nothing less than the forfeiture of their existence. If it were not so, I would not have been made aware of their names.

"What's with you man? Why are you sitting there watching me?" Lanky barked.

"I have business with one of you."

"Who the hell is that?"

"Maybe you."

Lanky shrugged as if he didn't care, but his face flushed and his fists clenched telling a different story. I looked from one side of the trio to the other. Sonny Links pulled out a pack of smokes and lit up as he watched. He looked calm and relaxed with that coffin nail dangling from the corner of his mouth. But all coolness vanished when he noticed that he already had a cigarette burning in the ashtray which he quickly mashed out. Cecil James had returned to the table from the jukebox and sat at one corner of the table. His calm exterior thinly veiled the nervousness that crept out through his eyes as they darted between players.

"What business?" Chuck asked.

"An unpaid debt."

"I can't help you there." After a hard stare, Chuck turned his back toward me and continued his cleaning behind the bar. I stood and walked to the counter and said, "Beer."

Chuck forcefully replied, "Why don't you get smart and take your money elsewhere before it's too late?" The felony faction stirred with anticipation.

"Come here, Chuck." He had made a suggestion, and I wanted to return the favor.

Stopping short of arm's reach with the counter between us, he said, "What?"

"Where's Icky?"

"Don't know, don't care."

"Here's my advice to you Chuck—leave while you can."

I walked back to my table and sat with the empty bottle in front of me. The faction smirked. Elements had begun to align, and evil tightened its grip on the joint. Over the span of thirty minutes, the trio and I were locked in an expressionless stare. When Chuck announced the last call, I would play my hand.

Icky's entry through the back door and slow gait down the hallway went unnoticed by everyone but me. He approached the bar and leaned against it. Was it a coincidence that he showed or had someone placed a call? After a brief conversation with Chuck, Icky turned and walked my way. I stood.

Icky was a thirty-seven-year-old man that had a known history of violence. He stood more than six feet tall, and my guess was he weighed in at about two-eighty. He wasn't the kind of guy you let get a jump on you.

He stopped with the table between us and asked, "Do I know you?"

"We haven't met, but Mona talked a lot about you. So much so, I feel like I know you and what you owe."

"Mona was a lying whore. She was working you for a fix."

"No doubt. She wanted money upfront, so I gave her some. Then she told me her story."

"For money or drugs, that girl would have done things to you that would make your head spin." He laughed as if he remembered specific details of his time with Mona. "You know she's dead, right?"

"I know. I was there when she died." I stepped away from the table and walked to the entrance of the hallway. Flippantly, Chuck said, "About time you left." The faction laughed, all but Icky, he understood what I'd said. I suppose they assumed I was leaving, but at the end of the hall, I pulled the door shut tight and gave the thumb turn on the cylinder lock a twist. The door latched assuring an uninterrupted opportunity to settle a score.

Reappearing by the edge of the bar, Chuck faded further away from the corner where I stood. Icky cleared his throat and stepped toward the middle of the barroom floor, his hands empty. He intended to answer my questions with his fists. "You've stuck your nose in where it doesn't belong."

"Vanessa asked me to pay you a visit."

"I don't owe Vanessa, Mona, or you anything. You got suckered."

Cecil James passed behind Icky and made his way to the jukebox. Flipping through the menu selection wasn't a convincing act. He'd taken an offensive position on my left flank. Lanky moved too. He joined Chuck on the opposite side of the bar's counter to my right side. Sonny Links remained at the table. Surrounded by criminals, Louis L'Amour couldn't have scripted a better old west stage setting than this.

Icky moved forward a few steps closing the distance between us. The jukebox was deathly silent. Cecil hadn't made a music selection. Moore's lungs strained with the booming of his voice, "This clown thinks he's entitled to collect something for the kid." The laugh that followed was phony just as the others were when they chimed in.

I shook my head and walked past Moore and to the front door like I owned the joint. Icky yelled, "Yeah, that's it, take off. You're all talk."

At the front door, I flipped the closed sign. Chuck shouted, "Can't do that it's still business hours."

"You're going out of business."

The felony faction had failed to contain me in their circle. The advantage was theirs in numbers and mine in position. Maybe Chuck was responding to my statement, "I don't want your kind of trouble in here," and gestured a backhanded wave in the direction of the door.

"Owen Moore, Cecil James, Sonny Links, and Teddy Simms— you're all cut from the same cloth. You all have to answer for what you've done."

Their mouths hung open, and they looked at each other and realized this was not a chance encounter. I was aware of their names. Chuck remained behind the bar while Lanky joined Icky in the center of the room. Links stood and stepped out from behind his table.

Chuck yelled, "If you don't leave I'm going to call the cops."

"Hang on, Chuck. This guy knows our names," Lanky said. "He's been following us for a reason. Maybe we ought to find out why."

"You're smarter than the others, Simms. All of you would go to jail if the cops showed up here."

"What do you want?" Icky demanded.

"I already told you what. I'm a debt collector, and I'm here to collect."

"Money? What?"

"I don't trade in money. You owe what you can never repay."

Cecil's eyes filled with fear. His hand slipped under the right side of his lightweight jacket. For a split second, the EastEnders parking lot shootout flashed a vivid recall. Premonition.

Cecil's eyes grew large as saucers. He stepped forward with two quick steps in my direction surprising everyone by his move. He'd drawn a small caliber revolver from his waistline and aimed in my direction but hesitated on the trigger. A novice move and a mistake he would not live to regret. Two rounds in quick succession from my .40-caliber knocked him flat. His gun bounced on the wood floor and slid away. I looked to my left to see Links with a bead drawn on me with another handgun. A bullet whizzed past my head. I spun, crouched, and shot, striking him, but it hadn't taken him out of the game. He dropped behind a half-wall that separated a portion of the bar from an antechamber. I immediately advanced using a few rounds of suppressive fire. Links collapsed to the floor. One shot had found its mark above the right eye. I turned to face Lanky who had picked up Cecil's revolver. We raised our weapons simultaneously and fired. I was spun, this time it wasn't by choice. A bullet grazed my hip. I fired a second time directly into Lanky's body core knocking him off his feet and to the ground. I heard the pump action of a shotgun and spotted Chuck aiming in my direction. It came back to me then, never trust the bartender in a shootout. The frontier towns of the old west were filled with stories of the shooter being picked off from behind the bar. I wasted no time firing in his direction. Then the blast from his weapon caught me in the right shoulder knocking my weapon from my hand. Chuck fell behind the counter. I was sure I'd made a kill shot that would bleed him out.

My Walther lay ten feet away. With Icky holding Cecil's revolver, the distance was insurmountable.

"Freeze! Put down the gun! Do it now." The booming voice commanded. Moore's attention was drawn to the front doorway that set ajar. Ware yelled again, "Put it down—do it!"

Icky Moore tossed the revolver on Cecil James lifeless body. "I'm not your problem, he's the criminal here," Icky pointed at me.

"On your knees. Hands behind your back and stay there," Ware directed Moore.

With his weapon at the guard, Ware moved to where my gun had come to rest. "This yours?"

I nodded. Ware reached into his suit jacket and removed a pair of latex gloves. "Why the gloves?" I asked.

"Evidence." Ware bent over and cautiously picked up my Walther. "How bad are you hit?"

"A couple scrapes." The wound to my hip area was superficial and bled slowly. The shoulder wounds were concealed from view by my leather jacket, and the bleeding was absorbed into the sleeve of my hoodie.

Ware checked James carotid artery for signs of life, repositioning his fingers and checking again. Ware continued to check vital signs on Lanky then on Sonny Links. Both dead.

"There's one more behind the bar."

Ware conducted a cursory check and shook his head, "Not a chance."

Holstering his handgun, he pulled the slide on my Walther back and checked for brass then removed the magazine. "Two shots left in the mag and one in the chamber, you were almost out of ammo."

"It was enough to finish the job."

Ware, who had pointed out Moore's location, needed no introduction. "Who are the rest of these yokels?" He asked.

"Habitual felony offenders and friends of Icky's in the same rehab program."

Ware turned his focus to Icky. "You're about out of friends Mister Moore."

"A real comedian! You're a cop, arrest this guy for killing these people, and take me into custody. Do what you are supposed to do!"

"Mister Moore, did you have Mona Lott killed?"

"You have to advise me of my rights to ask questions. Then I can tell you to cram it where the sun don't shine."

I was surprised he didn't implicate me after I'd told him I was there. His disdain for the law and his assumption that Ware was a cop dictated his reaction.

"You violently abused your daughter—"

Moore interrupted shouting, "No proof, I had nothing to do with it. My defense attorney recommended I take that Alford plea because Mona was a nut job and judged incompetent. She couldn't take part in my defense. No damn proof!"

"You used the system and took advantage of a plea deal."

Ware wasn't getting his questions answered, the reason he wanted to involve me. Icky, still on his knees, puffed out his chest and said boastingly, "I'll go back to jail for six months for a parole violation. Then, I'll return to my life. Nothing you or anyone else can do about it."

Moore faced me and smiled. He was right. Parole violators notoriously serve only a few months. Then, after a courtroom song and dance were granted a second, third, or more chances in society. It was bad policy.

Ware continued eye-balling my .40-caliber. I wondered if he liked the weight or feel of the weapon. Maybe he wanted to keep it as a trophy, a souvenir, or if he was trying to fit it in like a puzzle piece with past crimes he'd investigated. Without warning, he lowered my Walther and fired the round in the chamber into Moore's head. Without speaking a word, he unloaded the last two rounds into Moore's body. The slide automatically locked to the rear, Ware put the weapon on the floor next to me. "He had it coming," he said.

I was speechless. What was there to say to someone who finished what you had set out to do and at the same time save your life?

Ware looked at me, "I couldn't use my gun." He paused, "Besides, I figured I owed you that much. I'm ninety-nine percent sure it was you who stopped those guys in the parking lot."

Ware pulled out his phone and placed a call. "You better get in here."

Did he have a cop friend waiting outside to score a big collar, and had just called him in. He killed Moore with my gun and wore gloves when he did it. What defense would I have? Seconds later the front door opened and Hope, still showing signs of swelling and heavy bruising on her face, stepped inside.

"What's she doing here?" I asked Ware.

Hope didn't need anyone to answer for her. "Brandon came by to visit. We talked about my case and about you, Walter. I mentioned you were following up on the leads he'd given you about Owen Moore and he offered to help me locate you. I didn't want you taking out the trash by yourself."

"Great timing," I said.

Ware looked toward me, "You're alive aren't you?"

Hope continued, "When we pulled into the driveway, Brandon said, 'Muzzle flash,' and stopped his Impala there on the spot. When he leaped out the car door, all he said was, 'Wait by the phone' which is what I did."

Ware interjected, "Time to take off...and take him with you."

"I have a question that's dogging me?"

"Not telling you my reason for anything?"

"Not that, but how. How did you keep finding me? A sophisticated tracking device? I changed vehicles four times, and you found me every time."

"In my day we didn't have advanced tracking systems. We used knowledge and conjecture to track."

"Guesswork?"

He laughed, "More than that. You made a classic error. You went to the same shooting range all too often, and showed up in all the vehicles, except for the pickup which I already knew. I tailed you. If that didn't work out, I cruised the bar areas you were frequenting until I came across one of your vehicles."

I had pitted my skills against his and had to acknowledge he was better at cat and mouse than I was.

"If it's any consolation, you weren't easy. You beat me more than once at the game."

"You know how to make a guy feel better."

Hope had slipped out to the parking lot with my Jeep keys and brought the Wrangler to the back door. Ware helped me up from the floor, I hobbled to the back door on my own. Once inside the Jeep with Hope behind the wheel, we pulled onto the driveway where Ware had stopped his rig—the Impala was gone. Ware had left the scene to be discovered by natural process.

"Where to Walter?" Hope asked.

She made a point to say Walter for the second time. I preferred to discuss it at a later date but figured it was time to clear the air. "I am Walter. Hunter is an unfiltered version of who I am."

"Like a psychopath?"

"I'm sure the news would cover it that way. I turned in the keys to my apartment. My only other option is the condo uptown that I share with another person."

"That other person must be a female."

"Why do you say that?"

"Because you're being elusive."

"She is."

"Are you lovers?"

When I didn't readily answer she filled in the blank for herself'

"You are."

"She's not in Oregon right now."

Hope replied, "I'll be more relaxed taking care of you at my place."

"What about Sammie?"

"She's a nurse."

"A psych nurse."

"Maybe she can fix you for real?"

Hope and I had formed a business partnership with fringe benefits. She seemed fine with a superficial relationship.

Sammie's skills as a traditional nurse were rusty, but I'd been fortunate. Chuck had used birdshot. Sammie dug three pellets from the muscle tissue of my arm and leg. Three more pellets had passed through the tissue area. Sammie's ballpark guess was a week or more for recovery.

Sammie found it easier if we convalesced in the same bed. I didn't mind. On the morning of the third day, I checked my Palatini phone for messages. "We need a team," Anna said. "Thomas penetrated a cartel and intends to do what the Mexican government is not willing to do—

shut them down. Seymour has agreed to take his tug to the Mexican ports and use Palatini knights as crew. Maximillion is doing better, but I will continue to facilitate the project from here. Are you game?"

I turned to Hope, "Speak any Spanish?"

With a killer smile that spoke volumes she responded, "Si."

"That'll do."

www.ingramcontent.com/pod-product-compliance
Lightning Source LLC
Chambersburg PA
CBHW051532260626
47170CB00003B/900